Pack's Queen

Wolves of Crimson Hollow Book Three

M. H. Soars
Michelle Hercules

Pack's Queen © 2019 by M. H. Soars & Michelle Hercules

All rights reserved under the International and Pan-American Copyright Conventions. No part of this book may be reproduced or transmitted in any form or by any means, electronic or mechanical, including photocopying, recording, or by any information storage and retrieval system, without permission in writing from the publisher.

This is a work of fiction. Names, places, characters and incidents are either the product of the author's imagination or are used fictitiously, and any resemblance to any actual persons, living or dead, organizations, events or locales is entirely coincidental.

Warning: the unauthorized reproduction or distribution of this copyrighted work is illegal. Criminal copyright infringement, including infringement without monetary gain, is investigated by the FBI and is punishable by up to 5 years in prison and a fine of $250,000.

ISBN: 9781798811481

To all readers who gave this series a chance and shared their love for it. Thank you!

WOLVES OF CRIMSON HOLLOW SERIES:

RED'S ALPHAS (BOOK ONE)

WOLF'S CALLING (BOOK TWO)

PACK'S QUEEN (BOOK THREE)

CRIMSON HOLLOW: 13 DAYS OF CHAOS:

CROSSING TIME

Pack's Queen

WOLVES OF CRIMSON HOLLOW BOOK THREE

Website:
www.mhsoars.com
www.michellehercules.com

Newsletter:
http://mhsoars.com/sign-up/

Editor: Cynthia Shepp

Cover Design: Rebecca Frank

Chapter 1
Red

I don't tell Sam where I'm going once I leave his room. He's still exhausted from the battle, and he needs more time to recover from his wound. It's bad enough we're both worrying about Tristan's and Dante's fate. I don't need to add the situation with Alex to the plate.

Trying to control the beating of my heart, I walk toward Tristan's office where Alex is waiting for me. It's no use. It took me such a long time to get over the pain of our breakup. Now, having Alex suddenly drop into my life in this supernatural savior role is messing with my mind.

Voices coming from the entrance foyer below make me stop in my tracks. Approaching the railing with soft steps so as to not announce my presence, I find Alex's Dark Blades companions below. Max and Martin's sister are engaged in a heated argument, carried on through shout-whispers. *Please, don't they know shifters have enhanced hearing?*

"I don't like this at all, Max. Why won't they let me see my brother?" Martin's sister asks.

"You heard what Santiago said. Martin fell under

Harkon's demonic influence. The only reason his soul wasn't completely corrupted was due to the spell we used in his raven tattoo."

"He's not going to harm me." The woman crosses her arms.

Max moves closer, holding her by the shoulders. "Daria, I understand your frustration, but Martin knew about all the risks when he accepted his mission."

After pushing Alex's best friend away, she turns around and puts some distance between them. "I'm not frustrated. I'm angry. I don't understand why we had to drop everything to come help Alex's ex-girlfriend."

My spine goes taut when I'm mentioned. It's impossible to ignore the venom in the woman's voice. It's obvious she doesn't like me.

"Aren't you forgetting we're dealing with a major archdemon who has been obsessed with the same woman through centuries? That's right up our alley."

So they know about my past with Harkon. It seems I was one of the last people to find out I had a fucking demon after me. It figures. But Max said centuries. Does that mean I've encountered the monster more than once before?

Daria turns, her ponytail slashing around like a whip. "Why does it have to be Alex to come to the rescue? There are other Blades who could have taken this mission."

"Alex is one of the best. Plus, he never would have allowed anyone else to come. You know how he feels about Red."

My pulse flutters. What does Max mean by that? Alex

was the one who ended our relationship. He broke my heart. She snorts. "Yeah, we all know. One more reason he shouldn't be here. His feelings for the wolf princess will put the mission in jeopardy. We can't trust his instincts where she's involved."

"You're not being fair to Alex. He'd never let his personal business mess with his calling. I can't say the same about you."

She cuts him a glare. "What are you implying?"

"You know very well what I'm talking about. You either tell him how you feel, or you let it go."

"As usual, you're full of shit, Max," the woman spits, turning on her heels to stalk out of the house.

Max lets out a loud sigh before saying, "I hope you enjoyed the convo, Red." He turns to me then, a cheeky smile playing on his lips.

"You knew I was here all along?"

He winks. "I think you've let Alex wait long enough. The poor sod must be on pins and needles by now."

Shaking my head, I say, "You're still the same insufferable ass."

"Oh, no. I'm much, much worse."

With a laugh, he strides out of the house. I didn't get the chance to reply to his question. I did learn interesting things, but nothing gave me any intel about what I'm going to face in Tristan's office. *Come on, Red. Stop being such a coward.* I force my feet to move until I'm standing in front of the door, realizing I didn't think this through. Even from outside, I can smell Tristan's scent, and with it comes the sorrow again. My throat becomes tight while my eyes prickle. Curling my hands into fists, I try to keep my emotions in control. The anguish wave recedes a little, so I finally turn the knob.

Alex is standing with his back to the door, staring out the window. When he peers over his shoulder, my stomach ties into knots. I expect to feel a sharp pain in my chest as well, but the ache there is not caused by him.

Closing the door with a resounding click, I remain by it, not knowing what to say. He turns fully to face me, but also doesn't move forward.

"How are you?" he asks, his voice a little rough. It sounds almost as if he hasn't spoken in days.

"I've been better."

"Your scratches have healed nicely."

I touch my face. Yesterday, I had a scratch there I don't even remember getting. It's gone now. Some details of the battle in Shadow Creek are a blur.

"Perks of being a shifter."

Alex's expression becomes pinched, and emotion flashes in his eyes. It's gone too fast for me to discern what it was.

"So, you're a druid," I say.

"Yes."

"I guess it's safe to assume you were always a druid." My voice is neutral. Yet, Alex's expression turns into one of guilt.

"Yes. Like you were always a witch."

Oh, no. He didn't just turn this around on me.

"The only difference is I never knew I was one," I say

through clenched teeth.

"Touché." Crossing his arms, he leans against the windowsill.

I can't take this stilted conversation any longer, so I cut to the chase. "Why did you lie?"

Jaw hardening, Alex stares at me without saying a word. I can almost see the conflicting emotions bouncing inside of his head.

"I had no choice."

"Bullshit. There's always a choice."

"Really? Did you tell your friend when you were turned into a wolf shifter?"

My mood becomes sour in an instant. He had to go and mention Kenya.

"No." I imitate his stance, crossing my arms and sharpening my gaze.

"Humans can't know about the supe community, Red. I didn't know you had ties to the supernatural. If I had—" He shakes his head, breaking eye contact with me. "Maybe things would have been different."

I don't want to dwell too much between the lines of that statement. Playing what-if games doesn't lead anywhere, only to more heartache.

"You know what? It doesn't matter. You did what you had to do. Now, all I want to know is how you can help me find my mates."

Alex focuses on me again, his gaze now tense. "Our first priority is to find Harkon and deal with him."

"The hell it is. The first priority is to find Dante and

Tristan. Afterward, we'll deal with the archdemon."

Alex narrows his eyes to slits. "Harkon has Tristan, but your mate has been corrupted. And Dante could be in a million different dimensions. He could be dead."

Unfolding my arms, I take a step forward. My blood is boiling, my vision turning crimson. "Dante is not dead. And I don't care how long it will take to find him. I'll save him with or without your help."

"Do you even know where to begin searching? I'm not trying to be cruel, but the truth is you might not be able to save them both."

"What do you mean?"

"It will take time and resources to locate Dante. We have no idea what dimension he is in. My guess is he's in the underworld, which doesn't bode well for his rate of survival. As for Tristan, the longer he remains under Harkon's power, the more he'll succumb to the archdemon's malevolence. Harkon lost his vessel when you killed Valerius. Who do you think he'll use now?"

The blood drains from my face, while it seems like the floor opened up under my feet. "Tristan."

Chapter 2
Red

I'm faced with an impossible choice. Who should I save? Tristan or Dante? I can't make that call. But timing is running out for them both, so I have to decide quickly. After Alex dropped that truth bomb, I went in search of Dr. Mervina. If she can still sense her connection to Dante and Tristan, then she's the best chance I've got to locate both fast.

I find her outside the manor, rallying up the wolves left in our pack. If I have to guess, we've lost at least half our enforcers and a few youngsters as well. The mood is somber, but that's no surprise. When I step closer to the gathering, I fully expect the pack to watch me with hatred in their eyes, but I get something else entirely. They do stare, but almost as if they're in awe. Murmurs erupt among them, and I hear a few refer to me as the Mother of Wolves.

My trip down memory lane gave me undeniable proof I'm Natalia's reincarnation. Yet, I still can't wrap my head around it. The magical diary only gave me one glimpse of Natalia's life, and it left with me so many questions. But

I'm not sure if it would be wise to remember everything about my former life. I'm terrified of what that will do to my mental state. I wanted to know how to defeat Harkon, and that information I got. If people were meant to remember their past lives, then we would retain our memories. There's a reason why we don't.

Dr. Mervina pauses her speech, turning to me. "You arrived just in time, Red."

Frowning, I ask, "In time for what?"

"It's time to let the pack know the truth about the nature of your relationship with my sons."

My jaw drops. She's going to reveal I'm mated to Tristan, Dante, *and* Sam. In hindsight, it makes sense. Everyone already knows what I am. Besides, the biggest threats to the pack aren't around anymore. I killed that bitch Lyria. As for Seth, well, his time is coming.

I nod, then lean closer to whisper in Dr. Mervina's ear. "Do you mind if I tell them?"

There's hint of pride in her eyes. "Not at all."

Taking a deep breath, I address the pack. "I'm sorry that such horrible things have descended upon this pack in such a short period of time. It doesn't escape my notice, and I'm sure it has not escaped your attention either, that my arrival here triggered everything."

Once again, the crowd talks among themselves, this time in whispers of surprise. The atmosphere becomes tenser, so I'm quick to continue. "I'm terribly sorry for your losses, but I will not apologize for things I had no way of stopping, terrible deeds that were put in motion even before I moved to this town. But I will promise the monsters responsible for the death and destruction will pay for it."

I'm glad that most, if not all, of the pack aren't against me this time.

"What Dr. Mervina, your alpha, was about to tell you, is that I'm mated to her sons. All three of them."

Gasps of surprise echo all around, but at the same time, there are people who don't seem surprised. Maybe they sensed the mating bond or heard from another supernatural. The supe community doesn't want humans to know about them, but they sure like to gossip among themselves.

"Are you truly the Mother of Wolves?" a young girl asks.

"I—" I turn to Dr. Mervina, not knowing what to say.

"They should know the entire truth, at least as you know it."

"I believe so," I answer.

The girl smiles, then turns to her friend to giggle. I honestly don't know what that was all about.

"What does that mean for the future of the pack?" an elderly man with a bushy beard asks Dr. Mervina.

"It means I'll remain the alpha until Tristan and Dante return. Then, I'll step down in favor of my sons. We're getting three alphas."

The silence is so absolute, the sound of a pin drop could be heard. I'm staring openmouthed at Dr. Mervina. So that was her plan all along? My chest tightens. If my mates are the new alphas, what does that make me, the alphas' consort? Am I ready to lead these wolves?

"How are we getting them back?" Billy asks from all the way in the back. No wonder I didn't see him before. I'm glad he's okay.

I trade a worried glance with Dr. Mervina. We still don't know where they are, and Alex's words come back to haunt me. He doesn't think I'll have enough time to rescue both.

Dr. Mervina opens her mouth to reply when one of the sentries comes running toward our group. I immediately think something terrible has happened. Are we under attack again? My fear is not unique. I sense the shift in the mood of the other wolves, too. Damn it. Could Harkon have recovered from his defeat so quickly? My heart becomes unbearably heavy when I think about Tristan.

"What's the matter, Terrence?" Dr. Mervina asks.

"There's someone at the north gate requesting permission to enter. I couldn't reach you over the phone, so I had to run here."

I let out the breath I was holding, but I'm far from relaxed.

"Who's at our gate?" I ask.

"A Shadow Creek wolf," Terrence answers with enough venom in his tone to kill an elephant.

"Impossible. All wolves from Shadow Creek have been put in quarantine at Brian Kane's property," Dr. Mervina replies.

Terrence shakes his head. "It seems you've missed one. What should I do?"

A suspicious thought springs in my head. "What does this wolf look like?"

"She's a teen, dark hair, white as a ghost. She doesn't speak."

"Nadine," I whisper. "Please, let her in at once."

The sentry frowns, then turns to Dr. Mervina for confirmation.

"It's fine, Terrence. She's not the enemy."

"Yes, ma'am."

He pulls his cell phone from his utility belt, dials, and then gives the order to let Nadine in. I don't wait for him to finish before I head toward the gate. No one has heard from Nadine since the battle in Shadow Creek, which only makes me suspect more that the black jaguar who stopped Alex from fighting with Xander was her.

I meet Nadine and the sentry accompanying her in the forest behind the alpha's manor, halfway toward the north gate. He has his beefy hand wrapped around her arm, which pisses me off.

"Let her go," I order.

The young man's face twists into a chagrined expression. He does as I said, taking a sidestep for good measure. "I'm sorry. We can never be too careful. She's from Shadow Creek."

"So am I."

The sentry drops his gaze. "Yes, ma'am. May I return to my post?"

I'm taken by surprise by his deferential attitude toward me. It hasn't been that long since the wolves from this pack treated me like dirt. Has he already learned I'm mated to the future alphas of the pack? I don't feel deserving of any special treatment, though. My desire is to earn the pack's respect, not receive it by default.

"Yes," I reply.

With quick steps, the young wolf returns to the north gate, and I turn my attention to Nadine. My eyes scan her from head to toe. She doesn't have any visible wounds, but that means nothing.

I breach the distance between us, pulling the girl into a tight embrace.

"I was so worried about you."

Nadine curls her fingers around the back of my shirt for a second before easing off. Her green eyes are brighter, but she doesn't cry.

"Are you okay?" I ask.

She nods, then begins to signal with her hands. She points at herself, then at her lips.

"Do you want to tell me something?" I guess.

She nods again. Since the only way we can communicate telepathically is when I'm in wolf form, I begin to undress. But Nadine grabs my wrist, stopping me from pulling my shirt off.

"What is it?"

She takes a step back, then takes off the oversized dress she's wearing. I gasp when I catch sight of the multitude of bruises and scars on her skin. Nadine either pretends she didn't hear it or chooses to ignore it. She initiates the shift. I totally expect to see a black jaguar in the next moment, but I find a light grey wolf staring at me instead.

If Nadine wasn't the black jaguar, who was?

Chapter 3
Dante

The icy wind is the first thing I sense when I regain consciousness. I'm no longer in wolf form, and the gelid air against my bare skin feels like I was dunked into a frozen lake. Curling into a fetal position to keep warm, I open my eyes. Nothing around me is familiar. I can see jagged mountains framed by dark clouds out in the distance. But that's about it. There's no sun, no warmth. Propping on my elbows, I attempt to sit up. All my muscles protest, but I manage, barely. The cold is even worse in this new position, so I bend my knees, hugging them while I try to control the chattering of my teeth. I need to find cover, or I'll freeze to death.

Desolation is all around me. I'm in a valley where the ground is dark and uneven. Rough fissures show an orange glow underneath, something akin to lava. With a grunt, I get to my feet, then move closer to one. There's no heat coming from it. Curious, I pick up a small rock and throw it at the crevice. It fizzles as it disappears between the cracks. No heat, but whatever substance that is, it burns. I'd better stay clear of them. Oppressive mountains are on both sides, making me feel like I'm caged in. There's no sign of nature, of life. Where the hell am I?

Knowing I won't get answers by staying put, I force myself to move. I can't simply stay here and wait to freeze to death. Every step I take is torture, and I soon discover why. The ground is made out of sharp rocks that cut into my feet. I'm pretty much walking on broken glass. Fuck. I hope there isn't any wildlife here. They would for sure be able to smell my blood from a mile away. In my current weakened state, I'm in no condition to fight anything.

I try to ignore the pain, but there's a sharper ache in my chest. I can't sense Red anymore. The mating bond has gone silent, just like when Valerius took her captive. I don't want to think the worst has happened, but the longer I walk, the less hopeful I become. It's like this place is sucking out any positive thoughts, any joy, I have in me.

It doesn't take long for me to lose track of time. I know I must have been walking for a long while when I begin to lose the sensation in my fingers. Frostbite must be getting to me. I can't continue on like this. I have to shift. At least my wolf's fur will keep me warmer. The only problem is that I can't reach it. There has never been a time in my life when I haven't been able to connect with my wild side. The wolf's essence has always been in my core. It was a part of me. But now, the awareness is gone.

There's a shift in the wind. With the change comes the pungent smell of sulfur. There's a demon approaching. I pivot on the spot, trying to pinpoint from where the attack will come from. After a minute or so, I hear them, the grunts of animalistic beings that makes the small hairs on the back of my neck stand on end. I have to find a place to hide and fast.

As I run in the opposite direction, my attention is split between finding a spot to get out of sight and watching where I step. Tripping will only make my situation worse. But those rocky walls are smooth and impossible to climb. I can't see a nook or cave in which I can hide. The noise behind me becomes louder, more savage. Instinctively, I know the demons have caught my scent, probably already spotted the blood trail I left behind.

The ground dips as if the valley wasn't already sunken enough. Farther down, there's even less light. Spots of shadows provide the perfect hiding spot for any creature that wants to make a meal out of me. But I can also use it to my advantage. I'm running out of time. Pretty soon, whatever is pursuing me will break over the horizon and see me. The little bit of energy I have is quickly waning. My leg muscles are burning, protesting with the exertion.

When I plunge into the darkness, my accelerated heart increases its pace tenfold. It's hammering in my chest as my adrenaline level shoots to the top. I'm so worried about what's coming behind me that I don't expect to get hit by something straight ahead. A thick, corded net is launched at me, covering my head and dragging me down by the heavy weights tied to its ends. I can't keep my balance. As the momentum of the fall sends me rolling on the ground, I become more tangled with the net to the point I can't move my arms anymore. My face ends up pressed against the stony ground, and the sharp bite of a jagged rock digs into my cheek, drawing blood. At this rate, I'll bleed to death before frostbite ends me.

Breathing hard, I wait for my fate. This is the end, which brings bitterness to my mouth. Regrets are terrible things, and I have many. The biggest one is not having had the chance to tell Red how much she means to me—how much I love her.

Someone chuckles not too far away before something heavy—a booted foot is my guess—presses against my back, making the sharp ground cut into my cheek deeper.

"Well, well, look at what we have here."

"What is it, Dad?" someone younger asks. By the timbre of his voice, he's a teen.

"It seems we got ourselves a shifter."

"How do you know?"

"Oh, son, I just know. Quickly, help me get him on the mount before that horde catches up with us. I really don't want to deal with them today. We're low on arsenal."

I'm helped up quite roughly, and I can't contain my surprise when I come face to face with a human, not a demon.

"Who are you?" I ask.

"Your fairy godmother." The man whacks me in the head, sending me into darkness once more.

Chapter 4
Red

"So you're a wolf shifter after all," I say, more to myself.

Nadine stares at me with her amber wolfish eyes before shaking her head. She begins to shimmer again. I think she's returning to her human form when her fur becomes black and short, her features changing from wolf to jaguar.

My jaw drops as I gape at a black jaguar, the very same one that saved Alex from a deathly confrontation with Xander.

"Oh my God. How is that possible?"

"Son of a bitch," someone says from behind me, making my heart jump up to my throat as I pivot on the spot.

Zeke Rogers, the imp who has been helping me since the very beginning for reasons I have yet to discover, is standing not too far from us. Nadine peels her lips back. If she had the ability to use her vocal cords, I bet she'd be growling.

"Jesus Christ. What in the world are you doing here?" I ask.

"I came to see how you and Sam were doing. Spotted

you heading into the forest, so I followed you."

"You couldn't let me know of your presence beforehand?" Crossing my arms, I glare at the imp.

"Well, I didn't expect to come into a big secret like that." He points with his head to Nadine.

I glance over my shoulder, finding Nadine eyeing Zeke with keen attention. Turning back to Zeke, I say, "I guess a big thank you is in order."

Shoving his hands into the pockets of his jeans, he shrugs. "No need to thank me. If Tristan were around, he would tell you that everything I did was self-serving, and he wouldn't be lying. I was protecting my own skin."

His mentioning of Tristan puts a dagger in my chest.

Zeke switch his attention to Nadine. "I knew there was something special about you, girlie. But not in a million years did I expect a hybrid shifter."

"Hybrid shifter?" I ask, sounding as stupid as I feel.

"I didn't even know such a thing was possible," Zeke replies.

"Are you saying that shifters of different species never get involved?"

Zeke chuckles. "Oh, there are plenty of interspecies hook-ups among shifters. However, conception in those cases is exceedingly rare. Even if the offspring survives birth, they can usually only shift into one animal. As far as I'm aware, Nadine is the only one who can choose between species. The most peculiar thing is that, until now, we believed the Crimson Hollow's black jaguar pride had been exterminated."

"Exterminated how and by whom?"

"I…" Zeke pauses, then glances at Nadine. "I don't know."

He's lying. I can smell his bullshit from miles away. But maybe he doesn't want to talk about it in front of Nadine. He studies her for the longest time, and I don't like the calculating gleam in his eyes. He did just say that everything he does is self-serving. I can't forget he's a demon, even if a less powerful one.

"You need to swear you won't say a word about Nadine to anyone."

Zeke raises an eyebrow. "Oh? And what would you give me in return?"

Growling, I take a step forward. "How about I let you keep your tongue?"

Zeke covers his mouth with his hand, taking a step back. "Savage and a little insensitive as well, considering Valerius took his sister's ability to speak."

Ah, shit. The imp is right. Guilt squeezes my heart as I swivel to Nadine. She's shifted into human. In her eyes, I see the haunted expression has returned. I'm such a moron.

"Nadine, I'm so sorry."

She shakes her head before getting dressed again. It's so hard to read her when she's closed off like that. I just hope she doesn't decide to run again. We're not safe by any stretch of the imagination. Harkon will come back, more pissed off than before.

"You have to be careful with that one, Red," Zeke says, pulling me to the here and now.

I whip toward him, suddenly very much irritated. "Did you come here just to annoy me?"

He raises both hands as he widens his eyes innocently. "Of course not, but I'm an imp. Annoying people is in my nature, whether I want it or not. Actually, I came here because I think I know where Harkon sent Dante."

My heart stops beating for a second before it lurches forward with a jolt. "What? Why didn't say that first?"

"Because I got distracted by little Nadine there."

I cross the distance between Zeke, curling my fingers around his shirt's fabric and pulling him closer. "Where is Dante?" I growl.

"Whoa, watch the clothes, sweetheart. They're Italian."

I let go of Zeke and retreat, but continue to glare at him.

"I said I *think* I know where he is. I'm not one-hundred-percent sure."

Turning my hands into fists, I say, "Where?"

"Harkon didn't have access to all his power. He couldn't have conjured a portal to a dimension too far from ours. I believe he sent Dante to the Wastelands, an in-between realm where creatures from the underworld like to hang out. There are humans there, too."

"So, is that a limbo of sorts?"

"No. You're thinking about the Land of Lost Souls. That's where obsessive spirits are banished to if they refuse to do the crossing. The humans and supes living in the Wastelands are very much alive."

"So you think Dante is there?"

"Yes."

A flicker of hope flares in my chest. "So how do I get there?"

"Hold on, princess. Things are not that simple. The Wastelands is a dangerous place. We'll need help from someone on the inside."

"Damn it, Zeke. If this place is as dangerous as you say, we need to get Dante out of there as soon as possible."

Zeke loses all the levity from before. His expression turns serious as his facial muscles tense. I think he's finally realizing this is not a joke. "Okay, okay. I might know someone who can help us, but getting in touch might take a few hours."

"We don't have a few hours," I almost shout.

Zeke's eyes flash red before they return to their normal blue color. "Do you think I have a direct line to a hellish dimension? I'm afraid they don't have cell phone service there. While I try to reach my contact, you can call for an urgent meeting with your allies. Getting safe passage through the Wastelands will have a price."

"I don't care what the price is."

Zeke moves closer, his eyebrows scrunching while his eyes take on a dangerous glint.

"You might not care, but I'll bet a limb your druid and witch friends will."

Chapter 5
Red

After Zeke left to get in touch with his contact in the Wastelands, I went in search of Dr. Mervina to let her know about the conversation. I kept the fact Nadine was a hybrid shifter to myself. If Zeke is right and Nadine is a rarity among shifters, I want to keep the information contained. I still don't know who to trust to be completely honest. Seth's betrayal left me with a bitter taste in my mouth, and let's not forget the alpha of the Vancouver pack who was also working with Valerius. To protect Nadine, I'll keep her secret for as long as I can. I just hope Zeke keeps his mouth shut as well.

Nadine accompanied me when I went to talk to Dr. Mervina, and I was glad I didn't have to ask. I don't want to lose sight of her. The opportunity to really talk to her telepathically, to understand how in the world she's a hybrid shifter, hasn't come up. I wonder if she knows about her lineage and the truth about her pride.

Dr. Mervina looked troubled when I told her Dante could be in the Wastelands, but she didn't say anything to me specifically. She must know he's in a dangerous place. Instead, she went to make phone calls. Left with nothing to do but wait, I decided to get Nadine settled in one of the guestrooms in the alpha's manor.

Finally alone with her, I signal to the best of my ability, asking her if she wants to talk. She nods, so I shift. The process is more painful today, maybe because my body is still not one-hundred-percent recharged.

"Hey, are you okay?" I ask.

"Yes. I... I still can't believe Valerius is gone." She hugs her middle, making herself smaller. It's a habit I've noticed from her. I pray that one day she won't feel the need to do it anymore.

"I'm sorry, honey."

"Why?" Her gaze becomes hard, surprising me a little. "He was evil. He deserved to die. Did he suffer?"

"I don't know. I think so."

Tensing her jaw, she nods. The haunted expression in her eyes is gone, replaced by undiluted hatred. I can't say I prefer that emotion over the other. She's so young. It kills me that her own flesh and blood has put her through so much pain already.

"Have you seen Victor?" I ask.

At least one good thing came out of the fight in Shadow Creek. By some miracle, Victor had not been killed by our allies.

"No. He's in quarantine, and the druids are not letting anyone in besides their own kind and Dr. Mervina."

"She's doing everything she can to help those with chip

implants."

"It's no use. If she tries to remove the chips now, the wolves will die."

"How do you know that?"

"I've overheard Valerius talking with one of the doctors. The chip containing Harkon's signature has a destructive mechanism. If anyone attempts to remove it, the chip emits a signal that will kill the host's brain waves."

I feel the blood drain from my face. No wonder Martin insisted I had to have the regular chip. He knew about that destructive mechanism. Was he present when they implanted the chip in Tristan's head? Suddenly, I feel the urgent need to have a word with the man.

"There's has to be way to override that." I can't remain still, so I begin to pace.

"Maybe if Harkon is killed, then the chips will become regular ones?"

"Not if he's killed—when he's killed. I'll see to his utter destruction myself. But we need to tell Dr. Mervina about the chips."

"She knows."

"How?"

"I told them when I tried to see Victor."

Shit. When will the bad news end? I have to believe destroying Harkon will end his influence over the chips. But what if it doesn't? What if killing him doesn't disable the chips? The urge to howl is overwhelming, but it wouldn't do any good.

"I'd like to help rescue Dante," Nadine says suddenly.

I turn around so fast my tail hits the end of the bed. Damn it. It hurts. *"No. Absolutely not. You heard Zeke. The Wastelands is a dangerous place, and I can't put you in harm's way again."*

"I'm not a baby. I've survived Valerius's reign of terror on my own and without a chip implanted in me."

I wince a little. I don't think Nadine meant to take a jab at me, but I wasn't so lucky avoiding going under the knife of that butcher doctor.

"Why would you want to go there?" I ask.

"Because you'll need help from someone you can trust."

She has me there. I'm sure Zeke and Alex will volunteer to accompany me to the Wastelands, two people I can't bet my life on. Zeke is an imp. Only a fool would trust the guy. Alex is a man who betrayed my trust already.

"Let me think about it," I lie to stall her. I have no intention of agreeing to it. *"I don't even know if we'll be going there."*

In Nadine's eyes, I read that she intends to keep pestering me about the Wastelands, so I tell her I'm going to go check on Sam, then I shift and get dressed again. It's kind of ridiculous that I'm running away from a teenager, but I'm slowly beginning to realize I'll have a hard time saying "no" to her. What does that say about my future as a mom?

Holy shit. I pause in the middle of the corridor. Motherhood is another implication of my unusual relationship I hadn't stopped to consider before. I always wanted kids one day, but never in a million years had I expected to be married—or mated—to three men. I'm sure

Tristan, Dante, and Sam will want to start a family in the future, so does that mean they will each want to father one child? Ugh. Am I destined to become a puppy factory?

Stop it, Red. You're being ridiculous.

Leave it to my brain to come up with more stuff to worry about. As if what I have on my plate isn't already enough to give me premature wrinkles and a case of stomach ulcers.

Taking deep breaths to calm down, I open the door to Sam's room, finding the bed empty.

"Sam?"

The sound of the toilet flushing tells me where he is. Emerging from the bathroom in all his naked glory, Sam smiles at me.

"Hello, my love."

"How are you feeling?"

"Now that you're here, much better." He glances at his erection, then peers at me from under his eyelashes with a cocky grin on his lips.

I forget about our problems for a moment as my body ignites, answering a primal call, an urgent need that has me itching to get out of my clothes again. Sam and I move fast, breaching the distance between us with one stride each. His hands are yanking at my clothes as his lips find mine for a savage kiss. I let my hands go on an exploration of their own as well, touching every inch of skin I can find. The sound of fabric ripping alerts me that Sam has zero patience today.

Placing openmouthed kisses on my neck, he leaves a hot trail as he moves downward. One of his hands is already playing with my left boob when his tongue finds my right nipple. It was already pebbled, and when Sam sucks it into his mouth, using teeth as well, I let out a moan that's probably too loud. My body is tingling, my toes curling over the soft carpet. Can someone come from boob kisses? The thought is so ludicrous a bubble of laughter escapes my lips. Sam release my nipple with a pop, gazing up with heavy-lidded eyes.

"What's so funny?"

He's so damn sexy, even with a bandage over his eye. I already forgot why I laughed. Grabbing his face between my hands, I pull his lips back on mine. Our tongues mingle in a sweet and fervent dance while his hands find my butt to lift me off the floor. With my legs wrapped around his hips, his cock rubs right on the sweet spot. I'm not sure if I'll survive what's to come before I combust. Sam drops me on the bed without breaking the kiss. I shimmy up to make room before opening my legs for him.

He runs his hand down my side, brushing against the underside of my breast before continuing lower. I also try to do the same, but with him on top of me, it's hard to get access to what I want. His fingers graze the crease of my thigh first, a tease that drives me insane.

"Sam, please."

He smiles against my lips before deepening the kiss once more. Two can play at this game. Managing to wiggle my hand between our bodies, I curl my fingers around his cock. He hisses right before he swipes his thumb over my clit. Sweet mercy, the boy is good with his fingers. I arch my back, needing more contact. To get closer, though, I would have to mold myself to him.

Pressed against his body like that, it's harder to work his erection, but I try my best. Liquid has already pooled on the head, so I spread it around his length, using it as a natural lube as I begin to pump my hand up and down. With a growl, Sam sits on the balls of his feet, then rolls over before I can say a word. Knowing what he wants, I get onto my knees. He covers my body with his, biting my shoulder softly before he plunges inside my drenched pussy, bringing forth a small cry from my lips.

"Fuck, Red. I'll never get over how good it feels to be inside of you."

My response is something incoherent, garbled words that mean nothing. It's impossible to think straight when Sam is pounding into me. With each thrust, the pleasure doubles. I feel him become harder as he increases the tempo, the subtle change enough to initiate my own wave of pleasure. My skin tingles as I approach the inevitable plunge. Suddenly, Sam sinks his sharp teeth into my skin, drawing blood and sending me over the edge. I can't help it. I let out a loud cry, not caring who can hear us. Probably everybody in the house.

Sam keeps on moving in and out even after he empties his warm seed into me. My guess is he's trying to prolong the pleasure for as long as he can. Shit, if I had any control over it, I'd let it go on forever. Who in their right mind would want such a blissful feeling to end? It just proves nature knows best. No one would get shit done otherwise.

Sam finally stops thrusting, then collapses next to me.

"Damn it, love. I can't get enough of you. Even when our world is on the verge of total destruction, I crave you like an addict."

I roll onto my side, propping my head on my hand. "I can't explain what happened to me either. I was consumed by a raw energy, an overwhelming need to be with you. It was almost like a fever."

Sam turns his face to mine. His skin is flushed and covered in sweat. "It's possible you're close to going in heat."

"Uh, what?" I sit up.

Sam does the same, placing his hands on my thighs. "Mated female wolves go in to heat once a year."

My face becomes warmer, blush blazing. "What does that mean exactly?"

"It means your libido will go through the roof, and all you'll want to do is fuck."

I stare at Sam without blinking for several beats before I say, "How long does it last"

"It depends. Three to seven days."

"What? A week?" I push a strand of hair off my face with a shaking hand. Jesus fucking Christ. I can't imagine what having sex nonstop for that many days will do to my body. After one night of passion with Sam and Dante, I could barely walk. "I hope you're wrong. I don't have time to turn into a full-blown nymphomaniac."

"I have no experience in the matter. Only mated wolves go through it."

I let out a nervous laugh. "Well, that's good to know. So

does that mean if I go in to heat, only you and your brothers will be able to sense it?"

Sam leans forward to kiss me again. His tongue pushes the seams of my lips open. I naively believe it's going to be a quick one, but then his nails dig into my skin and my breathing turns erratic again. I have to force myself to end it.

"Sam, please don't start again. As much as I want you, we have things to do."

"Shit. Sorry, Red. I can't keep my hands to myself when you're around."

I jump off the bed, then head to the bathroom to clean up. While I'm busy with the task, the idea of having kids comes to the forefront of my mind again. I've never used protection with any of them. It hadn't even occurred to me since I get the birth control shot, and there's still two months until I need to take another one. But fuck, what if it's no longer effective thanks to me turning into a shifter? Damn it. I should have asked Dr. Mervina about this.

With my guts twisted into knots, I return to the room to search for my clothes. They're scattered on the floor and in pieces. Putting my hands on my hips, I glare at Sam. "Great. What am I going to wear now?"

"How about nothing?" He laughs.

My body is still reeling with desire, but until I get straight answers from Dr. Mervina, I won't succumb to his charms. I can't let our crazy wolf libidos take control. There's too much at stake.

"I didn't come here looking for booty, Sam. Zeke came to see me. He knows where Dante might be."

My mention of Dante works like a charm to sober Sam up. His spine goes taut, any trace of desire in his eye vanishing in a split second.

"Where?"

"A place called the Wastelands."

"I've never heard of it."

"According to Zeke, the Wastelands is an in-between realm."

Sam stands up, his body now coiled with raw energy. He's projecting his wolf nature to the max. "Let me guess. It's a dimension filled with demons."

"Yup."

"Okay, then. How do we get there?"

Chapter 6
Dante

When I regain conscience, I realize I've been thrown over the back of some kind of animal with my wrists and ankles bound. At least I'm no longer freezing to death. Whoever captured me was kind enough to throw a blanket over me. The fabric is rough and itchy, but it's better than the bitter cold from before. I can't really discern where we're going or make out more than the shapes of my captors as night has descended upon this strange place.

"Where are you taking me?"

"Oh, it seems Sleeping Beauty is awake," the youngster says.

"It doesn't matter where you're going," the other man replies.

"Who are you and what do you want with me?" I try to break free of my bondage, but it's no use.

"Don't even bother. Those are fae vines. Nothing can cut through them."

A growl rumbles from my chest, and the action stirs the wildness in me. I can feel my wolf again. Thank fuck. I'm torn between attempting a shift now and escaping or waiting until we arrive at our final destination. I'm pretty stuck between a rock and a hard place. I don't know how many people will be waiting where we're going, so my chances of escaping are greater now. However, my rate of survival decreases exponentially if I leave my captors. Without clothes and a sense of direction, I'll be dead before the night is over. I'll wait then.

"Fine. Don't tell me where we're going or your names, but can you at least tell me where the hell I am?"

"Pa, can I tell him?"

"I don't see the harm. It's his home now." The man chuckles.

Yeah, don't count on it, buddy. I'll find a way out of this hellhole.

"You're in the Wastelands."

"Wastelands? I've never heard of such a place."

"You're from the mortal lands, yeah? This is a different dimension," the youngster continues. "You're not in Kansas anymore, Toto."

"How do you know that expression? You're from there too, aren't you? Why are you here?"

"Uh—"

"Enough already," the father cuts his son off. "We've arrived."

Not too far from us, a soft light seems to be floating in the air. A second later, I realize a woman is holding a lantern. No, not a woman. Something other—maybe a fae. I've never seen one before to know for sure, but her ethereal, perfect beauty and pointy ears are a dead giveaway. They live in their own realm. Rarely ever do they wander into our world. The small light illuminates only her face, which is extremely pale. Swirling tattoos adorn her cheeks, and her hair is bound back.

"You're later than usual. You know it's not safe after sundown." Her eyes travel to me. "I see your hunting was fruitful at least."

"Oh, yeah. Your vision was dead on."

"But we almost lost him to the ghouls," the teen adds.

"Did they see you?" The fae's voice changes, a hint of alarm slipping through.

"No, relax, Maven. All is well." The man throws his arm around the fae's shoulder, then kisses her on the cheek.

Twisting her face into a scowl, she pushes the man away, which makes him laugh.

"Quickly, let's bring him inside. I'd like to take a closer look at him."

The man returns to the mount, then proceeds to untie me from the animal. He keeps my arms and ankles bound, though.

"You're not going to throw me over your shoulder, are you?" I ask.

The man snorts. "Sorry, darling. You ain't my type."

Suddenly, I begin to float, which makes me panic for a second until I realize the fae is using her magic to get me off the animal. The blanket falls off, and I try my best to cover my junk with my hands. This is already humiliating enough; I don't need my dick swishing back and forth like a damn bell cord.

She maintains levitating me as she walks, lantern in hand. Straining my eyes, I try to get my bearings, but outside the dim glow of light from the lantern is only blackness. I only know I've crossed an invisible barrier when I feel a tingling sensation all over my body. There's a blinding flash, then the darkness vanishes to be replaced by the interior of a big room softly lit by torches mounted on the carved rock walls. The walls contain built-in shelves of rough wood, filled to the gills with books.

The fae puts me on my feet in the middle of a cozy living room where a fireplace is lit. To my side, there's an ancient-looking stove where the fae is cooking something in a cast-iron pan. It smells quite nice, and my stomach growls in agreement. I feel like I'm stuck in a hobbit's lair. The scene is so surreal that I'm rendered speechless for a moment as I take everything in.

The fae approaches me, making my spine go rigid. She stares at me from head to toe appraisingly as if I were livestock.

"Not bad, not bad at all. He'll fetch a great price at the Shadow Market."

"Excuse me?"

"You didn't think we saved your ass out of the kindness of our hearts, did you?" the teen says, watching me with a satisfied, malicious glint sparking in his eyes.

"Are you planning to sell me as a slave?"

"Oh no, you're too fine to be a slave. We're taking you right up to the King of Bastards," the fae says, earning a cautious glance from the older man.

"Are you sure, Maven?"

Without taking her eyes off me, the fae smirks. "Oh yeah. I'm sure. Prythian will pay a fair price for the wolf shifter. That is, if he survives the ring."

She turns to the stove, going to check whatever grub she's cooking. The man and his son head off in the opposite direction of the room, presumably to unload their bags. This is my chance. I've heard enough. I can't just stand here and listen to these people talk about me like I'm a mere sack of potatoes they plan to sell at market. With a silent growl, I tap into my wolf. Slowly, I feel the shift begin.

"What do you think you're doing there, wolfie?" Maven turns, holding a spoon in her hand.

My bones crack and my muscles expand, but abruptly, the shift stops before reversing to the beginning. What the hell!

"Let me go," I say through clenched teeth.

"I'm afraid I can't do that. You see, the King of Bastards has been searching for a new champion for ages. Everyone knows he prefers pretty shifters like you, in and out of the arena." She grabs my chin between her cold fingers. Even though I want to charge her with my bound hands and all, I find myself paralyzed.

"After centuries of living in this forsaken dimension, I'm ready to leave, but I need coin to buy my way out. You're my ticket."

"He's our ticket, you mean," the man pipes in.

Maven drops her hand, taking a step back. "Of course,

darling. We're partners, remember?"

Shit. Is this fool buying the fae's bullshit? I can smell her lie from here. Whatever she's planning to do, she's doing it alone. How can I use her deception to my advantage?

Chapter 7
Red

"No, absolutely not," Riku Ogata says, crossing his arms and shaking his head.

"What do you mean by no?" I start to move forward, but Dr. Mervina puts a hand on my arm.

"We can't allow portals to hellish dimensions to open again in Crimson Hollow."

"You can't be serious," I say through gritted teeth.

"Oh, he's serious all right. Meet the most unbendable fox in the entire land—my father." Nina reaches for the table of refreshments, popping a snack into her mouth and completely ignoring the glare her father sends her way.

"It's not up to you, Mr. Ogata. If my brother is in the Wastelands, we're going there, whether you like it or not," Sam chimes in.

"The key word here is 'if'. You don't know if your brother is in the Wastelands. It's too risky to open a portal to that dimension without knowing you're in the right place. Do you realize what kind of horrifying creatures we could unleash in this town?"

"Oh, please." Nina rolls her eyes. "Stop with the dramatics already. Nothing is going to come out of the portal unless you open one in the middle of the Arena of Bastards."

"The arena of what?" I ask, then shake my head. "Never mind. I don't need to know."

"What if you had undeniable proof that my son is in that dimension? Would you still be adamantly against it, Riku?"

The man at least has the decency to look guilty. "How would you get that proof?"

"I can still sense the link to my son. If I have something from that dimension to use as a connector, I can find out if he's in the Wastelands."

Xander snorts. "And how are you going to get that without crossing over to the place?"

Nina takes a step forward. "Would this work?"

To Dr. Mervina, she presents a simple bracelet made out of copper.

"What the—" Xander's eyes fix on the object.

"How did you get that?" Riku says, a tone of disapproval in his voice.

Ignoring her father, she asks again, "Would this work?"

Dr. Mervina inspects the item, then raises her gaze to Nina. "Was this made in the Wastelands?"

Nina shrugs. "I believe so."

"Nina Ogata! How did you obtain that object?" The fox shifter pushes forward, now shaking in anger.

She twists to him, returning the glare she's receiving. "It's none of your concern how I got it."

"You crossed into that dimension, didn't you? You

ignored the Accords and opened an outer-dimensional portal."

"I did no such thing."

"You lie!"

"Dad! Enough." Leo Ogata, Nina's brother and also a member of Sam's band, slides in between his father and sister with arms raised.

His intervention does nothing to calm his father's nerves. With venom spitting out of his mouth, he addresses Nina, "You're a disgrace to our kind and this family. I was right when I banished you."

A flicker of hurt crosses the young fox's face, but it vanishes in the next instant. "That was the best day of my life. Truly."

Billy moves closer to the shifter, but refrains from touching her. I think everyone in the room has picked up on the vibe that touching the fox now would cause them a great amount of hurt. She looks ready to break some bones.

Riku turns his attention to Dr. Mervina. "I stand by what I said. I'm against opening any portal to the Wastelands with or without proof your son is there."

"Then I'm glad I don't need your vote," Dr. Mervina replies with steely coldness.

"No, but you need the druid's vote. Isn't that why you requested this meeting? You don't have enough power to conjure a portal."

Alex, who I had not seen since our meeting earlier, enters the room. He didn't come from the front door, but from down the corridor where the bedrooms must be. Is he staying with Brian Kane? Ugh. Why do I care?

"We have the go ahead from the Head of the Dark Blades. If your son is in the Wastelands, we can get him."

Sam growls next to me. "We? Who said you're coming?"

Alex's lips twitch into a smirk. "Let me put it this way. If the Blades don't come, you don't get a portal."

Santiago, who had been quiet until that moment, raises a hand. "Okay, okay. First, we'll find out if Dante is in the Wastelands. No sense wasting power to open a portal to the wrong dimension. If we confirm he's there, then a small group will do the crossing. However, not knowing Dante's exact location will make things more complicated. Ideally, you don't want to spend more than a few hours in a hellish dimension. The problem will be knowing when we should get you out of there. My guess is you can't open a portal from the other side."

"If we had a gadget that could store a spell, could we conjure an exit portal ourselves?" Sam asks.

"Do you think creating a portal is a simple spell?" Alex frowns. "It will require the combined energy of a witch *and* a druid circle."

Sam crosses his arms, projecting his pissed-off wolf aura. "Do you have a better suggestion?"

"Zeke Rogers knows someone in the Wastelands who can help us. If he has a way to contact them, then we could use the same method to communicate when we're ready," I say.

"Who is this creature the imp has access to?" Santiago

asks.

"I don't know. He didn't say. All he told me is it will cost us."

"Of course it will. That imp does nothing without expecting payment," Jared, Santiago's grandson, says.

"It's not Zeke who wants payment, but his contact," I clarify.

"When can we expect a word from the imp?" Alex asks.

"In a couple of hours. He knows we're pressed for time." I turn to Dr. Mervina. "How about Tristan? Zeke didn't say anything about him, but could he also be in the Wastelands?"

"That's very unlikely," Alex replies. "The Wastelands is too close to our plane, which means the demonic energy there is not as strong. Harkon, being an archdemon, would probably go all the way to the bowels of hell in order to restore himself."

My throat turns tight once more. I can't image what horrors Tristan is facing at the hands of that monster.

"Maybe we should try to rescue Tristan first?" I ask, feeling once more torn about who we should go after. This is an impossible decision.

"If Tristan is in hell, I'm afraid we can't get to him." Dr. Mervina's expression becomes troubled. Her words put a dagger through my chest.

"What are we supposed to do then? Nothing? Let Harkon consume his soul?" My voice rises to a shrill pitch.

She lifts her gaze to mine. "Harkon will return to Crimson Hollow for you. That's when we'll rescue Tristan."

"So you just want to wait?" I can't accept that solution. It's too cruel."

Sam touches my shoulder, squeezing it lightly. "You're underestimating Tristan. He's strong. He won't perish by spending a day or two in hell."

A rogue tear escapes the corner of my eye. I don't bother to wipe it off. "He has a chip, Sam. That changes everything."

It's obvious my words put a chink in Sam's confident demeanor. But we have no use for comforting lies.

"Carol, any word from Wendy yet?" Dr. Mervina asks.

"The stubborn lady wants to help, but her sisters are against it."

Dr. Mervina opens her mouth to reply, but Alex beats her to it. "We'll need a *full* circle of witches to create enough power."

"How many witches do you need for a complete circle?" I ask.

"Five," Carol replies.

"If Grandma can't join the circle, would I be able to take her place?"

Dr. Mervina stares at me with a glint of regret. "If you're part of the circle, you won't be able to use the portal."

My chest deflates as my hopes diminish. "Do we know any other witches then?"

Brian and Carol suddenly become tense, but it's their son, Jared, who sheds light on their peculiar reaction.

"Someone just crossed through the wards."

"Really? Again?" Nina says in exasperation.

"How can it be? We just reinforced it this morning," Brian mutters.

Frowning, Alex replies, "I don't sense a strong protective ward at all. Whatever spell you cast, it has lost power considerably."

Sam curses, and I sense his wolf nature is becoming more evident. He's ready to shift. I watch from the corner of my eye when Alex pulls out his special dagger. Max and Daria do the same.

"Is Harkon back already?" I ask. My heart is warring against hope and despair.

Hope that Tristan is with the archdemon, despair we're so not ready to face them.

Chapter 8
Tristan

I don't know where I am when I open my eyes, nor what happened before I got here. The most nauseating smell reaches my nose, making my stomach twist sharply as it tries to eject my last meal. Only there's nothing there but hollowness. My wrists are bound in chains. Once my eyesight adjusts to the gloom, I can make out shapes in my surroundings. Walls of jagged stones surround me, and there's moisture in the air. I'm in some kind of cave.

The sound of slithering in the background makes my skin crawl, but it's the unmistakable cry of someone being tortured in another chamber that twists my heart in fear. Cold sweat drips down my spine at the same time that pieces of my memory return to me. We went after Red through a portal and ended up in Shadow Creek. There was a battle and I… Fuck, I don't remember what happened.

I try to break free from the chains, but they're wrapped tightly around my wrists. All I do is rattle them, the noise echoing loudly. The slithering noise stops suddenly, as do the cries of pain. My skin breaks into goose bumps when

I sense a malevolent presence approaching. The awful smell increases until it threatens to suffocate me. My body begins to shake uncontrollably as panic sets in. I've never experienced something like this before, but I can't let my emotions control me. I can't.

The room suddenly changes color from almost pitch black to a red glow. The reason materializes at the entrance—a great beast, almost twice my size. Its skin is the color of charcoal, and it has protruding veins that glow a fiery ember color as if they're infused with lava. Twisted horns protrude from his forehead, spiraling upward to end in two sharp tips. His face is a cross between man and goat, and his eyes are two glowing red orbs that shine with pure evil.

My heart is beating at staccato, every pound louder than the one before. My mouth becomes dry as I endure the archdemon's stare.

"So we meet again, Robert."

"The name is Tristan," I say, not knowing how in the world I manage to utter those words with the way my tongue is stuck to my mouth.

The demon laughs. "It doesn't matter what name you answer to now. You've had many, despite the fact your puny human mind can't remember them. The only thing that matters is how much I'll enjoy torturing you until you're nothing more than a soulless, putrid carcass."

"Go ahead. Do your worse," I challenge the demon. I don't remember what happened at Shadow Creek, but if Harkon is wasting his time with me, it means he doesn't have Red. The longer I keep him distracted, the more time I'll give her and my brothers to forge the weapon that will end Harkon's existence for good.

"You don't know what you just wished for. Luckily for you, I have no intention of ending you so soon."

The demon snaps his fingers, making fire erupt from the ground below my feet. The flames lick my body, burning every piece it touches. The pain is unbearable, but I hold the scream that is stuck in my throat for as long as I can. I don't want to give Harkon the satisfaction. Eventually, the anguished cry escapes my lips, and it goes on until my throat is hoarse. The fire keeps eating away at my flesh, and the pain increases with each flaming stroke. I remain awake, but most importantly, I don't die. Now I know the true meaning of burning in hell.

As suddenly as it came, the fire vanishes. My body, which should be a charcoal mess, is whole again.

"Having fun yet?" Harkon asks.

"Loads," I breathe out.

"I have to say, you've gained balls in this new lifetime. Must be the wolf in you."

I don't have a comeback for that. In fact, I'm still reeling from the pain of being burned alive.

Harkon approaches, making my entire body tense. Clenching my jaw, I force myself to look right into his eyes. I won't cower in front of him. Crimson orbs that seem to be made out of pure lava stare back at me.

"I read defiance in your gaze. Pointless, I'm afraid. This is the end for you. No more do overs, no more new lives to make up for your past mistakes."

I don't have the chance to ask what the hell he's talking about before searing pain splits my skull in two, and I feel my life force being drained from me. My wolf rebels, churning inside my chest as it tries to claw his way out of the vortex that's sucking its energy. But it's no use. The force is too strong, and I'm too weak to fight it.

Chapter 9
Dante

The fae called Mauve forced me eat her special stew without telling me what it was. It didn't taste bad, and honestly, I need the strength. She seemed to think so as well, because she instructed her human partner to make sure I had enough blankets in my cell.

Once alone in my new quarters, which was in fact a small chamber carved into the rock, I attempt to shift again. But the wolf I felt stir before lays dormant, just as my bond to Red is nowhere to be found. I have to believe she survived the fight against Harkon. Even without the bond, I would know if she had perished.

I begin to pace in the small room, unable to rest even knowing I should preserve my energy. Mauve plans to sell me as a slave tomorrow, so I must attempt to escape before I'm in the hands of a new master. It will be much more difficult to run away then.

It's easy to lose track of time in this place, but if the weariness in my bones is any indication, I must have been running a hole through the ground for over an hour.

Suddenly, the magic barrier sealing this place parts in the middle, and Mauve enters. Now that she's not keeping her face hidden under a hood, I'm one-hundred-percent sure she's fae, which means, I have to be extra careful here. Her kind are known to be tricksters. They can bind someone for an eternal life of servitude if they say the wrong thing. Words have power in their hands.

"You're still awake. I don't like it."

"Tough shit."

I'm thrown against the wall. Kept there above the ground by an invisible force. I can't move a muscle.

"Do not disrespect me, wolf boy. I'm more powerful than you."

"Then why the hell do you need to sell me to this King of Bastards to buy your way out?"

The force disappears, and I fall like a sack of potatoes.

"The reason is not your concern."

"You can't leave, can you? You were banished, so now you need to buy a spell strong enough to free you."

She's on me in a split second, holding me by the neck in a vicious hold. Once again, I can't move, and I hate it.

"Watch what you say, wolfie. I might forget that you're worth a lot of coin and kill you now."

She releases me from her hold, and I gasp for air.

"If you need to get out of here so badly, maybe I can help you," I say as I clutch my throat.

She narrows her gaze to slits. "You? Who do you take me for? A fool? No one comes to the Wastelands by choice. If you're here, you're as trapped as I am."

"What do you mean?"

"Don't you get it? This is the banishment land, a place where unwanted beings are sent as punishment. In other words, this is a prison."

"I'll find a way out," I say, my voice now hoarse from her vicious grab.

"No, you won't. Now sweet dreams, my darling. Tomorrow is a big day for us."

She waves her hand, and I feel her magic descend on me, making me eyelids heavy. Before I succumb to her potent spell, I say, "For us, but not for your human friend and his son, right?"

The fae curls her lips into a cruel smile. "You're too perceptive for your own good."

※

When I wake up, I'm no longer in my small prison chamber, but on a carriage of sorts, moving. I'm also no longer naked. Strange clothing covers my sore body, a mix of rags and fur. My wrists and ankles are bound once more, but not by the same leather bindings. Metal chains keep me in place, rattling with every move the carriage makes.

Mauve is sitting across from me, her face the perfect expression of serenity. Her light hair is not tied back like she wore it yesterday, but braided on top of her head. Her clothes are simple, yet elegant, partially hidden by the thick cloak tied at her neck.

"Where are you taking me?" I ask.

"You already know, so stop asking pesky questions."
"To the Shadow Market."
"Yes."
"You think this King of Bastards will want to buy me. What makes you so sure?"
"You're his type."

I hear the implication loud and clear. "So, you're selling me as a sex slave, is that it?"

She snorts. "Prythian doesn't need to buy sex slaves. He receives plenty of attention from both genders for free. But he has a grand weakness, which is his gladiator games. He's always on the lookout for a new champion."

"What makes you think he'll deem me champion material?"

Mauve stares intently at me, and I have the uncomfortable feeling she's trying to read my mind.

"You're not a simple wolf shifter, that much I sense in you. You have another gift, and I have a feeling Prythian will be able to sense that as well."

I snort, but it's not to provoke the fae. She has no idea that my extra gift has a mind of its own, and I can't harness it at will. It would be great if I could since it tends to manifest when I least want it.

"You got it wrong, lady. I'm just a regular shifter."
"What you are is a terrible liar."

The carriage stops suddenly. A moment later, Mauve's partner sticks his head between the fabric partition to announce we have arrived at the Shadow Market. She gets out first, then orders me to follow her. It's hard to move at first with the chain's constrictions, but once I jump off the back of the carriage, it becomes a little easier.

We're at the entrance of a grand open market, where tents in different shades of drably colors are spread out. Once again, the sky is overcast, no sign of the sun. I wonder if their sun is the same as ours. I sense stares aimed in my direction, some so malevolent that dread drips down my spine. I lock my jaw tight, lifting my chin as well. I'm might be bound in chains, but I won't let them intimidate me.

Mauve glances briefly in my direction with an air of approval about her. *I'm not doing it for your benefit, bitch.* It's a matter of survival. The crowd of demons and other underworld creatures part to allow the fae to pass. I sense power emanating from her, and my guess is she's using it to keep the rough crowd at bay. They stop looking in our direction, too. I have the sense that in the Wasteland, it's kill or be killed. Mauve's partner brings up the rear. He didn't bring his son with him.

Despite not being stared at by the demons roaming in this place, the sense of being watched remains. I let my gaze wander, searching for the creature who is spying on us. Beyond the square where the market is, there are several three-story stone buildings that could easily hide someone. With thatched roofs and stone walls, they remind me of houses in a medieval town—at least the ones I've seen in movies. I'm about to give up, when I catch a black shadow jump from one roof to the next. The creature is covered from head to toe in black, wearing a cloak that hides their features. However, I did manage to see the duo color of their ponytail—blonde and black—before it disappeared behind a chimney.

A little commotion ahead draws my attention away from the outskirt buildings to the grand construction looming at the end of the market. I can't help it when my jaw drops as I stare at a replica of the Roman Coliseum as it was in its former glory. How in the world did I not see that when we entered the market?

"It's a beauty, isn't' it?" Mauve asks.

"Where did that come from?"

"Prythian's Arena of Bastards only appears when there's a game or he's doing business."

"He's that powerful?"

Mauve's human partner laughs behind me. "You're in for a treat."

"What is he? An archdemon?"

"No, Prythian is definitely not a demon, but he's equally matched in darkness," Mauve answers.

Fucking fantastic.

As we approach the gates, guards wearing full-blown armor block our path.

"State your business," one of them says, his voice sounding nothing like anything I've ever heard.

They're both wearing helmets, but when I peer closely, I see the skin around their eyes is grey and rough. It's as if they're made out of stone.

"I'm here with an offering for your king," Mauve replies.

The guard's stare travels past the fae to land on me. "He

doesn't look like much."

"You wouldn't know the difference between a squirrel and a lion even if it hit you in the face. Now get out of my way before I lose my patience."

The guards don't take Mauve's threats lightly. They're almost shaking with anger, but for whatever reason, they move aside and let us pass.

Once we're out of earshot, I say, "This Prythian guy really needs to improve the guards he employs."

"Those two clowns are only for show. They aren't real, you know?" the human says.

"What are they, then?"

"Puppets made out of clay and stones. It doesn't take much to obliterate them to pieces."

"Tobias! Quiet," Mauve shout-whispers, and the man clamps his jaw shut.

Interesting. So it seems that information wasn't something I was supposed to get. It's filed away now for when I make my way out of here.

Once inside the building, Mauve drops whatever magic she was using to keep people from staring at us. There are less creatures here, but they turn to watch us progress through the hallway. Greek columns rise up to at least thirty feet, supporting an arched ceiling. Fresco paintings above depict different battle scenes, the mastery of the artist rivaling Michelangelo's.

Low murmurs follow us, and my enhanced hearing picks up every word, but the language is not something I'm familiar with. The crowd is diverse, ranging from creatures that can't be mistaken for anything else other than demons, to the ones who look human, but don't smell like them.

The grand hallway opens to a huge, spacious room, where the simple stone floor gives away to shiny marble and granite in an intricate pattern. I'm sure the design shows another battle, but the supernatural being sitting on the throne at the end of the atrium has my undivided attention. A male fae with long, dark hair is sprawled on the throne. He has one leg hanging over the arm of his ostentatious seat, while he leans his elbow on the other arm.

Mauve continues to walk, stopping only when she's a few feet away from the King of Bastards. She bends forward in a small curtesy, but I remain standing upright. Surprisingly, no one forces me to bow, but the fae on the throne does pierce me with an intense stare. I can't discern if he's angry or amused. This is one of the rare occasions where I can't read a creature. He's guarding himself well.

"Hello, dear Mauve. It has been a while since you've paid me a visit."

"You know I only come when it's worth your while."

"What makes you believe that puny wolf shifter is worthy of my arena?"

Puny? My spine goes rigid. It's a jerky reaction, but I'm pissed nonetheless.

Mauve snorts, a sound that's a contradiction to her pristine demeanor. "Don't you try to devalue the merchandise, Prythian. You know very well this is not an ordinary wolf. He's an alpha, and he also possesses another power. If I can sense that, so can you."

Prythian rolls his eyes, while the corners of his lips twitch up. However, the carefree gesture does nothing to erase the cold menace emanating from him. He must have lifted his glamour, because now I can sense the darkness and malice take over the room.

Sitting up straighter, he signals to one of his stony guards before speaking again. "You know the drill. I don't acquire anything before a demonstration. If your wolf can best my current champion, then I'll pay the price."

"That's crazy. Your champion hasn't lost a fight in a year," Tobias says, earning an irate gaze from Mauve.

Prythian just smiles at the human, a gesture so chilling that it makes my blood run cold. And that gaze wasn't even aimed at me.

"Tobias is right. It won't be a fair fight," Mauve intervenes.

"No. But I know the desires deep in your black heart, Mauve. And for what you want, the stakes are much higher. Don't worry, I'll give you some small compensation in case your specimen can't beat Ravenous."

A loud growl echoes in the chamber, putting me immediately on high alert. Even if Mauve decides she doesn't want to take the risk, I know it's too late to avoid this confrontation. Prythian will have his entertainment.

"Unchain me," I command.

Mauve looks into my eyes for a fleeting moment before she waves her hand. The chains disappear. My wolf flares to life inside my core like a burst of light. So the damn fae was indeed keeping it locked up. Sensing a predator approaching, the wolf springs forth without me willing it so, and the shift occurs in the blink of an eye. It's the fastest I've ever shifted in my entire life.

The fur on my back stands on end as my muscles flex, preparing to fight. The ground seems to shake as Prythian's champion approaches, a creature built like a tree, almost ten feet tall with muscles rippling with raw power. His skin is dark grey and hairless. Protruding from his shoulders are three dog heads. It's almost like Cerberos grew a giant's body. Goddamn it.

A piece of cloth hangs from his waist, kept in place by a golden chain belt. On each of his necks, the beast has a choke collar with spikes. Leather cuffs wrap around his wrists. All those accessories have a purpose. They have thick chains attached to them, and Prythian's guard is gripping their ends. He's keeping the monster on a leash. Does that mean the King of Bastards can't control his monster? No, that's not it. There's too much power surrounding Prythian. I bet he could snap his champion's necks with a flick of his hand.

I smell fear coming from Mauve's associate, and from others in the assembly as well. Shit, I should be terrified, but despite the size and the deadly intent coming from Prythian's monster, I'm not afraid. In fact, I'm looking forward to the fight. Where the sense of confidence is coming from, I have no fucking clue. I still haven't recovered from my ordeal at the hands of Harkon. Until a minute ago, my body was infused with weariness. In my wolf form, it's all gone.

Ravenous's handler releases the chain, and the monster

charges. I hold my ground until the very last moment before leaping out of the way. As I suspected, what the beast has in size, it lacks in agility. It whirls around slower than I would have with his three jaws open wide as he roars, showing canines that could probably cut me in half in a second. I need to stay clear of those. He comes at me again, pulling one of his arms back to deliver a clawed blow. Once again, I wait until the last second to get out of his range.

The same dance continues for another minute before Ravenous finally wises up. He charges in the same manner, but when I leap to the right, he changes course last minute, swinging his clawed hand at the spot I jumped to, hitting me square on my shoulder. The impact sends me flying across the room, the fall jarring my bones. Pain shoots up from where I hit the stone floor hard, rendering me paralyzed for a couple of seconds, enough time for Ravenous to reach me. Knowing I can't move out of the way fast enough, I leap for his leg, viciously sinking my teeth into his skin. Foul blood fills my mouth, almost making me gag, right before Ravenous yanks me off his limb, sending me careening on the floor.

Before he can attack me again, I leap to my feet, realizing the time for tiring the monster out is over. I need to go one hundred percent on the offensive. His chains clink against the floor as he turns, and an idea strikes me. I see how I'm going to end this. His handler fucked up. Instead of releasing the chains from the monster, he simply let go. My guess is fear of getting too close to the monster made him commit that error, which I'm sure he'll pay for with his life, being real or not.

I need to get behind Ravenous in order to get those chains, but he's too tall for me to leap over his three heads. So I must go between his legs. As he comes at me, I run in his direction, dropping onto my belly right before he can swat me with his powerful arms. The momentum makes me slide across the floor, right between his legs. Now comes the risky part, the partial shift. I need my hands for my next move. My wolf protests, but I force through the shift until I have opposable thumbs again.

Ravenous begins to turn, moving the chains out of my reach as he does so. I leap on the ground, managing to hold on to the chain attached to one of his necks. Back on my feet, I yank at it hard, making the beast stumble backward. He doesn't fall, though, but it doesn't matter. That's not what I planned to accomplish anyway.

Securing the chain with my mouth, I shift into wolf form, then start to run in circles around Ravenous as fast as I can until the metal chain is wrapped tightly around his gigantic body. The monster tries to break free, but his attempt only brings his downfall in the end. He falls on the ground with a loud noise, and I take that opportunity to end it. Dropping the chain, I jump on his back and clamp my jaw around his right neck, slashing a main artery open. Dark blood seeps from the wound, but the creature doesn't stop struggling. In fact, it's still trying to get up. *No fucking way, Jose. You're going down.* I slash his left neck open next, hoping that will do the trick. I can't get to the neck in the middle, so I leap off the beast.

He's now surrounded by a pool of his own blood, his growls becoming weaker with every passing second. Finally, the beast stops moving, and his three pair of eyes shut forever. Prythian's champion is dead.

Chapter 10
Samuel

I position my body in front of Red, keeping my wolf at bay but ready to spring free. From the corner of my eye, I catch that fucking druid move to a position where he can easily defend Red as well. I should be glad for the extra protection, but Red is my mate, mine to protect. I don't need her ex getting in the way.

Peeling my lips back, I let out a snarl while I stare at the guy. With an eyebrow raised, he looks at me, then shakes his head as if my attitude is childish or something. Red touches my lower back, easing off some of the tension in my body, but not by much. I don't think I'll be able relax completely until this is all over.

When the doorbell rings, there's a collective gasp, and then my friend Armand asks, "Okay, since when are demons polite?"

Santiago lets out an impatient sigh. "Jesus, aren't we a bunch of jumpy idiots? It's Albert and Madison."

"Then why did the wards flicker a warning?" Jared frowns in his grandfather's direction.

"We never thought to add their signature to the white list." Carol shrugs. "After the Accords were signed, Albert and Madison kept to themselves, not wanting to have anything to do with the supernatural community."

"Even so, they wouldn't have been able to simply breach the barrier like that." Brian rubs his chin. "Something has caused the wards to weaken faster than usual."

There's a loud knock on the door, and Alex, of all people, is the one taking the lead to open it as if he owns the house. What an arrogant bastard.

"You're new," I hear Albert say from the entrance foyer.

A moment later, Alex is leading the way, followed by my former high school history teacher, and his wife Madison.

"Hello, I hope we aren't interrupting anything." Albert smiles in a friendly way, but I sense an underlying tension coming from him.

Brian breaches the distance between the newcomers, opening his arms to hug Albert and then his wife. "It's good to see you. It's been too long."

"You know where to find us, Brian," Madison replies, then her gaze stops briefly on Red before she turns to Dr. Mervina. "I'm sorry about what happened to your sons. If there's anything we can do to help…"

"How were you able to break through the wards?" Nina asks, eyeing Albert and Madison with suspicion.

With a pinch of her eyebrows, Madison replies, "There was barely any resistance."

The confirmation that Brian's wards are shoddy turns the mood in the room even more somber. He has reason to be concerned since he's keeping the Shadow Creek wolves here. But I have other priorities.

"Did you bring the sacred stone?" I ask Albert, cutting straight to the chase. I hope he came for that reason.

He watches me through slits, while his lips become nothing but a slash. "I've protected this stone for over twenty-five years. I'm not keen to part with it until I know what exactly you plan to do with it."

Red takes a step forward. "We need it to forge a weapon strong enough to defeat the archdemon Harkon."

Albert trades a glance with his wife before facing us again. "One stone won't be powerful enough to kill an archdemon."

"I know. We have a second one."

"Two might work," Madison says before she turns to Santiago. "Are you forging the weapon, Donal?"

Demetria Montgomery also called Santiago by his real name before. I bet there's an interesting story behind his new moniker. As much as I would like to say I've always been involved in the community, the more complicated things become, the more I realize I know shit about the other supes. Fuck, I didn't even know Albert had come from the past, and he was my history teacher in high school.

"No, my son Brian is. He's more experienced when it comes to weapons."

"Has your stone been linked to one of you?" Brian asks.

"Yes, to both of us." Albert reaches behind his neck, unclasping a delicate, very feminine necklace with an ember stone pendant. The piece of jewelry looks like it belongs to his wife. Maybe it did.

"I'm afraid we'll have to break the connection you have with it," Brian replies.

"What will that do to us?" Madison asks, frowning.

"I'm not sure to be honest."

From the corner of my eye, I catch Red biting her lower lip as she drops her gaze. I wish I had Dante's power to link to her mind without needing to be in wolf form. Since I can't, I lean closer to whisper in her ear. "What's wrong?"

Shaking her head, she gives me a pitiful smile. "Nothing."

"Don't lie to me, sweetheart." I put my hand on her lower back, and holy cannoli, the contact sends a flare of lust up my arm. I'm suddenly on fire, and the urge to take her again is overwhelming.

"Jesus Christ. Keep that shit contained, fuck boy," Nina says from across the room, glaring at us.

Red's face resembles a tomato as she steps away from me, keeping her gaze glued to the floor.

"I'm afraid that answer is not good enough for me. I won't risk Madison." Albert curls his fingers around the necklace, hiding it from view.

"Knock, knock." Zeke Rogers sticks his head into the room, keeping part of his body hidden behind the entry foyer wall.

"Great, now the imp is here," Kirian, Jared's younger brother, mutters, "Dad, you need to fix your wards ASAP."

"Wards, what wards?" Zeke's blue eyes are widely innocent, but the corner of his lips twitch up. "Oh that pesky little spell you put around your property? I was able to break it, easy-peasy."

He walks into the room like he owns it, wearing his usual rainbow attire. Today, it's a light pink sharp suit. Underneath, he has on an iridescent shirt that's glued to his body. He's another arrogant bastard, but at least he has a sense of humor.

"Did you speak with your contact in the Wastelands?" Red asks, bringing the focus back on the situation.

"Yes, I did. It was easier than I expected. And get this, I also have confirmation the King of Bastards has acquired a new champion for his wicked gladiator games, a wolf shifter."

Red gasps loudly before whispering Dante's name.

"I guess we don't need to run a location spell anymore, Mom," I say.

"No, but we still need a full circle of witches to open the portal," she replies.

"But with Grandma still recovering, aren't we short a witch?" Red looks from my mother to Carol.

"I can step in," Madison announces, and her husband makes a disapproving face.

"Maddie, are you sure? You haven't practiced witchcraft in years."

She touches his face with a small smile. "It's like riding a bicycle. I'll be fine."

Zeke claps his hands together. "All right. Everyone is on board. Fantastic. Now, about the payment."

"What does your contact want?" I ask.

The imp turns to Albert and Madison, making the couple tense on the spot. "She wants that beautiful piece of jewelry you have there."

"Are you out of your goddamned mind? We can't give a sacred stone to a demon," the dark-haired girl standing next to Alex says. I think she's with the Dark Blades, but I'm not sure. I haven't had the chance to get all the details of what went down in Shadow Creek.

Zeke raises both hands. "Hey, I'm just the messenger. But if you think you can navigate in the Wastelands without a guide, be my guest."

"We do need a guide, Daria," the third member of Alex's alley of clowns, a long-haired dude who resembles a stoner more than an elite fighter, chimes in.

"Why does she want a sacred stone?" Red asks.

"Why do you think, blondie?" Daria puts her hands on her hips, glaring openly at my mate.

A low growl bubbles up my throat, but I manage to swallow it when I sense Red's angry wolf essence lash out at the druid girl.

"What's your problem?" she asks.

Zeke jumps in between Red and the other chick. "Whoa. Let's bring this crazy aggression down a notch, shall we? We're all friends here. I should have made myself a bit clearer. Trinity doesn't want a sacred stone in its pure form. She wants a stone that's been fine tuned to fight evil."

"Did you say Trinity?" Madison asks, her tone taking on a different edge.

"Yeah. Why do you ask?"

"Is she a succubus by any chance?"

Narrowing his eyes, Zeke watches Madison closely now. In fact, everyone's eyes are on Albert's wife. Where is she going with these questions?

"Yes. Do you know Trinity?"

Instead of answering Zeke, she turns to Albert. Without words, they share something between them. I don't think they have the ability to communicate mind to mind, but my guess is after so many years of marriage, one glance is enough.

"No, Maddie. Absolutely not."

"I didn't say anything yet."

"I know what you're thinking. I'm not giving my stone to her."

"So you *do* know Trinity," Zeke says.

"Yes. We do." Madison spares one meaningful glance at her husband before turning to Zeke. "Why does she want the stone?"

"She didn't say. My guess is she's running away from someone, and she needs the stone to help hide her demonic signature. It's the only reason a demon would want an incorruptible stone."

"But the stone is still linked to Maddie and me," Albert argues.

"So what?" Zeke replies.

"So what? We don't know what it will do to us if she uses it, and no one here seems to know how to safely unlink the stone from us."

"This is a waste of time. The succubus can have the

stone I found in the Midnight Lily grimoire," Red says, not hiding her exasperation.

"I'm sorry. I can't give you that stone. I've already harnessed its essence to be used as a weapon. It wouldn't do the succubus any good," Brian replies.

Okay, I've heard enough. Taking a step toward my old teacher, I don't keep my wolf chained. "While we're here discussing what-ifs, my brothers are missing, with one in the hands of a fucking demon that is doing God knows what to him. I need that stone, Albert."

The man won't budge—or cower—under my wolf stare. I'm about to pry the damn necklace from his hand when Zeke gets in between us.

"For fuck's sake. Do I have to do everything here?" He touches both Albert's and Madison's shoulders. Suddenly, purple light envelopes them. Zeke's appearance changes to his true demonic form—greenish skin and red pupils. Madison lets out a gasp right before Zeke screams from the top of his lungs, letting go of the couple. He doubles over, then falls to his knees.

"Bloody hell!" Albert says.

Mom runs to Zeke, kneeling next to him. "What did you do, you fool?"

He raises his head, his expression scrunched in pain. Breathless, he replies, "I've broken the link."

"How?" Red asks.

"You crazy bastard. You could have been killed." Santiago approaches the imp, helping him get onto his feet.

"*Mon dieu.* This is more interesting than the that show

about the demon hunters brothers." Armand is staring at the scene like he's indeed watching a TV show.

"How did you break the link?" Albert moves toward Zeke with hands curled into fists.

"I attempted to corrupt the stone by blasting all my demonic energy at it. It didn't work, naturally, but it was enough to break the connection you two have with it."

"Bullshit. If it were that easy, then any linked stone could be unlinked."

"You forget something, Albert. That stone was never really tuned to you or Madison. You inherited it. The original bearer was someone else, wasn't it?" Zeke replies.

The blood seems to drain from Albert's face. Damn. More secrets. Where's my popcorn?

Madison takes a deep breath, then pries her husband's hand open, retrieving the necklace. He doesn't resist. She then attempts to give it to Zeke, but he shakes his head.

"Hell no. I've suffered enough on account of that damned stone."

"You mean blessed," Kirian pipes in, earning a glare from the imp.

"I'll take it." Red reaches for the jewelry.

"We need to move fast." Alex commands everyone's attention again, and my jaw hardens automatically. Yeah, I don't like the guy. Period.

"When is your contact expecting us, Zeke?" I ask before the douche canoe has the chance.

"She's on stand-by, waiting for word from me."

"Just one second," Red interrupts. "If she's in the

Wastelands, how can you communicate with her?"

The imp's lips turn into a crooked smile. "Thank you, Red, for being the first one to ask that. Have you ever heard of the Mirror of Briseis?"

Obviously, she has not, just like I haven't heard about it either. But it seems Alex and his friends have if their murderous glares at the imp are any indication. Daria takes a step forward, unsheathing her dagger. The tension in the room skyrockets once more, and I brace for it to snap completely. So much for the Dark Blades help.

Chapter 11
Red

"You have the Mirror of Briseis?" Max and Nina ask at the same time, then they frown at each other.

"You should not be in possession of such a dangerous artifact," Alex chimes in. "It belongs with the Council of Druids."

Zeke snorts, crossing his arms. "Yeah, keep dreaming I'll hand over the mirror to those old farts. I won that mirror fair and square. I'm not giving it up."

"Then we'll have to take it from you by force." Daria raises her dagger.

The imp loses his usual carefree demeanor as his lips curl into a snarl. "You can try, sweetheart."

"Everybody needs to calm down," Santiago intervenes. "Nobody is taking anything from anyone."

"Can somebody explain why those Dark Blades over there are losing their freaking minds over a mirror?" Sam asks, earning glares from Alex and his companions.

"The Mirror of Briseis is an enormously powerful artifact. It can be used for many things, including communicating with people in different dimensions, even those who have passed on to the afterlife," Dr. Mervina explains.

"Exactly, and it can be deadly in the wrong hands," Daria continues. "An imp shouldn't be in possession of it. He could open a portal to a hellish dimension with it."

"Oh, my Satan. Do you know for how long the mirror has been in my possession, girlie? Centuries. If I wanted to open a portal to hell, I would have done so already. Besides, why in the world would I want to do that? I left the underworld, and I ain't never going back."

Nina watches Zeke with a calculating gleam in her eyes. I don't know what she's thinking, but instinct tells me she's plotting something. I don't really care; I've reached the limit of my patience.

"Enough already." I speak loudly enough so everyone pays attention. "Every minute we waste having idiotic arguments, Dante's and Tristan's chances of survival diminish. Zeke, you'll reach out to your contact in the Wastelands. We should probably go with you and open the portal as soon as she's in place. Where are you keeping the mirror?"

"Do you think I'm going to give that information so the druid girl can steal it from me?"

"We need to conjure up the portal out in the open anyway," Carol says.

"Fine. Are you able to bring the mirror here?" I rest my hands on my hips.

Zeke clenches his jaw before sighing. "Okay, I'll bring

you to where the mirror is. I'll figure out another place to hide it afterward. Who's actually going to the Wastelands?"

"Red and I, obviously," Sam replies.

"I'm coming, too," Jared announces.

"And me." Armand takes a step forward, then turns to Leo.

Sam's friend switches his attention to his father, and I can read the turmoil in his expression.

"You don't need to come, Leo." Sam cuts the tense moment.

"Yeah, don't worry. I'll represent the family." Nina smirks, earning another glare from her father.

"Wait? If you're going, I'm going, too," Billy announces.

"No way, Jose." Sam pierces Billy with a domineering gaze. "You're staying here. I don't have time to babysit."

Billy opens his mouth to protest, but Alex cuts in. "Stop right there. What do you think this is? A trip to Disneyland? We're going to an in-between hellish dimension. We need to keep the party small to avoid detection. Ideally, only the Blades should go."

Anger surges through my veins. "You're crazy if you think I'm going to stay behind."

Alex exhales loudly. "I said ideally. I know you and your mate are coming. Unfortunately."

"Watch your tongue, pal," Sam snarls.

I turn to Zeke. "What are we waiting for? Let's go get your mirror."

"Where are you planning to conjure up the portal?"

Albert asks. "If the wards are not working properly, shouldn't we find another location?"

"This is madness." Riku Ogata, who had been quiet for the last half hour, finally speaks up again. "I'm not going to stand here and watch you break the Accords."

"Don't let the door hit your ass on your way out." Nina glares at him.

The man walks out of the room, spitting fire from his nose. I notice Leo, Nina's brother, watch his father leave with regret in his eyes before he turns to his sister. "You didn't have to be so rude to him."

"Bite me, Leo." The fox moves away, getting closer to Billy, who looks downcast now that Sam basically called him a child.

"Going back to Albert's question, if you're looking for a place to open the portal, I know the spot," Zeke says.

"The ground must be blessed to prevent demons from using the opening to jump into our dimension. Our forest is the ideal place," Carol replies.

"We need to make sure the wards hold this time." Santiago turns to Brian. "Do you think maybe the wolves from Shadow Creek, or more precisely, the chips in their brains, are disrupting your spell?"

"I didn't think about that, but it's possible."

"Then we have to get those wolves the hell out of here," Kirian chimes in.

"We still need to set up protective wards wherever they are. No, the only solution is to create stronger wards." Brian turns to Alex. "Do you think you can help out with that?"

Alex pinches his lips while he narrows his gaze. It's his trademark "I don't like this idea" face. He glances briefly in my direction, then turns to Brian. "Do you need all three of us? I don't think it's a good idea for Red to be roaming about Crimson Hollow unprotected. Harkon can return at any moment."

"Red will be protected by me." Sam takes a step toward Alex, his body shaking with anger. I hold his arm, pulling him back. The heat surges again upon the contact, so I drop my hand fast.

I also open my mouth to protest, but Dr. Mervina speaks before I can. "I agree with Alex. You have a target on your back, Red. You have to be careful."

Knowing I can't argue with that logic, I drop the argument.

"I thought I was clear I don't want any druids near the place where I keep the mirror," Zeke points out.

Alex moves closer to the imp, holding his stare. "You have my word I won't try to take the mirror from you, nor will I disclose its hiding place."

"Alex!" Daria raises both her eyebrows. "You can't do that."

He doesn't glance at his companion, but keeps staring at Zeke. Finally, the imp sighs loudly. "Fine, you can come."

"Really? Just like that?" Sam asks.

Zeke shrugs. "Hey, if Harkon reappears, he's going to be gunning for everyone. I'd rather have the protection of a druid fighter on my side. I can always change the mirror's location later."

He heads to the front door with Alex following behind him.

"I couldn't offer to come with you to the Wastelands, but I've got your back while you're here," Leo says to Sam.

"Thanks, man."

"Well, I can't come for obvious reasons. We have to make sure the wards hold longer," Jared says.

"Let's get going, people." Nina makes a shooing motion to her brother and Armand.

"You're coming, too?" I ask.

The woman turns to me with a sardonic smile. "Of course, I'm dying to have a look at the famous Mirror of Briseis."

"I can't image why," Sam mutters under his breath.

When Nina is out of the house—followed closely by Billy—I lean closer to Sam. "She's planning on stealing that mirror, isn't she?"

"Yup." Sam turns to me, smiling wide enough that his dimples make an appearance. My stomach does a backflip while my heart turns into a drumming machine. His gaze has turned hotter than a desert, and I become lost in it. Someone pulls me away from him. Dr. Mervina.

"What is it?" I ask.

"I need a quick word with you and Sam," she replies.

"Why?" My voice has a hint of alarm.

"Mom, what's the matter?" Sam moves closer to me, and the need to touch him becomes overwhelming.

"Are you feeling more aroused than usual when you touch each other?" she asks, and my face bursts into flames.

"What?" I squeak.

"Just a moment ago, Sam touched you, and the scent of the mating bond flared up," Carol adds.

"Wait a minute. You could sense it, too?" Sam asks. "I thought only shifters were able to smell the bond."

"Usually so, but if I picked it up, then it means Red is going into heat."

My eyes widen in embarrassment. I want the floor to open and swallow me whole.

"What does that mean?" I ask.

"It means you'll feel an overwhelming urge to, well…" Dr. Mervina starts.

"To fuck," Carol cuts in.

"Oh my God." I cover my face, unable to look at Sam's mother or her friend in the eye.

"Sweet mercy, Carol. I'd forgotten you have no filter," Dr. Mervina says.

"Okay, not that I don't like the idea, but this couldn't have happened at a worse time," Sam replies. "Is there any way we can delay the heat period?"

"Unfortunately, no," Dr. Mervina replies with a shake of her head. "The best you can do is try not to touch each other, and most definitely abstain from sex for as long as you can."

I peer at Sam, finding him sporting a frown.

"Just for the record, I don't like this one bit," he says.

Since I'm already embarrassed, I might as well get some answers. "I have a question. I, uh, took a birth control shot a month ago, but with everything that has happened, I didn't even stop to think if it was still effective."

Sam's eyes become rounder as he takes in the implications. I don't blame him for his reaction. This is a big deal.

"You don't have to worry. Shifters can only conceive during the heat period," Dr. Mervina replies.

A wave of relief washes over me, and I see the same emotion in Sam's expression. But I still need to know if it's possible to avoid getting knocked-up during the heat period. I'm not ready for motherhood yet.

"Yo, are you coming or not?" Zeke reappears, and the question gets lodged in my throat.

Shit, I hope he didn't hear this conversation.

Chapter 12
Tristan

I have no fucking clue how long it has been since I was taken by Harkon. It's impossible to keep track of time in this place. I'm still bound in chains, and I haven't eaten or drunk anything since I arrived. However, I don't feel hunger or thirst. It's almost as if my body doesn't need sustenance in this place. There's a high chance I'm dead and my soul was sent to hell, but would I still hear the strange buzzing in my head, something I believe is the controlling chip embedded there?

Dead or not, it's a paramount effort to keep my thoughts my own. There are moments when everything is a dark void. I don't remember what transpired in those moments of darkness.

Harkon comes to visit me often. Each time, he has a different type of torture for me, one crueler than the next. I sense his approach even before his stench reaches my nose. My spine goes taut, my body beginning to shake uncontrollably. I can't imagine what he has in the works now for me. I've been skinned, burned, gutted, and had every bone in my body broken, only to find myself completely healed by the end of each session. The memory of the pain, however, lingers for hours.

He appears today not in his demonic form, but as a human, someone who stirs something in my memory. The man in front of me appears to be in his sixties, with silver hair and a trimmed beard. His clothes are tailored, but they're not from this century. A suspicion begins to nag at me.

"What's this now?" I ask.

"I thought I would change things up a bit today since breaking your body is getting kind of old."

"Who are you supposed to be? An extra from *Poldark*?"

"It seems I haven't made you suffer enough since your sarcasm is still intact. You don't know who I am? Maybe I should refresh your memory."

He grabs my head between his hands, then digs his fingers into my skin. Splitting pain robs me of air, and a coarse scream escapes my mouth. Suddenly, the dungeon disappears, and I find myself alone in a forest. The air is chilly, the bright orange and red on the trees telling me it's fall. Where the hell am I?

I spring to my feet when I hear the shouts of men and the barks of dogs out in the distance. Then a woman breaks through the tree line, running without looking back. Her dress is torn and dirty, her ginger hair disheveled. In her manic race, she doesn't see the exposed tree root in her way. She trips, falling hard on the ground. I attempt to move from my spot to help her, but I find myself paralyzed.

The men pursuing the woman catch up with her, surrounding her as they shout obscenities. Their hunting dogs jump on her, ready to tear the woman apart with their sharp teeth when a man with silver hair appears. Fuck, it's the man Harkon was portraying, and next to him, Robert E. Saint.

Is this another trip down memory lane?

The dogs retreat upon their master's command, and the woman, who is now crying, lifts her gaze as she leans on her forearms. "Please, I've done nothing wrong."

"You're a filthy demon, and you will pay for your sins."

"I'm not a demon." She switches her eyes to Robert. "Tell them!"

The man next to Robert turns to him. "Do you have anything to tell me, son?"

I see the conflict in his gaze, but his jaw is clenched tight. "No," he says after a moment.

What the hell is he doing?"

The girl on the ground begins to cry anew, begging for mercy to no avail. The man Harkon was impersonating whistles, and his dogs attack. Robert just stands there, watching everything like a fucking statue.

Did that really happen? Was I the kind of man who would let an innocent person be ravaged by a pack of ravenous dogs?

The scene dissolves. Now, it's only Robert and the dead girl in the forest. The ruthless men are gone, including the silver-haired monster who referred to Robert as his son. Howling in the distance announces the approach of a pack of wolves. Robert pulls a gun from his holster. A white wolf breaks through the shrubbery first. Before she reaches the dead girl, she shifts into Natalia Petroviski, Red's former incarnation. With a solemn expression, she drops next to the girl, letting out a wail. Then she lifts her tear-streaked face to mine.

"How could you stand there and do nothing? How could you let her die?"

I want to tell her there was nothing I could do, but I don't have a voice. The only thing I feel is the grand sense of shame and failure that sweeps over me, dragging me under a dark wave of regret. Robert was a monster in his previous life, the same way I'm a monster in this one. There's no hope for me. There's only the certainty I'll hurt Red and my brothers in the end. The pain caving my chest in is worse than any physical torture Harkon has put me through. The agony is relentless; it has no end.

The forest vanishes and I'm back in the dungeon cell, bound once more to the cold chains. The sharp bite of the metal against my skin feels more acute than before. My cheeks are wet, and it takes me a second to realize I've been crying. A chilling laugh sounds from the corner of the room, and Harkon appears, still wearing the human's form.

"Wasn't that fun?"

"What the hell was that?"

"Your memories."

"Bullshit. I'd never let an innocent girl die like that."

"The lies you tell yourself to survive. It's a pity that humans don't retain the memories of their previous lives, isn't it?"

I don't reply because a rush of memories floods my brain. Harkon is telling the truth. That girl was a supernatural, and I allowed my father-in-law to slaughter her. I was trying to protect Natalia, lead the hunters away from her pack. But she saw what I did, and she never forgave me. I'm such a despicable creature.

"Yes, you are. What do you think will happen when Red remembers what you did? Do you think she'll ever be able to forgive you?"

"No," I breathe out.

"Exactly. It's futile to struggle. Give in to your grief, to your despair."

I have no fight left in me. My wolf howls in pain. My body sags against the chains while my chin dips. I don't flinch when Harkon holds my head between his cold hands, but I do scream when he splits my brain in two.

Chapter 13
Red

My face is still in flames when I walk out of Brian's house because I'm almost one hundred percent sure Zeke overhead the end of the conversation. I caught him smirking at me with a knowing glint in his gaze. Nosey imp.

Alex is waiting for us, leaning against a black SUV with his arms crossed. He seems annoyed. "What took you so long?"

I'm not about to announce to everyone what the hold-up was, so I simply glare at him, imitating his stance. "We're here, aren't we?"

Zeke moves toward his car, the famous Unicorn-Cupcake Mobil, a vintage RV the imp converted into the most outrageous food truck in the world. The body of the car was painted in different pastel tones that glitter under the sun. A big unicorn cupcake sits on the rooftop, surrounded by small sparkling lights that Zeke keeps on no matter the time of the day.

"I can fit four people in the Unicup Mobil. So, who are going to be the lucky ones?"

Alex peers at the colorful food truck with a wrinkled nose. "I'll pass, thanks."

Zeke shrugs. "You don't know what you're missing."

"I'll come," I say. "I've always wanted to see what the inside looks like."

"Well, that means I'm coming, too." Sam moves closer, his arms outstretched to wrap around my waist, but he seems to remember the conversation we just had about my situation and drops his arm at the last second.

It doesn't matter. His close proximity is enough to send my hormones into overdrive. How long do I have until I become a crazy wolf in heat?

"Oh, can I come?" Billy asks with a hint of excitement in his tone.

Zeke looks him up and down with an eyebrow raised. "Oh, so you're joining us, huh? Does that mean sweet Nina Ogata will also be riding in the Unicup Mobil?"

The fox rolls her eyes. "Please. I'm not joined by the hip to the kid."

Zeke chuckles. "Really? Whatever you say."

"I'll go," Armand says, and Billy seems a little disappointed that Sam's friend took the last spot in Zeke's truck.

Alex, who already has the door of his SUV open, glances in Nina's and Leo's direction. "You can ride with me."

"No, thanks. I got my own mode of transportation." She turns to Sam. "By the way, you still owe me."

A flash of irritation crosses Sam's expression. "I haven't

forgotten. You'll get your payment when I return from the Wastelands. She's not going anywhere."

He enters Zeke's truck before I can say a word, leaving me with a bunch of questions in my head. I follow him with every intention of asking him what that was all about, but my mind gets completely diverted by the sensory overload. While the outside of the van was painted in soft hues, inside is full-on rainbow central. Right below the truck's wide window, there's a cupboard where Zeke keeps his cooking supplies. There are colorful boxes carefully labeled, but the names don't make any sense to me. What the heck is "Spritz Glue" for example?

Opposite the window, there's a counter and above it, more cupboards. Sam has already taken one of the small seats near the truck's back door, and I'm glad the remaining seat is opposite him, not next to him. We have to keep our distance.

He's still sporting a frown, the gesture pulling at his eye bandage, which reminds me I wanted to ask about Nina's remark.

"What was Nina talking about just now?"

"Nothing." Sam can't hold my stare, choosing to fix his gaze on the floor.

"Don't lie to me. What did you promise her?"

Hunching his shoulders forward, he lifts his face. "I hired her to get intel on Valerius's territory when you were his captive. I wanted to find a way in. In return, she asked for my Ducati."

"Why would she ask for your motorcycle? Can't you

pay her in cash?"

"I did offer to pay more than the Ducati is worth, but Nina loves to push people's buttons. She knows how much that motorcycle means to me. It was a gift from my father."

"Oh, I see."

I didn't know what to make of the fox shifter before. There was something about her that rubbed me the wrong way, but now I know the reason. She's a bitch.

"I don't get why you tolerate her if she's so mean."

"Well, for starters, she's Leo sister. But that's not the only reason. We were friends before."

"People change, though. She clearly has."

"I don't think she has. To be honest, I believe her terrible attitude is a mask."

Sam's thoughtful insight about Nina gives me pause. It's the first time he's showed me this other side of him, the one where he's not cracking jokes or being a hot head. It's a nice surprise.

He cocks his head to the side. "Why are you staring at me like that?"

"I didn't realize I was staring."

"Hmmm, if you want me to keep my hands to myself, you can't do that, sweetheart." He smiles in a cheeky way, making my heart skip a beat. Damn his flirty ways.

"Oy, is it safe to enter, or are you kids about to suck face?" Armand sticks his head in.

"I'm afraid you'll have to come sit in the front with us," Zeke, who is already behind the wheel, says.

"Oh, thank heavens." Armand closes the truck's back

door, then continues. "The sexual tension in there is strong enough to give the dead a boner."

My jaw drops, and Sam laughs at me.

"Shut up."

"What? You forget you're around by supernaturals, Red. It's hard to keep things private. Just go with it."

Pouting, I cross my arms in front of my chest. "I don't think I'll ever get used to it."

We begin to move. Soon, I forget about my embarrassment when worry takes its place. There are so many things stacked up against us. It's hard for me to remain positive. Closing my eyes, I focus on the new energy that's now next to my wolf's essence. My witch powers. Dr. Mervina told me that I need to practice in order to be able to control them, but where's the time to do so?

"What are you doing?" Sam asks, making me open my eyes again.

"I'm trying to understand how I can use my new powers. Your mother told me I have to practice in order to wield them, but I'm not sure when I'll have the chance before I actually need to use it against Harkon."

"I'm sure you'll figure it out. You're strong, Red. More so than you realize."

Sam's words make my chest feel warm, but the self-doubt still lingers, as well as the feeling I'm not completely in control of my life. Since I've been changed into a shifter, I've been told I'm this or that. Am I nothing more than a pawn in all this?

"How is your eye?" I change the subject, not wanting to

dwell on my dark thoughts any longer.

Sam touches the bandage for a brief second before letting his hand drop. "Sore. Does it bother you?"

I frown, not understanding his question. "I don't follow you."

"The fact I'm no longer the hottest motherfucker you've ever met." He gives me an impish smile, and I fight the urge to roll my eyes.

"Are you fishing for a compliment? Really?"

"Hey, I was once told my eyes were my biggest assets. I have to know."

"Whoever told you that was a fool. Your heart is your biggest asset, Sam."

The easy-going smile vanishes from his lips, while his eye watches me with such regard it makes me squirm on my seat.

"My heart is all yours, Red. It will always be, even when I'm no longer in this plane."

"No. I don't want to hear you talk about death. You're not dying on me."

"Eventually, we'll all die."

"I know, but it won't be any time soon. Besides, when we're old and wrinkled, I demand to go first."

"So you want to leave me to deal with the pain, you wretched woman."

"Of course." I smile, and the force that links us feels stronger. It's not only lust that's pulling me toward him, it's pure love.

Sam lets out a growl. "This sucks. I want to kiss you so

badly right now. Why couldn't you go into heat like a week from now?"

"Wait? Red is going into heat?" Billy asks from the front seat, and I want to die.

I level Sam with my hardest glare while grinding my teeth. I had completely forgotten the back of the truck had no partition between the front.

"That explains a lot," Zeke adds.

"You have to promise me you won't open your big mouths to anyone else, especially you, Billy," I say.

"Why are you singling me out?"

"Because you have a weakness for a certain fox."

Sam, Armand, and Zeke chuckle at the same time.

"Why are you laughing now?" Billy snaps.

"Trust me, I'm not laughing at you, kid," Sam replies.

"I don't get it." Billy swivels in his seat to peer at Sam.

"I can't speak for Zeke or Armand, but I noticed how Nina is with you. I don't know what you did to her, but she's smitten."

"You really think so?"

"Oui, for sure," Armand chimes in.

Suddenly, Rihanna's *We Found Love* reverberates inside the vehicle so loud I can feel the beat inside my rib cage. Zeke begins to sing along, then Armand. Surprisingly, Sam join him.

"What are you doing?" I ask.

He shrugs, "We're a few moments away from venturing into a hellish dimension. We've got to stock up with good vibes, Red."

"This is really not funny," Billy grumbles.

I suppose Sam is right. With so many terrible things awaiting us, we should enjoy every moment of levity we can.

As if Zeke had timed it perfectly, we arrive at our final destination as soon as Rihanna's song ends.

"Blackwood's Storage? This is where you kept the Mirror of Briseis hidden?" Billy asks.

"What did you expect? Some heavily warded dungeon in the middle of nowhere?" Zeke opens the door, then steps out of the truck.

Sam reaches for the door handle, then jumps out first as if he expects danger to spring on us out of nowhere.

I follow him, not picking up anything out of the ordinary. There are only a few cars in the parking lot, and very few spots for bad guys to hide. The large warehouse building is right behind Crimson Hollow's high school. From the parking lot, we can see the football field.

Alex parks right next to us, followed by Nina in her red Mustang. Her brother Leo decided to ride with her. By the stormy expression on her face as she exits her car, I could bet they just had an argument.

"Something wrong?" Billy asks as he approaches Nina.

"Nope." Shutting her face off, she turns to the warehouse. "So, the mirror is here."

"For now." Zeke narrows his eyes. "Don't be getting any fancy ideas."

She turns to him with a sardonic smile playing on her lips. "I wouldn't dream of stealing from you, if that's what you're worried about."

"Yeah, right. And beige is not a vomit-inducing color." Zeke's reply makes me snort, but then I remember why we're here and the thought sobers me up quickly. The imp ventures into the building. One by one, we follow him. There's a front desk with a clerk who seems to be falling asleep on his chair. He barely glances in our direction before turning his attention to his computer screen.

Zeke flashes his card key against the panel mounted on the wall, and the gliding door swishes open. Several narrow corridors greet us, and I get a horrible sense of deja vu. This reminds me of the facility where Valerius had his lab. A shiver runs down my spine as our steps echo in the deserted space.

We walk for about a minute, making so many turns that I soon lose my sense of direction. Good thing there are signs everywhere. It would be so easy to get lost here. Zeke finally stops in front of a steel roll-up door, which is secured by a regular metal lock. He drops into a crouch. Using a key he pulled from his jacket pocket, he opens the lock. Before he opens the door, he glances over his shoulder.

"Now, I didn't object to so many people coming in here, but I'm not crazy to let you all see what's inside this storage unit. Especially you, Nina."

She pouts. "Why? Do you have a treasure on the other side?"

Zeke turns his eyes to slits. "I'm not answering that. I'll allow Red to come in. The rest of you should head back to the end of the corridor."

"If you think I'll let Red go in with you alone, you're sorely mistaken," Sam replies.

Zeke rolls his eyes. "Fine. You can come. But that's it."

"I don't need to see what you're hording here, imp. I'll wait for you at the end of the corridor. We should split up, make sure both ends are covered, just in case," Alex says.

"Sounds good to me." Armand shrugs, and Leo does the same.

Zeke waits until the group splits in two and heads in opposite directions before he finally rolls up the door. My jaw drops when I take in the size of the storage unit. I have to do a double take.

"How is this possible?" I ask.

"Imp magic." Zeke chuckles and walks in.

His storage unit is easily triple the size of what it appears to be on the outside. It has to be huge in order to store all the stuff he has here. There are carnival games, a giant unicorn made out of papier-mâché, pinball machines, several clothing racks bursting with the most outrageous and colorful costumes, and mannequin heads sporting different-styled wigs. There's barely any room to walk to the back of the unit.

Zeke pulls the door shut, and then makes a beeline toward a solid wood armoire. It's tucked between stacked-up boxes and a table where a miniature model of Crimson Hollow is. Strange markings are carved on the doors of the armoire, but I can't discern a pattern. It looks like random scribbles from a toddler. The moment Zeke touches it, the armoire vibrates, then changes into a mirror just as tall, encased by a golden, decorated frame.

"It looks like an ordinary mirror," Sam says.

The imp throws him a droll glance. "What did you expect? A mirror made out of cotton candy?"

I move closer, feeling an odd pull toward it. "How does it work exactly?"

"I've never quite figured it out. When I came into possession of it, I tried every spell I knew to make the bloody thing work. Then suddenly, out of the blue, when I was only using the mirror to check out my new outfit, Trinity appeared on the other side. Scared the shit out of me, to be honest."

"Are you saying she made the mirror work?" I pull my gaze away from the object.

"Maybe. Now, whenever I want to talk to her, I simply stare at the mirror and think about her. Like this."

We wait a moment, but nothing happens. Then the mirror's surface wobbles for a couple of seconds. Instead of our reflection, we see a young woman covered from head to toe in black fur, blending almost completely with the black background. Where the hell is she?

Zeke smiles. "Hello, Triny."

"What took you so long?"

"It has only been a few hours since we last spoke."

"You know how time here flows differently."

"Well, I have some good news."

"You secured the stone?"

"Yes. We're heading your way as soon as the witches open the portal. I need a visual of where you are."

There's a moment of silence before Zeke continues. "Is that the arena?"

"I don't see anything," I say, but Zeke raises his hand to signal me to wait.

"Yes. You need to hurry. Prythian has announced the start of new games, and he raised the prize, which is attracting more powerful contestants. I honestly don't think the wolf shifter will be able to get out of those games alive."

My chest becomes tighter with the news.

"Can't you create a diversion, something to stall the beginning of the games?" the imp asks.

"Fuck, Zeke. I don't know what I can do."

He opens his mouth to reply when the acrid smell of smoke reaches my nose.

"What—" A loud knock on the door cuts me off.

"We need to get out of here. The building is on fire!" Alex yells.

Sam runs to the door, bringing it up with one hard pull. The hallway is already filled with smoke.

"What happened?" Sam asks.

"I don't know." Alex covers his face, coughing.

Zeke sticks his head out to check the corridor himself. "This isn't an ordinary fire."

Following Zeke's line of vision, I see Nina and Billy hurtling in our direction, running away from blue flames that are licking the walls fast.

"Oh my God. What's that?" I point at the strange flames.

"Impossible," Alex mutters.

"Look! It's coming from the other side, too," Armand

points out.

"Maybe if we run fast enough, we can get to the exit," Sam says.

"No!" Zeke holds his arm. "You can't let that fire touch you."

"Why not?" I ask.

"Because that's clingfire. It's conjured by black magic. It can't be put out. It will burn until there's nothing left. If it touches you, you'll burn to death."

"Fuck. Does that mean we're trapped here?" Billy asks.

"Is there any other way out?" I turn to Zeke.

He lets out a string of curses before adding, "Everyone in. Now!"

We all cram inside the storage unit, and then Zeke shuts the door. What good that will do against the fire is anyone's guess.

"That won't keep the fire at bay," Alex says, speaking what's on my mind.

"No shit, Captain Obvious." Zeke strides back to the mirror, then stares at it for a few seconds.

"What are you doing? The fire will be upon us in less than a minute," Leo says.

"Zeke, please tell me there's another way out of here." Nina moves closer to the imp.

He turns to her. "Yes, but it's not exactly what you have in mind."

"Spill it already, man." Sam runs a hand through his head in an exasperated motion.

The smoke is getting thicker, making it harder to breathe

and see anything. My eyes are burning already.

Zeke switches his attention to Sam, then to me. "We must use the mirror to open the portal to the Wastelands."

Chapter 14
Samuel

"Come again?" I ask. I must not have heard the imp correctly.

"What are you talking about? We need a full circle of witches, plus druid power to open the portal," Red says.

Zeke switches his attention to Alex, who is watching the imp through slits. "You know it's possible."

Clenching his jaw so hard I can hear his teeth grind together, the Dark Blade turns to Red. "The imp is not lying. The Mirror of Briseis is known to have the ability to open doors to different realms."

"Why wasn't it the plan from the get-go, then?" I ask.

"Because it's very dangerous, and there's no guarantee where you will wind up if you use it."

"I hate to break it to you, but if we don't make a decision soon, we'll be toast." Armand glances at the door.

"What do we need to do?" Red takes a step closer to the mirror, regarding it with intent.

"Since we already have a connection to the Wastelands via Trinity, the chances we'll end up in a different dimension are slim," Zeke replies.

"But there's still a chance, right?" Leo asks.

"It beats turning into fox barbecue," Nina chimes in, then turns to Zeke. "You'll need to feed the mirror with your demonic energy. You know what that will mean."

A shadow crosses Zeke's eyes. For a split second, I think I read fear in them. "I gotta take the risk. But only my energy won't be enough. I'll need Red's and Alex's assistance."

Red whips her face toward the imp, her green eyes turning as round as saucers. "I don't know how to use my witch powers at will, yet."

"You'll have to try, sweetheart." Zeke places a hand on her shoulder, then drops it quickly when he feels my glower.

"There's only one problem with this plan. How are we getting back? We won't be able to open a portal from the Wastelands, and no one will know what happened to us."

"Anyone got a cell phone?" Armand asks, then glances once more at the entrance of the unit. Flames are already licking away at the roll-up door. "Shit, never mind. Let's get the hell out of here."

I sense the panic increase in Red's eyes as she stares at the flames. The urge to touch her in a reassuring manner is overwhelming, but I can't risk getting her derailed by lust. I'll have to resign myself to capturing her gaze instead. "You can do it, Red. I believe in you."

She nods, then briefly glances at Alex before focusing on Zeke again. "Tell me what to do."

"I want you and Alex to stand on each side of me as we face the mirror."

They get into position, then Zeke offers his hands to Red and Alex. "Now, touch the mirror."

"Now what?" she asks.

"Close your eyes and let me be your guide."

Alex makes a disgruntled sound in the back of his throat, but that's the only sign the druid is not happy about Zeke taking the lead on this. When the imp's appearance changes to his true form—a demon with light green skin—and his demonic aura flares to life, my wolf's protectiveness wakens with a vengeance. On instinct, I take a step forward, ready to yank Red from Zeke's grasp, but Nina wraps her fingers around my arm and yanks me back.

"Don't interrupt them. We'll turn into a crisp in the next minute if we don't escape."

My canines have descended, and I feel the wolf's wild energy churning inside of my core. This doesn't feel right.

"Nothing is happening," Leo says with a hint of alarm in his tone.

Then Red lets out a gasp, and if it wasn't for Nina still holding me in place, I would have pulled Red away from the mirror—as crazy as it sounds because that would mean certain death for all of us. The surface is now moving, as if it has turned into liquid. The blurry reflection on it is terrifying.

Red

The moment I clasp hands with Zeke, a malicious power zips up my arm. It takes everything in me not to pull away from him. My wolf churns wildly in my chest, protesting the demonic energy that is now coursing through my body. It probes as if searching for something, and it takes me a second to understand what exactly it is looking for. My witch powers.

As soon as Zeke's energy gets near my core, my new powers awaken, stronger than I have ever felt them. It fights against the imp's demonic invasion, pushing it away.

"Don't kick me out completely!" Zeke's voice sounds in my head.

"How did you get through my mental barriers?"

"He didn't. The Mirror of Briseis has linked our minds," Alex replies.

"That's just great."

"Please, let's save the bickering for when we're out of the fire. I need you to focus all your energy toward the mirror, having in mind only one idea, the Wastelands."

"That's too vague. We need a visual," Alex contests.

A second later, I'm looking at a desolated landscape, a desert of sorts, but much crueler and lifeless.

"Is that the Wastelands?" I ask.

"That's the image Trinity sent me," Zeke replies.

"It fits the name. Okay, what's next?" Alex asks.

"Now pour all of your energy into opening a door into

that dimension."

Zeke's power increases, wrapping around my body, but not invasive this time. I also feel Alex's druid powers mixed with it, something wild and raw, similar in a way to my wolf's essence. I realize in a split second I've never been closer to him than I am now. Despite myself, my heart breaks a little, and I don't understand where the sentiment is coming from.

"You're not focusing hard enough, Red," Zeke says, his voice sounding a little constrained now.

"I'm trying my best."

The witch powers begin to spin out of control. As hard as I try to mold it to my will, it seems to slip through my fingers. Then another energy gets closer—Alex's this time—circling around the vortex that's threatening to suck me in. Slowly, the spinning loses momentum until it becomes something tangible, a power I can actually harness.

"What do I do now?" I ask.

"For lack of better words, hurl that power sphere at the mirror with the command to open," Alex replies.

"Let's do it together," Zeke says. *"On the count of three. One, two, three, now!"*

I push the power ball out of my body with all my strength, grunting in the process. It mixes with Zeke's and Alex's own spheres, those three different energies converging until they become one massive orb of magic. It hits the mirror's surface in the next second, going right through it. Nothing happens for a moment until the mirror's frame turns ice cold against my hand. There's a ripple in the surface as it gradually turns pitch black, then sharp white teeth appear slowly, as if the mirror has become a giant shark mouth. I gasp out loud.

"*Oh my God. What is that thing? Did we do something wrong?*" I ask, but Zeke and Alex don't reply.

I try to let go of the mirror's frame, but it seems my hand is stuck there. I begin to slide on the floor as an invisible pull begins to drag me toward the monster's gaping mouth.

"Alex," I scream, not in my head this time.

"Red! Hold on." It's Sam who replies to my call.

His arms wrap around my waist, then he tries to move me away from the mirror, but it's no use. We're both devoured by it in the next second. I close my eyes, bracing for the sharp pain of those teeth sinking into my skin. Sam is yanked from me, and my eyes fly open only to see nothing but darkness. I scream his name, but it gets swallowed up by the void.

Chapter 15
Red

I open my eyes with a start, feeling lost for a couple of seconds. My head is fuzzy as if my brain has been stuffed with cotton. Gray sky greets me, but there aren't any clouds.

What the hell happened?

The memories return in a flash. We had to use the Mirror of Briseis to open the portal to the Wastelands. Someone set the warehouse where Zeke kept the mirror on fire, and we had no other way of escaping. Shit, if the mirror was destroyed in the fire, how the hell are we getting out of here?

Slowly, every single sense returns to my body. The first thing I notice is the coldness that seems to seep through my clothes and straight into my heart. Despair begins to take a hold of me as if any happy thought I've ever had disappeared. This is indeed hell.

I'm on my back, the uneven, rough surface digging into my skin. As I try to move, the small pebbles pinch me with their sharpness. Jesus fucking Christ, did I fall into a valley of razors?

"Red? Where are you?" Sam's voice echoes in distance.

"Shut up, you fool. Do you want to alert every single demon in the vicinity of our presence?" Alex replies sharply.

Careful not to cut myself on the rocks, I get up. I'm in a ravine of sorts, surrounded by steep rocks on all sides. A shadowy figure appears on top of the hill. Even though I can't see the stranger's features, I know it's none of my companions. My wolf stirs as it senses danger. The figure leaps from boulder to boulder, descending fast toward me, the only detail visible is a blur of blond and black hair.

I retreat until my back hits the rock wall behind me. The stranger lands in a crouch in front of me, slowly rising to its full height. A young woman peers at me from under her lashes with lips twisted in a chilling smile. Trinity.

"You must be Red," she says in a melodic voice. Without a doubt, it's obvious the tone could put me under her spell.

"You're Trinity," I say.

"Yes. How did you get here so fast?"

"There was a fire. We had to use the Mirror of Briseis."

Her eyes turn rounder in surprise. "Wait? You used the mirror to travel here? That's insane."

"No kidding." I shudder, remembering how the mirror changed into a monster's mouth.

"Do you have the stone?" She cuts right to it.

Alex was the one chosen to carry the precious offering. But I don't tell Trinity that.

"You'll get your payment once Dante is safe."

She narrows her eyes as she takes a step forward. "That wasn't the deal."

My lips peel back as I show my sharp teeth. I won't be intimidated by her. "I don't care what Zeke told you. You'll get your payment once we rescue Dante."

"Red!" Sam shouts from above before he leaps off the edge.

"For fuck's sake. Can your mate keep his voice down? He's not in Crimson Hollow anymore." Trinity turns to glare at Sam, who is already upon us.

He spares the demon a nasty glance before he stops in front of me. "Are you okay?"

"Yes. Did everyone make it through the mirror?"

"Yup. Is that Zeke's friend?" He turns to Trinity, staring at her up and down.

"Yeah, it's her."

She's no longer paying attention to us. Instead, she's looking up at the sky as if she's smelling something.

"Damn it. We gotta move. Thanks to your mate's big mouth, we got company."

She bends her knees, then jumps high enough to clear out of the ravine.

"Shit. I didn't know succubi could do that," I say.

"Maybe she's *the* Trinity." Sam smirks, making me roll my eyes.

"You heard her, let's go."

Not possessing Trinity's handy *Matrix* jumping skills, Sam and I climb out of the ravine as fast as we can. Once we reach the top, we find the rest of our party. I exhale in relief. They've all made it. Nina is watching Trinity through slits, but Leo, Billy, Armand, and even Alex, have completely different expressions on their faces. It's almost like they've been enchanted by her. Zeke and Sam are the only males who seem immune to her charm.

"You'd better zip up that succubus energy right now before I shove it down your throat," Nina speaks with a growl.

The woman smiles sweetly at Nina. "Oh, I'm trembling in fear, little fox."

In the blink of an eye, Nina is on Trinity, pressing a small dagger to her throat. "Don't push me, demon."

The amused smile vanishes from the succubus's face as she takes a step back. "Gee, relax. I have no interest in harvesting the soul of your precious little pup." She turns her face toward Leo and Alex. "I can't say the same about those two."

"So, I'm of no interest to you, huh?" Armand says in a casual way.

Trinity turns to him with her nose scrunched up. "You're a vampire. You don't have a soul."

"Ouch. I'm wounded." Armand presses a hand over his chest.

Dread drips down my spine as I pick up a very dark energy approaching. "Guys, we need to move now."

Trinity glances out in the distance, her expression turning somber. "Damn it. Ghouls. I hate those motherfuckers. Follow me."

She takes off at run without bothering to see if we're following her. No one hesitates to do so. I guess I'm not the only one who can sense the evil hoard of ghouls fast approaching.

I have no idea where Trinity is leading us. We're in middle of a deserted field. There's no hiding spot in sight. The closest mountain range is too far for us to make it before the ghouls spot us.

Suddenly, Trinity disappears. It's not until I reach the spot from where she vanished that I see the small fissure on the ground, wide enough for a person to slip through. It's pitch black down there. I hesitate in following her.

"What are you waiting for? Want to be eaten by ghouls?" comes the echo of her voice from below.

Armand is the first to jump, followed by Zeke, Leo, Billy, and Nina. I'm still frozen when Alex turns to me.

"Go."

I glance at Sam before taking the plunge. The fall is short, but my knees still jar when I land in the chamber below. A second later, there are two consecutive thuds next to me. Sam and Alex made it down, too.

I don't dare to speak, afraid the echo of my voice will reach the ghouls up on the surface. Everyone must be thinking the same for absolute silence reigns in our party. Slowly, my eyes adjust to the gloom, and I begin to discern the shapes of my surroundings. We're in an underground cave of sorts.

"They've lost track of our scent," Trinity finally says from somewhere in the chamber. In the next moment, the entire room illuminates, revealing a great cave with a high ceiling. Sharp stalactites cling to it.

Armand whistles as he pivots slowly in a full circle.

"This is amazing. I was expecting fire and brimstone, not a magical cave."

"Where are we?" Alex asks.

"The place I've called home since I left Prythian's side."

"Who's Prythian?" Billy stares intently at the succubus. I don't think she turned down her powers enough.

"The King of Bastards," she answers.

Billy begins to inch closer to her. My guess is he doesn't know he's doing it. Nina grabs his arm, pulling him back, before leveling Trinity with a glower.

"I told you to keep your succubus's powers contained."

"They *are* contained. Fuck, it's not my fault you haven't given your puppy what he wants."

"He's not my puppy," Nina growls.

"Billy, snap out of it," I command. Surprisingly, he seems to respond to my words. Blinking fast, he stares at me and then at Nina, seeming a little confused.

"Why are you glaring at me like that?"

Trinity raises an eyebrow. "I didn't realize you're a she-alpha, Red."

"She's a what?" Alex bursts out, surprise lacing his words.

"I'm not an alpha," I reply through clenched teeth.

"Could have fooled me."

"What's the plan? How do we get to the King of Bastards arena from here?" I ask, trying to bring the focus back to why we're here in the first place.

"This cave connects to a tunnel that will lead right below the arena. The problem is the arena is protected by a powerful fae glamour, and we'll only be able to enter once Prythian makes the arena visible."

"I thought he was about to start the games soon." I cross my arms.

"He has sent out his lackeys to spread the word through the Wastelands, but the doors to his arena will only open when the games commence. By then, it will be extremely difficult to rescue Dante."

"So what are supposed to do now? The longer we stay here, the more the demonic energy in this place will do us harm." Alex stares hard at Trinity.

"There's a way we can gain early access to the arena, and to the area Dante is being held."

"Well, spill it already," Sam snaps.

"Some of you can enter the games as Prythian's champion's opponents."

"What happens to his opponents?" Alex narrows his eyes.

Trinity shrugs. "They have to fight among themselves. Whoever wins fights against the champion. Let's say, they're the opening act of the games."

"That's out of the question. It's too risky." Alex shakes his head.

"Maybe too risky for you. It might be our only chance to rescue my brother. I volunteer," Sam replies.

Trinity pinches her lips. "You can't. Prythian will smell your connection to Dante from a mile away."

Zeke glances at Alex, who in turn nods. Leo catches the gesture and says, "Wait. You're going to volunteer?"

"He doesn't need to. I'll do it." Billy lifts his chin.

"No. You're not ready for such a challenge," Nina protests.

Billy's eyes turn to slits. "Stop treating me like I'm a kid. Dante needs our help. If Sam can't go, then I will. I can't let a druid risk his neck for my pack while I wait on the sidelines. There's no honor in that."

"So you'd rather die instead?" Nina almost yells.

Billy rolls his eyes in a typical teenager gesture. "I'm not going to die. Have a little faith in me."

"The wolf pup will be good bait. Prythian's handlers will probably underestimate him. But I think the druid should come as well. We might need the magic."

"I'll go then," Alex announces.

"And who is going to present the new contestants to Prythian?" Leo asks.

"It has to be me," Trinity says with a sigh.

"Are you sure?" Zeke asks.

"Do you have a better idea? I'm the only one here who is not a stranger to Prythian."

"No offense, but I don't trust you. I'll come as well," I say.

Trinity raises any eyebrow. "Are you offering yourself as bait?"

"No. I'm coming as your partner."

Chapter 16
Dante

Since I killed Prythian's former champion, I expected the King of Bastards to come pay me a visit in my new quarters, which is still in a dungeon but an upgraded cell. I haven't forgotten Mauve's implication the fae enjoyed male company. But he never came.

A commotion outside my cell draws my attention, and I spring to my feet. A couple of Prythian's handlers are rattling the other prisoners, egging them on. The growls and snarls that come in response make me break into a cold sweat. I won the fight against that three-headed monster, but that doesn't mean I can keep winning against the other demons.

One of those stony-faced handlers stops in front of my cell, then pulls a set of dangling keys from his belt. It's odd that in a place filled with extraordinary magic like this, the cell doors are still kept locked in the old-fashioned way.

I brace myself for what's to come, my wolf stirring in my chest. The dark magic that surrounds this place has once again made it impossible for me to shift at will. What's up with these fae messing with my shifting abilities?

"The king requires your presence. Move, mongrel."

The guard makes a grab for me, but I leap out of his reach, coming around his back to deliver a roundhouse kick. He staggers forward, hitting his helmeted head on the far wall. I break into a run, but I don't take more than a couple of steps before I'm blasted by an electric current that pushes me down on the floor, rendering me immobile.

A set of consecutive hard kicks on my ribs comes next, and I hear a loud crack before terrible pain erupts from the place of impact.

"Stop, you fool. That's the king's champion."

"He doesn't look like much of a champion to me."

I wince when I'm brought back on my feet in a jerky movement, then I'm dragged out of the dungeon by two guards. Their clawed hands dig into my skin, but that pain is nothing compared to the burning in my side. Fuck. If I didn't think I could win the king's wicked games before, there's no chance in hell now.

Despite the pain, I pay attention to where the guards are taking me. We leave the foul-smelling dungeon behind, going up a set of endless spiraling staircases that are illuminated by torches hanging on the walls. They emit an unnatural light. It looks like fire, but it's green instead of golden.

The air changes when I step out of the dungeons. Instead of the stench of decay, the fresh smell of flowers reaches my nose. The décor rivals any palace I've seen depicted in pictures showcasing royalty grandeur. High vaulted ceilings show frescos painted on them, just like they did in the audience chamber where I defeated Prythian's champion. The granite and marble floor glimmers, and it could be pain-induced hallucination, but it seems the image depicted in its pattern is moving as if it were alive.

A grand staircase looms ahead. Above it hangs an enormous glass painting of the King of Bastards sitting on his throne. The guy is as conceited as they come. I force my legs to move, but with each passing moment, breathing becomes harder. Damn it. I think one of my fractured ribs is pressing against my lungs.

A set of double doors heavily decorated with golden swirls opens by itself. We enter a luxurious room where the stone flooring gives way to plush, silk carpet. A variety of couches are spread out among other pieces of expensive-looking furniture, all leaning toward classic luxury. The paintings hanging from the walls are encased in frames that are just as astonishing as the artwork themselves. At the end of the room, a massive fireplace is roaring with the same greenish fire I saw earlier in the dungeon.

I don't spot Prythian in this colorful setting until he moves. His dark hair swishes around with the movement. He's wearing a patterned robe that blends with his surroundings.

"What's the meaning of this?" he asks in a deadly quiet manner. "What have you done to my champion?"

"He tried to escape, my lord."

With a wave of Prythian's hand, the two guards next to me break into pieces. It happens so fast they don't have time to scream. Without their support, I fall to my knees, clutching at my side.

Prythian is in front of me in the blink of an eye, but I'm in too much pain to lift my face to properly glare at him.

"You must be regretting the absurd amount of coin you paid for me now."

I sense a strange magic wrap around my body. It's not evil, but it's not good either. The pain in my torso vanishes. With its release, the ability to breathe normally returns.

"Rise," Prythian commands.

Clenching my jaw, I unfurl from the kneeling position. Prythian is watching me with a peculiar glint in his eyes.

"Why am I here?" I ask.

"I wanted to inspect my investment closely."

He begins to circle me, standing close enough that if I wished, I could strike him. However, instinct tells me I'd be dead before I touched the fae. The power emanating from him is contained, that I much I can tell. I don't want to be anywhere near him when he unleashes it entirely.

"I'm afraid you made a terrible one. I'm not a champion."

He throws his head back and laughs. When he's over his amused fit, he replies. "Most lie through their teeth to convince me they're champion material. Surviving in the Wastelands alone is impossible for any type of creature. I'm the only one who can guarantee safety. But you wouldn't know that, would you? Your soul is uncorrupted still. You just got here."

The urge to throw in his face that I don't plan to stay long is great, but I bite my tongue. Let him think I'm just going to accept my fate.

"Truth is, you aren't anything like any of my previous champions. I sense some great power in you, something that even you can't totally grasp."

My spine goes taut. If Prythian finds out I have visions of the future, he'll never let me go.

"You don't want me to know what it is, do you?" He chuckles. "I could force it out of you, but there would be no fun in that."

Turning away, he veers for a glass and metal tray not too far away where several different bottles are spread out. He picks up a crystal decanter with a deep red liquid inside. At first glance, it appears to be wine, but here in this hellish dimension, I can't be sure of anything. Prythian fills out two glasses, then offers me one. The smell that reaches my nose is akin to wine, but stronger. I don't take the beverage, though.

Prythian's expression turns into something feral. At the same time, his purple irises begin to swirl. "You dare refuse me?"

Before I can brace myself for his wrath, I'm blasted by a great force, causing my knees to buckle. Grabbing a chunk of my hair, he pulls my head back to force the drink down my throat. Stubbornly, I clamp my jaw shut.

"You're a fool for defying me. Do you know what I could to you, little wolf?"

"Do your worse," I reply.

I must have lost my damn mind. Why am I challenging this being? I don't want to die in this forsaken place. Then it happens... My entire body begins to tremble, and it's not something the fae is doing to me. Letting go of my hair, he pulls away to watch me with his keen eyes. I double over, trying in vain to keep the vision contained, but knowing it's futile. I can't control my gift. Of all the times for it to manifest, it had to be in the presence of the King of Bastards.

In a manic motion, I begin to search for something I can use to paint the images that are coming to my mind.

"I need paper and a pen," I say with effort.

With a swish of his hand, the materials I requested appear in front of me. Once I have possession of them, I get lost in my gift. As usual, I don't know how much time elapses before the sense of normalcy returns to me. The pen slips from my fingers while I stare numbly at nothing.

Prythian bends to retrieve my newest piece of art. Shit, I wish I had the forethought to glimpse at it before he got the paper. He seems frozen as he stares at the drawing. His expression can only be described as one of utter shock and vulnerability. His hands are shaking slightly. With a clench of his jaw, he turns the piece of paper to ashes.

"How did you know?" he asks, his gaze not trained on me, but lost and far away.

"Know what? I have no idea what I just drew."

He looks at me then. "Good. Then I don't have to kill you." Returning to his forgotten wine, he drinks it all. "Do your visions always come to pass?"

I don't answer right away, not knowing what the King of Bastards wants to hear. In the end, I decide to go with the truth. "I don't know. Some have, others not yet."

Curling his fingers around the cart handle, he leans on it for a moment before turning to me. "You won't say a word to anyone about what transpired here. In return, I'll let your friends live."

"My friends?"

"They've come to rescue you, those little fools. They don't realize nothing happens in the Wastelands without my knowledge."

Fear spikes my chest. Did Red come after me? If she did, then why can't I feel the bond?

Chapter 17
Red

We must have been walking for a least thirty minutes when Trinity raises her hand, signaling for us to halt.

"This is the tunnel that will lead to the basement of one of the stores in the Shadow Market."

"I thought we were going to request an audience with the King of Bastards," Leo points out.

Trinity stares at him with pinched lips and furrowed eyebrows, but her glare doesn't last for more than a few seconds.

"Like I said before, Prythian keeps his arena hidden most of the time unless there's a game in session."

"And how are you going to let him know you have contestants to enroll in his stupid games?" I ask.

Trinity's face remains impassive, but an odd emotion flickers in her gaze when she says, "Prythian and I go way back. He'll sense my presence."

"Oh, I bet there's an interesting story here." Armand rubs his hands together. His comment is cheeky. I don't think he meant anything by it, but Trinity's eyes flash red for a second nonetheless.

"One you'll never get to hear," Trinity replies sharply.

Armand's eyebrows raise as he whistles. "Oops. Touchy subject?"

Zeke shakes his head. "You have no idea."

"I'll have my payment now, druid boy." Trinity looks straight at Alex.

How did she know he had the stone? Can she sense it?

"I already said you'll get your payment once Dante is rescued," I reply.

She turns her ire in my direction. "And I never agreed to it. Besides, I need the stone before I come face to face with Prythian again."

Suspicion sneaks into my mind. Narrowing my eyes, I ask, "Why?"

"The King of Bastards has a hold on you, doesn't he?" Alex asks.

I see the truth in the way Trinity's facial muscles become tenser. "It's not as strong as it used to be, mainly because he wished it so. If he suspects I'm there to betray him, he'll tighten the leash. And then we're pretty much fucked."

With a sigh, I turn to Alex. "Just give her the stone."

"Red, that's not wi—"

"You heard her. Give Trinity the stone," Sam snaps, projecting his wolf aggression toward Alex.

There's a moment of undeniable tension in the air, so much so that Nina steps farther away from our group, pulling Billy with her. Does she think Alex and Sam will come to blows? I can't let that happen, so I step in front of

Alex, lifting my hand, palm up.

"The stone, please. The longer we waste arguing about it, the more we risk Dante's life."

Alex's dark gaze turns calculating. But as it had always been even when we were dating, I can't read what's going on in his head. The fact used to drive me insane because he never had that problem with me. He used to say I was an open book.

With a resigned sigh, Alex reaches inside his jacket and retrieves the necklace with the ember stone pendant that used to belong to Albert and Madison. When he drops it into my hand, I sense the power within. The energy is not the same as the stone I retrieved from the grimoire. The second stone was raw, the energy almost felt like it was untamable. The essence in this one is much calmer, but no less powerful.

When I turn around, I find Trinity watching me closely, but when I approach her with the stone, she seems tense, almost fearful.

"Here." I offer her the necklace.

There's a visible hard swallow on her part before she opens her hand. When the jewelry drops into her palm, the stone glows bright red before returning to its natural subdued ember hue. Trinity curls her fingers around it, closing her eyes for a second. When she peers into my eyes, hers are shining with a great sense of relief.

"You didn't know how the stone would react to you, did you?" I ask.

"I was afraid it would fry me on the spot. I sensed the goodness coming from it. It has been fine tuned to serve the angels."

"Isn't that what you want?"

"Yes."

"I don't get it. Why would a demon want a sacred stone blessed to do good?" Billy asks, then quickly adds, "No offense, Trinity."

She doesn't answer Billy, so Nina replies for her. "Because she doesn't want to be a demon anymore."

"Really? Is that even possible?" I ask.

"I wasn't born a demon."

"True, but something tells me you weren't human either before you were changed," Nina chimes in.

Trinity looks away, and Zeke clears his throat. "All right. Now that we've taken care of all the formalities, let's get cranking. The longer we stay here, the more vulnerable to corruption we'll become."

"Meaning we can turn into demons?" Billy asks with a hint of fear in his voice.

"You'd have to sell your soul to become a demon. But the miasma in this place will make you become darker, meaner, evil."

A shudder runs down my spine. "What's the plan?"

Trinity puts the necklace on, but hides it from view, sticking it underneath her clothes.

"Now we head to the Shadow Market. The owner of the tavern where this tunnel leads to is a friend of mine, so we don't have to worry about discovery. Those who are not coming inside the arena right now should wait and remain hidden."

"You don't expect us to stay hidden the entire time you guys are dealing with the King of Bastards, do you?" Sam asks.

"Yes, that's exactly what I expect. If everything goes according to plan, you won't need to do a thing."

"And what if things don't go according to plan? How would they even know?" I ask.

"If the Games start, you'll know we failed."

Trinity turns around, disappearing through a small crack in the cavern's wall. It's barely big enough for one person to squeeze in. I follow her next, and I'm relieved to find out the tight space is only at the beginning of this new tunnel. It widens a little after a couple of steps, turning into a wider tunnel instead. Up ahead, Trinity is holding a torch, the only source of illumination here. A staircase has been carved on the ground, leading up.

Our ascension is silent save for the sound of our steps hitting the stony ground and echoing around us. My legs are burning by the time Trinity stops in front of a door. Gee, how far down underground were we? She pulls a skeleton key from one of her jacket pockets. After the lock rings free, the sound of old hinges crack as Trinity pushes the door open. A second later, right before I follow her inside the tavern's basement, the hissing sound of fire being extinguished by water reaches my ear, then, it's blackness.

Sam bumps into my back, then he lets out a low curse. "Watch it you, will you?"

"Are you talking to me?" I ask, kind of surprised.

"Of course not, my love. I'm talking to druid boy behind

me."

"Can you idiots be quite for one second?" Trinity hisses from farther ahead.

A moment later, she turns on a flickering light. Maybe turn on isn't the correct term. Instead of seeing a dangling lamp bulb, a mason jar hangs from the ceiling. Inside, several winged insects bounce inside their glass prison.

"What are those?" Billy asks.

"Pixies. Nasty little buggers," Trinity answers from her higher position. She's perched on another set of stairs, those made out of wood, which I imagine leads to the tavern's main floor.

"How do you make them glow like that?" I ask, oddly fascinated by their manic movements.

"They smelled the blood in your veins. It puts them into a frenzy." She shrugs.

"Are you saying they drink blood?" Sam asks.

"Yup. They're like piranhas with wings," Zeke replies, making sure he's not standing directly under them.

"Wonderful," Alex says.

"Hey, what are in these wooden barrels?" Billy touches the one nearest to him.

"Demon beer," Zeke says with a tone of reverence.

"Demon beer? Is it any good?" Billy asks.

"It's delicious." Zeke strokes a barrel as if it was something precious to him. I'm not sure I like the glazed expression in his eyes.

"Zeke, step away from that barrel," Trinity commands, then curses under her breath.

"What's going on? Why is Zeke acting like that?" Leo watches the imp with caution now.

"I don't know. But he can't come with us. So make sure he doesn't drink any of that beer. Got it?"

"Yeah, no problem." Armand wraps his hand around Zeke's arm, then pulls him away from the barrels.

Trinity cocks her head as she appraises Armand, and then Leo. "Come to think of, I think the vampire and the fox shifter will be better offerings to Prythian. The druid should stay behind."

"No. You'll need my powers if things get dicey."

"What are you saying?" Leo raises an eyebrow, staring hard at Alex.

"I don't think druid boy has a lot of faith in our abilities." Armand's friendly demeanor changes to something savage. His features become sharper, as if he were carved from stone. His eyes turn a fiery red as he peels his lips back to show off his impressive fangs.

"I second the Blade staying behind, even if I have to suffer his company," Sam adds, earning an annoyed glare from Alex.

"Why can't *I* come?" Nina asks.

Trinity rewards the fox spy with a haughty look. "Because I don't like you. Don't worry. I won't let anything happen to the young wolf."

She turns to Billy, winking at him. The teen turns bright red before lowering his gaze.

"Oh, and one more thing. The warning to stay away from the demon beer is for everyone. One drop of that on your tongue, and say bye-bye to your free will."

Trinity disappears up the stairs. I take a step to follow her, but Sam pulls me back. "What—"

He grabs the back of my head, bringing me to him for a crushing, toe-curling kiss. I want to yell at him. We're not supposed to be touching. But as our tongues mingle together, the desire that wraps around my spine and spreads through my body erases all common sense. Suddenly, my clothes feel suffocating, even itch. I need to get them off.

I'm yanked from Sam's arms, and it takes me a moment to see through the lust gaze that Leo and Armand are holding Sam in place.

"What the fuck are you doing?" Trinity pops her head back into the basement. "I could sense the primal desire from all the way up in the store. You're going into heat."

"Ah, that explains," Nina says.

"You can't touch her, you idiot," Alex shout-whispers from behind me. He's the one who yanked me away from Sam, I realize now.

"Let her go," Sam growls, his eyes turning wolfish amber.

Sanity is slowly returning to my head, and with that, mortification.

"I'm good, Alex," I whisper.

He steps away, letting go of my arms. I can't make eye contact with anyone here, so I turn around and climb the stairs as fast as I can.

Chapter 18
Tristan

Those who say personal inner demons are worse than outside forces trying to bring someone down are correct. Harkon did everything in his power to break my spirit, but ultimately, it was my guilty conscience that did the trick. As I hang from the cold, steely chains wrapped around my wrists, I'm ready to fucking die. I don't care about anything. Red, my brothers, my mother, the pack, they're all better off without me.

It is in that state of misery that Harkon finds me, this time wearing his true demonic shell. I can't even summon the energy to fear him.

He laughs, an evil sound that echoes in this hellish chamber and reverberates all around me.

"So, you have given up already. Pity, I was looking forward to torturing you more. But there's no pleasure beating down a man who's hopeless. You disappoint me, Alesandro."

Alesandro? Who the hell is Alesandro? Another one of my previous lives? It doesn't matter. I'm sure I fucked it up, too. I don't bother correcting him. He can call me whatever he wants.

"Just end this already," I say.

"No, that would be too merciful. It might not be fun anymore to inflict pain on you, but you're not completely useless to me."

He approaches, and my numb body becomes colder. Once again, he grabs my head between his sharp claws and the excruciating pain assaults my brain. I hold off the scream in my throat for as long as I can, but like the other times, I can't keep it bottled in. Something different happens this time. I lose complete sensation of my body. It's as if my soul has wandered off from its broken shell. Peering down, I see my chained-up body with Harkon in front of me.

Suddenly, that image vanishes. In its place, I see another person chained to a pole. A woman wearing a white robe. I can't see her face from this angle, only her dark blonde hair flapping against the wind. She's standing on a rock, facing a turbulent sea. Great waves crash below, splashing water all over the ridge where she stands, drenching her. She must be a sacrifice. Behind her, a big crowd has gathered. Not too far from where she is, a dais has been raised where an imposing grey-haired man sits on a throne. Standing next to him, there's a young man wearing a red-and-white Greek style toga. I know that face.

With a jolt, I'm back in my body. The strange scene I just witnessed turns foggy, as if it were just a dream. But I force myself to latch on to it. I know it's something I must remember.

Harkon's laughter forces me to focus on my surroundings once more.

"You didn't scream as loudly this time. Perhaps I'm not inflicting enough pain on you."

Or maybe you don't know that my soul left my body for a moment, and that I felt no pain while I was floating in the nether. But I'm not about to tell him that. The fact I might have the upper hand infuses me with hope. The sense of complete despair dissipates a little. Harkon has not broken my spirit yet.

"Or maybe you're not as strong as you think," I say.

The blow comes so swiftly I don't have time to brace for it. My head is thrown back with tremendous force, and it's a miracle it didn't pop right off my neck.

"I should gut you and make you eat your own entrails for that comment. But I have a prize to collect."

He's talking about Red. I want to tell him he'll never have her, but my jaw is still burning from his punch. Goading him will serve no purpose.

"What? Are you out of cocky remarks?" Harkon continues. "It doesn't surprise me. You've always been weak, and you'll always be weak."

"You mean when I was Robert."

The demon stares at me as if he's amused. "You know nothing, puny human. Maybe one day, I'll make you remember it all. When I'm ravaging your mate in front of your eyes."

My wolf, which had been silent until now, resurfaces, and a loud growl comes from deep in my throat. My reaction only seems to amuse the demon.

There's another sharp pain in my brain, but not caused by Harkon this time. It's the damn chip. I had forgotten about it while in captivity. I shut my eyes when sudden pressure outside my skull threatens to turn my head into a pulp. *What the hell is going on?*

The horrible sensation doesn't last long. When I blink my eyes open, I'm no longer in that dark dungeon cell, but back in the human world. To make sure I'm not dreaming, I dig my nails in the hard ground beneath me, feeling the rough texture against my skin. Then I take a deep breath, and the scent that fills my nostrils give me the undeniable proof I'm out of hell. I smell Shadow Creek wolves.

My body protests when I attempt to stand up, but I force my legs to obey. Right in front of me is the charred remains of the gazebo where Valerius burned his alpha alive.

A great sense of uneasiness takes a hold of me. With keen eyes, I search my surroundings. The square is deserted. However, I know I'm not completely alone. Harkon is near. I can smell his stench not too far away.

A second later, I feel his demonic aura right behind me. Turning around, I ignore caution and glare at the demon, who still can't become corporeal in this plane.

"Why did you bring me back here?"

"Valerius's premature demise put a wrench in my plans. But now that I have you, I can finally finish what I've started."

My stomach clenches in a vicious manner while my throat becomes tight. "You want Red."

He laughs again. "She won't escape me this time."

Curling my fists, I take a step toward the demon, not realizing for a couple of beats that I'm growling and my canines have descended. I've partially shifted without noticing.

"You'll never have her. I won't let you."

"Oh, so it seems I didn't break your spirit after all. It's of no consequence. You're my new puppet, and you'll do exactly as I command."

White-hot pain shoots through my brain again. It's the controlling chip, stripping me of my free will. My legs fold, and I'm down on my knees. My body begins to change, my muscles contract, and my bones crack. Some foreign power is forcing the shift.

When I open my eyes again, I'm looking at everything through my wolf's eyes, but that's the only thing I can do. I break into a run, not knowing where the hell I'm going. It's as if I'm stuck inside a car ride where the driver has gone rogue.

I keep on running until I leave Shadow Creek behind, entering the Thunderborn's territory. Harkon is not far away, and I begin to understand his relationship with Valerius. Harkon used Valerius's life force to be able to linger in this plane. And now he's doing the same thing to me. We're linked somehow. I can't read his mind, but I can sense his intent. All the time he spent torturing me in hell had one purpose—breaking me so he could take possession of my soul. And with the chip in place, my resistance is even weaker.

I pick up the scent of bears nearby, a mother and a couple of cubs. My fur stands on end as the demon's intent becomes clear in my mind. He plans to feast on those bears through me, and there's nothing I can do to stop him.

Chapter 19
Red

In my haste to escape the embarrassing scene in the basement, I forgot for a moment I'm not in Crimson Hollow, but in a place where demons roam freely. I realize my mistake when I reach the landing of Trinity's friend's tavern. I'm at the back of a dark room, and at first glance, the place seems empty, but there's a malevolent aura that's impossible to ignore. A shiver runs down my back as cold tendrils of air curl around my spine. I shouldn't be here.

My heart leaps up my throat when someone covers my mouth and yanks me back, making my adrenaline levels shoot through the roof. My wolf instincts take control, and I begin to shift automatically.

"Relax. It's me, Trinity."

I stop struggling, but I'm far from relaxed. I don't think anyone who is not a demon could relax in this hellish dimension.

She uncovers my mouth, then turns me around to glare. "What the hell do you think you're doing? You can't simply walk out without a disguise."

"Why do I need one? Everyone will know I'm not a demon."

"You can't look like you just came through the human realm if you want to convince Prythian that you're my partner."

I cross my arms, feeling irritated. "You should have mentioned that before."

"Did you give me a chance? Besides, I'm the one who has reason to be pissed. You're going in heat, and you didn't consider telling me?"

My face becomes unbearably hot, especially now that Billy, Armand, and Leo have joined us in the back of the tavern.

"I didn't think it would matter," I whisper.

"Are you out of your mind? Shifters in heat lose their self-control. They operate on pure animalistic instinct, which wouldn't be completely terrible if their wild nature had any objective besides fucking."

Curling my hands into fists, I try to rein in my temper. "I'm not in heat yet, so you don't have to worry I'll turn into a deranged nympho."

Trinity shakes her head, laughing without humor. "You don't understand. If any demon suspects you're going in heat, they'll take you."

My throat becomes unbearably dry. "Take me for what?"

"I think you can guess."

"Maybe you shouldn't come with us, mon chérie. We won't leave this place without Dante. Promise," Armand offers. I appreciate what he's trying to do, but I can't stay behind.

"No. Dante is my mate. He's here because of me. I have to see this through. I have to come."

Trinity opens her mouth, but before she offers a counterargument, I continue. "Unfortunate will be the demon who tries to take me against my will."

The succubus watches me through slits before she replies. "Okay. If you're *that* determined to come, then I won't stop you. But let me make one thing clear. If things get complicated, don't count on me to bail you out."

"Are you saying you're not going to help if shit hits the fan?" Leo asks.

"Nope." Trinity shakes her head.

"That's fucking stupid if you ask me. You agreed to help us so you could get out of the Wastelands. If you bail on us, who's going to help you then?" Billy raises an eyebrow with an air of arrogance.

Man, he has changed so much. I'm as proud of him as if he were my own kid, especially when I see a flash of doubt cross Trinity's eyes.

"I'll use the stone to get out."

Billy laughs. "I hope your intel about the Wastelands is better than your knowledge of the sacred stone. You won't be able to use it to open a portal out of here, not when it's fine-tuned to fight evil."

My jaw drops. How does Billy know so much about the sacred stone?

Leo smiles at Billy before raising his hand for a high-five. "Nice burn, bro."

"Ugh! I'm regretting this arrangement already." Trinity strides away, disappearing into the darkness.

"Are we supposed to follow her or..." Armand starts, but Trinity returns before he can finish his sentence.

She throws some type of garment at me. The fabric is heavy and rough. "What is this?"

"A hooded cloak. I don't have time to procure other clothes for you, so this will have to do. Try to keep your modern clothes hidden underneath it."

She turns to the guys, and then I see the shackles and chains in her hands. "Now for the fun part. Raise your arms, boys."

Grumbling, they do as she asked. Trinity is enjoying turning them into her captives too much.

"Hey. Why do these shackles have to be so tight?" Billy complains.

"Do you want this ruse to be believable or not?"

I put the cloak on, making sure the clasp is tied properly. When I pull the hood over my head, I do feel a little bit better that my features are partially hidden. I know I'm a supernatural now, but I still feel very much human and vulnerable.

"Listen up. This will be our cover story. I met Red when we were staying at the River's Quadrant—"

"What's the River's Quadrant?" Billy interrupts.

"It's not important what or where it is," Trinity hisses.

"Uh, I think it kind of is, especially if you met Red there," Billy insists.

"Billy, let her continue," I say.

"As I was saying, we were staying at the River's Quadrant, an inn run by sprites, when it got attacked by a band of ghouls. We fought and escaped together, then decided we should partner up for safety."

"That's fine, but what's my backstory? How did I wind up here?" I ask.

Trinity shrugs. "You never told me, so if Prythian asks, you'd better have your story ready."

Armand leans closer to Leo and whispers, "How does one end up in the Wastelands in the first place?"

"Well, Dante got here because Harkon sent him, but obviously she can't use the same story." Billy motions his hand in a gesture that could be easily be translated to 'duh'.

Both Armand and Leo give Billy a droll look which, thankfully, he misses.

"I'll think of something. Can we go now?" I wave my hand impatiently.

"Wait a second. How did we end up being caught by you?" Leo asks.

Trinity moves closer with a smirk on her lips. "Like all males, you couldn't resist the charm of two gorgeous women." She runs her long nails over his chest, making the fox shifter tense on the spot.

"Well, you're a succubus, right? It would be pretty hard for any male to resist your powers," Billy says, his eyes glazing over a bit.

I pull Trinity away from them. "Cut it out, Trinity. This is not the time for games."

The woman turns to me, sporting an innocent

expression. "I wasn't doing anything."

"Whatever. Can we go now?"

Trinity leads the way with the guys sandwiched between us. I'd prefer if I was in the middle to keep them as far away from the succubus as possible, but that wouldn't look right for the purpose of our ruse. One thing is sure, I'm glad Trinity caught me before I ventured farther into the tavern. This is definitely not a place one should be roaming alone.

At first glance, it looks exactly how I'd imagine a tavern from the Middle Ages would look like, at least the ones I've seen depicted in movies. There are long picnic tables spread throughout the establishment where creatures sit at leisure drinking and eating. The walls are dark and rough, and without examining them too closely, my best guess is they are constructed out of stone. There's the hint of a brimstone smell in the place, which should be enough to clue anyone in that this is a hellish dimension. But there's something else as well, a terrible feeling of doom that has sneaked into my heart, squeezing it tight. The sensation is stripping away all my confidence, all my positive thoughts. How long until it begins to corrupt my soul as well?

My worry for Dante doubles. He's been here for two days. Is he still the same kind of person I fell in love with or has this place already turned him into a cold monster?

A tall, two-headed creature walks around the main counter and heads in our direction. Her necks are long, and she possesses features that remind me of a reptile. Only she's not completely hairless. Dark hair falls to her shoulders, and she's rocking sharp bangs as well.

"Who's the two-headed dino wearing the wigs?" Billy, who is the closest to me, whispers.

"Shh. Let's try not to offend any of these demons," I reply.

"Trinity. It's been a long time." The demon stops in front of the succubus, blocking our way.

"Yes, indeed, Rhonda."

The demon looks over Trinity's head, her attention riveted on our captives. "I see you're now into trading. I thought you abhorred the job."

Trinity shrugs. "There's not much one can do in these lands. This is easy, and it pays well."

"You could always go back to the king's court."

Trinity doesn't reply for a couple of beats, and I notice the patrons have taken a keen interest in the conversation. Finally, the succubus answers, "Maybe I will."

"Are those specimens for Prythian?"

"Yes. I've heard he's got a new champion."

"He does. A powerful wolf shifter. He defeated Ravenous with the blink of an eye, at least, that's the story everyone in the Shadow Market has been regurgitating. Mauve was sure lucky to come across that specimen. I'm sure Prythian paid her handsomely."

My entire body becomes tense at the mention of the demon who captured and sold Dante to the King of Bastards. She'd better be far away from here, because if we cross paths, I'll kill her.

"Mauve is a sneaky bitch. I'm sure she didn't move a muscle to capture the wolf shifter. Doesn't she still employ that human and his son?"

"Oh yeah. The idiot fancies himself in love with the fae." Rhonda laughs. "Humans are so stupid. It's no wonder they're so easily corrupted by us."

"Yo, Triny," someone calls from the middle of the tavern.

Trinity glances in the voice's direction, but from where I stand, I can't see who spoke.

"If Prythian doesn't want your load, I'll buy the wolf pup. I haven't eaten shifter meat in a long time."

Billy turns rigid at the same time a low growl escapes his lips. I lift my hand to touch him in a reassuring manner, but then I remember he's my captive.

"Quiet," I command. I hadn't thought I had spoken that loudly, but I suddenly sense several pairs of eyes aimed in my direction.

Rhonda, who up until that point had not even glanced my way, is staring at me now. "And who is that one? She smells like a shifter, too, but different."

"She's my new partner." Trinity's tone is hard as if she's angry that Rhonda is now asking about me. Maybe I should have kept my mouth shut and not drawn attention to myself.

"You never had a partner before."

"She slaughtered ten ghouls in one fell swoop during the attack at River's Quadrant, and she doesn't get on my nerves. I decided to give it a try."

"She has killed ten ghouls by herself?" Rhonda's tone is of incredulity. Around the room, I hear similar murmurs. Fuck. Why did Trinity have to paint me like I'm some sort of wolf warrior?

"Yup. I'd better get going. Need to unload the merch." Trinity shrugs.

Rhonda nods with both her heads, then brushes past Trinity and heads to the back of the tavern. She cuts me a curious glance as she walks by, but the movement is fleeting. It's not until she disappears into the darkness of the back room that it occurs to me Trinity never told her friend about Sam, Alex, and Zeke who are hiding in her basement.

I wait until we're out of the tavern to ask the succubus about it, but once outside, I realize I won't be able to talk freely with her at all. We're smack in the middle of a busy market where the number of demons and other supernatural creatures is ten times larger than the patrons inside the tavern. Once again, our group garners too much attention for my liking. My wolf stirs restless inside my core. I wonder how fast I can shift in case I need to protect the guys who, bound like they are, are defenseless.

It takes a great effort on my part not to cower under so many demonic auras. I summon all the strength I have in me to project a menacing wolf energy. I'm not sure if I'm doing it right, but so far, no one has done more than watch us. I have no idea where we're going, but I wish Trinity would circle around the busy market instead of taking us right through the middle of it. The place is too crowded, and it's hard not to brush against others. Every time I touch someone, I get colder and my resolve to remain strong diminishes.

Damn it. I wish I were closer to the succubus so I could

question her actions. The concentrated demonic energy is not doing us any favors. When I hear a hiss coming from Armand, the small hairs on my neck stand on end. Shit. When he turns his face to glare at a creature who got too close to him, I see that he has turned full vamp. The question is, did he do that on purpose or is he already affected by the corruption of this place? Oh man. I hope I don't have to fight with Sam's friend. I have no idea how to subdue a vampire.

"Is it just me or is the crowd is getting a little rougher?" Billy says under his breath.

"They're definitely getting a little too bold for my liking."

No sooner do I utter those words than a creature with long gray hair and skin that resembles bark makes a grab for Billy. "I like this one. I claim him."

She yanks at the chain, and Billy stumbles to the side. Without stopping to think, I swing my arm around, hitting the crooner with a clawed hand, sending her to the ground. "Don't fucking touch him," I growl. My canines have descended and my vision has changed, which means my eyes must be glowing amber.

The demon scooches back while clutching at her face. Dark blood oozes from the wound I inflicted. She scrambles onto her feet and flees. After that, the demons that were crowding us ease off.

"Thanks, Red," Billy whispers.

I can't reply, but this encounter has left my blood boiling. I'm done following along with whatever it is Trinity is planning. I stride past the guys to bring the succubus to a halt. Grabbing her forearm, I pull her closer. "What the fuck are you doing?"

"Let go of me," she says between her teeth.

"Not until you tell me why you're bringing us to the busiest part of the market. Do you want us to be attacked? Is that your plan?"

"Don't be foolish. No one is going to attack us."

"Oh, so I just imagined swatting away an uglier version of Snow White's witch?"

"That was Crazy Mirtle. Harmless."

Narrowing my eyes, I continue. "You haven't told me why we're in this part of the market."

Trinity opens her mouth to reply, but a commotion ahead draws my attention. Trinity turns toward it as well. The air on the other side of the market begins to vibrate, and then, a great building appears on the horizon. Prythian's famous arena.

Chapter 20
Red

The appearance of a Coliseum-style building out of thin air is something incredible. The market grows silent for a moment. It seems to me everyone is frozen on the spot. Then, the creatures in front of us part, creating an open path for the approaching tall knights who stride toward us with purpose. From the corner of my eye, I catch Trinity squaring her shoulders as she lifts her chin higher.

"Are those guards friend or foe?"

"Neither. They're Prythian's minions."

The tallest of the trio stops a few feet away from us, flanked by his companions. He's nearly seven foot, and as wide as an armoire. The little bit of skin showing under his helmet is dark grey and brittle as if he's made out of rocks.

"So it *is* you." He addresses Trinity.

"Hello, Grunt. Miss me?"

"No. What are you doing here?"

"I've got some merch I'd like to present to your boss."

"He already got a champion."

"I know, but he needs other fighters before the grand act,

or has he changed the rules?"

The guard glances over Trinity's shoulder for a fleeting moment before returning his attention to her. "They don't look like much to me."

"Since when are you one to judge? You're obviously under orders to bring us inside the arena, or Prythian wouldn't have bothered sending you out anyway."

The big guy grunts, then pivots around to return where he came from. His two companions stay behind, but leave us enough room to pass. I think they're meant to bring up the rear.

"Is Grunt really his name?" Armand asks in a low voice so the guards can't overhear us.

"Pft. Of course not. Prythian doesn't give names to his creations, but it's impossible to tease them without differentiators."

"Wait? Creations?" Billy asks.

"Yes. Those stone faces aren't real. They're animated by Prythian's powers."

"What exactly is this guy? And if he's so powerful, why is he stuck in the Wastelands?" Leo asks this time.

"Stop asking me shit. You're going to blow our cover with your incessant questions," Trinity snaps before following Grunt.

I return to the end of the line, simply because I don't trust the king's guards. At least, they're good for something—keeping the crowd of demons at bay.

The closer we get to the arena, the more in awe I become. The construction is magnificent, a true architecture masterpiece. How in the world did the King of Bastards manage to get it built? I don't believe there are skilled workers around. So if he didn't hire people, did he build it with his powers? *Shit.* Leo's unanswered question comes back to haunt me. We have no idea what kind of forces we're dealing with. We should have demanded more intel about the King of Bastards from Trinity before we came here. Too late now. I hope we're not making a mistake by trusting the succubus.

More guards are stationed by the entrance of the arena, manning the double doors that seem to be made out of some kind of metal with an iridescent sheen. The guards all carry a long spear, and are also wearing brass armor, just like Grunt and the other two guards behind me. The ones in front of the gate move out of the way, and the great gate opens outward, revealing a dark void. Trinity enters without hesitation, dragging Armand, Leo, and Billy with her—she has the other end of the chain. I have no choice but to plunge through the darkness as well. But it's not air that greets me. The darkness is actually a barrier that feels like oil against my skin. The resistance is minimal, but I breathe out an air of relief when I'm through.

The air on this side is damp and cool, and the interior has none of the grandeur I witnessed from outside. Bricks made out of rough-cut stones make up the walls of the chamber. It does nothing to make anyone feel welcome. The place is illuminated by torches mounted on the walls. The flames are black in their core and green toward the end. Definitely not ordinary fire.

"What is the meaning of this?" Trinity's loud voice booms ahead, echoing around us.

The chain in my hand gets yanked. Since I wasn't holding it too tight, I lose it completely. Guards have taken control of it, and are now hurtling my friends to a different location.

"What the hell do you think you're doing?" I take step toward the guys, but two burly guards block the path.

Filled with my wolf's rage, I growl. "Get out of my way."

"We don't take orders from filthy slave traders." The one closest to me lifts his arm above his head as if he plans to slap me. Not being the fastest monster, I move out of his range, running around him toward Armand, Billy, and Leo.

They're putting up a fight as well, but only Armand is in his full vampire form. Billy and Leo have not shifted yet. What the hell are they waiting for?

"You have to shift," I say.

"We've tried. Something is blocking our powers," Billy replies.

"Leave my slaves alone." Trinity shoves the guard, who has one end of the chain, making him stumble.

Suddenly, the loud sound of a snake hissing gives me goose bumps. Trinity freezes before turning in the direction of the sound, cursing under her breath.

A small hooded figure approaches us. On instinct, I position myself in front of Billy, clawed hands at the ready. I don't want to completely shift just yet.

"Sashir. I should have known you were behind this

ambush," Trinity says.

"Ambush? Not quite, my dear. This is the treatment that all low-level slave traders receive. Or did you think the king would be waiting for your return with open arms?"

"Bullshit. I left in good terms with Prythian. Does he even know I'm here?"

The creature laughs before replying. "The king sees everything. But he's rather busy with his new champion. You know how he likes them pretty boys."

I don't mistake the implications in that statement. A low snarl emanates from my throat, drawing the hooded figure's attention to me.

"Ah, you must be Trinity's new partner. How peculiar that after all these years in the Wastelands, she deemed it necessary to have one. How peculiar indeed."

"Oh, just shut up already. I'm sick of hearing you talking, Sashir. Do you have any interest in my slaves or not? There are other motivated buyers, and I don't have the entire day."

"That's too bad, my dear. The king wants to inspect the new contestants one by one. I'm afraid you'll have to wait until he's done with the wolf shifter. He's been locked up with his champion for hours already, but you never know with the king…" The creature cocks his head, partially revealing his face. A snake. "Actually, my mistake. You do know all about the king's sexual appetite, don't you, my dear?"

"Fuck off," Trinity spits out.

Snakeman lifts his hand, and the guards once again

come for our fake prisoners. I hold my ground. "You're not touching them."

"Hmm, now I can see why you picked the she-wolf for a partner. She's feisty. Perhaps you would like to sell her as well?"

I glare at the Snakeman. "I'm not for sale."

Trinity turns to me, and I see in her gaze that she's considering the monster's offer.

"Don't even think about it," I shout-whisper.

"Are you sure? You're pretty, and just Prythian's type. You'd have a good life by his side," she replies in a nonchalant way, as if the scenario we're portraying is real.

"That wasn't the deal," I say through clenched-teeth.

The succubus simply shrugs before turning to Snakeman. "Give me an offer and I'll think about it."

"*What*? You sneaky bitch!" When I take a step toward her, I suddenly find myself surrounded by guards.

I shove the first one who tries to grab me, but there are too many of them and I'm surrounded. In the confusion, something cold gets clamped around my wrist, and I realize too late the guards had been a distraction. Trinity just shackled me. With my free arm, I try to claw her face off, but she leaps out of range and watches me with a smug smile.

Not for long, bitch. I'll bite that smile off as soon as I'm in my wolf form. I concentrate on shifting, but nothing happens. It takes me a moment to understand I can't shift. My wolf's essence is dormant. As a matter of fact, my claws have disappeared, and my teeth have returned to normal.

"What the hell did you do to me?"

"The chains, darling. They're fae made. They keep your shifter powers contained."

"I thought you wanted to get out of the Wastelands." She lifts her chin. "I will, and you are my ticket."

"I knew there was something fishy with these shackles when I couldn't tap into my wolf," Billy says, only a bit too late. I wish he had brought it up sooner.

"I really wanted to give you the benefit of doubt, Trinity," Armand says, his voice sounding defeated. "Such a shame."

A strange emotion flashes in the succubus's eyes, something almost like regret. But I must be imagining things.

Chapter 21
Tristan

Between the moment I realize Harkon's intent and when we arrive at the riverbank where the mama bear and her cubs are playing by the water, I tried and failed to gain control of my body. The shifter notices my presence when I break through the trees into the clearing. At first, she just peers at me in curiosity. She knows who I am the same way I know who she is. Leticia Rodriguez, Xander's older sister, which means those cubs are his nephews.

No. I can't do this. I can't allow Harkon to turn me into a monster and kill my friend's family.

I hear his laughter in my head before his putrid voice fills the void caused by the chip's interference in my brain waves. "You can't fight my will. You're not strong enough."

My wolf's and my human's conscience rebel against Harkon's grip, but it's no use. I peel my lips back just the same, assuming an aggressive stance. Sensing the danger, Leticia lets out a roar and stands on her hind legs. Her cubs stop guffawing around in the water and freeze, staring at the scene. *Get the fuck out of here, you fools*, I want to yell at them. Bear shifters can also communicate telepathically when in their animal forms, so Leticia must have sent the command to them. So why aren't they moving?

Despite the sheer size difference, I know that with Harkon feeding me his demonic energy, the bear won't be a challenge for me. I break into a run, ready to attack. Leticia is not having any of it, so she charges as well. However, I change course in the last second, going after the cubs in the water. Thanks to the momentum and her size, Leticia loses precious seconds before she can adjust her trek. She won't reach me before I have one of her sons in between my jaws.

Forgive me, Xander, I think a second before I pounce on the smaller cub. Pain explodes on my side when a great force collides with my torso and sends me flying down the river. I sink like a dead weight, hitting my head against a rock. Everything turns dark for a moment. Then my body is dragged out of the river before I drown. Coldness takes a hold of me as I cough out the water I swallowed.

"Get up!" Harkon screams in my head.

Blinking my eyes open, I find his massive smoke form hovering above me, the only thing with any substance being his red glowing eyes. His voice is loud and piercing, but the hold he had on my body a second ago has slackened. The roar of two enraged bears draws my attention away from the demon. Xander has joined his sister, and they're gunning for us. Good. I hope they succeed.

The excruciating pain comes again before Harkon says, "You're not getting out of this so easily, Tristan. I won't allow it."

"Fuck you."

My entire body begins to convulse as an electric current runs through it. Harkon is using the chip to torture me into obedience, and just like it happened in his dungeon, my soul detaches from my body and I feel no pain. Hovering above the scene, I see that Xander is going straight to Harkon. But he can't see the invisible miasma the demon has around him. If Xander touches or breathes any of that contaminated air, he will die. Maybe if I return to my body and do as Harkon commands, I can draw my friend away from the toxic cloud.

But as hard I as try to go back, my soul remains floating above my body. Did I die? If I did, why am I still lingering here? Xander will reach Harkon and his miasma in the next couple of seconds. I have to do something. But as long as Harkon keeps torturing my body, my soul won't budge. With a grunt, I finally move, not back to my wolf form, but toward the demon's shadow. I zoom at him, head first, not thinking for a second what colliding with the demon will do to me.

I pierce through his ethereal form, finding complete darkness inside. It feels like I'm swimming in tar. Then comes the roar in my head. In the next moment, I'm hurled out of Harkon's shadowy body back into mine. He's no longer torturing or controlling me. I get onto my paws, ready to escape, but Harkon wraps his cold claws around my middle, and then jumps into a portal right before Xander can reach us.

My body slams against the stone wall in my dungeon cell, and I feel every bit of the impact. I'm back into my human form. Harkon is on me in the next second, lifting me off the ground with his hands. They burn against my skin.

"How dare you try to defy me? You're nothing but a weak, pathetic human who failed the person you loved in every one of your lives."

Like a deranged person, I laugh. I must have hit my head harder than I thought. I can't stop laughing even when Harkon begins to punch and kick me. My bones break, I bleed, but the more I hurt, the more I laugh. Eventually, the demon gets tired of punishing me. I imagine he's not having as much fun today. He's so furious that he doesn't put my body back together this time. Despite lying broken on the cold floor, I still maintain my smile. Harkon doesn't know that when I was inside his demented consciousness, I took something with me. A thread, a connection. I'm not sure how I'm going to use it, but I won't be his puppet anymore.

Chapter 22
Samuel

I don't like one bit that Red is off with the succubus, but I do feel better that my friends and Billy went along with her. I don't care that her ex is supposed to be this super-skilled druid fighter. I don't trust him near Red. I've caught him staring at her with a wistful expression in his gaze several times. It's obvious he's still pining for my mate.

"Could you please be a little more subtle with your glaring?" Nina stands next to me, huffing in exasperation.

"The whole point of glaring is to be obvious."

"I get it. You're suffering from retroactive jealousy. I don't blame you. The druid is hot, and he was your mate's first."

"What?" I turn to Nina, my spine going as taut as a guitar string. "Where did you hear that? Did Red tell you?"

"Riiight. Like she would ever tell me anything. She hates my guts, and I can't really fathom why. Nobody told me. It's a logical conclusion. They were high school sweethearts, weren't they? And she wasn't a blushing virgin when you hooked up."

Nina is probably right. Damn it. Now I have one more reason to hate the guy. I return to my glaring. The idiot is still doing the same thing he was doing a minute ago, staring at the mason jar full of pixies. I don't get why he's so fascinated with those blood-sucking buggers. He finally drops his gaze, pinching the bridge of his nose.

"You know all that glowering is not harming me in any way, right?"

"Maybe not, but how about a punch to the jaw, then?"

The druid rolls his eyes as if I'm of no consequence.

"Why are you being so childish? Red is *your* mate. You won. Get over it." Nina throws her hands up in the air, then scans the basement. "Wait a minute. Has anyone seen Zeke?"

Alex glances behind him. "He was sitting on that chair just a minute ago."

My ears prickle with the noise of someone swallowing, and then alarm bells sound in my head. "Shit. Zeke has gotten hold of the beer."

Nina curses loudly before turning a corner of stacked-up boxes. When I follow her, we find Zeke sprawled on the floor, holding a clay jug in his hand. By the idiotic expression on his face, there's no doubt in my mind he just drank a gallon of demon beer.

"What have you done, you fool?" Alex asks.

"Oh, don't be so dramatic," Zeke slurs before letting out a loud hiccup. "I just had a sip."

Nina crouches in front of the imp, wrinkling her nose as she takes the jug from his grasp. "A sip? More like you had a bath in beer. You reek."

"That's exactly what we need, to babysit a drunk imp." I place my hands on my hips, aiming my glower at Zeke now.

"If only that was the only problem," Nina chimes in.

"What do you mean?" I cut a glance in her direction.

She opens her mouth to answer, but Zeke leaps to his feet, looking left and right like a maniac. Before anyone can stop him, he begins to throw boxes out of his way, making a ruckus we don't need.

"Zeke can't handle the demon stuff. He gets completely deranged and out of control."

As if he needs to make Nina's point, Zeke howls as he waves a broom in the air. He then puts the thing between his legs, apparently pretending he's Harry Potter.

"Get him. We're supposed to stay hidden."

"Fat chance of that happening now." Nina winces when Zeke breaks something.

When Zeke runs by me, I tackle him to the ground, but damn, the demon is stronger than he appears. He flays under me, then manages to elbow my nose and slip from under me.

"Goddamn it." I whip my face, catching blood on the tips of my fingers. Stupid imp. If missing one eye wasn't enough. The idiot had to give me a broken nose, too.

Zeke is still running wildly back and forth, but Alex manages to clock him in the face, knocking him out.

"Nice punch," Nina says, but her celebratory expression changes in an instant when the sound of feet approaching puts all of us on high alert.

"Get him out of there," I order Alex while I hide behind

a stack of beer barrels, waiting to jump whoever comes down the stairs.

"What in hell's name happened here?" someone mutters.

"We have company," another creature replies.

What the fuck? There are two of them? I swear I only heard the noise of one pair of feet.

"Trinity. You can't trust that succubus. Always brewing trouble."

"Whoever you are, come out now before I get very angry."

Nina, who had been standing across from me, steps out of her hiding spot. "I don't want any trouble."

"My, oh my. What do you we have here? Another fox shifter?"

Now that Nina has the creature distracted, I chance sticking my head out to get a glimpse. I need to know what we're dealing with here. A two-headed demon almost seven-foot-tall is standing near the stairs, blocking our way out. It has long dark hair, which is an odd contrast to its reptilian appearance. It looks like a lizard wearing a wig. Despite its almost comical appearance, I don't miss the sharp talons that peek from underneath the sleeves of the demon's robe.

Nina doesn't seem one bit intimidated by the strange creature. However, she's keeping both her hands clasped behind her back.

"Yes. So what?" she asks.

"Did Trinity forget you?" one head asks.

It's second head promptly responds. "No. That succubus is too smart. If she didn't take you to the king's arena, then it means you're not worth it. But you sure look good enough to eat. My patrons haven't had fox in a long time."

The demon makes its move, reaching for Nina with both clawed hands. She jumps out of reach, pulling her arm back to throw something on the floor. Purple smoke takes over the basement, and the demons begin to shriek like mad.

"Come on. Let's go," Nina yells.

I follow the sound of her voice while covering my face to protect myself from whatever the hell this smoke is. Someone bumps into me, and I prepare to go on defense mode when Alex's face appears in my line of vision. He's carrying Zeke over his shoulder.

"Get the jar with the pixies," he says.

"What? Whatever for?" I cough.

Meanwhile, the two-headed demon seems to be having a helluva of a bad time. She's banging against the boxes Zeke managed to leave intact.

"Oh, for fuck's sake. Never mind. Here." He transfers Zeke onto my shoulders, then disappears again into the smoke.

"Come on, guys. What are you waiting for? My fog won't last for much longer," Nina urges from the top of the stairs.

Cursing under my breath, I head to the exit. That stupid druid better come out of this basement alive. As much as I don't like him, if he were to die under my watch, I know Red wouldn't forgive me.

I hear hurried steps right behind me, hoping it's the idiot. Once we reach the landing, I see it was indeed Alex who followed me. Glaring, I say, "I hope those pixies were worth the trouble."

He hides the mason jar inside his jacket pocket. "I'm not sure yet, but they might come in handy."

"How hard did you punch Zeke? He's still dead to the world."

"He should be coming around soon."

"I hate to break up your chitchat, but I sense several very nasty demons coming our way. We need to find the back exit of this place," Nina says.

"How do you know there's a back exit?" I follow her down a dark corridor.

"All taverns have back exits."

"That's comforting. What if this one is different?"

"Then we're screwed." Nina stops abruptly when the corridor splits in two opposite directions. "Damn it."

A loud shriek echoes against the walls, giving me chills. The two-headed demon must have recovered from the effects of Nina's fog.

"Let's go right," I say.

"Are you sure?" Nina casts a glance over her shoulder.

"No, but I got a fifty-fifty chance of being right."

"Fucking great." She takes off down the corridor in the direction I suggested.

Man, in times like these, I wish I had Dante's gift. If my hunch is wrong, we'll soon become demon chow. Luckily, it seems I got it right. There's a door at the end of the corridor, and Nina doesn't waste any time. She kicks it open, clearing it completely off its hinges. The pungent smell of an alleyway greets us, and I have never been so happy to walk out onto a filthy street.

"Did you have to kick the door?" Alex asks.

"It worked, didn't it?"

We don't slow down as we continue to put distance between us and the tavern. So much for Trinity's friend. We run for about a minute before we slow to a brisk pace, stopping completely only when there's no sign of pursuit.

"Damn, that was close." Nina braces her hands on her knees, a little short of breath.

"Are you okay?" I ask.

"Yeah, I just need a minute to clear my lungs. I'm allergic to fox fog."

"Oh, so that's what it was. I bet that demon had a worse reaction than you." I smirk.

Nina flips me off before standing up straighter. Alex is gazing into the distance with his eyebrows furrowed.

"You got something on your mind, druid boy?"

He turns to me, eyes narrowed to slits. "Yes. Trinity said the tavern keeper was her friend. Obviously, that was a lie. What other lies has she told us?"

My heart skips a beat. "Do you think Trinity led Red and my friends into a trap?"

"I wouldn't put it past her."

Hissing, Nina pulls a pendant from underneath her clothes. "Fuck, fuck, fuck."

"What now?"

She's staring intently at the coin pendant. "I gave the other half of this magical medallion to Billy when he went to investigate his brother. It works as a distress signal when activated." Nina lifts her gaze to mine. "He just used it. They're in trouble."

Chapter 23
Dante

Prythian didn't send me back to my cell in the dungeon. Instead, he left me in his luxurious private room and disappeared soon after he dropped the bomb my friends had come to rescue me. The first thing I did when I was alone was to try to escape. However, every time I got near any door or window, I felt an invisible barrier that prevented me from going farther. Damn fae magic.

I've been sitting for the past half hour in one of the many comfortable couches spread in the room, pondering about everything that has happened to me since I arrived in this forsaken dimension. I wish I knew what was in my vision that made the powerful fae king so rattled. Frustrated, I run a hand through my hair. Why I can't remember it? What good is my gift if I can't control or retain the information in my brain?

My wolf is quiet, dormant, and that's thanks to the strange magic that keeps my shifter powers bound. Lifting my gaze, I survey my lavish surroundings. How can Prythian have accumulated so many riches in this bare land? Is he able to leave this dimension at will?

Fuck. I can't just sit here alone with my thoughts. I stand up suddenly, my body filled with restless energy. The urge to trash this room is immense. It's an ugly feeling, not born out of frustration. It swirls and fester in my chest, like a virus that has the sole purpose to corrupt me. It's wrong, it doesn't belong to me, but at the same time, I don't want to contain it. On the contrary, I want to unleash the dark energy that surrounds my heart. My eyes land on the fancy drink cart. Before I know it, I'm making a beeline for it. I pick up the crystal decanter from which Prythian poured me the drink he forced down my throat. It did make me feel better, but at what cost?

I hurl the fancy bottle at the oil paint portrait of the king. It shatters against his smug face with a loud crack, smearing the canvas and the surrounding wallpaper with the dark liquid. A satisfied grin spreads on my face, but it only lasts a couple of seconds. The smear disappears at the same time the shards of glass fly through the air, reconnecting until the decanter is whole once more and standing on the drink cart as if I hadn't destroyed it a moment ago.

My mind is reeling as I stare at the perfect object for a couple of beats. Growing up, I've heard stories about the mysterious fae race. They keep to themselves in their own realm. Most of the tales about them are about naughty children who were kidnapped by them if they misbehaved. But all the books I've read on the subject didn't seem like they contained any real information. They read like fables. However, a recurring theme in all the stories was that some of the most powerful fae had the power to bend reality. What if everything I'm seeing right now is an elaborate illusion? What if Prythian was cursed to this dimension and is now trapped like me?

The ugliness in my chest relents. Rubbing my face, I begin to pace. Once again, my thoughts wander to the vision I had. What had I seen? The sudden tug of the bond makes me freeze mid-step. Red. She's here.

Prythian's words come back to haunt me. If he knew she came to rescue me, does it mean he captured her already? All the questions bouncing in my head won't do me any good. I have to get out of here.

I sense a disturbance in the air, and then the fae king enters the room. He changed clothes, opting for an all-black ensemble devoid of any embellishment. But that's not all that's different. His hair is all white instead of the pitch black of before, and his eyes are no longer dark purple either, but a lighter grey color. Even his aura is different, not as dark. However, there's no mistaking it's him. His scent is the same.

"You've tried to tarnish my beautiful room." His gaze drops to the decanter.

"You've had a hair job done. It seems we've both been busy since the last time we saw each other."

Prythian lifts his chin, his hard stare meant to break someone's will. I grind my teeth, refusing to yield to his power. Narrowing his eyes, he seems to sense my defiance.

"Those rags you're wearing won't do." With a flicker of his hand, the rough fabric pants and shirt disappear, and now my ensemble is almost the same as Prythian's save for the color. Instead of black, my pants and the tailored tunic are in a deep blue color.

"Why do I need to look presentable? I'm only a mere slave, aren't I?"

"You're my champion. I can't have you looking like a beggar. Besides, we have an incredibly special visitor today."

There's a knock on the door, and Prythian's expression lights up. "Ah. She's here."

The double doors open. A woman comes in wearing leather and fur. Her hair is in dual colors, white blonde and black. It takes me a moment to get a read on her aura. I have to concentrate hard in order to sense the energy surrounding a person or a supernatural being. Most of the time, I don't bother, relying solely on my sixth sense. The newcomer is not human. Her energy flickers and changes colors, as if it can't decide what it wants to be. My focus converts to her sternum. There's concentrated energy in that particular spot. She must be wearing a magical necklace.

"Prythian," she says in the most melodic voice I've ever heard. It moves me. It makes me yearn for something. I just don't know what.

The king turns his back to her as he pours wine in one of the glasses. "I'm surprised to see you back in my court, Trinity. You vowed never to return."

"You're not surprised. As a matter of fact, your last words to me were exactly these. *I'll let you walk out of my arena, Triny, but only because I know you will return to me.*

So, why don't you cut the crap and just say I told you so."

Prythian chuckles before bringing the rim of the glass to his lips. The energy surrounding him changes, turning almost untainted.

"I missed you," he says.

The strange supernatural turns her attention to me for a second. "I seriously doubt that. I gotta say, your new champion is rather attractive. Are you sure you want to risk his pretty face in the arena?"

I turn to watch Prythian's reaction. Sure enough, his aura becomes darker as his amused expression vanishes. "You brought me some goods, I hear."

"Yes. Two shifters, a fox, and a wolf. Plus, a hybrid vampire."

Damn it. Trinity's bounty must be Sam, Leo, and Armand. But if Sam decided to enroll his bandmates in a rescue mission, why didn't he bring Jared, the only member of Sam's band who has an actual shot in fighting the strange magic in this place?

"Hybrid you say? Interesting. What is his other heritage?"

She shrugs. "Beats me. I'm sure you can figure it out."

"That's not all, is it?" Prythian takes another sip of his drink.

"No. I've also got another wolf shifter, a female. Your champion's mate to be exact." Trinity's lips twist into a wicked smile as she stares into my eyes.

Son of a bitch. How did she know Red was my mate? My vision becomes tinged in crimson as fury surges through my veins. My worry for Red's safety overrides everything. Suddenly, my wolf's essence breaks free from its bindings. In the back of my mind, I know I didn't break Prythian's spell. He must have released his hold on me.

Growling, I take a step toward the woman. "What did you do to Red?"

Trinity's eyes widen before she turns her attention to Prythian. "Aren't you going to contain your wolf?"

"Nah, I'm quite enjoying this. You shouldn't poke the beast if you can't face it."

"You're a jerk."

Those are the last words she throws at Prythian before I have her by her throat. "Where's my mate?"

My claws dig into her skin, drawing blood. I feel the bloodlust taking control, and it mingles with the darkness in my chest. I almost don't want her to answer so I can crush her airways.

The woman suddenly stops struggling. No. She can't be dead already. Pain explodes in my abdomen next, forcing me to let her go as I double over.

Prythian laughs as I try to ride the pain. Fucking bastard.

Trinity is massaging her neck when I raise my head. She also throwing daggers at the fae king with her eyes. "I see you haven't lost your sadistic ways."

"Oh no, my dear. If anything, I've just gotten better at it. What else is one supposed to do in such a place? I must keep myself entertained."

"Well, I'm not staying long. I just came to sell you some new amusement, and then I'll be off."

"Where exactly do you plan to go, Triny? Didn't all the years you spent away from me teach you anything? There's nothing for you out there."

"I'm not staying in the Wastelands. I want to return to the human world."

Prythian's hair changes from white to black in the blink of an eye as he advances on Trinity. She takes a few steps back as her face becomes paler. She should be scared. The king's face has acquired new edges, he's crueler. He's also projecting his dark aura at full strength. Even the densest of humans would be able to sense it.

"I warned you about this place, and yet, you chose to come with me."

"That was a long time ago. I was a naive fool, and you..." Her lips tremble as her voice becomes choked up. My attention is riveted on the scene. I don't want to miss any nuance, any detail.

"And I was what?" Prythian moves closer to the woman.

"You weren't the carbon copy of the people you hated the most."

Prythian pulls his arm back with a roar, and Trinity braces for the impact of the blow. He stops in the last second, swinging around and moving away from her. Without making eye contact with me, he heads for the drink cart. He fills his glass with more wine, then he swallows it in one gulp.

"I don't have the power to send you back," he says, still not facing her.

"Bullshit. I know there are less powerful beings here in

the Wastelands who can open portals to the mortal lands. Didn't you pay Mauve a handsome fee for your champion?"

Prythian laughs without humor, then glances over his shoulder. "All clever lies. There's no way out of here. You would need an artifact of great power to conjure a portal from this side."

Trinity pulls out the necklace she had hidden underneath her clothes. "Something like this?"

Prythian swings around. "That's a sacred stone. Where did you get it?"

She hides the jewelry once more. "It doesn't matter how I got it. And you can't have it either. It has been fined tune to fulfill the will of the angels."

Prythian doesn't say anything for a couple of beats, then he eyes me. "Your mate must really love you."

"So are you going to pay my price or what?" Trinity continues.

"You didn't name your price."

"Yes, I did. I want you to help me open the portal."

Prythian presses his forefinger against his lips, seemingly in deep thought. After a moment, he says, "I'll consider it after I inspect the merchandise myself. I'm mostly curious about the she-wolf. Is she pretty like you, Triny?"

I take a step toward Prythian, the urge to protect Red stronger than ever, but I can move no farther. Prythian has rendered me paralyzed once more.

"She's just your type."

Chapter 24
Red

"I knew that succubus was up to no good. I knew it." Billy paces in the small chamber we were thrown in together after Trinity betrayed us.

"Whatever, *petit* wolf. You were going gaga over her. I saw you watching the demon with googly eyes," Armand replies.

Billy swings around, his gaze wide and outraged. "I was not!"

"Don't feel bad, Billy. Few can resist the pull of a powerful succubus." Leo stares at the ceiling as if he's searching for something.

"This is all my fault. I was the one who told Alex to give the stone to Trinity. With her payment in hand, she really didn't need to stick around, did she?" I curl my fingers around the metal bars that seal us inside. At least they didn't stick us in a completely closed-off cell.

"It's not your fault, *ma chérie*." Armand lays a hand on my shoulder. "If anyone is to blame, it is Zeke."

"Oh my God. Of course. I'm so stupid." Billy slaps his

forehead, then reaches inside his T-shirt.

"What do you have there, kid?" Leo asks.

Billy growls in Leo's direction. "I'd really appreciate if everyone would stop calling me a kid. I'm nineteen for crying out loud."

"Exactly, you're still a puppy." Armand laughs.

"Cut it out, guys. Billy is only two years younger than me. If he's a puppy, so am I."

"Truth is, you really *are* only a puppy," Billy replies with a shrug.

"What the hell! Is that the thank you I get for defending you?"

"I mean, in wolf years. You've just been turned," he adds with an apologetic tone.

"Whatever. You were excited about something a moment ago." I sigh, moving away from the metal bars.

"Right. I just remember I have the dual-sided medallion Nina gave me. I can let her know we're in trouble."

"How does that work?" I peer closely at the small object in Billy's hand.

"I just have to press the medallion down in the middle. Nina will be alerted by the other half, which is in her possession."

"Ingenious," Armand says in awe. "Why don't we all have one of those things?"

"Because knowing my sister, that gadget is most likely rare. The question is, why did she bother giving Billy that magical medallion?" Leo's attention is riveted on Billy's face now.

"Maybe she likes me." Billy smirks.

"You?" Leo scoffs. "Get your head out of the clouds, kid. My sister would never get involved with you."

Billy's expression falls in a way that ignites my protective instincts. He can be a brat, but I don't want to see him get his heart broken.

"Why is that? Because of my age?" he asks.

"That and the fact you're too wholesome. Nina has always preferred the bad guys."

"Maybe I'm not as good as I appear. She didn't seem to mind my wholesomeness when I kissed her." He puffs out his chest.

"You kissed my sister?" Leo's eyebrows shoot up to the heavens. The expression would be comical if we weren't stuck in the King of Bastards' dungeon.

"*Mon Dieu*. The dramatics in this group rival any daytime soap opera. All we're missing is the ominous soundtrack," Armand points out.

"Guys, can we focus on our situation for a moment? While alerting the others we're in trouble is good, how are they going to get in this place? The building won't be visible until the games start," I say.

"Ah, *merde*. I had forgotten about that." Armand rubs his face while scrunching his eyebrows.

"We only have one solution for our problem." Billy's gaze becomes hard. "We must ensure the King of Bastards starts the games."

"It means we all have to fight in it," I say. I hate Billy's solution, but I'm unable to think of a better alternative.

The sound of steps echoing down the corridor makes my entire body tense. Cautiously, I approach the metal bars once more, craning my neck to see who is approaching. I sense a cold presence before I get a visual of the party coming our way. On instinct, I move toward the back of the cell, dragging Billy with me. A man dressed in an all-black ensemble—tailored pants paired with an Asian-style suit and a cape—stops in front of our cell. He doesn't need to say a word for me to know he's the King of Bastards. Extraordinary power oozes from him, dark, yet alluring.

It's hard to maintain eye contact with him, but I try nonetheless. His features are all about sharp angles in perfect symmetry. He's the most handsome man I've ever seen in my life, though also the coldest. A cruel beauty. Flawless. Even his black hair gleams under the torch lights.

I can't tell the color of his eyes, but they're so intense that I feel uneasy standing under his watchful gaze. It is as if he could invade my thoughts with that powerful stare. *Shit.* I'm not sure he can't. A hard breath billows from my lips as I make sure my mental shields are in place.

"You must be Red," he says in the smoothest of voices, making goose bumps break out all over my skin.

I have no idea why I'm reacting to him this way. He's evil, and he has Dante as his prisoner. Either he has some kind of supernatural power over me, or my wolf hormones are already going crazy.

"And you must be the King of Bastards. Fitting name," I reply, not knowing how I was able to make my voice sound strong.

The corners of his lips twitch up into a perverse grin. "Feisty. Just like your mate."

The mention of Dante makes my chest feel tight. Trinity must have told Prythian everything. That bitch. She'll pay for her betrayal.

"Where's Dante?" I ask.

"You'll see him soon enough."

The king switches his attention to my companions. As infuriating as his dismissal is, I feel a million times better now that the pressure of his gaze isn't on me. I wasn't imagining things. He was doing something to me.

"A fox and another wolf shifter. Interesting. I've always enjoyed shifters immensely. Your kind brings a raw energy I don't get to see among demons. It's quite providential I acquired not one but three specimens in the same week. The forthcoming games will be exhilarating."

"You're a sick bastard." Armand takes a step forward, baring his teeth. He has changed into full vamp. Bizarrely, he now resembles the King of Bastards.

Prythian doesn't move for several beats as he studies Armand. Finally, after what felt like an eternity, he asks, "What are you?"

"You can't tell by my fangs? I'm a vampire."

"No, you're more than that," the king says, sounding almost in awe.

I don't like one bit how he seems to be in a daze of sorts. The comments from the king's henchmen about how Prythian enjoys pretty males blares in my head. Maybe he has set his sight on Armand this time.

"Where's Trinity?" I ask, trying to distract Prythian from Sam's friend.

He turns to me, narrowing his gaze. "You were the one who gave her that sacred stone. What a foolish thing to do."

Sadly, I have to agree with the guy, but I'll be damned if I let him know that. "She made a terrible mistake betraying us. She can't open a portal to the human world from here. Only our allies on the other side will be able to do so. She just lost her ticket out."

I realize as I say those words that even if—by some miracle—we manage to free Dante and escape Prythian's arena, we have no way out of here either. The original plan was for the witches to open the portal. Since we had to use the Mirror of Briseis—an artifact that most likely has turned to ashes by now—no one knows where we are.

"Trinity may have many flaws, but stupidity is not one of them. I can open a portal to the mortal lands."

"I thought you were also trapped here," Billy says. "If you have the power to get the hell out of this place, why would you stay?"

Prythian's expression twists into one of rage for a fleeting moment. Billy must have found his Achilles' heel.

"Trinity has the sacred stone. You, on the other hand, have no way out. She told me how you used the Mirror of Briseis to get here. There's no one on the other side ready to create a portal for you."

"Trinity knows nothing," I say through clenched teeth. "Do you seriously think we would tell her all about our plans?"

Prythian laughs, the sound echoing around us like a bad omen. "It's of no consequence to me if she doesn't know everything. You should consider yourselves lucky I'm the one acquiring you. If you hold on to your wits and prove to be excellent entertainers, you might actually enjoy living in my court. I tend to reward my favorite fighters very well."

"Not in your life, pal," Leo spits, his eyes and hair changing from dark brown to ember.

"I'm bored of this conversation already. It's time to see what you lot are capable of."

"What do you mean?" I ask, apprehension dripping down my spine.

"It's time for a demonstration."

Chapter 25
Samuel

"How in the hell are we going to get in the King of Bastards' arena? Doesn't it only appear when the games are on?" I ask.

"Maybe if druid boy hadn't hit Zeke so hard, he would be up by now to help us." Nina glares at the douche.

"Great. So now it's my fault we're in this situation. If I had gone with Red as was the original plan, I doubt they'd be in trouble now."

"Are you saying Red got taken because my friends didn't step up to the plate?" I curl my hands into fists, getting into the druid's personal space.

"That's exactly what I'm saying. You were the first one to agree when Trinity decided to use your friends as baits instead of me. I'm actually going to lay all the blame for this royal fuck-up on you. If you weren't so insecure about the idea of me spending time alone with Red, this wouldn't have happened."

I feel the shift descend on me as fury spreads throughout my body. Nina grabs my arm, pulling me away from Alex.

"Damn it, you two. Now is not the time for a testosterone contest. We all fucked up. I should have suspected the succubus was up to no good when she didn't let me join them."

I rub my face while I try to process this utter failure.

"You're right. We can't fight among ourselves. We need to focus on the end game, which is to find a way inside the King of Bastards' fortress and save our friends."

"Why are you talking so loudly?" Zeke asks from the place where I dumped him.

"Oh, great. You're awake. We have a serious problem. Your friend betrayed us. Now we have to storm Prythian's arena and save everyone," Nina replies.

"What are you talking about?" The imp rubs his eyes.

"Am I speaking in Japanese? Your succubus friend sold us out."

"That's impossible. Why are you saying that? Did the games start?" Zeke attempts to stand, but he's too wobbly on his feet and ends up falling back on his ass.

"Oh, for fuck's sake. Here." I offer him my hand.

"The games didn't start. Billy alerted Nina they are in trouble. There's also the fact Trinity's friend, the tavern's owner, tried to eat Nina," I say.

"No kidding." Zeke stares at Nina with a slightly confused expression on his face.

"All because of your stupid addiction to demon beer." She glares at the imp.

"Wait? I drank some of it?" His eyes look sincere, but I ain't making the same mistake again by trusting any of these demons.

"Not some of it. An entire jug," Alex replies.

"Wow, I remember nothing. Okay, fine. The tavern's owner wasn't exactly nice, but don't you think jumping to the conclusion Triny betrayed us is a bit much?"

"No," we all answer in unison.

"It's best if we go in with the assumption your friend stabbed us in the back. But how are we getting inside the arena if it's not visible?" Alex stares out in the distance.

We managed to find a hiding spot in a putrid alley, but considering this is a hellish dimension, we're far from safe.

"If our original ruse was discovered, we can't pretend again we're here to fight in the games," Zeke muses.

"What kind of creature is this King of Bastards? A demon?" Nina turns to the imp.

"No. He's high fae."

"High fae? Are you sure?" Nina's voice turns different, less confident.

"Yes, I'm sure. Triny told me as much. Only a high fae would be able to hide an entire arena."

"Do you know from which court he is?" Nina continues with her interrogation.

"She never told me that."

"Who cares about all that? He's powerful. We get it," I say, irritated we're wasting precious time here.

"Only a fool wouldn't want to get us more information about the enemy." Alex sneers, renewing my urge to punch him.

"High fae are known to be excellent at mind games.

Maybe Prythian's arena is nothing but an illusion," Nina continues.

"If his arena doesn't exist, where the hell is he hiding then?" I ask, letting all my frustration show in my voice.

"He's probably in a different pocket of this dimension," Zeke replies as his gaze turns inward.

"You've lost me completely," I breathe out.

"Of course." Alex snaps his fingers. "It makes perfect sense. If the King of Bastards is high fae, he would be powerful enough to carve an inter-dimensional pocket in this dimension."

My irritation escalates when no one seems inclined to explain shit to me.

"We would need a spell to reveal a doorway for us," Nina adds, then glances at Alex. "Are you able to cast such magic?"

"It shouldn't be too complicated. We used to create similar hiding pockets during my time at the Dark Blades Academy."

Still not understanding what the hell they're taking about, I say, "Great. We have a plan. We just need to know where exactly this arena appears."

"It's at the other end of the Shadow Market. Trinity showed me the spot," Zeke replies.

"Okay, let's get going then." I step away from the group.

"Wait. We can't simply head into a market filled with demons without hiding our identities first. If this Prythian guy is so powerful, I'm sure he has eyes everywhere," Alex says, once again grating on my nerves.

I glare over my shoulder to give him an angry retort when Nina adds, "Good point. Can't you cast a cloaking spell around us?"

"Who do you think I am? Harry Potter?"

"Technically, Harry Potter never cast a cloaking spell; he simply owned a cloak of invisibility. Pretty handy accessory if you ask me," Zeke chimes in.

"Wendy Redford was able to cast one without a problem," I say with glee.

"She's a witch. I'm a druid. We don't work magic the same way."

"Oh, quit your whining, you two. This reminds me too much of when I took my one and only babysitting job. Wait here. I'll get us something to wear."

Without waiting for our reply, Nina takes off, leaping over a wall to get to the roof of the nearest building. Then she vanishes from sight.

"I don't like this at all. We shouldn't be splitting up." Alex frowns in the direction she disappeared to.

"She's a fox spy. If anyone can navigate undetected in a sea of monsters, it's her." Zeke is quick to defend my friend. I watch him closely. He seems recovered from his manic behavior, but I gotta make sure.

"Since we're not going anywhere until she returns, would you care to explain what the hell was that stunt you pulled in the basement?"

Zeke drops his chin, staring at his shoes. His once-pristine pink suit is smeared everywhere with soot and other stains. "Many, many years ago, when I was still a mere cog in the underworld machine, I discovered demon beer. It was the only thing that could abate the apathy I'd developed. It turns out, the picture in the brochure was nicer."

Without realizing, I glance over at Alex, mouthing the question, "Brochure?". He simply shrugs. It's a gesture I could easily see Dante making, which turns my mood grimmer. I can't fail him or Red.

"I didn't realize how addictive the stuff would be," Zeke continues.

"Did it always make you act in that deranged manner?" Alex asks.

"No, never. It made me happy, or as happy as one can be in hell. It was only when I was already living in the human world that the stuff began to affect me badly. I think that by hiding my demonic nature, I developed an intolerance for it. I know if supernaturals drink it, it can turn them into mindless shells. It's deadly to humans."

"If you know all that, why did you drink it then?"

"I couldn't stop myself. I don't even remember grabbing the jug, much less drinking from it." Zeke finally meets my eyes. "I am truly sorry for that."

"Here's one thing I've always wanted to know. How does someone become an imp? Isn't it done by choice?"

Zeke pinches his lips together, pulling the lapels of his jacket closer. "The usual stuff. I fell for the wrong girl, yadda, yadda. Before I knew it, I had sold my soul to the devil."

I don't buy that his story is simple for a second. He doesn't want to tell, which doesn't surprise me. He's always been a big mystery.

Someone lands softly behind me, making my heart skip a beat. I swing around, ready for a fight, just in time to catch Nina unfurl from her hero-landing position, carrying a bundle of clothes.

"You're back already? You've only been gone for a couple of minutes."

"Gee, Samuel. You sound like you don't know me at all. Here, I grabbed the first items that crossed my path."

I take the cloak made out of rough material that reminds me of a burlap sack. It smells like horse manure. My stomach twists as I fight the urge to gag. Covering my nose, I say, "Oh my God, I think I'll die if I wear this."

"You'll definitely die if you don't. The place is crawling with demons and other nasty creatures. Word has gone out that there will be a game soon, so every shady character in this forsaken dimension has come out."

Trying to not breathe through my nose, I put on the garment, knowing I'll have to burn the clothes I'm wearing if they survive the day. I might have to shift at a moment's notice. In fact, I'm itching to get onto four paws and bite something.

The others have also donned similar attires. All except Zeke, who is eyeing his cloak as if it has done him great injury.

"I'm not wearing this." He tosses it aside.

"Didn't you hear anything I said?" Nina replies.

"Yes, I heard you, but you forget I don't need to hide my features, not here."

He shakes his head, and his appearance changes. His skin takes on a greenish tinge, and his pupils are now red. The hair remains the same white-blond color, but small horns peek from the short strands.

"I don't think I've ever seen you like that before, at least not a full-on glance. Freaky," I say.

"I'm lucky I got to retain a semi-human shape. Other imps aren't that fortunate."

"Now, how do we find the exact locale where Prythian is hiding his arena of illusions?" Alex asks.

"At the end of the market is my guess. It's where most of the demons were veering toward," Nina replies.

"All right. We shouldn't plunge right into the market. Let's circle back," Alex adds, but Nina shakes her head.

"It will look suspicious. Besides, I saw great beasts wearing armor guarding the perimeter. We'll draw less attention if we mingle with the crowd."

"Let's go then… before the stench of this cloak kills my sense of smell." I move in the direction the noise is the loudest without waiting to see who is following me. There's a new darkness swirling in my chest, and it's not only worry. This place is already getting to me.

Chapter 26
Tristan

My eyes are closed when I sense Harkon's presence nearby. But I'm not asleep. I haven't been able to do so, even knowing I need the rest. During the first few hours after I returned from Shadow Creek, I was in too much agony to succumb to slumber. Once my body began to regenerate slowly and the acute pain to lessen, it was my mind that kept me up. If Harkon has recovered enough in order to return to the human world to continue his nefarious plans, then I'm running out of time.

What, though, kept him from terrorizing our world before that? He still can't fully take form above ground, but he was so easily able to open a portal out of hell. I might not be obsessed with Crimson Hollow's history like Dante is, but I know several measures were taken to prevent demons from escaping their hellish dimensions.

"I see that your body is fully put back together. Good. I'm in the mood to break every single bone you have once more."

"You must not have anything better to do then. What's

the matter, Harkon? Can't go back to the surface?"

Grabbing a fistful of my hair, he yanks my head back. Soulless eyes stare at me. "You deprived me of a meal, now I must make you suffer."

"That's the ticket, isn't it? You must feast on defenseless shifters in order to gain your strength."

"How very observant of you. But you missed one key factor. It's not about the flesh nourishment—it's about the pain. The more I make my prey suffer, the stronger I become. That mother and her cubs would have been perfect."

"Better luck next time."

He punches me straight on my jaw, filling my mouth with blood. I think he knocked out some of my teeth, too.

"You filthy mongrels think you're so smart. Your antecessor also thought he could use me to gain power and not deliver his end of the bargain."

"I'm nothing like Valerius," I spit.

"Oh, but you are. You're both pathetic in your need to feel superior. Valerius craved power, but he knew he lacked the strength to challenge his alpha. So he came to me, sold his soul to eternal damnation in exchange for the brute strength to achieve what he desired the most."

"What did you get in exchange?" I ask.

Harkon laughs, as if he was waiting for my question. "A way to claim what was due to me. I knew she was walking among mortals again. I could sense when she was born."

"Who? Red?"

"Yes, the woman you craved since the beginning of

times, but you were always denied. In a way, we're the same in that regard. The only difference is, she will be mine in the end, and you will be obliterated to nothing."

"You will never have her." I strain against the chains around my wrists, feeling the wolf stir inside of me. Harkon, for whatever reason, is not keeping my wolf bound, and the chip in my head is silent.

"Pitiful shifter. When are you going to learn you can't fight destiny? Even the bargain your mate made in order to escape me backfired. In fact, that vow is what keeps putting her in my path over and over again." The demon laughs again as he begins to pace. "And to think the actions of that servant of hers put everything in motion for me this time around."

"Servant? Who are you talking about now? Seth?"

"That vermin? Another pitiful creature who coveted more than he deserved."

Harkon faces me, his mouth turning into a malicious grin. "Since you're not going to live that much longer, I'll tell you, but only because it's probably going to make you suffer more by knowing."

My heart begins to beat in an erratic manner as my mouth turns dry. Who Harkon is going to reveal as the new traitor?

"What are you waiting for? The cue from the soundtrack guy?"

"I suppose that's meant to be a clever jab. Perhaps being tortured for days has finally affected your brain. I'm referring to the witch Wendy Redford. "

"Wait? Are you implying Red's grandmother betrayed her?"

"Wasn't she the one who sent Red into the woods knowing there was a rogue wolf on the loose? The same rogue Valerius sent with the purpose to turn Red into a Shadow Creek wolf?"

"That doesn't make any sense. Are you saying Valerius and Mrs. Redford were working together?"

If that's the case, then I'll kill the old lady with my bare hands.

"That's enough talking for now. It's time for my favorite part of the day."

He moves so fast he turns into a blur. Then his clawed hands are on my head again. With the touch comes the searing pain. I close my eyes, hoping I'll be able to escape the worst of the torture by hurling my soul out of my body. I don't know how many times I'll be able to do it before my soul detaches completely and I end up dying.

This time, however, I don't float above my body, but straight in Harkon's head. Just like when I entered his shadow form in the human world. The sensation is just as unpleasant as before. It feels like I'm swimming in crude oil.

Suddenly, I'm no longer stuck in that putrid darkness. I'm alone on a beach at night. The smell of the ocean reaches my nose as the soft, warm sea breeze kisses my skin. I'm wearing a toga made of soft fabric. The sky is clear, but it's the new moon, so darkness is almost absolute, save for the soft glow on the sand. Turning around, I see the source of the illumination. Giant torches are lit in front of a temple, the flames reflecting against the statue of a woman holding a bow and arrow surrounded by wolves. Artemis. The name just pops into my head. A forgotten memory?

A dark silhouette slips out of the building, then heads in my direction. The breeze changes, and the scent of the person approaching reaches my nose. Desire and longing hit me all at once, and before I know it, I'm running toward the mysterious woman I don't yet recognize even though my heart does.

We stop short of colliding with each other, and I have to take a step back to steady myself. The woman is wearing a hood. With impatient hands, I push it back. The most beautiful creature stares at me. I want to capture her face between my hands and kiss her until the end of time.

She wraps her arms around my waist, resting her cheek against my chest. "Alesandro, you came."

"Of course I did, my love."

"I can't stand this. Why must we hide our feelings? Why can't we be together?"

I ease off the embrace, holding her shoulders. Her big, dark eyes are staring at me with a mixture of sadness and love.

"We'll find a way."

She shakes her head. "Uncle will never accept us. Let's run away. During the festival, there will be so many people in town. We can easily slip off. No one will notice we're gone until we're far away."

A terrible weight settles on my chest. There's nothing I would like more than to take Calisto away. But that's an impossible dream. "You know we can't run away, Cali."

She steps away from my touch, her delicate eyebrows furrowing. "We can't or you don't want to?"

"What? That's nonsense. Of course I do."

"Lena said you met the Spartan princess during your last trip. She's said to be a beauty. Have you fallen for her charms, then? Is that it?"

"Lena is a lying old hag. I never met a princess on my last trip."

"But you don't deny your father wants an alliance with Sparta."

I open my mouth to defend myself, but Calisto, the woman I'm desperately in love with, swings around and runs back to the temple. I want to go after her, but it's futile. No man can enter the temple of Artemis.

The scene disintegrates, like a sand castle being blown by the wind, and then I'm inside a building. This time what I'm seeing is not through the eyes of my former self. The thoughts bouncing in my head are horrible, dark, and depraved. I must be reliving a memory from Harkon.

Hooded figures approach me, keeping their gazes down. Their robes are a dull grey color besides the one man in the middle. His clothes are darker, made of finer fabric, and there's a braided golden belt at his waist.

"You've summoned me, Eneas. Does that mean you have finally decided to pay the price for your riches?" Harkon says, his demonic voice echoing in the grand space.

The man pulls his hood back, revealing the same man I've seen in my previous vision. "Yes. Just please stop sinking our ships."

"I want the fair maiden you harbor in your court. The beauty who has caught the eye of your son."

"Calisto?"

"Yes, I want your niece."

No! I want to shout, but I have no voice. So the woman I was in love with was my cousin? Was that why my father was against our relationship?

Instead of rage, a chilling smile appears on the man's face. "Consider it done."

"So cold. And they call me the monster. Tell me, Eneas. You have no regards for your own blood?"

"Not when it stands in the way of building an empire."

Chapter 27
Samuel

The farther we venture inside the Shadow Market, the more my skin crawls, and I'm not talking about the itchy-as-fuck piece of garbage Nina gave me to wear. I try to keep my gaze down and not make eye contact with any of the creatures in this place, but the market is so crowded I must watch my step to avoid bumping into anything. We decided to let Zeke lead the way, since he's the only one who's actually a true demon and sort of belongs here. Of course, I'd never tell that to his face, especially after hearing how he became addicted to demon beer.

Growing up, I always considered demons to be the ultimate bad guys, creatures to be avoided at all costs. At least, that was the way it was taught to us. After the Thirteen Days of Chaos, no one can blame the survivors for having a deep distaste for demons. I'm not sure how Zeke managed to convince everyone he was harmless.

A commotion up ahead puts me on high alert. The small hairs on the back of my neck stand on end while a low growl escapes my lips. *Shit.* Why is my wolf trying to come out like that? What is it sensing that I can't? A loud shriek makes our entire party freeze, and it sends the monsters surrounding us into a curious frenzy. I lift my head in time to see something fly in our direction, a blur of black feathers and extremely sharp talons.

"Thief! I curse youuu!" A bedraggled woman emerges from the crowd. She's wearing rags that look filthier than what I have on. For a split second, I think she's accusing us of stealing her clothes. She's headed straight for me, a wooden staff raised above her head. I'm too stunned to react fast enough, not completely moving out of her path. She shoves me to the side with an immense force for an old creature, making me stumble and collide with Alex of all people.

"Jesus freaking Christ. What the hell was that?" I step away from the druid.

"A banshee," he says, still focused in the direction the crazy demon went.

"She was freakishly strong for an old hag."

"Yeah, and that's her advantage. People underestimate her due to her appearance. Honestly, I'd rather face a three-headed dog than that thing."

Nina comes closer to me, then pulls my hood over my face none too gently. I bat her hand away. "What's the matter with you?"

"Your stupid face was showing, and creatures were staring." Her jaw tenses visibly. "Come on. Let's go before they realize we're not from around here."

From the corner of my eye, I catch Alex curl his hand

around the scabbard of his blade, which is concealed by his cloak. A memory of it glowing comes to me—when he'd wielded it during the battle in Shadow Creek and Red ultimately used it to kill Valerius.

Curious, I ask, "What does that blade of yours do besides glow?"

"It can cut through the thickest demon skin, and it also destroys barriers."

"Barriers? What kind of barriers?"

"The demonic kind." Alex smirks, making me roll my eyes. I don't get what Red saw in this douche canoe. He sounds like an arrogant ass.

"Hmm, I like the sound of that. Where can I get one?" Nina asks from ahead of us.

"Only Dark Blades receive one upon passing the trials. The blade won't work for anyone else."

"It worked for Red, though," I say.

"The blade was already active. Plus, Red had the same goal as I did, which was to kill Valerius. That's why she was able to use it."

"Pity. It means it's not worth it to steal one then, huh?" Nina says in a nonchalant way.

"Stealing is never worth anything. Period," Alex replies in a hard tone.

"Whatever, Mr. Nice Guy. Like you've never done anything bad in your entire life," she continues.

Alex doesn't reply. Instead, his jaw tightens as he diverts his attention to the lovely scenery. I do the same. The crowd is getting thicker the closer we get to the other side of the market. It becomes impossible to avoid jostling against creatures of which I don't wish to know their kind. We huddle together, moving as a unit. It doesn't take long for my ears to pick up the sound of brutes barking orders.

"When are the games starting?" I hear someone in the crowd ask.

"The games will start when the games start," replies one of the tall armored guards.

He's easily eight-feet tall and as wide as an ancient tree. We definitely want to keep a low profile around those dudes.

"Okay, guys. It seems we're not getting any closer to Prythian's arena perimeter going this way," Nina says.

"Why are all these demons excited about these stupid games anyway? Don't they have anything better to do?" I mutter, not really expecting an answer.

"No. They've been banished here, remember? I supposed Prythian found a need in the market and took advantage of it," Alex replies.

Nina cranes her neck, trying to look over the sea of monsters in front of her. I doubt she can spot much, considering she's five foot nothing.

"What are you looking for?" I ask.

"A way out of this jam."

Zeke glances over his shoulder, startling me for a second. Damn. I'm not used seeing him in his true demonic form yet.

"I've got it. Follow me," he says, then begins to elbow his way through the crowd, creating a path for us.

Mercifully, none of the demons shoved aside complain

about it. At least until he finds something that does. Another alpine monster type with dark grey skin and not a single strand of hair on his shiny head glares at the imp from his vantage point. What's up with these demons being so fucking tall?

"Where do you think you're going, imp?" the creature asks.

"None of your business. Now move aside," Zeke replies without an ounce of fear in his voice.

The grey-colored monster narrows his black eyes, then his nostrils flare as he takes a big whiff of Zeke. "I know you. You're the imp who betrayed Lord Kurthan."

Zeke takes a step back, his body going rigid. But we're right behind him, and there's nowhere for him to go. "You've mistaken me for someone else."

The creature lets out a horrific laugh, and as he does so, glyphs appear on his skin, glowing red. Oh man, I think he's a troll. I only know one, Baldwin, the bartender at Hell's Hole. But he's half human. So it means his mother slept with someone who resembled that motherfucker. The thought makes me a little nauseated.

"I know it's you, imp. Lord Kurthan has issued a reward for your head. A ticket out of this dive, and I intend to claim it." He grabs Zeke by the collar of his shirt, lifting him off the ground.

Many things happen at once. Flexing my legs, I begin to shift, but before I leap on the troll, I catch Alex unsheathing his blade, which is now glowing blue. I can't see what Nina's doing. She has disappeared. Then the troll lets out an enraged roar as his legs fold and he falls to his knees. Zeke, however, is still trapped by the giant's grip. Without wasting any time, I strike the troll's forearm, severing his hand from the rest of his body with my claw.

Alex glances at me in surprise before switching his attention to Zeke, then Nina, who is standing behind the fallen troll.

"Come on. Let's go!" She swings around, brandishing orange fire from her hand.

Leo once told me about the power some fox shifters have to summon foxfire. I never knew Nina possessed it. By some miracle or sheer luck, no one follows us as we blaze through the market stalls and merchandise. Maybe it's the crazy fire wielder in our party, or the fact we've just slain a pretty big guy. I'm not going to question the whys.

There's a barbed wire fence up ahead, which I find extremely odd in this place where everything else is reminiscent of the medieval era. Using the already-extinguishing fire in her hand, Nina opens a hole in the wire big enough for us to pass through. Then we find ourselves once again in a narrow and fetid alleyway. The good news is there's no one here. No demons or guards.

"The arena should be that way." Zeke points farther ahead.

We run in that direction. It seems to me all we've been doing since arriving in this dimension is run. Zeke stops abruptly when the alley ends. He sticks his head out, scanning left and right before signaling with his hand for us to follow him. A great desert looms in front of us, going on for miles until it disappears on the horizon. The land is completely flat, unlikely the terrain we came through when we got here.

"Do you sense that?" Alex asks.

"I don't sense anything," Nina replies.

"Me neither," I say.

Zeke narrows his gaze before waving his arm in front of him. "I feel a barrier. It's very faint, though."

"No, it's not faint. It's actually quite obvious to me. Maybe I'm sensitive to it because I'm a—"

"A druid. We get it. You're a special snowflake. Do you think that's where Prythian's illusion starts?" I ask.

"It's highly likely. Only one way to found out." Alex makes a slashing motion with his dagger, and the air glows slightly as it ripples.

"Okay, so we found the perimeter of Prythian's arena. Now what? How do we get in?" Nina takes a step forward.

"Now I do my thing," Alex replies, closing his eyes and holding the hilt of the blade with both hands. He doesn't move for a few beats, and my patience begins to wear thin.

"Come on, already," I say under my breath, but Nina shushes me.

"Hey! What do you think you're doing there?" a soldier yells at us from not too far away. Fucking A.

I turn to Alex. "Whatever you're doing, you'd better hurry up, pal."

"Stop being a dick. You're not helping." Nina pushes past me, positioning herself between the fast-approaching guards and Alex.

With a growl, I follow her lead, but I only allow a partial shift. I have no desire to lose my clothes and be forced to prance around naked in this place. Besides, it's getting kind of cold already. Alex finally raises his dagger above his head, then brings it down with great force against the invisible barrier. A hole appears, like a tear in the fabric of space, revealing the inside of a room

"It's now or never, guys," Zeke says before jumping through the small fissure.

Alex motions to Nina and me. "Go on before the opening closes again."

I wait for Nina to go first, then I follow. A second later, Alex slips through the opening just before it seals shut.

We're in a wide hallway with walls made from stone brick. Mounted torches burn the unnatural fire we've seen before, green with a dark core. Spooky as hell and exactly what I expected to find in such a place. The air is stale and humid, which makes me think we're underground.

"Great. You had to open a portal to the underbelly of the King of Bastards' domain," I whisper.

"It wasn't like I had a map of the place," Alex replies through his teeth.

"Ouch," I say as I feel a pinch on my arm, then swivel to find Nina staring daggers at me.

"Stop acting like a ridiculous child. When are you going to grow up, Sam?"

My mouth opens and shuts, but no sound comes forth. I don't have a smartass comeback because Nina is right. We're in the territory of extremely dangerous fae, and we have no idea where Red, Dante, and the others are. Yet, here I am, bickering with Red's ex. I'm an idiot. Truth be told, the reason I'm so jealous of Alex is because he's everything I'm not. What if Red realizes he's the better guy and decides to say to hell with the bond after all this is over?

Chapter 28
Dante

Prythian has been gone for almost half hour, leaving me alone with his former lover, the succubus who betrayed Red. She's keeping her distance from me, but she doesn't need to worry. The King of Bastards' magic is still in place even in his absence. I can move, but I can't get near her. Lucky for her because the longer I stay in her presence, the more I want to do her harm.

"You've been glowering at me for the past thirty minutes. If looks could kill, I'd be dead. Come on, ask me."

"I don't need to ask why you betrayed Red. You already said everything. Prythian can get you out of here, and you thought Red couldn't."

Trinity stands, striding toward me with her gaze narrowed. "Zeke told me you were the sensitive one, the one with the sight. If that were true, you would know."

"I would know what?"

She shakes her head, then laughs without humor. "You must have already figured out this place is magical."

"As if the fact his arena appears and disappears were not

a dead giveaway." I give her a droll look.

"So you must understand that everything we do and say, Prythian knows about it." Trinity stares right into my eyes, a meaningful glance that gives me pause.

I push aside my animosity toward her for a moment, concentrating on my ability to speak mind to mind. I've never attempted to connect with another being that wasn't a wolf, but if I'm reading the succubus correctly, that's what she wants me to do. At first, I feel nothing, no matter how hard I concentrate.

"Try to think outside the box, wolfie."

I peel my lips back and growl, but then I do try a different approach. Instead of attempting to find the beginning of her barriers, I pull back into my head, drawing in energy as if I had cast a net, and now I'm collecting the bounty. At first, nothing happens, but then a different signature brushes against my mind. I lower my shields partially, allowing only the two-way-communication channel to flow.

"Explain yourself," I say.

"I didn't betray your mate. I had to gain Prythian's trust. The only way I could do it was if I pretended to sell Red and your friends out."

"Let's say I believe you. How do you plan to get us out of his clutches?"

"I've spent centuries with Prythian. I know how he operates. He's taking his sweet time inspecting the new merchandise only to torture you. Any minute now, he'll come back and announce we're having a demonstration."

"And if he doesn't?"

"He will."

"And then what? What's the plan?" I scowl, doubting everything she says.

"I can't tell you. If you know, you're going to try to stop it."

"Why is that?" I ask, narrowing my eyes. At the same time, I try to get the information Trinity is withholding. It goes against my morals, but I can't worry about it now.

"I've told you enough already... and only because I don't want you to aim for my neck once you're free of your compulsion. Now, he said something remarkably interesting a while ago. You had a vision about him, didn't you?"

"How do you know about my gift if you've been trapped here since before I was born?"

"Please." Trinity waves her hand. "I didn't come here without having a way to communicate with the outside world. Zeke told me all about you and your brothers."

"Are you saying you volunteered to come to this forsaken place? Were you that in love with Prythian?"

"Who says I was in love with him?" She fidgets uneasily.

"Only a fool in love would do such a thing."

Her lips turn into nothing but a thin, flat line. "Yes, I was a fool once, but never again will I let my heart make the decisions for me."

"What made you want to leave? Did you finally see what an utter prick your beloved is?"

Trinity's expression changes from outraged to sad.

"Prythian wasn't always like that. He was tormented, but he was never cruel. This place changed him. It turned him into the monsters he despised."

The succubus's words make me focus on the darkness inside of me, which seems to be growing more powerful as the time goes by.

"How come you didn't become corrupted as well?"

Trinity drops her eyes. "I'm different. This place doesn't affect me as much."

In that moment of vulnerability, Trinity drops her mental shields more, allowing me to read the actual truth. *"Your love for Prythian kept you from turning into a monster like him."*

Her fiery gaze connects with mine once more. "Snoop much?"

"I can't help reading what's right in front of me."

In an instant, she brings her shield back up. "Yes, I suspect my love for him kept me protected somehow, but ever since I left his side, it's been harder to resist the darkness." She pauses, then stares out the window. "Many years ago, before I became this...monster, I was once filled with undiluted rage. It was the horrible feeling that ultimately sealed my fate. I don't ever want to have that hate in me again. That's why I need to get out of here."

The door opens suddenly, making me jump on the spot. Trinity simply turns around, doing a much better job of hiding her surprise. Or maybe she's not surprised at all. She did say she knows Prythian very well.

"I hope you're ready, Dante. I've met your mate, and

she's lovely. Now I must see if she has the power to match her looks. It's time for a demonstration."

When I peek at Trinity, I find her smiling smugly at me. I hope her confidence extends to the rest of her plan as well.

"Emotion has made you speechless? Oh my poor champion. It's a pity I must now make you watch her fight for her life."

Chapter 29
Red

I'm not sure what the deal is with villains who just make an ominous announcement and then bail. Do they all attend the same school for bad guys? Prythian said it was time for a demonstration and then took off, leaving us hanging.

"What do you think he meant by 'we'll have a demonstration'? Like is he going to make us fight monsters and shit?" Billy asks.

I want to reassure him and say no, but that would be a lie.

Leo crackles his knuckles, his expression turning into something quite feral. I don't know the guy at all, but based on the little information I got from Sam, Leo is supposed to be the level-headed voice of reason in their group. He doesn't look like the voice of reason now.

"If push comes to shove, will you shift into a fox to fight?" I ask, because during all the battles I faced with his sister Nina, not once had I saw her shift.

"We're different than wolf shifters. Foxes are not aggressive by nature. Our strength relies on stealth and tricks."

"I see. What kind of tricks are you talking about?"

"Some can summon foxfire. Nina is one of them. My specialties are diversion and illusion. I'm sorry I can't offer brawn to the table."

I shake my head. "Don't be sorry about that. I suspect we're going to need your gifts in this place since we don't have Alex with us."

Out of nowhere, I feel a tug in the bond. I'm not sure if I'm sensing Dante or Sam, but the feeling makes me happy despite our situation. It's short-lived, though, when a sense of dread drips down my spine, freezing my blood. The hissing of a snake gives me goose bumps. I turn on the spot. A second later, the small hooded figure who was part of our welcome committee earlier appears in front of our cell.

"What do you want?" Armand takes a step forward, curling his hands into fists and showing off his fangs.

"The king has instructed me to escort you." The creature unlocks the metal door, stepping aside as it swings open on its own. "Don't try anything foolish." His face is profiled in the torch light, giving us a glimpse of his features. The head of a snake peeks out, and an involuntary chill runs through my body.

"I hate snakes," Billy whispers to me.

"Me too."

"Do you think his fangs are venomous?"

"Most likely, so don't try anything."

I throw a meaningful glance in Leo's direction as well, catching his gaze. I'm sure he heard what I told Billy—

shifter-super hearing and all—but it doesn't hurt to reinforce the message with a look. Unfortunately, Armand is still staring at Prythian's minion, his aggression obvious in the way tension seems to coil around his body.

To make sure Armand doesn't do anything foolish, like jump the snake man, I walk ahead of him, exiting the cell first. The fact this creature came along without guards is enough to make me extremely cautious. He's probably able to take on the four of us. Or maybe, Prythian *wants* us to do something foolish. Neither scenario will be to our advantage.

Armand is close behind me, so it's easy to sense his desire for violence. It's coming off in waves. I've picked up on certain moods from other supernaturals before, like Xander when he was eyeing Nadine in an unfriendly way, but I don't think I was ever so in tune with someone who wasn't a wolf. Is this a side effect of this place or does Armand have so much contained energy that even a mummy would be able to sense it?

I look over my shoulder, and it's no surprise that I find Armand still in full-vamp mode. Once again, I notice his resemblance to the King of Bastards and it's a little unnerving, to be honest.

"Are you okay there?" I ask.

"I'm fine," he replies through clenched teeth, his gaze fixed on the hooded figure ahead.

"Don't even think about it," I warn him.

"I can't help wanting to separate his head from his body with my bare hands."

A shiver runs down my spine. "Thanks for the specifics."

His red-pupil eyes lock with mine. For a moment, they return to his natural brown color, retaining only a reddish tint at the edges. "I'm sorry. I don't know what's going on with me. I can usually control my vampiric instincts better. I get more aggressive when I drink a lot of blood at once, but not even when I accompanied Tristan that night when he went to claim you in Shadow Creek did I feel this urge to kill."

"You were there, too?"

Armand increases his pace to walk next to me. "Yes, Jared, Leo, and I. We didn't know what was going to happen that evening. I thought for sure we would have to fight Valerius and his wolves then."

"I'm glad it didn't come to that. You were grossly outnumbered. But thanks for coming."

"Don't mention it. Sam is a good friend; I'd never leave him hanging." Armand doesn't speak for a moment, then continues. "How is he doing, by the way?"

"What do you mean?"

"Sam likes to play tough and joke around, but it's all an act."

I've noticed this about Sam as well, but I don't comment on Armand's remark. After a moment, he continues.

"He's the vainest person I know. I can't imagine what the loss of his eye must be doing to his ego."

I'm taken aback by this observation, getting irritated instantly that Armand would make such a cruel comment about Sam. But when I glance at him, I see the corner of his lips are turned upward. He's joking, only I don't know if it's for my benefit or his.

The conversation hits a lull, so I focus on our surroundings instead. Nothing changes for the next minute. We're in a long and narrow corridor with empty cells on each side. Our steps echo around us, making this walk even more dreadful. We don't know what awaits us. I focus on my core and the dual energy that resides there. My wolf is quiet—too quiet for my liking—but my new witch powers are brighter than I've ever felt them before. It's keeping the creeping darkness at bay, but how long until I begin to have uncontrollable murderous thoughts like Armand?

"What's up with all these empty cells?" I ask Snakeman, hoping he will answer me.

"That's where the contestants in the games stay as they wait for their turn for glory or eternal damnation," the creature replies.

"How many contestants are there usually in a game?" I continue since the snake is feeling chatty.

"It depends. Since word got out that my master has acquired a new champion, hundreds of demons have come."

"Hundreds, huh?" Billy says. "Where are they?"

"Eager to meet your opponents, little wolf? I suppose you have a death wish."

Billy lets out a growl, moving closer to us. I lift my arm, blocking him from getting closer to Prythian's servant.

"Calm down, Billy. He's just trying to get a rise out of you," I say.

We finally reach the end of the corridor. Snakeman veers left where thick double doors made from wood and reinforced with metal bars along their length open when he approaches. We enter another corridor, this one much wider and also not as gloomy. High windows with colorful glass run along the walls, granting the space its illumination. The decorated glasses depict different scenes, one more intricate than the other. In some, there are people dancing. In another, knights are battling a great beast. I see everything at a quick glance for Prythian's servant has increased his pace.

This is a shorter hallway, which ends in another set of double doors. But this time, they don't open on their own. Instead, the creature passes right through them. I stop in my tracks, not knowing if I should follow or not.

"Is this a trap?" Leo asks.

"I don't know." I focus on the door, trying to pick up on anything that could indicate danger. But I don't know what I'm doing or if I'm even able to sense magic like that.

Then the stone walls on each side of the door move. From them, guards in full armor, each holding a spear, step out.

I gasp as I take a step back, bumping into Billy.

"Where do you think you're going? There's only one way and it's forward." One of the guards points at the closed doors.

"Are we supposed to just walk through them?" I ask.

"I don't know about you guys, but I'm getting a serious HP vibe from this," Billy whispers.

"I'll go first." Armand takes a step forward, but I stop him.

The bond just became stronger, so much so that I know exactly who is on the other side of those doors.

"No. I will," I say, leaving no room for arguments.

Taking a deep breath, I step straight into those doors. On instinct, I close my eyes so not to lose my nerve in the last second. A tingling sensation runs through my body. When I open my eyes again, I let out a sob. Dante is here.

CHAPTER 30
RED

I blink fast, almost not believing Dante is in front of me and in one piece. My heart is beating at staccato rhythm. I let out a gasp as I prepare to break into a run toward him, but guards I hadn't noticed before step into my way, using their spears to block my path.

"Red." Dante takes a step in my direction, stopping short when he's yanked back.

It's when I notice the choke collar around his neck and the chain attached to it. Prythian, who is sitting on his throne with a bemused expression on his face, has the end of Dante's leash.

"Isn't this marvelous? You're finally reunited with your mate."

"You monster. Let him go!" I curl my hands into fists, trying to call on my wolf powers, but I can't feel it right now. Some kind of magic is keeping it contained.

Dante's eyes are pained, filled with longing and regret. It's almost as if he feels guilty for being in this situation. I open up my channels, hoping he's trying to talk to me telepathically. But there's no familiar touch on the other side. Maybe the same force that is keeping my wolf powers contained is also affecting Dante's ability to communicate mind to mind.

"I love how fearless newcomers are. It's a breath of fresh air not having people tremble and cower by my presence alone."

"Unfortunately for them, your amusement only lasts a few seconds," Trinity replies, and I catch a hint of criticism in her tone.

"Yes. I get bored very easily. You know that better than anyone else." Prythian cuts her a glare, and the succubus stands up straighter.

Dante turns to Prythian. "Please let them go. You've already got me. I'll do anything."

My heart breaks by seeing Dante on his knees, begging for that hateful fae to let us go. My vision becomes tinged in red as power surges within me, spreading through my limbs. The tips of my fingers tingle, right before a crackling sensation goes up my arm. This is not my wolf at work.

Prythian's eyes widen a fraction as he leans forward. "What's this?" He turns to Trinity, who is standing on the other side of the throne.

"I'm not sure I know what you're asking," she replies innocently, making me want to punch that phony look off her face.

The King of Bastards waves two fingers, and the guards in front of me step aside. This is it, my opportunity to strike the monster. Pulling my arm back, I feel my power concentrate on the palm of my hands. With a roar, I hurl the energy sphere in the king's direction, but the ball connects with an invisible barrier before fizzling to nothing.

Prythian's hair changes from white to black at the same time his pupils change color as well, glowing a deep purple. "You're not only a simple wolf. Who are you?"

"I'm Amelia Redford, the woman who's going to kick your ass if you don't release Dante at once."

"You will tell me who you truly are whether you know it or not."

White-hot pain flashes in my temple while my vision turns blurry. Prythian's form seems to pulse as he projects his powers toward me. No, not his body; his energy is pulsing. In an instant, he's able to penetrate through my mind shield as if they were made out of butter. My legs fold, and I find myself kneeling on the ground. All sounds become muffled. I grind my teeth, tasting blood when I bite my tongue by accident. I have no idea what he's doing, what he's seeing. All I can do is pray he'll leave my head before I faint. I see one glimpse through the pain, though. The image of a woman with dark blonde hair who's tied to a pole. She's wearing a simple, Grecian-style dress, and there's defiance in her gaze. The image vanishes, and another heartbeat passes before the pain recedes as if it were a tidal wave. I don't know what I saw, but deep down, I realize it's important and Prythian was the one who unearthed the memory.

Even breathing through my mouth and nose, I can't seem to get enough air into my lungs. I lift my head, discovering Dante is breathing hard as well. His face is red and covered in sweat. The veins on his forehead are throbbing. Did Prythian also make him feel the same excruciating pain I did? The King of Bastards' eyes are no longer glowing, but his hair is still black. I'm not sure why his appearance changed like that. It didn't seem to me it was something he did on purpose, more like a reaction to his emotions. Now he's regarding me with his unnerving dark eyes as he rubs his chin.

"You bear her mark," he breathes out.

"Bear whose mark?" I ask through clenched teeth, and its sounds more like a growl. Is my wolf awakening? I don't sense the familiar churning in my chest.

Prythian throws his head back and laughs, the sound echoing in the concave ceiling of the grand room.

"What's so funny?" I rise slowly.

The raw energy I felt before begins to converge once more in my core, almost as if my rage is fueling it.

"What's funny is that you don't even know where the strange power you have is coming from."

"I was told Red is a witch. Is she not one, then?" Trinity asks, frowning in my direction.

Prythian cocks his head to the side, narrowing his eyes a little. "I can see how that power could be mistaken for those of witches. But no, she's not a witch."

"That's a bunch of bullshit. You're trying to mess with my head, but your fae tricks won't work on me."

"Let her go," Dante says in a strained voice as if it cost him a great effort to do so. "Please."

"No. I brought your mate here because I want a

demonstration, and a demonstration I shall have. Sashir, bring out the first challenger."

The snake man makes a small bow, then says, "Of course, my lord."

He moves through the room as if he were gliding, the only sound coming from him is the fabric of his long robe rubbing together. He presses his hand against a narrow door with carvings on it. It opens forward. Through it, a beautiful female enters—not human—wearing a billowing dress. The fabric is gauzy, making the dress see-through and revealing a flawless body underneath. I switch my attention to Dante, but by the way his lips are curled into a sneer, he couldn't care less if she's parading naked.

Her wrists are bound together by thin vines, not chains. There's no doubt they must have some kind of magic in them. When she turns her face to Prythian, her eyes flash with undiluted hate and the tips of her pointy ears peek from her long hair. She's fae as well.

"You are a filthy snake," she hisses at Prythian.

He laughs in an odious manner, making her even more furious. "Mauve, my dear. I expect a better insult coming from you."

"I gave you a champion, and this is how you repay me?" She lifts her bound wrists.

Wait. She was the one who captured and then sold Dante to the King of Bastards? The knowledge does something to me. It brings forth an ugliness that's more than simple fury. I want to tear her to pieces. I want to see her blood spilled on Prythian's beautiful marble floor.

The King of Bastards leans forward, his eyes turning feral, dangerous. "You came into my home and tried to steal from me after I paid your price. No one steals from me, my dear."

The fae seems to turn paler, her eyes widening a fraction. But her emotion only lasts a split second before she regains her composure. "I had no choice. Your coin wasn't enough to buy a way out of here."

"You went to the Carver, I presume?" Prythian raises an eyebrow.

"Yes," she hisses. "How did you know? I cloaked myself."

Making a tsking sound, Prythian shakes his head. "Indeed you tried. I've always thought you were one of the smart ones, Mauve. Nothing happens in the Wastelands without me knowing. Now, enough talk. I'm feeling benevolent today. If you can fight that shifter and win, you're free to go."

The fae turns to me, her eyes assessing. "Who is she?"

"My champion's mate. Isn't she wonderful?"

Mauve regards me from head to toe. After she's done with her scrutiny, a chilling smile slashes her face. "You want to me fight a wolf shifter? That's not even a challenge."

"Perhaps you want to fight me instead." Armand takes a step forward, prompting one of the guards to make a grab for him. He sidesteps with ease before hitting the creature square on the chest, sending him careening onto the floor. I hadn't realized he was that strong. He turns to the next guard, but then he freezes. The guard swings his spear around, hitting Armand on his shoulder, sending him down. I let out a cry, but I can't move either. What the hell is going on? I sense a shift in the air, a crackling of sorts. I can't move my legs or arms, but my neck isn't affected by Prythian's spell. I face the throne in time to see the high fae stand up, pull his arm back, and send a purple fire lance through the air. It hits the guardian's back, piercing through his metal armor as if it were made from paper. The guard disintegrates, turning into a mountain of pebbles. Prythian just killed his own minion. Why?

Once the rage subsides and his face returns to normal, he seems just as shocked by what happened. His gaze is glued to the remains of his guard. No one utters a single word. He then switches his attention to Armand, who I'm glad to see isn't harmed and is already getting to his feet. He's clutching at his shoulder, though.

"Why would you kill your own guard?" he asks.

"Because I could. You ought to remember that. I appreciate the bloodlust, though. You'll get your turn if your friend survives."

I've had enough of Prythian's games. If he wants me to fight the bitch fae who sold out Dante, I'll do it. In fact, I'm looking forward to it.

"Release me," I say.

"Aren't you eager now, Calisto?" He smiles sardonically. That name. It stirs some long-forgotten memory in my brain. What did he see when he invaded my mind?

"The name is Red," I reply.

He waves his hand in a dismissive way. With that

gesture, I feel the invisible bindings around my body vanish. My wolf springs to life, ready to be set free. The vines around Mauve's wrists also disappear. She gives me no chance to shift before she attempts to bind me once more with her fae magic. I can almost see the tendrils of her power circling my body. My wolf lets out a whine as it begins to lose strength.

Hell to the fucking no. I won't let this bitch tame my wolf. Using my new powers, I slash through the fae's spell, sending it rebounding to her. She's thrown backward, hitting the wall behind her with a loud thud.

"Yeah! Go, Red," Billy shouts, but it's too soon to be celebrating.

The fae staggers to her feet, her eyebrows furrowed in determination. I pissed her off royally, and she's going to bring her A game now. I can't let her try anything, so I shift as fast as I can, ruining the clothes. Screw them. I leap on her, but she moves out of my way in the last second. With the momentum, I can't stop myself before I hit the wall.

The woman laughs, the sound grating on my nerves. Growling, I come at her again, not sensing before it's too late that her taunt was a lure to her trap. Vines explode from the floor, curling around my limbs and ensnaring me. The more I struggle, the harder the unnatural plant squeezes my body.

I whine as the pressure brings me down. One of the branches finds my neck, wrapping tightly around it. Damn it all. She's going to choke me to death.

"Red! Get up," Dante yells from behind me before he

grunts as if in pain.

I'm unable to look in his direction, but I can guess Prythian hurt him somehow. *No.* I won't let these creatures, high fae or not, hurt my mate and my friends. I'm better than that. I'm stronger than they are. Ignoring the contracting force around my neck, I delve my attention completely into the force that lives in me now. I will it to expand, to burn through my body. A faint blue glow surrounds me, similar to the one that wraps around the great wolf apparition. But the ethereal beast is not coming to the rescue. The glow is coming from me. As the light burns brighter, I become stronger. The vines slacken until, with a flash of blinding light, they snap with a loud crack.

"No. That's impossible." Mauve retreats slowly, not taking her eyes off me.

I don't hesitate. Free from the fae's deadly vines, I launch at her, breaching the gap between us in a second. Once I find her neck, I slash it open with my teeth. Her nails claw at my shoulders as she makes a strangled sound, but she has no chance of surviving the attack. I've got her. Her strange blood fills my mouth, fueling my need to take revenge, to end her existence, but then, a familiar touch brushes against my mental shield. I would know his signature anytime, anywhere, so I lower my barriers.

"Red, sweetheart, let her go."

"No. She sold you to that monster."

"I know, but she's dead. However, you don't know what swallowing her blood will do to you."

Damn it. He's right, and I've already ingested a few

gulps. But the rage won't subside, and my wolf is still happy to mangle her body further. I'm thrashing the fae's corpse as if it were a rag doll. I don't think I can stop.

Then, a scream filled with rage and despair sounds in Prythian's chamber, clearing the bloodlust enough for me to let go of the fae and lift my gaze. A man with shaggy hair and a beard is standing on the other side of the room. He's dressed as if he's a ranger of sorts. Everything happens in slow motion next. He pulls a gun from inside his duster, takes aim at me, and shoots.

Chapter 31
Samuel

"Any idea where we should head to?" I ask.

Zeke turns to me with eyebrows raised slightly. "Shouldn't we be asking you that question?"

"What's that supposed to mean?"

"Your bond to Red. Can't you sense her?" Alex replies, eliciting a growl from me.

Nina clears her throat, drawing my attention to her. She gives me a meaningful glance, reminding me of what she just told me a minute ago. I need to stop bickering with Alex.

"No." I turn on my heel, biting my tongue.

The urge to say something nasty to Alex is great, but I can't blame my foul mood on his question. It's the lack of answers that's the problem. Why can't I sense my mate? A great feeling of failure begins to fester in my chest, and it's hard for me to keep the doubts about my relationship with Red at bay. I love her more than life itself. She was the first and only woman I've ever said the L word to. But I know her case is not the same. She loved another man before—Alex.

Jealousy spears my heart, making it hurt like a mother. Why can't I shake off this feeling? Is it real or is this awful place amplifying my negative emotions?

We walk in silence for the next minute, treading carefully in enemy territory. It seems we're still in the bowels of Prythian's arena, but so far, we haven't seen any sign or source of life. I'm not sure if that's good or bad. When we come across a fork in the hallway, I have no clue where to go.

"Now what?" Nina asks.

"We can't keep walking blindly," Alex adds.

I'm about to give the druid an angry retort when I sense a ripple in the air. "Did you feel that?"

"Yes. What the hell was it?" Nina's gaze darts left and right before she pivots and peers behind us.

"I don't like this," Alex chimes in.

Zeke takes a couple of deep breaths, his nostrils flaring as he does so. "I smell wicked magic."

"Great. I didn't even know you could smell that," I mutter.

"Well, wherever it is, it's coming. We'd better get out of here fast. Let's just pick a direction and go," Nina says.

When I prepare to veer right, a tug in my chest makes me freeze. I place my hand there, not daring to believe what I felt is real.

"What is it, Sam?" Zeke asks.

"I can feel her. The bond… it's calling me."

I take off in the opposite direction I was going a second ago, not bothering to see if the others are following me. I can't risk losing the connection to Red. If I couldn't sense her before, then it's possible the wicked magic Zeke smelled a moment ago was blocking it. I don't know what lifted the barrier or how long it will last, so I sprint down the narrow corridor without a second thought. The torches are sparser in this section, placed farther apart until they simply vanish. When they do, I plunge into complete darkness. For fuck's sake. I slow my pace, focusing on my hearing and sense of smell since I can't see shit now.

"Are you sure this is the right way?" Nina asks, not too far from me.

"Yes. The bond is getting stronger."

I don't pick up anything different with my nose, but I can't smell magic like Zeke can, so I ask, "Are you still smelling bad magic, Zeke?"

"Oh yes, most definitely."

"Anyone got a cell phone that's working?" Nina asks. "Mine is dead."

"Who do you want to call, my dear?" Zeke asks with a chuckle.

"I don't want to use it as a phone, idiot."

I pat my jacket, but find the inside pocket empty. "Either I lost mine or I forgot it altogether."

"And I don't believe in cell phones," Zeke replies.

"Excuse me." Alex pushes me aside as he moves ahead. I open my mouth to give him a piece of my mind, but the complaint dies in my throat when a faint light springs from his palm.

"What? You don't have a cell phone either?" I ask.

"Dark Blades are taught not to rely on technology. It can easily be disrupted by magic, so we don't bother carrying phones." Alex takes the lead. Begrudgingly, I follow the guy.

"Is it me or is the corridor getting narrower and narrower as we go?" Nina asks.

"It's definitely getting more constricted and…ah, shit," Alex says.

I peer over his shoulder, finding the source of his frustration. It's a dead end.

"We have to go back and—"

"No, we can't. Red is nearby," I say.

"Unless you know how to walk through walls or have learned to blow them to smithereens with your bare hands, we can't continue," Nina replies.

"Hold on a second. Let me through." Zeke elbows his way until he's standing right in front of the stone wall. He stares at it for a second before patting the surface in an up and down motion with the palms of his hands.

"What are you looking for?" I ask.

"A fae holding wouldn't be complete if it didn't have fake dead ends and secret passages."

"All right. Let me help you look for it," I say, then I turn to Alex, who's blocking my way. "Do you mind?"

Clenching his jaw, he moves aside.

I begin to search for anything that could trigger the opening of a secret passage, but I find nothing but regular stone bricks. After a minute of doing that, I'm already frustrated.

"Ugh. We're wasting time. Let's just retrace our steps

and find another way," Nina says.

"Hold on. I think I found something," Zeke announces from his crouch. "Ugh, damn it. I can't get to it."

"What is it?" I ask.

"There's a small fissure on the rock. I sense a slight variation in the magic there. I'm almost sure this is the trigger."

"Let me see," I say.

Zeke stands, moving out of the way so I can take his place. I touch the lower corner of the wall with the tip of my fingers until I find the fissure.

"We need something sharp to stick in there," Zeke says.

"I can try with my dagger," Alex suggests, but I shake my head, lifting my hand to reveal sharp claws instead of nails.

"I got it."

Carefully, I insert the thinnest of them with bated breath. Another second and there's the clear sound of a click. The wall trembles before it slides open, revealing on the other side a much wider and brighter hallway. Before I step in, I take a deep breath, trying to pick up the scent of anything that might be dangerous—or Red's scent.

"The coast is clear," I say as I cross the threshold.

The passage slides shut as soon as our party is on the other side.

Nina whistles. "Wow. I guess we've left the bowels of Prythian's castle."

"We sure have." I don't know what to look at first. The contrast between this lavishly decorated hallway to where we were before is like water and wine. I've never been to the Versailles Palace, but I suspect this place is ten times more ostentatious.

"Is this really all an illusion?" I ask.

"Most likely. Where would the King of Bastards find those pieces of art, fine drapery, and furniture in this dimension?" Nina replies.

I shake my head to snap out of my stupor. Why am I in awe of the decor? It must be another trick from that damn fae. As soon as I realize I was under some kind of glamor, the sense of wonder vanishes. And I also pick up on Red's scent. She came through here.

"Let's go." I sprint down the hallway. The bond is not only becoming stronger, but there's also a feeling of impending doom that's beginning to crush my chest. Something is not right. Red is in danger. My wolf's energy is swirling inside of my chest, begging to be set free, but I can't shift now without knowing what we're dealing with. Shifters don't have a lot of defense against magic, which is a fucking pain when it seems all our problems are caused by magic, either fae or demonic.

However, even without a natural gift to fight against certain supernatural creatures or the ability to sense wicked magic as Zeke does, I can definitely see when the air right in front of us changes. It's almost like there's a barrier that has been disturbed. The air is rippling.

I come to a halt. "What the fucksicle is that?"

Two great marble statues of knights come to life in the next second, jabbing their sharp spears our way. They're just as tall as the guards we met outside.

"More of Prythian's creations is my guess." Alex pulls his dagger from its sheath, holding it at the ready.

"No offense, dude, but I don't think that little knife of yours is going to be very effective against them," I say, leaping out of the way when one of the knights swings his weapon at me. The tip of the spear hits the floor, creating a hole where I stood a second ago.

Alex slashes his dagger, hitting the statue on his weapon-wielding arm. It does exactly what I thought it would. Nothing. It's a miracle Alex's blade didn't break with how hard the idiot hit the creature.

"Sam is right. Your druid weapon won't be enough." Nina pulls something from her satchel, a red and pink canister of sorts.

"Is that hairspray?" Alex stares at it incredulously.

My jaw drops because I'll have to side with Alex on that one. What the heck does she plan to do with it?

"Stop gawking like a bunch of idiots and pull that curtain down," she yells at the same time she avoids becoming a shish kebab by the spear of the second knight.

It finally dawns on me what Nina plans to do. While Zeke begins to distract the guards by playing a game of tag, I make a beeline for the nearest curtain. I yank it, but the heavy fabric won't tear. I try to cut it with my claws, realizing the process will take too long.

"Hold on. Let me try." Alex strikes the curtain with his magical blade, and the fabric finally tears. Once it's cut halfway through, I give a final hard pull. It detaches from the top part. I stagger back as I try to keep my balance. Jesus, this damn fabric is heavy.

"I got the curtain," I tell Nina since she's busy running away from the stone knight.

"I need you to wrap it around the guards. Zeke, let's bring them closer together."

The imp nods and then runs in Nina's direction. They stop short of colliding. When the knights are almost upon them, Nina bends her knees, grabs Zeke, and jumps high enough to avoid the knight in her path. Prythian's creations are too heavy to slow down before they collide with each other. Alex and I take the opportunity to tie the curtain around them. As soon as we move away, Nina shakes the hairspray canister, then fires the flammable substance on the fabric at the same she ignites her foxfire, sending a jet of flame toward the tied-up guards. The curtain catches fire in an instant. I stare at the flames that erupt for a moment, before an excruciating pain in my chest has me gasping out loud.

The next thing I know, the sound of a gunshot reverberates through me.

CHAPTER 32
DANTE

Everything seems to happen in slow motion. Tobias—Mauve's human partner—appears out of nowhere just in time to witness Red kill the female fae. The roar that comes from deep in his throat is desperate and filled with rage. It's the sound of a person losing someone they love deeply. Never mind that Mauve planned to take off without him.

If I had any control over my gift, I would have foreseen the gun he pulls from behind his coat. Red won't be fast enough to avoid the bullet. My leg muscles tense as I prepare to jump. I forget the choke collar around my neck and the chain. Before Mauve's lover pulls the trigger, my body is already in motion, flying through the air. The boom of the gunshot echoes in the room, only a split second before I hear the sound of a bullet zap by my ear. I land on top of Red in an awkward manner, biting my tongue with the impact. The chain attached to me clanks loudly against the marble floor.

It takes me a moment to realize Prythian had this planned all along. I don't know what Mauve did to make Prythian incarcerate her, but the appearance of her lover in the exact moment Red killed the female fae was not a coincidence. Nor the fact Tobias had a gun on him. Prythian wanted this to happen. He even let go of my chain, allowing me to push Red out of the bullet's path.

All around us, mayhem commences, but the noise is muffled for all I can hear clearly is the sound of my pulse drumming in my ears. Red rubs her muzzle against my face, then licks my cheek. My heart goes off in a mad race, beating out of control in my chest.

She begins to tremble in my arms until she's human again. Lust ignites in my core so suddenly it robs me of breath. It spreads throughout my body like wildfire. I'm aroused like I've never been before. Common sense goes out the window. I don't care where we are or that in the background, Leo, Billy, and Armand are fighting with God knows who. My hands find Red's face, and then I'm kissing her like nothing else matters. She matches the tempo of my tongue, and her body mimics mine with urgency. If I don't stop in the next second, I'll take her on the hard stone floor. With a gasp, she pulls away, pressing her hands against my chest.

"Dante, snap out of it," she says with difficulty.

"What?" I ask, feeling confused.

"I knew it," Prythian says from somewhere in the room.

His voice is enough to lift some of the fog from my brain. And then it hits me, or better yet, the scent of Red's heat hits me. No wonder I'm so aroused. With great effort, I drop my hands from her face, scooching back for good measure. But the yearning remains, the need to mate overwhelming. Goddamn it. This is impossible. When female wolves go in heat, their mates can't fight the primal instinct.

Red sits up, bringing her knees up to cover her naked body. "I'm sorry, Dante."

"Why are you apologizing?"

"Red!" Sam's voice echoes in the distance.

I leap to my feet, then automatically reach over to help Red as well, but she moves away from me, her face twisting into a grimace. Denying the heat must be just as hard for her. There's a sudden hard yank on my chain, making me stagger. Furious, I whirl around, finding Prythian holding the end of my leash again. There's a smug smile on his face, which only fuels my rage more. I'm done being his puppet. I grab the link, planting my feet on the ground.

"Oh, so you want to play with me, little wolf?" he says.

"Prythian, come on. Is this really necessary?" Trinity takes a step in his direction with an arm outstretched.

"Oh, but the fun is only starting."

Sam doesn't come any closer to Red, but I can read in his eyes that maintaining his distance from her is killing him. Nina seems to notice his turmoil. She dashes toward us, but she doesn't reach the middle of the room. Instead, she's hurled back as if an invisible hand swatted her.

"Nina!" Billy goes to her, crouching next to her sprawled form on the ground.

The fox leans on her elbows, shaking her head. "I'm okay."

There's a shift in the air, a concentration of great power,

and it's coming from Red. She rises, facing Prythian. Despite her nakedness and the fae blood covering her body, she looks powerful and glorious. She lifts her chin while a chilling smile spreads on her lips.

"I declare these games over." She grabs the chain. Amazingly, an electric current shoots from her fingers, running up the length toward Prythian.

His eyes widen right before the electric current reaches him. He drops the chain with a grunt before falling to one knee. The metal around my neck cracks open. Without wasting a second, I pull it off me, slinging it far away.

Prythian's head is lowered, but his hair keeps changing color from white to black, without settling into one. Finally, it turns black. When he lifts his gaze, there's no doubt his retaliation will be mighty.

Careful not to touch Red, I step in front of her, using my body as a shield.

"How dare you defy me, little wench?"

"How dare you use us for your wicked games?" Red spits back.

Prythian laughs, and the unsettling sound of it makes the hackles on my neck rise. "You call my games wicked?" He glides forward, and the power leaking from his frame paralyzes me once more. "You don't know anything. This is nothing. You don't know what it means to be truly wicked, to be so evil you can't even fathom the meaning of light."

"Are you going to give us some sappy story of how tormented you were in your younger days? Are we supposed to feel sorry for you now?" Red replies, and I wish I could get a glimpse of her face.

Prythian falters at the same time his eyes lose some of the demented glint in them. The same thing happened when he saw the drawing from my gift. I don't know how my vision and Red's words are linked, but there's more than just darkness in the high fae. Maybe staying this long in the Wastelands corrupted his soul.

"Do you think I want to be pitied? How idiotic of you. You're not here to think, or to try to understand me. You're here to entertain me, and entertain me you will." Prythian swings his arm forward, sending an almost translucent ball of light across the room. Frozen as I am, I don't know who he aimed for. All I hear is a grunt.

The invisible bindings around my body snap, and the force sends me to my knees. I lift my gaze toward Red, but she's not looking in my direction. Her gaze is fixed on a young man who seems familiar, but I can't place him.

"Alex," Red whispers.

The man breaks into a run in her direction, and I fully expect Prythian to swat him away just like he did with Nina. He doesn't, and I understand why in the next second. Alex stops in front of Red, grabs her by the shoulders, and kisses her. A loud roar reverberates in the room, and I don't know if it's coming from me or Sam. The scent of Red's heat hits my nose with double strength, and my wolf goes berserk.

"What did you do?" I hear Trinity ask right before I shift into my wolf form. I will tear that son of bitch limb from limb.

Something hits me before I can reach the guy, keeping

me in place. In my mad need to protect my mate, I don't know what's holding me until I smell Zeke's scent. I try to shake him off, snapping my jaw at his face, but he keeps himself away from my sharp teeth while he holds me down.

"Somebody needs to do something. I can't keep Sam contained for much longer," one of Sam's bandmates says, but I can't tell who.

"Stop struggling, Dante. Don't let Prythian get into your head," Zeke says. He doesn't understand that reason has left my body.

"What's going on? Why doesn't Red push Alex off her?" Billy asks.

Exactly. Why? Did Prythian do something to her as well? Does he want to torture Sam and me by forcing us to watch Red mate with another man?

Trinity lets out a curse before running toward Red. The succubus pulls the man away from Red. Alex tries to grab her again, but Trinity kicks him in the stomach, knocking him down.

"Think very carefully about what you're about to do, Trinity," Prythian warns.

The succubus glares at him for a brief moment before she invades Red's personal space… and kisses her.

CHAPTER 33
RED

I thought I was imagining things when Alex was kissing me, because I could not, in full conscience, be kissing him back. But when Trinity pulls him off me to kiss me next, I know something is definitely wrong with me. It seems I'm feeling the full-bloom effects of going in heat, but why would I want to have sex with Alex? I thought I would only feel the urge with my bonded mates.

There's only one logical explanation—Prythian did something to Alex and me. He must have twisted my heat in a way that affected Alex as well. But whereas Alex's kiss was a real one, full of teeth and tongue, Trinity's isn't. She's holding my face in place, sandwiched between her two hands, while she seems to be sucking the lust out of my body. The entire experience doesn't last more than a few seconds. After she steps away, my mind is clear once more.

The succubus doubles over, holding her stomach as she wheezes. It sounds like she can't get air into her lungs. Alex doesn't make eye contact with me as he slowly gets onto his feet. Prythian has his eyes fixed on Trinity. His face is contorted, but I can't tell if he's feeling rage or pain. He does seem to be shaking.

"Damn it, you fool." Zeke lets go of Dante, then runs to his friend. She's on her knees now, bracing her hands on the floor with her head hanging between her shoulders.

He pulls her into his arms, turning her around.

"What's going on?" I ask.

"She used her succubus power to suck the lust out of you, but it was too much. Now she's suffocating in it."

Guilt sneaks into my heart. She betrayed me, but she also intervened in Prythian's wicked games. "Can't you help her?"

"I don't know how."

"Triny…" Prythian raises a supplicant arm. His hair is once again white, and his eyes are the clearest, brightest sky blue now.

I understand what he is now. He's darkness and light in equal parts. The thought comes to my head unbidden. Living in this hellish dimension must have suppressed his good side in the same manner it has been slowly poisoning my soul. I can't waste this opportunity. Before he reverts to his evil side, I stride in his direction without a care for my safety. Invading his personal space, I grab him by the lapels of his fancy jacket and shake the guy.

"Help her. Don't let her die."

I've never seen eyes more filled with sadness than his when he focuses on me. "I don't have much time. I can already feel the corruption returning. She needs to get rid of the lust she took from you."

"How?"

"She needs a victim."

"What?" I say.

"Of course. Why didn't I think about that?" Zeke mutters.

"My lord?" the snake man says, getting closer. I had forgotten about him. Behind him, I see the body of the human who tried to shoot me down. Prythian's eyes begin to change color. I'm losing him to the dark side, which means I'm running out of time. If he came to the human dimension with us, maybe he wouldn't return to that awful state. Why do I feel the need to save this fae after all the horrible things he did to us? Never mind that I have no clue how we're getting out of here.

Grabbing my hands, he then pushes me off him, but not roughly. He peers over my shoulder. "The stone. I need the sacred stone."

"What for?" Sam asks, moving closer to us.

"It's the only way I can open the portal to the mortal lands for you. It's the only way to save Triny. If any of you tries to help her here in the Wastelands, she'll become something she's been fighting against for the past fifty years. She'll turn into a full-fledged demon, and she'll corrupt the soul of her victim forever."

Trinity reaches inside her clothes, pulling out the necklace I gave her, then yanks it free. She throws it in Prythian's direction, but his minion, the snake man, jumps to intercept it. Alex's glowing dagger flies through the air, hitting the monster in his chest. He disintegrates before he hits the floor.

Prythian now has the stone in his hand, and the urge to pry it away from his fingers is immense. I made the foolish mistake of giving the stone to Trinity, and she betrayed me. Prythian is ten times worse and more powerful than she is. I have no idea how he's going to use the stone.

Someone grabs my arm, pulling me away from the high fae. It's Alex. The memory of his passionate kiss is still vivid in my mind, and if the growling of two very pissed-off wolves is any clue, it's vivid in Sam's and Dante's minds as well. I yank my arm from his grasp, afraid he's still under Prythian's lust spell.

Alex raises both eyebrows. As if understanding dawns on him, he lifts his palms up. "I'm back to normal, I swear."

Sam grabs the back of Alex's collar, then shoves him farther away from me. "You'd better stay the hell away from her."

"Whatever you plan to do with that stone, you'd better do it fast. Triny is getting blue," Zeke says from the ground where he has the succubus in his arms.

Clenching his jaw, Prythian stares intently at the stone until it begins to glow. The blue light becomes brighter and brighter, igniting the power inside of my core as well.

"Oh my God. That's amazing," Nina says in awe, moving closer to me.

On instinct, I let the energy flow freely from me toward Prythian, feeding whatever spell he's casting. I sense Alex doing the same. Remembering what we did to use the Mirror of Briseis to come here, I picture the alpha's manor. Slowly, a portal begins to form. On the other side, the familiar house, the place I call home now, materializes.

"What are you waiting for? Go!" Alex shouts.

Leo, Armand, Nina, and Billy run toward the portal, jumping one after another. Zeke carrying Trinity follows suit, but Dante and Sam won't budge.

"What are you doing? You must cross the portal!" I shout at them.

"Not without you."

A grunt from Prythian makes me lose concentration. My power recedes, and the portal begins to close.

"We have to go now," Alex urges.

"Let's go all together. Ready? Now!" I run to the portal, but only jump when Dante, Sam, and Alex are poised with me.

The travel through the magical portal only lasts a few seconds, and it's as strange as the first time we used it. I manage to land on my feet, then realize I forgot Prythian. Turning, I catch his face before the portal closes completely. He's smiling, not in a malicious way, but in a peaceful manner.

"Damn it. We forgot the stone," Alex says. A second later, the necklace with the sacred stone falls to the ground. Prythian somehow managed to return it before the portal sealed shut.

"Hello. I need help here," Zeke says.

Shit. Trinity.

Leo is the first to come to Zeke, kneeling next to him. "Tell me what to do."

Zeke stares at Leo as if he can't believe the fox shifter is volunteering. "Just kiss her."

"Don't do it, Leo. She'll suck away your soul." Nina takes a step forward, but her brother ignores her and kisses the succubus before anyone can stop him.

Chapter 34
Tristan

I don't remember returning to my own body after I witness the bargain between Eneas and Harkon. Nor do I know how long I've been unconscious. I hate I can't tell how much time has passed while I'm trapped in this dungeon. Has it been hours, days, weeks? No, not weeks. Harkon is too keen to return to the surface as soon as possible.

My mind is still reeling after what I discovered by peering into Harkon's memory. I have thought this entire time that my connection to Red started in the nineteenth century when she was the Mother of Wolves. But it isn't so. She was Calisto, the niece of an important man in ancient Greece. I was her cousin and deeply in love with her. My father offered her to Harkon as a sacrifice, which began the archdemon's obsession with her. But how did she escape him then? And what is Mrs. Redford's connection to all this? Harkon implied she knew Valerius had sent a mind-controlled wolf to attack Red. But I can't believe she would willingly sell her granddaughter out like that.

I could enter Harkon's mind again, try to find out more, but the idea makes me sick. His thoughts were vile, dark, and I can't bear to experience them firsthand again. No. I have to get out of this place and warn Red. We must recover all of our memories that involve Harkon, not only the ones pertaining to Natalia and Robert. And if I discover Red's grandmother betrayed her knowingly, I'll rip her throat out myself.

I'm sure by now Xander must have alerted the others that I reappeared and attacked his sister and nephews. But does he know I was under Harkon's control? The worst was avoided, but I don't think I can look into the alpha's eyes again after I tried to kill his family.

I test the chains around my wrists, see if they have somehow weakened so I can break them. It's an exercise in futility. Nothing has changed. My wolf is dormant, and I can barely feel my body. Suddenly, a great sense of sadness takes over me. Not too long ago, I was ready to die. I thought Harkon had crushed my spirit for good. But then, I managed to create a link with the demon, get something, a leverage he didn't know I possessed. That motivated me. But now I'm back to feeling hopeless again.

The worst part of my captivity is moments like this when I'm alone with my thoughts. I almost wish Harkon would pay me a visit, which is insane since every time he comes, I'm tortured to the point where my soul must detach from my body.

A tightness forms in my throat, and I'm ashamed to say I'm on the verge of crying. *No! Get your shit together,*

Tristan. You've never been so close to unveiling the truth and finding a way to defeat Harkon as you are now.

I grab the chains attached to the metal cuffs on my wrists, curling my fingers around them tight until the cold metal bites into my skin. The pain serves to awaken a fury inside of me. It's not my wolf's rage. It's my human's, and it burns. I've never experienced emotions that were separated from my wolf's before. It was easy to attribute the ferocity I felt all my life was linked to my animal nature. Only now that the wolf's essence is dormant can I see the savagery in my heart was from my human side. It comes from the pit of my stomach, born out of an old wound I've carried through several lifetimes. I don't need to remember all my previous lives to understand that. There's guilt and regret, and with every failed attempt to fix past mistakes, my resentment and rage grew.

From the few glimpses I was able to see of my life as Robert and Alesandro, it seems I've always succumbed to my fears and self-doubt. I was going down the same path this time around. I allowed that snake Seth to take control of the pack. I failed to protect my people because I was weak. This toxic pattern ends now.

Fueled by this new awareness, my body regains its strength. Using all my power, I pull at the chains, trying to break them free from the stone walls. The iron cuts through my skin, but I don't care. I hear a crack as the chain begins to loosen from their hooks. I'm close, so close. With a roar, I pull them as hard as I can. They finally detach. I fall forward with the momentum, banging my forehead on the hard ground. It doesn't matter. I'm free from my chains.

Crazy laughter bubbles up my throat, but my amusement is cut short when I sense a change in the air. I stop breathing for a second, anticipation making my heart skip a beat. A demonic energy is surrounding me. I expect Harkon to make his grand entrance any second now, but when he doesn't appear, I begin to worry this is another attempt to break me. The demonic aura is getting stronger, crowding around me, pressing on me from all angles. Then a great vortex forms above my head, sucking me off the ground. I'm spinning out of control at a great speed. The pressure is so terrible I honestly feel I'm going to get squished like a bug. But then it vanishes. With a jolt, I find myself on my back on a grassy ground. The terrible smell of sulfur is gone. Instead, I smell tree bark, wet soil, and flowers.

I dare to open my eyes, finding bright blue sky above. Am I dreaming? I inhale deeply, taking a good whiff of the different scents around me. I don't catch Harkon's signature stench, but that can't be. He wouldn't simply allow me to go free. The vortex that brought me here—I can't remember now if it had a demonic signature or not. It happened so fast. Is it possible I was actually rescued?

I sit up fast to get my bearings. I don't recognize the trees surrounding the clearing, but after I take another deep breath of fresh air, I catch the distinct scent of bears. Fuck. I'm back in Xander's territory. Now everything makes sense. If Xander finds me here, he'll try to kill me, no doubt about it. Is that what Harkon wants? He said he feeds on pain. Killing me won't serve his purpose, which means this must be a trap for Xander, not me. I knew getting out of hell was just too good to be true.

I spring to my feet, ready to get the hell out of Dodge, when I hear the distinct sound of a twig breaking nearby, followed by a roar. I turn around, finding Xander in his great bear form not too far from me. I raise my hands as a sign of peace, but his aggressive stance tells me he doesn't give a fuck about that. Instead, he stands on his hind legs, letting out another loud roar.

"Xander, listen to me. I didn't mean to attack your sister and nephews. Harkon was controlling me via the chip. You have to believe me."

He drops onto his four paws and charges. I have no choice but to run. Damn it, even with the newfound strength that allowed me to break my chains, I won't be able to outrun Xander on two legs. I have to shift. I try to connect with my wolf, without much hope I'll be able to. But it flares to life, surprising the shit out of me. It's as if the lid over it has been lifted.

Xander will be upon me any moment now, so I must shift at once. There's a fallen tree trunk up ahead. I aim for it, hoping the obstacle will buy me a few more seconds. Leaping over it, I shift in midair. When I hit the ground on four legs, I run like the wind. The forest turns into a blur.

I manage to put some distance between Xander and me, but he's still in hot pursuit and this is unfamiliar territory. It's only a matter of time before I make a mistake and the alpha catches up to me.

Focused as I am on not getting myself trapped, I don't

pick up on the scent of other wolves until I get a visual of them. There are five shifters in wolf form ahead, and one of them is Francois Boucher, the alpha of the Vancouver pack. Simon Riddle, the alpha from the London pack, is in his human form, carrying a tranquilizer gun with him. Fuck. Is this a trap? Are they also traitors?

I skid to a halt, then I prepare to fight. My aggressive stance is met with the same kind by the other wolves. They peel their lips back, growling as their bodies tense. I'm ready to attack when Simon lifts his hand and steps in front of the wolves. Francois turns to his counterpart, then howls. I don't think this was part of the plan.

"Tristan. I don't want to shoot you, but I will if you don't shift back."

What? He wants me to shift back? What for? To make it easier for them to finish me off?

The hairs on my back stand on end. Xander has caught up with me. I'm trapped.

My wolf wants to attack. It has been contained for far too long and it's thirsty for blood, especially if it is from traitors. But something in Simon's demeanor makes me pause. Maybe I shouldn't give in to the bloodlust. If Simon and Francois are traitors, it means they are working for Harkon. For all intents and purposes, I'm under Harkon's control, too.

Fuck it. I have to change and explain I'm in charge for now since I can't feel the chip anymore or sense Harkon's presence. Only it seems I hesitated too long, and Xander has no patience. He hits me on the side with his big bear paw, sending me flying. My Superman adventure ends shortly when I collide with a tree nearby. The impact stuns me for a moment, but it's enough for Simon to shoot me with the tranquilizer gun just the same. Damn it, here we go again. Back to darkness.

Chapter 35
Red

It seems everyone is holding their breath as we watch Leo and Trinity suck face. At first, he just presses his lips against hers without getting any reaction from her. She looked dead. But then, she arches her back, grabbing Leo's face with her hands. A red glow envelopes them both, and the scent of sexual arousal is impossible to miss. It stirs my own lust. Before I begin to feel the effects of the heat again, I cover my nose and step away.

"Let go of my brother, you filthy demon." Nina motions for the duo, but Billy wraps his arms around her, keeping her in place.

"You can't touch Trinity," he says as Nina struggles in his arms. "She might affect you, too."

"I don't care. Let go of me, brat." She elbows Billy in his stomach, making him slacken his hold on her. She leaps away, missing the distraught glint in Billy's eyes. Stupid fox. I want to throttle her for hurting him.

Trinity pushes Leo off her before Nina can reach them, then she jumps to her feet, breathing hard. "I've taken enough."

Leo makes a motion to approach the succubus again, and I notice how his eyes have gone out of focus. Oh man, I think he's still under her thrall. Nina grabs him by the back of his jacket collar, then shoves him to the ground. It doesn't do anything to clear his eyesight.

"Damn it, Leo. Snap out of it." She swings her arm, slapping her brother hard across the face.

Ouch. That must have hurt, but it seems to have worked. Leo shakes his head, then peers at his sister with a slight a frown.

"What the hell was this for?" He touches the sore spot.

"For acting like an idiot. Why did you let that succubus suck your life force?"

Leo's face hardens before he pushes Nina away and gets back on his feet. "Why don't you use your connection to my mind and figure it out?"

Nina's face turns white as her jaw drops. "What?"

"You heard me. You didn't think I would figure out that you can see through my eyes?"

"Leo, I—"

He raises his hand. "Save it, Nina. I don't want to hear your half-baked excuses."

"How did you find out?" She stands up, rubbing her hands on her leather pants.

"Oh, please. You knew Sam was mated to Red even though that information was told under Brian's silencing spell. There were other instances where you seem to know exactly what I was thinking. It took me a while, but I finally connected the dots. I can't believe you have that ability and you never told me about it."

"I'm sorry, Leo. At first, I didn't know how to tell you. Then, as we grew older, I figured it wouldn't be a big deal if I never abused our strange connection."

"Abuse our—" Leo shakes his head, letting out a pitiful laugh. "You invaded my privacy. Betrayed my trust."

"Never on purpose, I swear."

"Right. I believe you." Leo stares into the distance.

"Well, not that this little family drama wasn't fun, but what are you going to do now? Don't you have a demon to kill?" Trinity asks, appearing completely back to her former self.

I bend to pick up the jewelry with the sacred stone in it. It's not glowing any longer, but I can sense a faint trace of its power. It's not completely spent yet. When I lift my gaze from the stone, I realize everyone is staring at me.

"Let's find Dr. Mervina and the others."

"Aren't you forgetting something?" Trinity eyes the stone in my hand.

Nina huffs. "You're out of your mind if you think you're getting that now."

"I helped get Dante out of the Wastelands, didn't I?"

"You helped?" Nina's voice rises to a shrill. "More like you betrayed us and then got lucky that Prythian had a change of heart in the last second."

"No. The plan all along was for Trinity to betray you," Zeke chimes in. "It was the only way Prythian would let her back in his court."

"It's true," Dante adds. "She told me as much when we were alone. There was no reason for her to lie to me then."

I watch Dante closely, not because I doubt him, but because I can't believe I got him back. The yearning in my heart doubles, the deep seed of desire unfurling down below. *No*. I can't let my mind wander in that direction, not when Tristan is still in the hands of Harkon.

Suddenly, the front door of the alpha's manor bursts open and Nadine emerges from it. She stops on the front steps, her eyes wide as if she can't believe we're all back. Then she sprints down the steps and jumps into my arms.

"Hey, Nadine. I'm happy to be back, too."

She eases off the embrace, then begins to sign fast with her hands.

"Whoa, slow down."

"I can't believe you're back," Daria, Alex's companion, says as she emerges from the house, followed by Max, Jared, and Dr. Mervina.

"Dante!" she says before breaking into a run, stopping only when she's hugging her son. My eyes fill with tears. A rogue one rolls down my cheek, but I hastily wipe it off.

I sense Sam moving closer to me, but he stops short, leaving a gap between our bodies. It's futile. Like a magnet, I'm being pulled by his aura.

"I don't understand. Where have you been?" Dr. Mervina asks.

"There was a fire at the storage unit where Zeke was keeping the Mirror of Briseis. We had to use the object to create a portal to the Wastelands."

"I knew you could use the mirror to open a portal to a hellish dimension." Daria glares with accusation in Zeke's direction.

"We had no choice. It was either try to use the mirror or turn into ashes." I'm quick to jump to Zeke's defense, even though I'm still annoyed he kept us in the dark about his plans with Trinity.

"I don't know who started the fire, but they used clingfire, so it had to be someone with magical powers," Alex adds.

"We gathered as much. There was nothing left of the building. If not for the help of the Midnight Lily Coven witches, the fire would have gotten to the high school as well," Dr. Mervina replies.

"Wait? Are you saying that Mayor Montgomery actually helped?" Sam asks. "It must be the end of times."

"Yes, she came through. *Finally*. But let's continue the conversation inside. And we need to change the bandage on your eye."

We follow Dr. Mervina inside the manor. She gives me one of her white coats to wear, reminding me I'm butt naked. Funny how the prospect of certain death brings things into perspective. Parading naked now is the least of my worries. We head to the dining room where Brian, Santiago, Jared, Kirian, and another man I don't recognize are waiting for us. No sign of the ally alphas from Canada and England or Grandma, though.

"Jesus, you're back. Thank God," Brian says, scanning us as if he's counting if we're all here. Then he frowns.

"I see you also brought someone else back from the Wastelands."

I swivel to see Trinity has followed us with Zeke by her side.

"You shouldn't be here, demon," Daria says.

"I second that thought." Nina cracks her knuckles, as if she intends to start a fight.

"I'm not going anywhere until I get my stone." Trinity narrows her eyes, her chin jutting out stubbornly.

Santiago, who until recently I thought was a young sheriff deputy and nothing more, simply says, "Give her the stone."

"What? You can't be serious." Daria whips her face to the druid.

Leveling her with a calm, but serious expression, he replies, "Do you want her to start sucking the souls out of every single man in this room?"

"I'm not deranged like that." Trinity scowls, almost seeming insulted. "I can control my powers."

Santiago shakes his head. "Oh, no, my dear. You can't. I can see it in your aura. It's becoming darker and darker. Am I wrong to assume that's not what you want?"

"No," she replies quietly, almost in a whisper.

Santiago raises an eyebrow at me, expecting me to deliver the sacred stone to Trinity, but I still hesitate. A feather-light touch reaches my mind. *"I think you should heed Santiago's words. Trinity is a succubus, but she doesn't want to be one any longer."*

"We could use the stone to forge a weapon against

Harkon."

"If you don't allow her to have the stone, she'll eventually succumb to her demonic powers, and then she'll have to be dealt with."

"You mean they're going to kill her?"

"Active succubi are too dangerous. The supernatural community won't allow one to live."

Curling my hands around the stone, I close my eyes. It becomes warmer in my hand as if somehow, my power is charging it once more. I can't have her death on my conscience, and I did promise her the stone. I could justify keeping the sacred jewel by saying we need it more, but it wouldn't be right. No. I'll have to find another way to defeat Harkon.

I open my eyes again, then offer the stone to Trinity. "Here."

Trinity parts her lips as if she can't believe I'm actually giving the stone to her. Her eyes fill with tears, but she doesn't cry. Instead, she takes the stone from me, shivering as she closes her fingers over. "Thank you."

I nod, feeling immensely better that I followed Dante's advice. The petty feeling in my chest vanishes, and I suspect I was still under the Wastelands' effect. Nasty place.

"How did you manage to open a portal from the Wastelands? I didn't think it was possible," Jared asks.

"Prythian was able to with the help of the stone," I reply.

"Who is Prythian?" Kirian asks.

"The King of Bastards," Dante, Alex, and I answer in unison.

"Wasn't he the one who imprisoned Dante?" Kirian frowns, staring hard in Dante's direction.

"Yes," Dante answers simply, his gaze turning inward. He spent more time with the high fae than we did, so he might know more about that complex male than we do. I can't help but feel bad that we didn't try to get Prythian to come with us. If it weren't for his help in the end, we wouldn't be here. Maybe once Harkon is defeated, we can find a way to help him.

"How long have we been gone?" Alex asks.

"A week." Dr. Mervina replies.

"What? No way. We didn't spend that much time in the Wastelands." Sam's expression is incredulous.

"Time moves differently in the Wastelands," Trinity explains.

Dante rubs his face, then asks, "What happened after I was hurled through the portal? Where's Tristan?"

The mention of Tristan puts a chink in my heart. If we spent a week in the Wastelands, is he still alive?

"Tristan was seen a couple of days ago," Dr. Mervina replies, and my heart jolts inside of my chest.

"What? Where?" I take a step forward, unable to contain myself.

"In the Thunderborn territory," the man I don't know replies. "He attacked my wife and children." His face twists into a grimace as he curls his hands into fists.

"He's still under Harkon's influence," I mutter. Nadine moves closer to me, holding my hand in support. I appreciate the gesture.

"I don't care if he's being controlled." The bear shifter hits the table hard, cracking the surface.

"Derek, calm down." Santiago puts a hand on his shoulder, and the rage seems to lessen a bit.

"What happened?" I ask.

Derek lifts his face to mine. He might be a little more in control of his emotions now, but the rage is still alive in his eyes. "Xander showed up and saved my family. I don't know what happened to Tristan. He disappeared."

My hope deflates as worry consumes me. Did Harkon take him back to the underworld?

"Have we made any progress with the wolves under the influence of the chips?" Alex changes the subject.

I'm not sure if I should be grateful or resent him for it. When it comes to my mates, I'm a one track-mind person. The need to keep asking questions about Tristan is immense.

"No. We don't know how to remove the chip without killing them in the process," Dr. Mervina breathes out, sounding defeated.

I turn to Nadine. "Have you visited Victor yet?"

She shakes her head.

"We're keeping him sedated. He's the only wolf who hasn't shifted back to human. We don't know if it's the chip that's keeping him in that state or the trauma."

"I don't understand. Why did you have to sedate him? Was he violent?"

"No. But shifters who remain too long in animal form go crazy. We thought it best to keep him under considering what he went through." Dr. Mervina's gaze is apologetic. I'm sure she's trying her best, but I feel terrible for Nadine.

"Where are Simon and Francois?" Sam asks. "Did they leave already?"

"No. They've gone to the Thunderborn territory. They're searching for Tristan."

Once again, I feel the acute pain in my chest. "What do they intend to do with Tristan once they find him?"

"Bring him back here," Dr. Mervina replies.

Dante grunts as he leans forward, clutching at his middle. On instinct, I reach out to him, but before I touch him, Trinity pulls me back.

"Don't! I can't suck the heat out of you again."

Damn it. I had forgotten about that pesky detail.

"Dante, what's the matter?" Dr. Mervina touches his back as she watches his face closely.

He shakes his head with his jaw locked tight, then he leaves the room. Is he about to have a vision? When I glance at Sam, I notice he must have guessed the same thing. In silent agreement, we follow Dante, catching up with him in the hallway.

His hand is braced against the wall and his chin is dipped down. Careful not to touch him, I circle around, stopping in front of him.

"Dante, talk to me. Are you having a vision?"

"I—I don't know. I think the time I spent exposed to Prythian's fae magic did something to my gift. I feel a vision is about to come to me, but I'm able to fight it now."

"Why would you do that?" Sam asks.

Dante raises his head, his eyes swimming in pain.

"Because I can't keep having these visions in the most inconvenient times. I had one in front of Prythian, and I don't fucking know what I saw. He wouldn't let me see the drawing either. What if it happens in front of an enemy? If there's a way to fight it or better yet, to control it, then I have to learn."

I can contest Dante's logic, but it pains me to see him in this state. God knows what Prythian put him through. He needs to catch a break. Maybe now is not the time to attempt to control his visions. He's home after all, and we can easily go to his room, away from prying eyes. I'm about to suggest it when the front door opens and Simon Riddle, the alpha of the London pack, enters carrying an unconscious Tristan in his arms.

Chapter 36
Red

Someone makes a distraught sound in the back of their throat. It takes me a second to realize it was me. With my heart squeezed tightly, I break into a run, stopping short of colliding with Simon.

"What have you done to him?" I watch Tristan's face, searching for a sign he's breathing.

"Trust me, I didn't want to shoot him. But I had no choice. He was about to get into a fight against five wolves, including an alpha."

"You shot my brother?" Sam stops next to me, glaring at Simon so intently that I can feel his anger coming out in waves.

I don't sense Dante's approach. He must still be trying to keep his vision from taking over.

"I used a tranquilizer gun, but Xander did deliver a blow before I could stop the bear shifter."

As if summoned by the mention of his name, Xander stalks in, appearing more savage than usual. He stares at Sam and me, then his gaze travels past my head, no doubt fixing on Dante.

"I'm glad to see you're back in one piece and returned with Dante. That little Shadow Creek wolf was driving me insane with her worry," he says.

I try my best to hold on to the anger toward him, but Xander's mention of Nadine derails my thoughts.

"Why were you spending time with Nadine in the first place?" I ask.

Xander's eyebrows shoot up to the heavens. "It wasn't by choice. Somehow, I got stuck babysitting your pup."

"She's not anyone's puppy. And how dare you attack Tristan?"

"He's lucky it was me who found him and not my brother-in-law. It took great effort on my part to convince Derek to stay behind. Tristan would be dead otherwise."

Narrowing my eyes, I stare hard at Xander. Even when he returns the glare, projecting his beastly stance, I don't back down.

"Spare me your excuses and listen carefully. This is the first and last time you lay a hand on any of my mates without suffering the consequences. If you so much as touch one strand of their hairs, you'll have to deal with me."

"Is that a threat?" Xander takes a step forward, his eyes flashing amber.

"You bet," I growl, sensing my wolf is full on board with the idea of taking on the bear shifter. Funnily enough, I don't even think I'm crazy for my attitude. I can hold my own against him.

Sam jumps between us. "Whoa. Not that I don't think

your willingness to defend us is a hell of a turn-on, but let's not poke the bear with a short stick."

I snort. "I'm not afraid of him."

"Can someone please point me to Tristan's room? I'm in top shape, but Tristan is a big guy," Simon chimes in.

"I'll take you. Sam, could you please get your mother and let her know Tristan is home? She needs to check him to make sure he's okay."

"You got it."

Dante straightens when I walk past him. When I open my channels, his voice fills my head in the next moment.

"I'm coming with you."

"Okay. But how are you?"

"The compulsion to paint has passed for now." There's a brief pause before he continues. *"God, I want to touch you so badly, and it has nothing to do with the heat."*

"Same with me. As for my condition, I don't know when it's going to hit me full on. Whatever Trinity did to me delayed its progression somehow."

"I suspected as much. The urge to mate is strong, but not impossible to control. When Prythian amplified the heat, I thought I was going to die if I didn't take you."

I suppress a shudder as that scene replays in my mind, hating that Prythian could so easily manipulate and control my body. Never again will I let anyone do that to me. I'll do whatever it takes to gain the power to protect myself and my mates from that invasion.

Not wanting to dwell on the time we spent in the Wastelands any longer, I focus on Simon, who is following behind me.

"What happened here while we were gone? I didn't have the chance to get all the details from the druids."

"Besides the fire at the warehouse near the city's high school and your disappearance, nothing out of the ordinary happened. At least, not until Tristan showed up a couple of days ago and tried to eat a bunch of bears."

"It wasn't his doing. Harkon must have been controlling him. He has a chip, too," I say, hating that most likely his chip has Harkon's demonic signature, which means we can't remove it without killing Tristan in the process.

"That's a big problem. Francois didn't want to bring Tristan here. Instead, he wanted to take him to the location where the other wolves are in quarantine. But I made a promise to Dr. Mervina that I would bring her son back home. I never break a promise."

"Thank you for that," I say.

I grow silent, busy thinking of a way to destroy the chip in Tristan's head. Dr. Mervina managed to convince Simon to bring Tristan here, but I bet the others will have an issue with it.

When I enter Tristan's room, I have to control the swell of emotions that hits me all at once. The memories of the last time I was here with him are still fresh in my mind. I want to make an endless amount of new memories with him, Sam, and Dante. Will I have the chance?

Yes. I will fight for that. Fuck Harkon and anyone else who tries to take away what's mine again. A fire ignites in my core, mingling with my wolf. It fills me with strength and determination. I'll see this through.

Simon lays Tristan on the bed. The only piece of clothing covering his nakedness is the jacket someone was considerate enough to wrap around his shoulders.

"Thank you," I say.

"I'll be down with the others. And don't mention it. I would do anything for any member of the Wolfe family, you included, Red. Anthony Wolfe was a dear friend, and if I can help avenge his death, I will."

Dante approaches the alpha and then does the hug, pat-on-the-back thing. "I really appreciate it, Simon."

The tall man nods, then leaves. He exchanges a few words outside with Dr. Mervina before she enters the room, her eyes immediately zeroing on Tristan. Sam enters as well, and then closes the door.

Dr. Mervina takes a small flashlight from her jacket pocket, then peels Tristan's eyelids back to check his eyes. He doesn't move a muscle.

"I really wish Simon hadn't shot Tristan," Sam says.

"I'm more concerned with any injuries caused by Xander's brutality. I really don't like that guy." I huff, my fingers curling into fists.

"Don't worry about Xander. I had a talk with him about his methods already." Dr. Mervina turns Tristan around to exam his back. She frowns at the big mass of purple bruising right in the middle of it.

"Did Xander do that?" Sam asks.

"Yes, I believe this is Xander's handwork. He said he sent Tristan flying against a tree."

Sam cracks his knuckles. "I think maybe I should give him a piece of my mind." He gazes at me and continues. "That is, if you don't want the honors."

"Trust me, I'd love to punch that asshole's face, but I think we should all recover our strength first."

"Red is right. You can't go picking fight among our allies. We have enough enemies as it is," Dr. Mervina says.

"Speaking of enemies. What happened to Seth?" Dante asks.

"He managed to escape after the Shadow Creek battle. We haven't seen him or learned about his whereabouts."

"He'll resurface soon enough. Now that Harkon has lost part of his wolf army, he'll gather as many soldiers as he can," I say while bitterness pools in my mouth.

"One more reason to make sure everyone is in top shape. I know you didn't spend a week in the Wastelands, but it was too long anyway. I need to check to make sure you don't have any side effects from that place," Dr. Mervina says.

"And how are you going to check that, Mom?" Dante asks.

"We can perform a reading of your auras. I'll ask Brian to assist." Dr. Mervina addresses Sam. "I don't have my supplies here to change your bandage. You'll have to come with me."

"No offense, Mom, but can't that wait?" Sam glances longingly at me.

Dr. Mervina sighs deeply as if resigned. "Fine, I'll be right back."

She leaves us alone, and then I approach the bed. God,

Tristan looks so pale. He has lost weight, too.

"Oh, Tristan. What that monster did to you?"

I sit next to him. Ignoring caution, I touch his face. It's ice cold. The heat doesn't flare up, but maybe it's because he's deeply sedated.

He stirs in his sleep, and my heart jumps up my throat.

"Tristan, honey. Wake up."

His eyebrows furrow, and then he says my name in a whisper. Dante and Sam move closer to the bed, but I don't take my eyes off Tristan. Unable to resist, I lean down and press my lips against his.

A low humming comes from deep his throat, and then he lifts his hand, tangling his fingers with my hair. His lips part as our kiss deepens. My entire body begins to tremble as my desire awakens. Is this the heat or only regular longing? I pull away to make sure I'm not dreaming. Tristan's eyes blink open, a little unfocused at first, then they sharpen, riveted on my face.

"Red? Is that really you?"

"Yes. It's me. You're back home."

His grey eyes become brighter as they fill with tears. My gaze turns blurry as well, then Sam touches my shoulder. I don't even need to look up to know it's him.

"Welcome home, brother."

Tristan switches his attention to Sam, frowning a little. "What happened to your eye?"

"A parting gift from Harkon."

"How did you manage to escape?" Dante asks.

"I don't know. The first time I came back to Crimson

Hollow, Harkon brought me. He wanted me to kill Xander's sister and nephews. I tried to stop him, but he had full control of my body."

"We heard about it," I say, hating to see the grimace in his face. It wasn't his fault.

"This time, I don't know what happened. A great vortex appeared in my dungeon cell, and it sucked me out of there. When I came to, I was back in Xander's territory. I couldn't sense Harkon anywhere."

"That doesn't make any sense. How about the chip in your head? Is it doing anything?" Sam leans forward, watching Tristan intently.

"No. It has been silent for a while now. I can't help but think Harkon wants me to believe I'm free from his grasp."

"Couldn't that be possible?" I ask, daring to hope that somehow, Harkon's hold on Tristan has slacked.

"I don't know. I think we should operate under the assumption I can turn on you guys at any moment."

Tristan's eyes are serious, and my heart breaks for him once more. He's right, but I can't bear the thought of treating him like he's the enemy.

"I don't sense anything evil coming from you," Dante says.

"Harkon fed on my life energy. It's what gives him the ability to gain shape in this plane. He wouldn't give me up like that. He's planning something."

"Shit. If we only knew what exactly." Sam runs a hand through his hair, switching his attention to the painting above Tristan's bed.

"Something happened to me while enduring one of his torture sessions. My soul detached from my body, and I was able to see a scene from my previous life." Tristan looks into my eyes. "We were wrong to assume it all started when you were the Mother of Wolves."

My chest feels tight once more. "Prythian, the high fae who had Dante captive, hinted as much. He said I bore the mark of someone, a woman. I just don't know who."

"I don't know anything about another woman," Tristan replies. "All the information I got was you were an offering to Harkon centuries before. Your name was—"

"Calisto," Dante and I say at the same time, then we stare at each other in surprise.

I'm about to ask him how he knew that name when his face twists into a grimace. He leans forward, clutching his head with both hands as if he's in terrible pain. The vision he was able to stall must have returned.

Chapter 37
Red

"What's the matter?" I go to him, touching his back.

He grabs my arm as he staggers toward the chair in the corner of the room. Sitting down with his head dropped between his shoulders, he continues to grind his teeth.

"Just let the vision come, Dante. It's not worth this suffering," Sam says.

"What's going on? Why is Dante trying to fight his gift?" Tristan leans on his elbows, eyes riveted on Dante.

"He got into his head that he must learn how to master it. Is it even possible? Mom has a similar gift, and her visions also come unbidden."

"My gift is not like Mother's," Dante replies through his teeth. "I was wrong to assume so."

"Did Prythian tell you that?" I ask, remembering what the high fae told me about my powers.

"Not exactly, but he hinted at it."

"He did the same thing to me. He told me I didn't have witch powers. If I'm not a witch, then what the hell am I?"

"Calisto had a link to the Goddess Artemis. I'm not sure

if she was priestess or something else, but it's a place to start," Tristan replies.

"Who is Calisto?" Sam looks from me to Tristan.

"She was the niece of a powerful man in ancient Greece. He sold her out to Harkon, offered her as a sacrifice in exchange for power. But something happened, and she was able to escape that fate."

"The great wolf apparition told me I would find the answers if I searched where everything started. I assumed he was talking about Natalia and how she defeated Harkon."

"Yes, but she didn't defeat Harkon. She only hurt him badly," Sam points out.

"One of the memories I recovered was of Calisto exiting the temple of Artemis. It had a statue of the goddess surrounded by wolves. I'm sure there's where we should look. There's where we'll find answers." Tristan's expression turns into one of determination.

"A trip to Greece might be difficult right now," Sam replies. When Tristan glowers at him, Sam adds, "Oh, you weren't talking about actually going there. Okay, gotcha ya."

"How did you learn about Harkon's bargain with Calisto's uncle? Please don't tell me you were that uncle." Feeling wretched, I hug my middle.

Tristan closes his eyes, grimacing. "I wasn't the uncle. I was his son. I somehow managed to enter Harkon's mind. Saw the scene through his eyes. It was awful. The dark and perverted thoughts in his head are something I wish to forget completely."

"The cave," Dante breathes out.

"What about the cave?" Sam narrows his eyes.

"The cave where we went to get Natalia's diary. That's what my vision is showing me. I don't know why, but we must return to the cave."

"Are you out of your mind? Those poltergeists almost killed you, Dante." Sam makes an exaggerated motion with his hands.

"What cave are you talking about?" I watch them both.

"The one where we got Natalia's diary. The place was used to torture witches in the nineteenth century. There's an active spell around the area to prevent people from finding it," Sam replies.

"Do you think there might be other diaries there that will help us?" I ask.

"It's... possible," Dante grunts.

"Why didn't you take everything with you?" Tristan asks.

"I honestly don't know. It was a miracle those ghosts let us take one diary." Sam closes his eyes for a second, shuddering.

"Red, I must tell you something about your grand—"

A knock on the door interrupts Tristan. It's Dr. Mervina. Odd that she felt the need to announce her return. Did she think we were up to no good? When she enters the room, I see the reason. Grandma is right behind her.

My knee-jerk reaction is to go to her, but then I remember everything she's done to me, so I stay put.

"What's Mrs. Redford doing here?" Tristan asks with a frown.

"I came to check on you, young man. We have several concerned supernaturals demanding you be incarcerated with the other wolves from Shadow Creek."

"Over my dead body," I say, taking a step closer to the bed, positioning myself in between Grandma and Tristan.

"No one is taking my son away from me again. That's why I asked Wendy to check Tristan, to make sure he has no trace of Harkon in his aura."

"I already did that. There's nothing there," Dante replies.

"I'm sure your assessment was correct, but I'm afraid your word won't mean much to the mayor and Riku Ogata." Grandma moves closer to Tristan, and I notice he becomes tenser. I've never seen him act like that around her before. Is he afraid of what she might find?

"Don't tell me he went straight to the mayor to whine about us going to the Wastelands." Sam's expression morphs into one of disdain. His animosity is palpable, but it could be aimed at Grandma, too.

"Yup. He sure did," Dr. Mervina replies.

"This won't take long," Grandma reassures us, and then adds, "But I'd like to be alone with Tristan."

Suspicion makes my entire body tense. I don't like the idea of leaving Tristan alone with her. The feeling makes me sad. Grandma and I were close. I trusted her with many of my secrets in the past. She knows things that not even my parents do.

"Why can't we stay?" Sam asks.

"I need complete focus in order to peer deep inside Tristan's core."

Her answer only makes me want to say *no* to her request on the spot. It sounds like a terrible invasion of privacy. I open my mouth to protest, but Tristan beats me to it.

"It's fine. I don't mind."

"What? Are you seriously going to let Shady Grandma inside of you?" Sam asks.

"Shady Grandma, huh?" Grandma glances at Sam, neither laughing or glowering.

He shrugs. "You poisoned me."

She makes a tsking sound, and then focuses on me. "You don't have to worry, Red. I won't hurt Tristan."

"It's not as bad as it sounds. I would do it myself if I thought my word would be enough to appease Georgina and Riku," Dr. Mervina says.

"All right, then. But we'll be right outside." I finally relent, not feeling any better by Dr. Mervina's words.

I walk out of the room with a heavy heart. I don't know where this sense of foreboding is coming from. Am I worried Grandma will find traces of Harkon inside Tristan's core or is it something else?

─────

TRISTAN

Red and my brothers weren't happy to leave me alone with Mrs. Redford, but I have my reasons.

"How are you feeling, Tristan?" she asks.

"Like I've been attacked by a bear."

"You're incredibly lucky Xander was able to show some constraint. He could have easily cracked you in half."

I cut straight to the chase. "I don't sense Harkon's presence in my mind, and the chip has stopped emitting the annoying sound."

"That's good, but I must look deeper to see if the demon hasn't left a seed deep within your soul."

"Do what you must."

With a nod, she closes her eyes. A moment later, I sense her power grow. It feels like waves of air, resonating from her frame outward. When her power touches me, I become tense, an automatic reaction after having spent too much time with Harkon.

"You're fighting me, Tristan," she says without opening her eyes.

"I don't mean to do it, but it's…hard."

"He tortured you, didn't he?"

"Yes. Physically and mentally."

"I can see the scars he left on your soul. He fed on your aura. There are dark spots all around it."

"Is that irreversible?"

"No. You need time to recover, but you can't do that if you don't sever your connection to him completely. Now, would you let me in?"

"I'll try." I close my eyes, forcing my body to relax. Mrs. Redford's power is not malevolent like Harkon's was, but I can't help but remember his words, how she could be implicated in hurting Red.

She doesn't say a word for the next couple of minutes,

but it seems she's been probing for longer than that. Sweat pools on my forehead, and I feel every ache in my muscles and bones.

Finally, her power recedes from me, and I can breathe easily. "Did you see anything?"

She opens her eyes, watching me with her sharp gaze. "No. But the chip in your brain is still there, I'm afraid. I didn't sense a demonic presence in it, though. Brian and I have scanned some of the wolves in confinement, and the first thing we sensed was Harkon's demonic aura corrupting the brain waves of their victims."

"So does that mean I have the chip Red did? That's good news, right?"

"Yes, very good news. Your mother might be able to surgically remove the chip. Now, you must rest."

She begins to turn toward the door. "Not so fast, Mrs. Redford. I'd like a word with you."

"Oh? About what?"

"While in Harkon's captivity, I was able to see some of my past lives."

"You had another glimpse at Robert's life?" She seems mildly interested.

"Not Robert's. Alesandro's. Does that name ring the bell to you?"

She becomes paler in an instant. The muscles around her mouth tense, making her wrinkles sharper. But it's the scent of fear that's the most obvious sign she's hiding something.

"No. Why should it?" she replies.

Liar.

"Mrs. Redford, I'm only going to ask this once and you'd better answer me truthfully. Did you connive with Valerius to have Red turned into a Shadow Creek wolf?"

Her eyes widen as she lets out a loud gasp. "I can't believe you're asking me that. Of course I didn't conspire to turn my granddaughter into a Shadow Creek wolf. That's absurd."

Narrowing my eyes, I continue, "But you knew there was a rogue in the forest. Yet, you let Red walk right into Valerius's trap. You see where I'm having trouble believing you had no idea the rogue wolf belonged to Shadow Creek?"

"You think you're so smart, but you know nothing. You never have." There's fury in her eyes now, but her words only make sense if she knows more than what she's saying.

"I'm giving you the opportunity to explain yourself here. If you care about Red at all and you want her in your life, tell me what you know."

She lifts her chin. "I have nothing to say."

"Fine. Have it your way. We'll learn the truth, the *whole* truth, with or without your help."

We keep at the staring contest, then, finally, Mrs. Redford drops her gaze to the foot of the bed. "I'm nothing but a servant. I can only do as she commands."

"Who?"

She lifts her gaze. "The Goddess Artemis."

CHAPTER 38
SAMUEL

"What's taking them so long?" I ask as I continue to pace up and down the hallway.

Red has been staring at Tristan's door for the entire time without saying a word. Ignoring that I'm supposed to keep my distance from her, I move closer and touch her arm, bracing for the crazy lust to ignite, but all I feel is the normal need to be with her. Nothing I can't control. Trinity must have really done a terrific job. I hope Leo doesn't suffer many consequences for his action. Kissing a succubus like that was such a reckless act. I still can't believe he did it.

Red glances down at my hand, then lifts her eyes to mine. "I hope Grandma doesn't find any trace of Harkon in Tristan."

Wanting to distract her from her troublesome thoughts—and mine, too—I kiss her softly on the lips. A tingle runs down my spine. When a powerful urge stirs in my belly—the desire to whisk Red away—I hastily pull away, ending the kiss abruptly. My heart is jumping, and there's a buzz in my ears.

"You won't be able to fight this for much longer," Mom says, bringing me down to Earth.

I should be embarrassed she can sense my arousal, but there's no room for it in my head. Besides, we're shifters. It's kind of hard to hide that stuff anyway.

Red blushes, which makes her even more desirable in my eyes. My dick is rock hard, which sucks because there's no chance I'll be able to take care of it any time soon. Besides, a quick hand job won't do it either. Only Red can help me.

She cuts her stare to Dante, who is leaning against the opposite wall with his arms folded and face down.

"Are you feeling better now?" she asks.

He lifts his chin, focusing on her with eyes that are also filled with desire. Damn. I really shouldn't have touched her.

"I guess," he replies. "The compulsion to create art is gone, but I'm feeling a little unsettled I was able to fight off the urge."

"You were able to keep the vision from manifesting?" Mom asks. "How?"

"I don't know. I just blocked it."

"But why would you want to do that? Your visions have been a great asset to us, especially since Red came along."

Dante's demeanor changes. He watches our mother with a pained expression, and I feel that deep in my guts.

"Because I'm tired of having this ability control me. I'm tired of worrying when the next urge to paint will hit. It's the reason I rarely left my studio before. What if I got hit by a vision while driving or in the middle of the supermarket?"

"Damn, I never stopped to think about that," I say.

"Yeah, I know."

"What's that supposed to mean?" I frown, catching the frustration in my brother's tone.

"It means it's hard for anyone to understand it unless they've felt something similar. I'm not blaming you of anything, Sam."

I run a hand through my hair, feeling pretty bad for not once thinking about the burden Dante had to carry. God, and I used his strange gift to terrorize the other wolves in the pack when we were younger. I was such a stupid brat.

"Dante, I'm so sorry," I say.

"I know, Sam. Don't sweat it, okay? I'm not saying this to make you feel guilty." He speaks to Mom next. "What I wanted to say initially is that despite being able to fight the urge to paint, I was able to see something. I'm not sure if I had let the vision come through in art form it would have been different, but when I fought the compulsion to draw, a clear image popped in my head. The cave where Mrs. Redford hid all those old witch journals."

"Why would you see that, I wonder?" Mom presses a finger to her lips, seeming to ponder.

"I think we need to return to the cave with Red and Tristan. I got the impression there's more to unearth about Harkon's obsession with Red. It didn't start when she was the Mother of Wolves."

"It makes sense," Red says. "In both memories I retrieved from my life as Natalia, I got the distinct notion Harkon had been pursuing her for an extensive time, possibly more than one lifetime. She tried to kill him using one sacred stone, but it didn't work. There has to be another weapon that can kill him once and for all."

"But why does the answer have to be in that spooky cave?" I ask, hating the idea of returning there.

"I don't know, but there's only one way to find out."

Shuddering, I make a disgruntled sound in the back of my throat. With a smirk on his lips, Dante asks, "What's the matter, Sam? Are you still afraid?"

"Hell yeah. Aren't you? They almost choked you to death."

"I ain't afraid of no ghost," Dante sings, then cracks a smile. I'm glad his time with that freak King of Bastards didn't break his spirit.

"Once we return from this haunted cave, I'd like to visit the wolves in quarantine," Red says. "I want to bring Nadine with me. She told me you haven't let her see her brother yet."

Dr. Mervina shakes her head. "We're not letting any shifters near those wolves. Only the druids and witches have gone in. It's not the safest place right now. The wards aren't holding. "

"Do you think the chips are causing some kind of disturbance to them?"

"I can't think of anything else. Georgina offered to move the wolves to one of the coven's properties, claiming her witches would be able to provide better protection. We have dragged our feet for as long as we can, but if we can't create a ward that will last more than a few hours, I'm afraid we'll have to accept her offer."

"We must avoid that at all costs," Dante says. "We can't trust the mayor. She was siding with Valerius on the land dispute, and she threatened not to send help in case he attacked. That woman is a snake."

Red twists her face into a grimace, and I want to know why.

"What's the matter, my love?" I ask.

"I'm just thinking about the deal I made with Demetria Montgomery. I hope it wasn't a mistake."

"You meant to protect her oldest granddaughter? I don't remember her very well," I say. "She went to a boarding school out of town, and I don't think she visits often."

"Let's not worry about Erin Montgomery for now," Mom says. "As for your request, I think it's a terrific idea for you come see the wolves. Maybe you can help figure out how to diminish the chip's power."

"And Nadine? She's suffered so much. I really want her to see her only living relative."

"You know Victor hasn't shifted back to human. I'm not sure if he's able to do so anymore."

"I understand, but if he's getting worse, it's one more reason for Nadine to be able to visit him," Red presses, and I love her determination to help that poor kid. I don't know half the horrors Nadine went through at the hands of Valerius, and she deserves a break.

Tristan's door opens, and Mrs. Redford walks out. Her eyes briefly land on Red before she turns her attention to Mom. "I didn't find any traces of a demonic presence in

Tristan. However, the chip is still there."

"But you didn't sense a demonic signature in it?" Red takes a step forward.

"No."

Red lets out a loud sigh, clutching at her chest. "Then we could try to remove it. Right?" She turns to Mom.

"Yes. But I would need to bring him to the hospital. I'm not sure how deeply they embedded the chip in his brain."

The hope vanishes from Red's eyes. She knows that with everything going on right now, Mom most likely won't have time to perform a complicated surgery on Tristan. I also doubt my brother will want to spend the next few days recovering in bed. Harkon will come back soon, swinging harder than he did before, and Tristan has all the rights to fight that monster back. Harkon has taken so much from us already.

"I..." Mrs. Redford starts, but then rubs her forehead, frowning as if she's suffering from a major headache. "Tristan is waiting for you."

"Grandma, are you all right?" Red asks, worry lacing her voice. Shady Grandma is lucky that Red still cares about her well-being.

"I'm fine. I just need to recover my strength. Dr. Mervina, would you be so kind to offer me a hot beverage. Tea, perhaps?"

"Of course. Come with me. And once you feel better, I'm sure Riku and the others would like to hear your assessment." Mom steers Mrs. Redford away. When I drag my gaze from them, I realize Red has already entered

Tristan's room.

I'm the last one in. Tristan has gotten dressed, ready to head out despite the fact that he looked like death not too long ago.

Closing the door, I ask, "Are we going somewhere?"

"Yes. We're getting some real answers."

"Tristan, you're scaring me. What did you and my grandmother talk about? She seemed distraught, and I don't think it was all related to depleted energy levels."

"That's what I began to tell you earlier. Harkon's favorite method of torture was to plant the seed of doubt in my mind. He led me to believe your grandmother was in cahoots with Valerius all along."

"No, that can't be. She wouldn't do that to me." Red takes a step back, placing a hand over her chest.

"I asked her point blank if that was the case. I needed to know the truth, Red, because any way I look at it, she's guilty."

I see what Tristan's harsh words do to Red. She's gone paler, her eyes brighter. I wish I could come to her grandmother's defense and erase the sorrow from Red's eyes, but I can't do that.

"And what did she say?" Red asks in a small voice.

"She said she wasn't working with Valerius, but she did say her actions weren't voluntary."

"What do you mean?" Dante narrows his eyes.

"She's a servant of the Goddess Artemis."

"What?" I ask.

Tristan opens his mouth, but his reply is cut short when

Dante hisses, holding his head in his hands.

"What's the matter? Are you getting another vision?" Red asks, her body poised to come closer to Dante.

"I'm seeing that damn cave again. I think we need to head there ASAP." Dante raises his head, eyes glowing amber.

"Does that mean we need Shady Grandma's help getting there again? Remember the spell keeping the trail hidden?" I point out.

The amber hue fades from Dante's eyes, but not the intensity. With determination, he says, "No. I can find the way."

Chapter 39
Dante

I feel wretched. Every single muscle in my body hurts as if I've been working out too hard. But it's the sickness in the pit of my stomach that's making me feel so horrible. Twice in a row now I've felt the tingling sensation at the base of my spine. The telltale sign that a vision was about to come. And I fought with every fiber of my being to stop it from taking complete control of my body and mind. Usually, the artwork derived from one of my visions would be a scene, sometimes difficult to interpret. The vision of the cave manifested as a clear image in my mind. I'm certain we need to pay it a visit—all four of us.

To avoid bumping into anyone, we decide to take our exit via the clinic. I catch Sam messing with his eye bandage once, making me feel guilty. Mom didn't have the chance to change it, and I was the one who insisted we leave at once. But my gut feeling is telling me we can't wait. Plus, there's also the chance our allies will demand Tristan to be locked up despite Mrs. Redford's statement that he's not under Harkon's influence any longer.

Touching his arm once we're outside, I point at my head. I want him to lower his mental shields. Tristan and Red notice my gesture, but when I start the telepathic convo, I find no resistance from anyone.

"*Why did you have to ask us to lower our shields?*" Tristan asks.

"*Because my head is still a little jumbled thanks to me fighting the vision. I thought it would be easier if I didn't have to mentally knock. How bad is your wound, Sam?*"

"*It's itchy as fuck, but nothing that will kill me. Besides, I've already lost the eye, so whatever.*"

"*You can get an infection,*" Red chimes in, making Tristan gasp loudly.

"*When did you learn to do a group chat, Dante?*"

"*I didn't. I think Red is the link.*"

Tristan glances at Red in an odd way, giving me a bad feeling. Peering closely at him again to make sure there's really no sign of Harkon or any other malevolent force in him, I find nothing.

"*I wish we had a chance to shower. I feel kind of icky after spending those days in the Wastelands,*" Red says.

"*I second that. Nasty place. And you didn't even have to wear the filthy disguise Nina procured for us. Ugh. I can still smell it.*"

"*I guarantee it wasn't worse than the stench in Harkon's dungeon,*" Tristan replies with a snort, and I feel everyone's mood plummet.

Once inside the garage, Sam makes a beeline for the biggest truck there. Dad's. He doesn't hesitate before he opens the driver's side door and slides behind the wheel. Tristan asks me, *"Do you want to ride shotgun?"*

Glancing at Red, I allow myself to be a little selfish. I know Tristan just came back from hell, but I need to be as close to her as possible. I'm not sure where this emotion is coming from. It almost feels like I'm on borrowed time. Sensing my stare, she cocks her head at me.

"What is it, Dante?"

"Nothing." I focus on Tristan. *"I'm riding in the back with Red."*

The clench of his jaw tells me he doesn't like my answer. I'm about to say there's no need for him to ride up front with Sam, but the former sticks his head out of the car window and shakes his head. "No freaking way am I going to play chauffeur. I don't care who rides shotgun, as long as it's not Red."

"Hey. Thanks a lot." She pushes out her bottom lip, making me want to bite it. I swallow a groan, shaking my head to clear the instant lust.

"No, you're taking this the wrong way. I don't want you sitting next to me because it would be too much of a distraction."

Rolling her eyes, she shakes her head. "Fine. I'll ride in the back."

"You know that us sneaking away like this will look really bad." Sam opens the garage doors.

"Oh well. Tough shit," Tristan grumbles.

We're lucky we don't cross paths with anyone coming in, but as soon as the main gate opens, Mom will be alerted we left. Still, I let out a relieved breath when we exit the compound without any problems.

"Do you still remember the way?" I ask Sam, since I drove the last time.

"Yeah. You just need to tell me when get near the secret path."

"It won't be for another twenty minutes," I reply.

No one says a word for the next couple of minutes, but I don't attempt to read their moods by using my gift. I'm too busy trying to keep my hands to myself. I'm all too aware of Red's proximity to me even though there's a gap between us. My hand is resting next to me on the leather seat, so when her finger brushes against mine, it's feels like an electric current just went through my body.

"Dante," she speaks in my mind.

Swallowing hard, I shift in her direction. She's watching me with a tiny smile on her lips, even though I read worry in her gaze. I make sure the others can't hear our convo by blocking them out. Again, I don't want to share this moment with them.

"Yes, sweetheart?"

"I was so worried about you. Did Prythian hurt you?"

"No, he didn't hurt me. Considering the bad guys we've faced so far, he was on the tamer side." I smile at her. I'm not lying about him not hurting me. He could have easily done many terrible things to me.

"I'm sorry about the whole thing with Alex. I didn't know what I was doing or even who I was kissing."

Unable to keep from touching her, I curl my fingers

around hers and squeeze them tightly. *"Don't worry about it, Red. I know you had no control of what was happening to you. I still don't know who he is, though."*

"He's my ex."

My heart clenches sharply in my chest. I was never a jealous person despite my wolf's nature. I always thought the emotion was futile and juvenile. So the fact I'm reacting this way shows me how naive I've been about myself. I never loved anyone enough to be jealous.

"And I suppose you were serious with him?"

"Yes. We dated throughout high school. He was my first...everything." She bites her lower lip, hiding her face. Her reaction makes the pain in my chest more acute. What is she hiding from me?

I reach for her hair, running my fingers through a loose strand. *"Red, what is it? Do you still have feelings for him?"*

She whips her face to mine fast with her eyebrows raised. *"What? No. Why would you ask that?"*

"I... shit." I run a hand through my hair. *"Our relationship happened so suddenly that I wouldn't blame you if you still had feelings for him. I mean, you loved him, didn't you?"*

"Yes, but that was a long time ago."

"But it was natural. There was no bond in place, clouding your feelings."

She pinches my chin between her thumb and forefinger, making me face her. *"I love you, Dante, bond or no bond. When Harkon sent you through that portal, it felt like a piece of me had died. It was one of the most horrifying moments of my life. You, Sam, and Tristan are imprinted in my soul. You own my heart. No one will ever come in between us."*

A huge lump forms in my throat, and I have to fight the tears forming in my eyes, making everything blurry. Smiling, I cup her cheek and bring her face closer, crushing her lips against mine. I've barely touched her tongue when Sam complains.

"Yo. I didn't volunteer to drive so you guys could make out in the backseat of the car like two horny teenagers."

Red leans back, facing Sam to stick her tongue out.

"Please, don't do that, sweetheart, unless you want me to stop the car and have my way with you."

The scent of arousal fills the car, making me squirm on my seat as the bulge in my pants increases. Damn wolf libido all to hell.

"Jesus Christ. What's going on? Why are we all so turned on right now?" Tristan asks, but it sounds more like a growl.

"It's the heat. I feel it coming back," Red replies.

Tristan swivels around, watching her with his mouth hanging open. "You're going into heat? Since when?"

"It started right after the battle in Shadow Creek."

He rubs his face, cursing under his breath. "In regular wolves, the heat period can last days. We'll be completely vulnerable when it does."

Red covers her face with her hands. "Why must everything happen all at once?"

"It's all Murphy's fault. Fuck that asshole," Sam says, managing to get a chuckle out of Red.

The level of tension and arousal decreases a notch and in good timing. As I peek out the window, I realize we're approaching the bend with the concealed dirt road.

"Sam, the turn we must take is after that curve."

Sam slows, and I continue. "There. Turn right over there after that weird-shaped tree."

"Are you sure? There's no road there," Tristan asks.

"Yes. This is it. I remember now." Sam takes the road. It's clearly visible to me, but maybe not to everybody. From the corner of my eye, I catch Red grab the door's handle and tense, as if she's bracing for impact.

"Holy crap. That was a seriously strong concealment spell. I thought we were going to hit a tree for sure," Red says once we're through the illusion.

"Yes. Your grandmother really didn't want anyone to find this cave."

"She cast that spell alone?"

"Well, that I don't know. But she still has a lot of juice for an old lady," Sam replies.

"Do you think that maybe her powers aren't one-hundred-percent witchy?"

"What do you mean?" I glance at Red, not getting where she's going with that.

"Prythian said my powers were different. It seems the more I dig, the less I know about myself."

"I'm having the same doubtful thoughts. I've always assumed I inherited my gift from Mom, but what if that's not the case? She only gets visions; she's never felt the urge to paint anything or forgets what she saw afterward. When

I'm in the middle of one my trances, I don't know what I'm doing."

"I hate the feeling I'm not in control of my own destiny, that someone is controlling all the strings and I'm nothing but a puppet," Red continues.

"I'm not sure if we can ever have such control. It seems everything that happens in one's life is preordained," Tristan adds, turning the mood down.

"Good grief, Tristan. Snap out of that funk. You can't develop a woe-is-me attitude now that I've finally gotten used to your asshole ways."

Tristan snarls at Sam. "Are you ever going to stop with the stupid jokes?"

"Ah, that's better." Sam laughs.

"Hey, is that fallen tree trunk real or just another illusion?" Red points ahead.

"No. That's real." Sam parks the car, and we hop out.

"We walk the rest of the way," I explain.

"I've never been to this forest before. Not that I'm a big fan of hikes, but Grandpa used to take me out when he was teaching me how to shoot."

"You can shoot? I didn't know that." Sam watches her with a puppy-love glint in his eyes. I'm sure mine shine the same way whenever I gaze at her.

"Yes, I'm fairly good at it actually. Not that I'm going to have much use for it now, considering my instinct when I'm in danger is to shift, not to grab a gun."

"I wish our enemies thought that as well. Unfortunately, Seth didn't have a problem using guns against his own kind," Tristan says.

"I wonder where he is. He must be planning something," Red continues.

"The only time I ever mentioned Seth to Harkon, he laughed. I got the impression Seth is just another pawn the demon will soon get rid of."

"Yeah, but until Seth meets his demise, he can still do a lot of damage. I'd feel better if we ended him," I say, letting all my anger toward Tristan's former friend show in my voice.

"Don't worry, brother. If Seth ever shows up again, I'll gladly slash his throat." Tristan jumps over an exposed tree root, landing farther than he needed to in order to clear the obstacle.

A cold gush of wind comes barreling from the top of the hill, sending chills down my spine. Red trembles before she hugs herself. I'd pull her into my arms if that wouldn't make her go in heat faster.

"The cave is straight ahead." I point in the direction.

Less than a minute later, we arrive at the clearing where the cave of witches lays semi-hidden underneath some vines. Red stops suddenly, her body shaking a little. Her reaction puts me on high alert. Expanding my senses, I search for any malevolent presence nearby. I don't pick up on anything wrong, nor the presence of any ghosts.

"What's wrong?" I ask.

Hugging herself, she replies in a whisper, "I've been here before."

Chapter 40
Red

I don't know where the certainty comes from, but I have no doubt I've been to this place before. Maybe in my previous life as Natalia. I take a step forward only to be stopped by Dante, who grabs my hand and pulls me back. The touch sends a flare of craving up my spine, making me hiss. He drops my hand quickly, cutting me an apologetic glance.

"Careful. The last time we were here, your grandmother had to cast a spell to be granted access. There are wards protecting this place."

"I can sense them. I can almost see the power strands of their make up."

"Can you undo the spell?" Tristan asks.

Raising my hand, I let my power ebb freely through me until it whooshes from my fingers. It goes right through the barrier without a problem.

"I believe so," I reply.

Taking a deep breath, I head for it, sensing the barrier's resistance when my body connects to it. It's weak, and I barely have to do a thing to breach it. But once I'm through, I discover it was only the first layer. I sense two more. Another gust of chilly wind wraps around me, sweeping my hair in different directions. It takes me a moment to realize it's not a natural occurrence. The wind is sentient.

"So, you've finally returned to collect what's rightfully yours," a disembodied voice speaks, giving me effing chills. Oh man, I think I'm going to side with Sam and say I don't like ghosts either.

"Who is this?" I ask.

"You don't remember. Pity." A woman materializes in front of me. She has light brown hair that flows unnaturally around her, and she's wearing a beautiful deep blue gown. I guess it's from the nineteenth century, but I'm not an expert in historical fashion.

"There's a lot I don't remember. I'm here because I'm tired of being in the dark."

The ghost smiles, but it's sinister as hell. "Yes, she didn't want you to remember everything. She's afraid."

"Who is afraid?"

The ghost cocks her head, then peers over my shoulder. "I see you brought company. The one with the deepest frown I remember from lives past. The other two came with the old hag not too long ago."

"You know Tristan?" I ask, guessing he's the one the ghost referred to first.

"Of course. However, we can't allow them to enter. The secret you seek can only be unveiled to you alone."

"Why?"

"Because she commands it so."

"Who does? My grandmother?"

The ghost laughs. "Child. You truly know nothing."

I bristle at her comment. "I'm doing my best to remedy that."

"Before we allow you to come farther, you must prove you have the power to do so."

"Why?"

"Because without it, you can't find what you're seeking."

"Red, what's going on?" Sam asks.

Why is he asking me that? Oh wait. "They can't see you, can they?"

"I thought it was best if they didn't. The youngest wolf boy almost soiled his pants the last time he came here."

I try to smile reassuringly at Sam. "It's okay, Sam. I'm just trying to break through this ward."

His jaw hardens as he tells Dante. "I don't like this."

I switch my attention to the ghost. "All right. What do I have to do?"

"You have to breach through the next ward."

I raise my hand, feeling a stronger resistance in this second barrier. When I try to break through, my hand receives an electrical shock. "Ouch." I yank it quickly away.

The ghost laughs again, making me angry.

"This isn't funny."

"Oh, but it is."

Ignoring her, I focus on the strands of energy in front of me. The longer I study them, the clearer they become. This is so strange. Why can I see magic like this? I was never able to do it before. *You can think about that later, Red.* The strands form intricate knots, creating a net all around the perimeter. If I can undo some of those knots, I might be able to open a hole in the barrier.

I start with one knot at first. Using my powers, I imagine them becoming loose. Nothing happens for a few seconds, but then a strand finally moves. I put all my energy into it, until the first knot is undone. Once I get the hang of it, undoing the remaining knots happens in the blink of an eye. My intention had been to only create a hole big enough for me to pass through, but I end up unravelling the entire thing.

"Not bad," the ghost says. "Let's see how you fare in breaking the last barrier."

There's a hint of malice in her tone, which makes me suspect this last one won't be so easy to clear.

I reach for it with my hand first, just like I did with the first two. Only this time, I find something solid, an invisible wall. When I focus my power on it, the tips of my fingers turn hot, but the barrier won't give. Damn it.

The ghost chuckles. "Lena definitely had no intention of ever letting you in here."

"Lena?" Why does that name sound familiar?

"How about I give you a hint?"

I expect the ghost to tell me something, not to barrel through me and get into my head. Not prepared for the assault, the mental shields I have in place are useless against her. With a gasp, I fall to my knees. Then, the forest vanishes, and I find myself in a strange room illuminated by torch lights. With a quick glance, I notice the four-poster bed where sheer fabric is draped on top. It's covered with some kind of animal skin and white sheets. There's a fire roaring in the fireplace on the other side of the room where a woman wearing a simple robe is crouched.

"What am I going to do, Lena? Alesandro does not wish to run away with me. Do you think he no longer loves me?" I say, even though I have no conscience of forming the words in my head. *Am I relieving a moment of one of my past lives?*

The woman unfurls from her crouch. She's fair with blonde hair pulled back by a single side braid. Wisps of curly hair have escaped and are now framing her face. She's young—my guess in her mid-twenties. But it's her eyes that give her away. She's Grandma.

"He is not only a man, Calisto. He is a prince. I have warned you about the dangers of giving your heart to him."

Calisto was hoping for kinder words, a pretty lie, not her friend's blunt truth. My heart squeezes tightly as she stares blindly at a random fixture on the wall.

"I did not wish to fall in love with him. I do not even remember how it happened. When I realized, I was already in the middle of it."

"It is not your fault. You lived most of your life away from Eneas's house and its depraved ways. If anyone is to blame, it is Alesandro. He used his experience and malice to seduce you."

Calisto glances once more at the woman, fury coursing through her veins. "Alesandro is not cruel like that, Lena. He loves me."

"If he did, then he would defy his father and ask for your hand instead of doing exactly what the king commands. Alesandro is a spineless coward who does not deserve you. You should pledge yourself to the goddess like I did."

Calisto shakes her head. "I was not born to a life of prayers and lack of human touch."

"You mean the lack of a man's touch. Have you been foolish enough to have lain with Alesandro, Calisto?"

It's impossible to miss the judgmental tone of her question.

Calisto lifts her chin. "Yes, I have. And spare me the lecture. I do not regret it."

Lena's face twists into a grimace. She opens her mouth to protest, but a loud knock on the door interrupts her.

"Who is it?" Calisto asks.

"It is Hector. King Eneas requires your presence in the audience room."

Calisto frowns as a shiver of apprehension runs down her spine. I'm stuck inside her head as a spectator only, but I know the request is strange. It's late, and the king has never once requested her presence at this hour. Glancing at Lena, Calisto finds her focused hard on the closed door with her face twisted in suspicion.

"I will be there in a moment," Calisto replies, scanning around her room in search of something.

"I am under orders to escort you now."

With shaking hands, she tries to smooth out the lines from her simple dress. Then she fidgets with her hair. The braid is still in place. Lena heads for the door, but waits for Calisto to give her the signal to open. She does so with a nod.

Hector is the head of the king's personal guard. Once again, the knowledge enters my mind as if it has always been there. It's easy to see why he was selected for the position. The guy is huge, with muscles that could rival solid rock. But I suspect it's his brutish facial features that makes him a person not to be messed with. He has a face only a mother could love. His eyes are spread too far apart, framed by a thick unibrow. His nose is large and crooked. My guess it has been broken in the past, maybe more than once.

Calisto keeps her gaze down as she walks out of the room. I wish she would lift her chin so I could get a glimpse of her surroundings. She doesn't because she once made the mistake of looking into Hector's eyes, and the soulless glint she saw there made her terrified of the man. It's surreal how I can retain my own thoughts, yet also feel exactly what Calisto is thinking.

The trek down the gloomy corridor doesn't last long, and then I'm crossing the threshold of double doors that are already open. Two guards are stationed there, one on each side. The king—Calisto's uncle—was a very suspicious man, afraid there were assassins lurking in every corner, ready to slit his throat. So he always had guards securing any room he was in.

Through Calisto's eyes, I see him sitting on his throne, and a spear of anguish goes through my heart. I can't breathe as my airways become constricted thanks to the bolt of panic that takes a hold of me.

With a gasp, I'm hurled into my own body in the present time. It takes a moment for my senses to return, but when they do, I hear three men shouting my name while the ghost laughs and laughs.

I throw her a glower before I get back on my feet. "Can they see you now?"

"They sure can. I couldn't resist."

I hold out my hands in a reassuring gesture, trying to smile at my mates. "I'm okay. She didn't hurt me."

"What happened?" Tristan asks.

"Another trip down memory lane." I wipe the dirt from my pants.

When they all continue to stare at me like I'm going to break or something, I feel the need to comfort them. "Truly, guys. I'm okay."

"I'd feel better if we could get to where you are. Why can't we cross the wards?" Dante asks.

"I don't think these wards are the same as the ones you've encountered before," I say on a hunch.

"You mean Shady Grandma came back here and changed them?" Sam asks, but then shrugs. "Well, that doesn't surprise me."

I try to reconcile what Sam just said to what the ghost made me see. She said Lena didn't want to let me in the cave. But Lena is Grandma. Why would she keep me away? What is she hiding from me? My chest becomes so heavy it's hard to draw in air. What if Grandma remembers her past lives? Did she do something she doesn't want me to remember? It would fit what the ghost said a moment ago. Damn it. I have to break through this ward. I need to learn the truth.

When I try the barrier once more, it's still the same solid, impenetrable wall. Focusing on the strands of magic, I don't see knots to be undone. The energy is making a sleek and impenetrable shield. Well, if I can't unravel it, then I will have to break it.

I curl my hands into fists, concentrating all my power there. For good measure, I borrow part of my wolf's essence as well. Once my fists become as hot as if they were on fire, I hit the wall, grinding my teeth when my knuckles crack with the impact. White-hot pain shoots up my arms, but I swallow the scream. I don't want to worry the guys even more.

My knuckles don't break, though. What does crack is the barrier. It splinters like the windshield of a car when it gets hit by a pebble at a hundred miles an hour—in this case, my now-throbbing fists. Fissures expand in a spider-web pattern. Since I don't wish to injure either hand, I finish destroying the barrier with a powerful kick to its middle. It shatters completely, falling to the ground like raining glass.

Without waiting another second, I hurry forward just in case the barrier decides to rebuild itself. I don't want to punch it again. Lifting my chin, I stare at the ghost.

"Well, now what?"

She cracks a smile. "Now you get to meet my friends."

CHAPTER 41
DANTE

"Are we supposed to just stand here and do nothing?" Sam asks when Red disappears inside the cave, following the ghost.

"No," Tristan and I answer at the same time.

"What's the plan, then?" Sam lifts his hand, then pulls it back immediately when sparks of electricity ignite. "Ouch!" He shakes his arm out. "That thing just zinged me."

"We'll have to break through the barrier." I stare ahead, not seeing anything, but definitely sensing the power coming from the invisible shield.

"And how are we going to do that? We're shifters. We don't have magic mojo." Sam glares in my direction, placing his hands on his hips.

"We don't, but Dante does," Tristan replies.

Scrunching my brows in confusion, I peer at him. "I don't think my powers will help in this situation."

"You don't know that." Tristan narrows his gaze as if he's trying to read my mind. Maybe he can sense my turmoil and doubt.

I rub my face, glancing away from his knowing stare. Since the time I've spent with Prythian, I've been questioning the origins of my peculiar gift a lot. Mom once told me it's extremely rare for male descendants of witches to inherent their powers. It's usually only passed on to women. I've always assumed my case was different because of my shifter nature. But what if my powers have nothing to do with hers?

"I have no idea how I'm going to break down this barrier. It feels different than when we came here with Mrs. Redford," I say.

"I'm certain the old hag changed something. I'm telling you. She's hiding shit." Sam's posture tenses.

"You're right about that. She claims she's only a servant of the Goddess Artemis, and that she pretty much didn't have free will in certain matters."

"I call that bullshit. People always have a choice; they just choose the path of least resistance," Sam replies.

"Isn't Artemis supposed to be the protector of animals, wolves in particular?" I ask as an idea takes hold in my head.

"Do you think I know anything about goddesses?" Sam says, exasperated.

"She is," Tristan replies. "But I don't follow where you're trying to go with this train of thought."

"If Mrs. Redford answers to Artemis, it means she's real and she can be reached somehow. I want to try to communicate with her."

Sam laughs, and when I simply stare hard in his direction, he asks, "Wait? Are you serious?"

"More than anything. Tristan, you said you got a glimpse of Artemis's temple in ancient Greece, right? Maybe if I link our minds and we focus on that precise image, we can summon her."

"Don't you think this idea is a bit out there?" Tristan asks.

"Out there? Oh no, we've passed out there five exits back," Sam chimes in.

"I can always hurl you against the barrier to see if it breaks," I reply, twisting my lips into a smirk.

"We have nothing to lose. Let's give it a shot," Tristan says.

Sam opens his big mouth again, but Tristan cuts him off. "Enough already with the ill-timed jokes, Sam."

As it has always been with the three of us, Tristan loses his patience with Sam first. I expect Sam to talk back or flip Tristan off, but surprisingly, he doesn't. His face is dead serious now.

"All right. Just one question, though. What makes you think we have a shot of reaching out to a goddess like that?" he asks.

I take a deep breath. The idea didn't just spring into my head out of the blue. "Many years ago, I had a vision about a woman with flaming hair. She carried a quiver of arrows and a bow. She was surrounded by two wolves."

"You never showed us this painting before."

"No. It was one of my first visions. I believe I was ten or something like that. The painting was abstract at best, very confusing. No one has ever seen it, not even Mom."

"Why did you keep it hidden?" Sam arches his eyebrows.

"Because I was embarrassed. I didn't remember painting it for starters. As my visions came with more frequency and Mom eventually found out about them, I had forgotten all about my first painting."

Tristan turns to the cave again, his eyebrows and jaw set tight. "If what Mrs. Redford said is true, then finding out if you have a connection to Artemis is definitely worth a shot."

"I need you to open your mental shields, just like when I start a regular telepathic convo."

I close my eyes, but not because I need to. Talking to my brothers mind to mind has always been natural to me. But now I want to avoid their curious and expectant stares. I'm going completely blind here, and I need every ounce of concentration I can get.

"Okay, Tristan. I need you to picture that image from your recovered memory."

A temple built of large white stones appears before us. I can only see the front where the torches are lit. The statue of Artemis is in front of it. It's so similar to the painting of my first vision that chills run down my spine.

Besides the initial thrill of recognition, I don't sense any familiarity. There's nothing for me to grasp. I call her name, ask her to give us a sign that she's at least listening, but nothing happens.

"This isn't working, is it?" Sam asks.

"No," I reply, frustrated.

"I think we need to lower all of our shields, not only the

outer layers," Tristan suggests.

I hesitate, sensing Sam doing the same. "We've never done this before. If we do, we all be privy to one another's deepest thoughts and fears."

"I know, but I can't think of anything else to do. Trust me, I'm not looking forward to you and Sam poking around my head freely."

"Oh, Tristan. There's probably nothing interesting in that boring head of yours anyway." Sam chuckles, but he can't fool us with his humor now, not when we're linked like this.

"I suppose you have?" Tristan fires back.

"Hell yeah, I do."

"Seriously? Are we going to do this now? Focus, guys," I say. "We don't know what the hell is going on inside that cave. Red needs us to come through for her."

I lower all my shields completely, setting the example. Sam and Tristan follow suit, and it takes me a second to not get overwhelmed by the overload of information. It feels like I'm inside a carnival ride where I'm strapped to a wall and the thing keeps spinning and spinning while the world becomes a blur. I see my brothers' thought fragments as they move at incredible speed in front of my eyes.

"Jesus Christ. I'm glad I haven't eaten in a while. I'm getting seriously dizzy."

With a grunt, Tristan replies, "We need to focus on the same thing."

The first thing that pops in my head is Red. I hold on to her image. Bit by bit, the other images begin to slow, then fade into the background.

"Good news. We all still have our priorities straight," Sam says.

I know exactly what he means. The first thought that popped in our heads was Red, but in order for this to work, we must think of another person—no, not person, deity.

"This is the woman in my painting." I show them the memory of it, feeling a little exposed as I do. I guess I still have the same insecurities I buried deep down as a child.

At first, I train my thoughts on Artemis's face, but then something prompts me to lower my gaze to the wolves at her side. I don't know why my attention is riveted on them. My body suddenly feels light as it seems I'm falling toward the painting. No, that's not what's happening. I'm being sucked into one of the wolves' eyes.

In the background, I hear Sam's voice ask what's happening, but it sounds far away.

"Dante," comes the faint voice of a woman. "Why do you call me? You made your choice."

"Artemis?" I ask.

"Yes. Don't you remember my voice anymore?"

"No," I answer truthfully. I'm guessing I can't really hide anything from her.

"As it was meant to be. You wanted to be with my protégé. And because you were one of my favorites, I could not keep you against your wishes."

"I don't understand."

"You are not meant to understand. You and your brother made a bargain with me. Go be with her. Forget all about Mount Olympus and me."

"Are you referring to Red?"

"Yes, she goes by that name now. I wish I did not have to check up on her from time to time, but she also made a bargain with me."

"What bargain?"

"That is between her and me. Remember, you are not meant to remember."

Frustrated, I raise my voice. "But I have to remember! She's inside a cave filled with vengeful poltergeists, and we can't break the through the barrier. She's our mate, and we have to protect her."

The disembodied voice makes a tsking sound. "Lena was overzealous, but I am afraid it is more for her benefit than mine. She does not wish anyone to know about her shame."

"Lena? Do you mean Mrs. Redford?"

"Yes."

"Are you saying you don't care if we enter the cave?"

"I want to answer that I do not care, but I do. Those ghosts are tormented, and they can no longer discern between good and evil. They will tear you to pieces if you cross their domain."

"They didn't harm me before."

"That does not mean they will let you live this time."

"Please, can you break the barrier or not?"

The silhouette of a woman shimmers in front of me. When her features become sharper, a bolt of recognition hits me straight in my core. Artemis.

"Holy cannoli. Is that her?" Sam asks.

"Hello, Samuel. I have missed you as well." She smiles in Sam's direction.

"How come I have the feeling we've met before?" he asks.

Wait. Did Sam miss the beginning of my conversation with Artemis? And where's Tristan? I can't sense him anywhere.

"Your older brother cannot hear or see me. He is not bound to me, nor do I have any appreciation for him. To be quite frank, he is lucky Calisto loved him so much. I would have struck him down when he betrayed her in the most crucial moment."

"Typical Tristan. Always pissing everyone off," Sam muses.

"Can you undo the spell Mrs. Redford put in place or not?" I ask.

Artemis takes a deep breath. "If I do this, then I would need something in return."

"What?" I ask, uneasiness coiling within me.

"When your time on Earth comes to an end, you must return to me. Both of you."

I frown, not really understanding how that would work. My father's soul was collected by a reaper and then taken by an angel.

"You are thinking about your father. He was not like you, Dante. He was not one of my wolves."

"Is it nice where you live?" Sam asks, eliciting a smile from Artemis.

"Yes. It is wonderful. You used to love it."

"Then why did we choose to be born as shifters if it was so grand?" I ask, suspecting Artemis is omitting the truth.

"You both became fascinated with Calisto's reincarnation. She was called Natalia, I believe. It was the first time she was born a wolf shifter. But the power she carried inside of her was not from the witches."

"You gave her the power that allowed her to become the Mother of Wolves, didn't you?" I ask.

"Yes. Just like I gave you the gift of sight, and Samuel the gift of joy."

"Okay, now you know your powers are definitely not like Mom's," Sam chimes in again.

"Indeed not. As for Calisto, when I made the bargain with her, I became bound to my word to help her vanquish the foul creature Harkon. Sadly, the power I bestowed upon her was not enough. It was then that you and Samuel decided to live among humans and help her."

"I'll return to you if you help us now," Sam says.

Deep down, I know I'll regret this bargain, but if something happens to Red in that cave, I won't be able to live with myself. "I will, too. Now please, help us."

Artemis smiles, victory shining in her golden eyes. "Consider it done."

When she vanishes, the forest becomes visible again, but from the wrong angle. I'm lying flat on my back. Tristan appears in my line of vision, bug-eyed and panicked.

"Dante? Oh thank God you're awake."

I sit up, rubbing my eyes. "How long I have I been out?"

"A few minutes. You and Sam just collapsed to the

ground out of the blue."

Sam staggers to his feet, wincing as he does so. He lifts his hand, carefully probing the air in front of him.

"She did it. The barrier is down." He smiles, but it vanishes in the next moment when a woman screams. Red.

Chapter 42
Red

I follow the ghost into the dark cave with my heart stuck in my throat. For all my bravado, my palms are sweating and I'm having a hard time controlling the shaking of my body. I never enjoyed horror movies, and the last one Kenya convinced me to watch was *Thirteen Ghosts*. It scared the living shit out of me. I couldn't sleep for days. Now I get to meet a bunch of them. Fucking fantastic.

The cave is damp and cold, and it reminds me of the tunnels we had to take in the Wastelands. I barely returned alive from that hellish dimension, and here I am again, braving a place filled with evil poltergeists. Funnily, though, I wasn't as terrified then as I am now. *You weren't alone either, Red.* I wish Dante, Sam, and Tristan were here with me.

The walk down the narrow tunnel doesn't last long. It ends in a wider chamber, which is illuminated by torches mounted on the walls. It's still a little gloomy, and it takes a moment for my eyesight to adjust. When it does, I notice the ground has been disturbed right in the middle of the cavern.

It is as if someone tried to dig a hole or something. Come to think of it… can ghosts light torches? Shit, what if someone is here?

I begin to search the perimeter, barely taking note of the weird apparatuses spread throughout the place. A cold wind comes from out of nowhere. A second later, I feel their presence. The other ghosts. The woman who met me outside is floating above me, watching my freak-out moment with glee.

Phantom hands touch my body and mess with my hair. It takes herculean effort to stay rooted to the ground instead of bolting out of this place.

"Welcome back, Natalia. Or is it Amelia now?" one of the ghosts asks, then cackles away.

Digging my nails into my palms, I force myself out of the grasps of fear. I won't be controlled by it. It's ridiculous to be afraid of a bunch of poltergeists when I didn't hesitate to charge an archdemon.

"Stop touching me," I demand when I finally find my voice.

"Ooooh, she's still feisty," a disembodied voice says.

"Leave her alone," says the ghost who appears in front of me. She seems so young, almost a child still, but I won't be fooled by her innocent face.

I don't understand why these ghosts remain here. Why can't they find peace?

Watching her intently to try to guess what she has in store for me, I catch movement through her semi-transparent body. Straining to see more clearly, I spot a person lying on the floor. It only takes a moment for recognition to pierce me—spurred by the sight of yellow hiking boots, the ones Grandma loves.

"Oh my God. What have you done to her?" I break into a run, but before I can reach her, I'm snatched away by an invisible force.

"She's not your concern. You came here for one thing, and that's all you're going to get."

I ignore the ghost child. "Grandma! Wake up."

Several ghosts emerge from the ground and the stone walls, screeching and laughing. They begin to taunt me, pulling my hair and flying through my body. I try to bat them away, which is pretty fucking stupid considering their ethereal nature.

Crawling, I try to get closer to Grandma again, but this time, a cold hand wraps around my ankle and drags me to my starting point.

"Did you kill her?" I ask.

"She's not dead, but why do you insist on helping her? Don't you know what she's done to you?" the child ghost asks.

"She doesn't remember a thing. That's why she needs the treasure that one over there hid here," the first ghost replies.

"I don't care what she did in a previous life. She's my grandmother. I have to help her."

Grandma moves, then she lifts her head. "Red, is that you?"

"Yes. It's me. Are you okay?"

"Just a little dizzy." Slowly swinging toward the ghost child, Grandma's expression changes. "Get away from my granddaughter, you little leech." She raises her hand, and a little sparkle crackles between her fingers.

"Oh, you're not going to use that trick on us again." The ghost in the blue dresses zaps toward Grandma, but before she can reach her, Grandma sends a spell her way. The ghost shrieks when the electric blast hits her. The other spirits begin to circle above us in a frenzy.

Grandma leaps to her feat, then runs to me. "Come on, Red. Let's get out of here."

I stagger to my feet, but stop. "No. I came here seeking answers, and I won't leave without them."

Grandma's eyebrows furrow while her lips become a flat line. "They'll kill us if we don't leave." She grabs my arm and starts yanking me out of the chamber, using tremendous force for someone her age.

Her attitude snaps me out of my initial shock. I pull my arm free from her grasp. "I'm not leaving. You can if you want to."

"You're not supposed to be here. She doesn't wish you to know."

"Bullshit. It's you who is afraid of the truth," I say, guessing Grandma is referring to Artemis. I address the ghost child. "Where is it?"

She points to the site where someone—*Grandma*—had already started to dig a hole. I run to it, dropping to my knees when I'm in front of it.

"Please, Red. I'm begging you. Certain truths are not

meant to be learned."

It sounds likes she's crying, but I block it out as I start to dig with my bare hands, breaking nails and scratching my palms in the process. The ground is made out of packed mud and rocks. *No.* There's gotta be an easier way to do this. If Grandma hid something valuable here, she would have concealed it with magic, not simply buried it.

Reaching for the power deep within me, I bring forth a ball of energy. It literally erupts from my chest, going straight toward the small hole in the ground. It disappears inside, cracking the surface around it. The light begins to expand until it encompasses the entire chamber. It's blinding, forcing me to close my eyes. My skin tingles as a whooshing sound fills my ears. Afraid of the disruption I caused by accident, I open my eyes again. Instead of the ghost-filled chamber, I'm now in Calisto's head. Back to that scene where she was summoned by the king.

Chapter 43
Red

Calisto's body is shaking, and she tries in vain to hide it by folding her hands in front of her.

"Good evening, my lord," she says, her voice small and almost without any substance.

"Calisto. The most beautiful woman to ever grace my palace. Isn't it, my son?" The king turns to a man Calisto had not yet seen, for he was hiding in the shadows behind the king's throne.

When he emerges, Calisto's heart skips a beat. She's in love with the prince, her own cousin. I don't recognize him at first. He's an attractive man for sure. Tanned with dark hair and a face carved to perfection. I suspect the great artists of the time used him as inspiration for their creations. Busy as I am taking notice of his features—and also trying not to drown in Calisto's affections for this man—I don't see what's right in front of my eyes. It's Tristan.

Now my own heart skips a beat—or it would if I had any sensation of my body. So this is where everything started. This is the beginning. Natalia's and Robert's lives were not what the great wolf apparition meant. And Grandma was too happy to allow me to believe it was.

"Yes, the most beautiful woman I have ever set my eyes on."

He's gazing at Calisto with the profound adoration only a man deeply in love can summon. Her body reacts accordingly, then she goes and remembers the night they made love for the first time. Just fucking great. I don't need to experience secondhand horniness. I have my own to deal with.

"Calisto, you're like a daughter to me. I want you to know that."

"Thank you, my lord."

The king waves his hand. "Let's not bother with those formalities tonight."

"Yes, Uncle."

"And as a member of this family, you also have duties to fulfill. You are to obey my wishes without second thought."

A sliver of fear drips down her spine. She glances at Alesandro, but he misses the gesture. He's busy staring at his father with his eyebrows furrowed.

"Yes, Uncle. I am ever your dutiful subject."

"Good, for it is with a heavy heart I must deliver you this news, my dear. You know our city has been plagued with ill fortunes. We have lost countless ships, and our people are dying of mysterious illnesses. I have spoken with my spiritual advisors and with the oracle. Through them, I learned that until we appease the demon that lives in the bowels of the Aegean Sea, our people will continue to suffer."

Oh my God. The demon. It must be Harkon.

"What are you saying, Father?" Alesandro asks.

"The demon demands a sacrifice. He has requested Calisto."

"No," Alesandro screams, but Calisto remains frozen. She doesn't utter a single word.

"I won't let you do that," the prince shouts. "There must be another way to appease the demon. I will slay the beast if necessary."

The king stands, towering over his son. "You will do no such a thing. I have already made the pledge, and preparations are in motion. To try to stop it would only unleash an even bigger evil upon our land. Is that what you wish, Alesandro? For your own people to perish and suffer?"

The king's words seem to take the steam out of Alesandro. With eyes filled with regret and anguish, he takes in Calisto's stricken countenance. But he doesn't try harder to convince his father. He does nothing but stare at her. I want to scream at him.

Calisto finally lets out a sob, covering her face.

"Hector, take her to her room. Under no circumstances is she to be let out."

"Is she your prisoner now?" Alesandro rounds on his father.

"Despite her promise to obey me without question, I find that when one's life is in jeopardy, duty and honor become scarce."

Hector grabs Calisto by her arm, ushering her away. I

wish I could control her body for I would have pulled free from his grasp. I'd forgotten for one second that what I'm seeing has already passed, and I can't change the outcome. Once again, I'm here hoping Alesandro will come after Calisto, but he doesn't. The poor girl cries the entire time she is herded to her room. I don't know why I keep thinking about her as if she were an actress in a movie. She's me—or I was her. Ugh. It's beginning to get confusing.

Lena is waiting in the room for Calisto, but when Hector enters and scans the space, his gaze travels right past the woman and he doesn't even blink. Did she cast a cloaking spell? He leaves soon after, locking the door behind him. Calisto runs to Lena's arms, sobbing incoherently for a good minute.

"What happened, Callie? What did the king want?"

Through her sniffles, Calisto tells Lena everything. Once she's done, she's no longer crying. Her renewed determination is finally apparent.

"I refuse to become a sacrifice. I will not die for my uncle. It is not fair."

"I have heard whispers the king has sold his soul to this demon. Saving his people is not his desire. He is doing it because he wants power. He wants to conquer the neighboring kingdoms."

"One more reason for me not to go through with it. Lena, I know I was never as devoted to the Goddess Artemis as you are, but I need to plead my case to her. Maybe she can help me."

Lena moves toward the fire. "I do not know if I can

summon her. She only appears for us when all the priestesses call upon her together to deliver offerings."

"Please, Lena. She is my only hope."

Lena whirls toward Calisto. "What about your prince? Can he not help you?" There's a tone of malice in Lena's question, but Calisto doesn't notice. Was that what Grandma didn't wish me to see? That she was jealous of her friend?

Calisto's eyes fill with despair, but she lifts her chin. "Alesandro has forsaken me. He barely pleaded my case with his father before he gave up."

"I will refrain from saying I told you so, and I will try to help you." Anger fills me on Calisto's behalf at Lena's self-righteous statement, but once again, Calisto doesn't seem affected by it.

Lena continues. "But you must come with me to the temple. Tonight."

"How are we going to slip out? Uncle has me locked inside this room."

"The king, for all his obsession with security, does not know half the secret passages in his own home."

Lena presses a hand to a brick next to the fireplace, and the entire wall rotates, revealing an opening.

Calisto's eyes widen. "How did you know about that?"

"My grandfather designed this place, and I was lucky enough that he did not think women should not learn things."

Calisto's thoughts wander back to Alesandro. If she'd known such secret passageways existed, she would have used it to meet with him. I can understand her logic, but her life is at stake, for crying loud. *Girl, priorities.*

Lena picks up a torch, then glances over her shoulder. "We need to go now."

Calisto follows her with her heart going a mile a minute. She doesn't know if she's shaking because of the death sentence hanging over her head, or if it's the idea she'll actually have to speak with a deity. *I wish I could fast forward this scene because being stuck in Calisto's head is torture.* The moment the thought enters my mind, the dark corridor vanishes and I'm inside a temple. *Whoa. I didn't know I could do that.*

Calisto is kneeling in front of an altar where a statue of the goddess stands. There are two wolves at her heels, and those animals stir something in my chest. Candles are lit all around the perimeter, casting a soft glow on the sand-colored stone steps. Lena is on her knees next to Calisto with her eyes closed. She's murmuring words, and my guess is she's praying to the goddess. *Shouldn't Calisto be praying, too?*

Lena lifts her head, then gestures at Calisto. "Now you must offer your sacrifice."

What's with these people and sacrificing shit? Calisto reaches over to the dagger that is standing in front of her. Her grip on the handle is tight when she slashes across her palm, drawing blood in an instant. The pain is sharp, but Calisto doesn't seem to mind it. She curls her fingers, squeezing the drops of blood onto the altar.

"Oh Supreme Goddess Artemis, champion of nature, protector of women in peril, please accept my blood as an offering of eternal servitude."

Nothing happens for a couple of beats, then the statue in front of them shimmers and comes to life. Artemis is beautiful with her flaming red hair and perfect facial features. Her clothes are weaved in a fabric so fine I can easily see the contours of her body. As stunning as the goddess is, my attention is drawn to her wolves. They have also come to life. Two beautiful pure white wolves. Oh my God. Dante and Samuel.

My mind is reeling. Everything I thought I knew about the Wolfe brothers was wrong. I never once considered that maybe I also had a previous connection to Sam and Dante, not only to Tristan.

"You seek my help, child. But I have never once heard your prayers before."

Calisto bows her head. "I was a fool for ignoring my duties to thee. I did not understand the importance of nurturing my soul. I was vain, concerned only with material things."

"And carnal things as well."

Calisto's face becomes hot, but she keeps her gaze down. "Yes. That, too."

"I did not want to come, but Lena prayed so vehemently on your behalf I got curious."

That surprises me. Lena, up until now, hadn't acted like a true friend. I sensed a lot of resentment on her part. But I still don't know why.

"Thank you," Calisto replies.

"What is it that you want from me?"

"I want to escape the fate my uncle has decided for me."

"Only the most fanatic devotees will willingly offer themselves as sacrificial lambs. What a foolish man. Why tell you beforehand that he plans to slaughter you?"

"I do not know."

"His ego is bigger than his brains. He does not believe Calisto will attempt to go against his will. Or this is a trap to test his son's loyalty," Lena replies.

"Ah, yes. The young prince. What would you have me do, Calisto?"

"Can you kill the demon?"

"No. That I will not do. I do not meddle in the squabbles of mortals and lower beings such as sea demons."

"Then help me escape."

"Oh, child. That will not help you at all. If the demon has his eyes set on you, he will follow you no matter where you go."

Calisto lets out a shaky breath, and desperation begins to take hold of her. Meanwhile, I sense Artemis's gaze on her. Finally, after what it feels like an eternity, she speaks. "Then help me defeat him."

Calisto jerks, eyes flying to Artemis's face. "Defeat him? Am I capable of doing that? Tell me how."

"You do not mean that, Calisto. You cannot possibly fight a demon."

She stares defiantly at her friend. "Do not underestimate me, Lena."

"What would you give me in return if I provided you the weapon to defeat Harkon?"

"Anything you want," Calisto replies. I get that she's

desperate, but no one should simply say that to a deity.

"Will you pledge yourself to me in this lifetime and in the next ones to come?"

"Yes."

"Think wisely, child. I demand much from my servants."

"I would rather serve the great Goddess Artemis than suffer eternal damnation at the hands of a demon."

A wolf howls, drawing Calisto's attention to it. Artemis notices her stare, but continues. "I do not like the comparison, but I believe my wolves have taken a liking to you. Very well."

Artemis reaches behind her, then pulls an arrow from her quiver. In her hands, it glows a bright blue. Both Calisto and Lena gasp.

"This is one of my sacred arrows. It's a powerful weapon, capable of killing gods. You must aim it at the heart of the demon when he comes for you. You cannot miss."

Artemis holds out the arrow. Seeming mesmerized, Calisto reaches for it, cradling it almost reverently.

"I am going to need a bow," she pronounces, then shifts toward Lena.

Then I see what Grandma tried so hard to hide from me. Pure jealousy shines in her eyes. But Calisto doesn't notice it. If she had, she wouldn't have said the following, "Lena, you can help get the bow, right? When they tie me to the sacrificial pole, you can hide the bow nearby."

"And how are you going to free yourself from your bindings?"

Calisto bites her lips. That's a problem she hadn't

considered.

"Use the tip of the arrow to cut through the bindings. Not even the thickest iron can withstand its power," Artemis says.

"Then all I have to do is make sure I hide the arrow well," Calisto says, feeling hopeful for once.

She curls her hands tighter around the arrow. I'm ready to speed these memories to the moment she tried to kill Harkon when loud screaming pierces my ears. I'm hurled back into my body, and then I feel something sharp prick my finger. I glance down to find Artemis's arrow in my hand, or what's left of it anyway. It's broken in two pieces.

The poltergeists are once again agitated, circling above me and screeching like banshees. They aren't aiming their wrath in my direction, though. Tristan, Dante, and Sam are in the cave, braced for a fight.

Chapter 44
Samuel

I'm seized by a moment of panic when I see all those crazy ghosts circling above Red, like sharks in a frenzy. But I fight against the feeling. I was one of Artemis's wolves for fuck's sake, and Red is in danger. The bond manifests, stronger than ever before. With it comes the need to protect my mate. My wolf stirs savagely in my chest, ready to be set free, and I want to give in to the animalistic side of me.

"Don't shift," Dante's voice sounds in my head. *"It's futile against them."*

I growl louder, pissed I can't let loose. Red takes us in with wide eyes, then switches her attention to the right. I follow her line of vision, and look who we have here. Shady Grandma. In the flesh. How the hell had she gotten here so fast? I thought she was still at the alpha's manor drinking tea with Mom.

Red jumps to her feet, holding something in her hand. I think it's a broken arrow. That's the treasure Shady Grandma didn't want her to have?

"Come on. Let's get out of here." She runs toward the

exit, but one scary ghost barrels down on her.

"Watch *out*," I yell too late. The ghost pushes Red to the side, and the force sends her rolling.

"Damn it. How can they touch us?" I ask, searching for a path without any crazy ghosts flying around.

Red jumps to her feet, sticking the broken arrow inside her shirt. I'm so focused on her that I don't realize her grandmother has moved closer to us.

"I'll distract the ghosts. You grab Red and get the hell out of here."

"Why are they acting like that?" Tristan asks. "Did you set them on us?"

"I didn't set anyone off. You did that on your own when you barged in here."

Furrowing her eyebrows, she raises her hand. Sparks fly from the tips of her fingers, converging between her hands until they form a sphere of power. The ghost we saw outside, the woman wearing the blue gown, notices what Shady Grandma is about to do and lets out a scream so high it almost pierces my eardrums. She then flies in Red's direction, not noticing until too late that Red's ready for her. She hurls a blue sphere at the ghost, hitting her square in her chest.

I see a disruption in the attack. That's our chance. I break into a run toward Red with my brothers following closely behind me. The ghost of a child appears suddenly, blocking the way. I skid to a halt, not wanting to run right through her.

"You should not have come. Now you must pay the

price." Her jaw opens in an unnatural way, revealing razor-sharp teeth as if she were indeed a shark.

"What the fuck is that?" I ask in horror.

"A true poltergeist, bro," Dante replies.

She comes at me faster than lightning, making me really wish I had shifted. Another power sphere smacks her, and she vanishes into thin air.

Red sprints the rest of the way, barreling straight into my arms. "Let's go."

"You don't need to say it twice, my love." Lacing our hands together, I spin around and aim for the exit, but once again, those fucking ghosts get in the way.

"Keep going," Shady Grandma calls. "I'll handle them."

"No, Grandma. You have to come with us."

"Listen to your grandmother, Red. She can take care of those ghosts. We can't," Tristan insists.

Red hesitates for a brief second, and it's enough for me. I pick her up, throwing her over my shoulder.

"Sam, what the hell! Put me down."

"Not a chance." I speed toward the chamber's exit. Despite Shady Grandma's efforts to keep those ghosts at bay, some still get to us. They scratch and pull at our clothes, but I suspect these are the weaker ones.

I don't stop until we're out of the cave and a safe distance from its entrance.

"Sam, if you don't put me down this second, I'll kick your ass." Red hits my back with her closed fists, but instead of feeling pain, all I feel is the awakening of the mating bond. It must have struck her at the same time because she stops struggling.

I set her down. It's only with great effort that I manage to take a step back from her. When I glance at my brothers, they're frozen statues save for their labored breathing.

"Is this happening now?" Red asks.

"I'm afraid so," Dante replies.

"The cave is not protected. Those ghosts are free to get out and attack us," Tristan replies, his voice tight. Shit. He must be having a hard time controlling his desire as well.

"What are we going to do?" Red's gaze bounces among the three of us.

Loud shrieks come from the cave, getting nearer. Red's grandmother comes running out, clutching at her shoulder. I can smell her blood from here.

"She's hurt." Red tries to go to her. On impulse, I hold her back. Big mistake. The urge to mate becomes the only thing I can think about.

Shady Grandma stops suddenly, facing the cave. A couple of the ghosts escape, but when she raises both her hands, I can almost see the barrier repairing itself. Once it's done, she throws a harried glance over her shoulder. "What are you waiting for? Go. You don't have much time before you're consumed by lust."

"Come on." Dante touches Red, pushing her into motion, but I can see it was a bad mistake, so I grab him by the back of his shirt and pull him away from her.

"What the—"

"Snap out of it. The lust is taking over your senses," I say, thinking how ironic it is that I'm the voice of reason in this moment.

"Sam is right. We should avoid touching Red at all costs."

"How did you manage to break the barrier?" she asks, not slowing down.

"Dante managed to get us a meeting with the Goddess Artemis," I answer.

"What? You spoke to her?" Red stops suddenly, not hiding her surprise when she pivots around.

"Only Dante and Sam were granted an audience," Tristan replies.

"Hey, don't be a hater because you weren't invited." I smirk at Red. "Apparently, Tristan managed to piss Artemis off in one of your past lives."

"Enough about me. It's getting harder and harder to keep my hands to myself," Tristan says.

"Where are we going?" Red asks, right before our car becomes visible when we round the bend.

"Oh my God. Do you think it's wise to get confined in a car with Red? My dick is already about to explode." I try to rearrange my erection into a more comfortable position without any luck.

"I'm not going to give into the heat out here in the forest," Red replies through clenched teeth.

"Why not? We're wolves," Dante argues before I can.

"Because... I, ugh. Do you really want to have an orgy so close to that haunted cave?"

I don't know about the others, but the idea puts a wrench in my libido, albeit a really small one. I've never been so aroused in my life, not even when we rescued Red and had our first threesome in Xander's hideout.

Red stops next to the driver's door. "Who has the key?"

"I do." I throw it to her. Can't risk getting any closer.

"All right. I'll drive, and you all sit in the back." She unlocks the door, then slides behind the wheel before we have a chance to say anything.

"Where to?" she asks once we're all in the car.

"Fuck. We're at least twenty minutes from town." I glance out the window, making sure no ghosts are coming after us.

"There's a bed and breakfast on exit twenty-two," Dante says.

"You want to go to a B&B? Are you out of your mind?" Tristan glares at Dante, who is sandwiched in the middle.

"Do you have a better idea?"

Red puts the car in drive and takes off. "I don't care where we're going. As long as it has a roof over our heads, I'm game. It's getting painful to resist what's happening to me."

"And it's not healthy either. Wolves who fight off the natural instinct to mate can go crazy," Dante remarks.

"Great," Red mumbles under her breath.

"Gee, Dante, we know you're a textbook with arms, but must you part with your knowledge all the time?" I glare at him.

"What? Do you want me to lie and tell her everything will be okay?"

"Exit twenty-two you said?" Red asks. I notice she's

holding the steering wheel with such force her knuckles are white.

"Yeah. It will come up after the bend," Tristan replies.

"Do you think…" Red pauses, and the strain in her voices tells me we don't have much time. "Do you think Grandma will be okay?"

"Yes," we all answer in unison.

"Don't worry about her, sweetheart. She can handle a few ghosts," I add.

"I found her unconscious inside the cave."

"They probably caught her by surprise. She had the situation under control when we left," Tristan replies, watching Red as if he's about to leap to the front seat.

"Exit twenty-two straight ahead." I point at the road.

"Oh, thank God," Red breathes.

She takes the exit, and it's another two minutes before the sign to the bed and breakfast appears. But when we turn into the driveway and see all the cars parked there, we realize this was probably a huge mistake. The parking lot is full, which means they might not even have a room for us.

Red parks right in front of the main building, then rests her forehead against the steering wheel. Her face is flushed and sweaty while her breathing is shallow. God, she's hurting, which only makes it harder to resist the pull.

"Wait here. I'll go see if they have a room available." Tristan exits the car, then plucks at his pants, trying to hide the bulge there.

"A few more minutes longer, honey," Dante says with difficulty.

"I can't stay in the car any longer. It's taking every ounce of my self-control not to jump to the front seat." I open the door, my muscles protesting as if they have been put through the ringer. It feels like I have a terrible fever.

I take a deep breath of air sans the mating scent, which should help, but it doesn't. My wolf knows his mate is inside that car, hot and ready. *Ugh. No. Don't think about it, Sam.*

Tristan trudges out in the next moment, not looking happy at all.

"What is it?"

"They don't have any rooms available, but after I paid a huge sum of money to the owner, he agreed to lets us use the barn."

"He didn't ask what for?" I raise an eyebrow.

"He's also a shifter." Tristan's hard reply tells me there's more to the story.

"What kind of shifter?"

"A squirrel."

"Come again?"

"You heard me. Now let's get going." Tristan knocks on Red's window. The moment she lowers it, her scent hits me on full blast. How Dante is able to stay put in his seat is a mystery to me. I find myself inching closer without realizing I'm doing it.

"Drive around the main building and park in front of the barn," Tristan tells her, his voice more animalistic than human.

Red's eyes are glazed already. She manages a nod, then drives off. Tristan and I follow on foot—more like run after

the car, actually.
"I've never met a squirrel shifter before. Did you tell him why we needed the barn?"
"No need. He guessed. That's why he charged me so much money. Little rodent."
When we get to the building, Red and Dante are already inside. The place is not a five-star accommodation, but it's only being used to store hay and other farming materials. Regardless, the ground could have been covered in manure and I wouldn't have noticed. All I can think about is the woman in front of me and how many times I can make her come.

Chapter 45
Red

Getting out of the car is a struggle. My legs feel like jelly, and my breathing is erratic thanks to the accelerated beating of my heart. I enter the barn first, all too aware of Dante following close behind me. As soon as I cross the threshold, I begin to undress. My clothes are suffocating me, chaffing my skin. I hear Dante's footsteps, but I don't move. I'm afraid if I do, I will combust on the spot.

"Red…" he whispers, and I finally have the courage to face him. My clothes are scattered on the ground, yet my skin still burns.

"Dante, I think I'll die if you don't touch me now."

"Me too, my love. Me too."

I don't need to ask what's keeping him from attacking me. It's respect for his brothers. He doesn't want to start this without them. The door to the barn bursts opens, and Sam and Tristan fill the entrance. Both stare at me with so much desire it's enough to send me over the edge. I don't realize what I'm doing until my own fingers find my clit. I climax before my mates breach the distance between us. Who lifts me off the ground or whose mouth is where is a mystery. All I can do is focus on the pleasure their caresses and kisses are giving me.

My back hits a bed of straw, and I open my eyes. Tristan is between my legs, licking and sucking my clit as he fucks me with his fingers. Sam is busy playing with my tits, running his tongue around my nipple while he kneads the other with his hand. His erection is pressed against my hip. Dante kisses my neck at the same time I'm assaulted by another orgasm. I cry out, not caring who might hear me.

"That's it, my love. Come for us," Dante whispers in my ear.

I reach for Sam's cock, barely squeezing him once before his warm seed spreads all over my hand. He lets out a groan, which only prompts me to keep pumping him. At the same time, Tristan's mouth moves away from my pussy. I open my mouth to protest, but when he spreads my legs farther apart, bringing my knees up, I turn to Dante.

"I want your cock in my mouth."

"Your wish is my command, my queen."

He changes position, bringing his erection closer to my lips. My mouth waters in anticipation. Curling my hand around his length, I bring his cock into my mouth, loving the taste and the smooth velvety texture on my tongue. At the same time, I feel Tristan's head at my entrance. I'm so wet that he slides in with ease. An amazing sensation begins to rebuild inside of me, curling around my spine to travel through my limbs in a tingling wave. I've never been so coordinated before, but I somehow manage to work Sam with my hands and Dante with my mouth without skipping a beat.

Tristan is merciless. He keeps on pumping in and out, faster and faster with each thrust. I arch my back when I can't keep an orgasm from hitting me again. In the most beautifully orchestrated symphony, Tristan, Dante, and Sam also climax.

All three collapse around me, but I'm far from satisfied. I'm covered in sweat, and I've lost count of how many times I've orgasmed so far, but my body wants more. I roll onto my belly, then slowly get onto my knees to better see my three beautiful, sexy wolves. I honestly can't tell who I want more. I want them all. Now.

But I move closer to Dante, choosing him at random. He seems to guess my intentions.

He rewards me with a lazy smile. "I love seeing this wanton side of yours, sweet Red."

"What? Was I too vanilla for you before?"

"No, far from vanilla," Sam replies.

"Maybe I should ride you next then." I wink at him.

"Oh no, no, no. Come here." Dante wraps his arm around my waist, pulling me on top of him. His cock is hard once again, and with a quick rotation of my hips, he slides in.

I let out a contented sigh before I begin to move, slowly at first, but it's impossible to be patient when my body is on fire. Sam and Tristan aren't satisfied to just simply watch. The kneel next to me, one on each side, and run their hands and tongues all over my skin. Dante, however, won't let me fuck him. Wanting control, he grabs my hips and thrusts upward.

"What? Wasn't I doing a good job?" I ask between breaths.

"Yes, too much so. I just can't help it. You feel so good, Red. So damn good."

"Oh my God. Are you getting bigger?" I ask.

Dante answers with a grunt, his fingers digging into my skin. His eyes roll back into his sockets for a second. Despite the lust haze clouding my mind, worry sneaks in. Is he having a vision?

"Dante?" I stop moving, bracing my hands on his chest.

Sam and Tristan must not notice my hesitation since they keep finding ways to torture me into oblivion. Sam is sucking one of my nipples hard. Tristan runs his hot tongue down my spine.

Dante's eyes fly open, glowing bright amber. "Fuck, Red. I'm so sorry."

"What fo—" My train of thought gets derailed when his cock becomes impossibly large, the tip hitting my G-spot. Dante lets out a howl, arching his back as he finds his release once more.

"I'm going to come again," I say, closing my eyes this time as I'm swept under a wave of unending pleasure. I try to move, but I can't. It's strange, but damn it, this feels too good, so I'm not complaining.

Dante's cock pulses inside of me as he empties himself. I might be imagining things, but it seems to go on forever, just like my own orgasms are lasting longer than the former.

Dante finally opens his eyes, his gaze still infused with lust.

"What were you apologizing for?" I ask.

"For knotting. I didn't know it could happen while I was in human form."

I don't know what he's talking about, but I don't have a chance to ask because Tristan grabs a fistful of my hair and brings my face to his. His kiss is as hot as lava, his tongue merciless and wicked. Dante's cock is still sheathed in me, but now fingers find my clit—I don't know whose.

Sam pulls me away from Tristan's kiss to capture my lips. This is by far the craziest experience I've ever had in my life, but also the most sublime. I'm a lucky woman to be loved by three amazing wolves. My heart is full, filled with joy and love.

I feel like I'm floating on air. In my haze, I realize I'm now on my back without knowing how I got there. Sam's body covers mine, all slick skin and velvet touches. Then he's in me, filling me to the hilt. He's huge, bigger than I've ever felt him before. The word *knotting* comes back to me. It's a fleeting thought, because with Sam fucking me like there's no tomorrow, I can't hold on to my sanity any longer. It all becomes a blur of sweet bliss and love. I'm high on ecstasy. My body shatters again, and then I do surrender to the wolf's heat completely.

Chapter 46
Tristan

I wake up first after I don't know how many hours of non-stop sex. Propping myself on my elbow, I scan the barn first. Soft morning light breaches through the cracks between the wood panels, giving the rustic environment a cozy feeling. It's morning, but of what day exactly? A female wolf's heat can last days. My eyes drop to Red, who is sleeping tucked between the three of us, Dante and Sam still in their wolf forms.

Maybe sensing my stare, she stirs in her sleep before lazily stretching her body. When she finally blinks her eyes open, it's clear of the lust fog from before.

"Hi." She smiles, making my heart soar. It's a smile that, deep down, I know I don't deserve.

"Hey, how are you feeling?"

"Sore everywhere, but incredibly happy." She glances at Sam's and Dante's sleeping forms.

"When did they shift? I don't remember."

"At one point, we all did."

She turns to me with her eyes as rounder as saucers.

"Did we, you know… in wolf form?"

"Are you asking if we mated as wolves?"

She blushes, which makes me chuckle. "Yeah, of course. Once you gave in completely to the heat, it was only natural that your wolf would spring forth. Don't worry. We didn't engage in bestiality."

She lets out a shaky breath. "That's a relief. I must confess I'm feeling a little embarrassed by all this. I mean, it was pretty wild." She frowns suddenly. "Wait, how long have we been here?"

"I don't know. I just woke up."

A loud knock on the door makes me tense on the spot. The sound also awakens Sam and Dante. They both jump onto their paws, growling at the door.

"Hello, are you guys alive in there?"

"Do you know who that is?" Red whispers to me, searching for something to cover herself.

"It's the B&B's owner. He's a squirrel."

"Huh?"

"A squirrel shifter," I clarify.

"Oh. I didn't know they existed." Finding her T-shirt under a pile of hay, she wrinkles her nose at it. "This looks like it has been chewed by a cat."

"Better a cat than any of those creatures in the Wastelands," Sam replies, standing naked in the middle of the barn with his arms folded.

Red puts her shirt on, then her eyes fix on him. She must be taking note of all the scratch marks on his arms and back.

"Did I do that?" she asks, confirming my suspicion.

Sam smirks at her. "Sure did, sweetheart. But don't worry. I enjoyed every second of it."

"Can I come in? I brought breakfast," the squirrel calls.

I turn to Red, making sure she's fully dressed. She found her pants as well, which is a shame. I didn't have enough time to appreciate her body post-sex marathon.

"Yeah, you can come in," I reply.

The door swings open and the squirrel comes in, carrying a large tray in his hands. The scent of fresh-brewed coffee, eggs, and bacon hits my nose, and my stomach grumbles in response.

Sam approaches the guy, then inspects the spread. "Nice. Thanks, man."

"It was the least I could do since I couldn't provide you with a room."

"But charged us ten times more for the barn." I spring to my feet, not caring I'm still naked.

The man's eyebrows shoot up. He has the gall to look offended by my remark. "I had to. It was a lot of work to keep the guests from wandering over here when they started to hear strange noises."

"Oh God." Red covers her face with her hands.

"How long have we been here?" Dante asks, having shifted back to his human form as well.

"Thirty-six hours, give or take."

"What? We've been gone for that long?" Red gets onto her feet, then begins to pace. "Everyone must be wondering what happened to us."

"Don't worry, sweet pea. Per Tristan's instruction, I

contacted Dr. Mervina."

Sam takes the tray from the squirrel. When he won't leave, he says, "Go on. I'm sure you have loads to do."

"I'm sorry. I've never been around a female wolf mated to three shifters at once." He continues to gape in Red's direction, making my protectiveness flare. Moving in front of her, I growl.

"Now you've seen it. Move along, squirrel, before I decide to have you for breakfast."

"The name is Tico," he hisses through his teeth, like his angry retort has any effect on me. He swings around, adding, "This is the last time I help ungrateful shifters."

Yeah, right. One thing I learned about dealing with smaller shifters like Robert is that what they lack in muscle power, they make up for in cunning. Just look at the foxes.

Sam places the breakfast tray on the ground, and we all sit around it. There's plenty of food to feed a family of five, but I know it won't be enough to make a dent in our hunger. We attack the food without regard for manner or the proper use of utensils.

"Oh my God. I've never tasted anything more delicious in my life." Red sticks an entire slice of bacon in her mouth before shoving a piece of muffin in, too.

"I thought my cock was more delicious," Sam teases.

Dante and I roll our eyes.

"It's yummy in a different way. Sadly, it won't give me sustenance." Red laughs.

"So, we've only lost a day and a half. Not bad," Dante says.

"I hope everything is okay at home. I'm really worried about Grandma." Red's forehead creases, her eyes unfocused.

"Did you discover why she was so keen on keeping you out of that cave?" Sam asks.

"Kind of. I saw glimpses of my former life as Calisto, the niece of a powerful man in ancient Greece. I don't know exactly the time of those events, but he was a king. It's strange, though. I thought oligarchy was how countries were governed back then."

Dante rubs his chin before he speaks. "He may have been part of the Argead Dynasty."

I stop chewing to stare at my brother. After twenty-five years, I shouldn't be surprised he's a walking encyclopedia, but he always finds a way to astound me.

"Come again?" Sam asks.

"The Argead Dynasty was an ancient Macedonian royal house of Dorian Greek provenance," Dante replies, but when we all keep staring at him, he adds. "Alexander the Great's royal house."

"Ahh, why didn't you say so from the start? There's no need to prove your superior intellect, nerd." Sam shoves another piece of bread in his mouth.

Dante narrows his eyes, but before he throws an angry retort at Sam, I ask Red, "What did you see in your memories?"

She turns her attention to me. "I saw you. Calisto was madly in love with Alesandro, one of your former incarnations."

I drop my gaze, afraid Red also saw how cowardly I was in that life.

"Man, I'm beginning to get jealous of your super-deep connection with Tristan." Sam pouts, and I feel the urge to slap him upside the head. He can be such a nimrod sometimes.

Red faces him and Dante with a little smile. "Don't fool yourselves. My connection to you and Dante is just as meaningful and strong. You were Artemis's favorite wolves, and yet, you chose to be with me."

"You know that?" Dante asks, and Red nods.

"Yes. You came with Artemis when Calisto called upon the goddess. I recognized you immediately."

"What happened during that meeting?" I ask. "What did Calisto promise Artemis?"

Red lets out a heavy sigh as her shoulders sag forward. "Calisto promised to be Artemis's servant for all eternity. I think that's why Natalia became the Mother of Wolves. Artemis granted her special powers so she could protect Artemis's favorite animals."

"But what did Artemis grant Calisto in return?" Dante asks.

"One of her arrows." Red searches around her. "Shit. Where is it now?"

I help her look, then spot the tip sticking out from under another pile of hay. "It's over there. I'll get it."

Leaping to my feet, I stride across the dusty barn, trying my best to ignore the stench I hadn't noticed until now. But it's all I can sense. The arrow is almost completely buried under the haystack. How in the world did it get there? Bending, I lift the stack to pull the arrow out without damaging it. If it's from ancient Greece's time, it must be fragile.

When I touch the shaft, an electrical shock runs up my arm. I scream in agony as my knees fold. Red yells my name, but it sounds far away.

"Let go of the arrow," she pleads, pulling at my arm. I can't move. My fingers seemed to be glued to it.

Then there's a flashing light, and the pain ceases for a moment. My body is floating on air. No, not my body, my soul.

"What the hell is going on?" Sam asks from nearby.

Swiveling, I find not only Sam has followed me into this ethereal plane, but also Red and Dante as well.

"Where are we?" Red asks.

"I don't know." We are surrounded on all sides by white fog.

"You are in my domain," a woman answers before her form materializes in the distance. The first thing I notice is her flaming red hair. When she comes into full focus, wearing a beautiful toga dress and carrying a quiver of arrows, I realize she has to be Artemis.

"Why are we here?" Dante asks.

"To be quite frank, I do not know. I sensed your presence, so I came to investigate. I definitely did not invite that one here."

She's glaring straight at me.

"Why do you hate me so much?" I ask.

"Because you are weak."

Artemis's words hurt as much as if she had run a spear through me.

"Tristan is not weak." Red quickly comes to my defense.

Artemis raises an eyebrow. "Oh, so he has managed to finally redeem himself after all these centuries? I observed your mortal lives in the beginning, but it got tedious after a while."

"Oh, great to know that fighting for our lives bored you," Red replies, not hiding her annoyance.

"Watch your tongue, child. Do not forget your place. You are my servant, just like Lena is."

"Okay, let's all calm down for a second." Sam flies in between Red and Artemis. "Since we got here by accident, can we at least see how Calisto managed to escape Harkon's clutches the first time? You know, for educational purposes."

Artemis's fiery expression softens. Sam and Dante were indeed her beloved wolves before, and she still cares about them. I hope that will keep her from unleashing her wrath on Red and me.

"Sure, if you want to see how your big brother and Red's grandmother crumbled in the most crucial moments of their lives."

Sam cuts his eyes to me, the expression of pity there making me angry. I don't need his sympathy.

"I'm ready," I say, but in reality, I'm far from it.

Chapter 47
Red

Still thinking about Artemis's harsh words to Tristan, I'm not prepared when we leave the white fog behind and are hurled to an ancient coastal city. We're still floating above it all, having a bird's-eye view of the beautiful coastline. The blue-green color of the Aegean Sea is a dark blue today, and its usual serene waters are violent. Waves crash against the jagged rocks in a show of white foam. If Harkon was a sea demon, then I'm sure he's responsible for it.

I scan the scene fast, searching for Alesandro and Calisto. It seems the entire city has gathered to see her slaughter. How those people can just stand there and do nothing brings bile to my mouth. Finally, a loud clamor erupts from the crowd, cheering on guards who wear helmets and carry long spears. They cut through the masses, carving a path to allow King Enea's chariot to pass through. Calisto stands next to him, pale as a ghost. She's wearing a simple white gown. For the life of me, I can't see where she could have hidden Artemis's arrow.

Alesandro follows behind the chariot on his horse, appearing tall and proud. My heart breaks a little. For a man who is about to witness the love of his life being sacrificed to a demon, he doesn't seem affected at all. I twist slightly toward Tristan, who is floating next to me, but not too closely. His eyes are riveted on the scene below, and his jaw is a rigid line.

"Wow, bro. I guess you've always had that arrogant countenance, huh?" Sam says in a light tone.

"Artemis gave you the arrow, but how are you supposed to shoot the demon without a bow?" Dante asks.

"Lena was supposed to hide the bow next to the sacrificial pole."

I search for her in the sea of people, but I don't find her anywhere. The chariot stops by the steps that lead to the jutted cliff where a pole has been erected. Already waiting there for Calisto are two hooded figures. The king has the gall to kiss Calisto on the forehead before sending her off to die. Alesandro remains on his horse, his face a stony mask.

"Is he not going to do anything?" Sam asks.

Suddenly, Alesandro climbs off his horse and runs to Calisto. King Eneas blocks his path, and they engage in a heated argument. I wish I could hear what they're saying.

"Can't we get any closer? I can't hear a thing," Sam says, scrunching his face as if he's trying something. With a grunt, he adds, "Damn it, I can't move."

"I don't think Artemis wants us to do more than watch," Tristan replies. "It doesn't really matter."

It's impossible to miss the bitterness in Tristan's

comment. I can't move down, but I can fly closer to him. "Tristan..."

"I'm okay, Red. As hard as it is to see you being betrayed by your own family and me, I have to watch so I won't make the same mistake again."

"You're not Alesandro. You're not Robert, either. You're Tristan, the grumpy wolf shifter I love. Don't let the past define who you are."

Sam cuts in. "Hey, something is happening."

Alesandro is no longer arguing with his father. He's sprinting up the stairs to where Calisto is. The hooded figures have already chained her to the post. They try to block Alesandro from speaking to her, but he lifts one of them off the ground, shaking him. God, I really wish I could hear what he's saying. When he drops the man to the ground, he and his companion scatter, running to where the king is.

Alesandro glances at the chains wrapped around Calisto's wrists before attempting to break her free from them. She shakes her head, and I'm betting she tells him about her plans. Alesandro pulls her face to his, crushing their lips together. He doesn't see that the king has sent Hector and another guard to the sacrificial ledge. Hector grabs Alesandro from behind, locking him in a chokehold. Alesandro tries to free himself, but he's no match for Hector and his alpine arms. In no time, Alesandro passes out. I'm not sure Hector didn't kill him.

Calisto becomes frantic as she tries to reach Alesandro. The other guard raises his arm, then slaps her hard across the face. Tristan, Dante, and Sam let out a growl. Even in this ethereal form, I can sense their aggression.

The guards leave Calisto alone finally, dragging Alesandro with them. The hooded figures light up a bonfire at the base of the rock, apparently starting the ceremony. The sea becomes more violent. The waves crashing against the cliff begin to reach higher and higher until Calisto is drenched from head to toe. Then a water vortex forms, its center as dark as tar. The wind changes, the sun disappearing behind the clouds. Harkon is coming. The crowd becomes restless when the shape of Harkon's horns emerge from the sea.

No one is looking in Calisto's direction. She takes that opportunity to pull the arrow from under her dress. She must have had it tied around her thigh. Like Artemis had promised, the tip of the arrow cuts through the metal chain, but Calisto makes sure they are still wrapped around her wrists. She shifts slightly to the left. With her foot, she moves a rock that concealed a fissure on the ground.

Harkon is already half out of the water, and even though he can't see me now, my spirit trembles. His skin is dark and scaly, covered in crevices that reveal a glowing ember beneath. Huge, spiraling horns protrude from his goat-shaped head. He doesn't resemble a demon that lives in the depths of the ocean at all.

Fear spikes my heart, not my own, but Calisto's. In a flash, I'm inside her head, seeing everything through her eyes. *What the fuck!* Why now when Harkon is here? My panic mixes with hers when she doesn't prepare to shoot the demon with Artemis's arrow. When I cease freaking out for a second and actually pay attention to what's going on, I see the fissure where the bow was supposed to be is empty. Lena didn't fulfill her part of the plan. Was she discovered by the king? No, if they knew she was trying to hide a bow by the sacrificial rock, they would have searched Calisto as well.

Oh, no. Grandma. You never brought the bow. Why? Was that the truth you were trying to hide from me?

A great shadow looms over Calisto. When she sees the great monster that's standing in front of her, she screams from the top of her lungs. Harkon laughs, and his putrid breath makes Calisto gag. Her fingers are still curled tightly around the arrow, but now she has no way of launching it at the demon. She does the only thing she can—she runs away. Harkon roars behind her, a terrifying sound that sends the crowd into a mad race to get out of the square.

Calisto doesn't slow, not even when King Eneas orders her to be shot down. The archers positioned at strategic points on higher ground take aim. The first arrow flies, missing Calisto by an inch. The second does find its mark, piercing her shoulder. She falls, and the sucky thing about being stuck in her head is that I feel the whole thing, the burning pain on her shoulder and the impact of her hitting the ground.

She manages to lift her upper body by leaning on one elbow. Her vision is hazy, but she doesn't miss the scene in front of her eyes. Alesandro is engaged in a sword fight with Hector, but the king, the odious man responsible for this mess, is nowhere to be seen. He probably fled. The fucking coward.

Calisto tries to get up, only to be caught by a gigantic clawed hand. Harkon's talons pierce her skin as he begins to squeeze the life out of her.

"Let me go!" She struggles against his hold, but the more she moves, the deeper his talons dig in.

"Calisto!" Alesandro shouts her name, and she manages to turn in time to see Hector's sword come down in an arc, cutting Alesandro straight down the middle.

"*No*," Calisto screams again, and her feelings are pure agony. I don't want to go through this again. I try to get out of her head, but it's in vain. I'm stuck there, and I bet this is all Artemis's fault. That bitch.

Harkon laughs as he brings Calisto closer to his face. "You're mine now. I look forward to making you suffer for all eternity."

"Never!" Calisto raises her arrow-wielding hand, then strikes when she's close enough. The arrow pierces his right eye, then blue lights bursts from it. Harkon drops Calisto to the ground, and I'm finally free to soar away.

I return to where Tristan, Sam, and Dante are. They circle me as if they want to embrace me somehow, but since we don't have bodies, it's kind of hard.

"Where have you been?" Sam asks.

"Somehow, I got stuck in Calisto's head. I couldn't get out until now. It was awful."

Gazing at the scene, I discover why I was suddenly released. When Harkon dropped her, she fell from a great height, hitting the stone steps and breaking her neck. Calisto is dead, and so is Alesandro, slain by his father's soldier.

Harkon has retreated to the sea. He managed to yank the arrow from his eye, and discarded the weapon—which is now broken in half—close to Calisto's body. A tingling sensation on my body warns me this trip down memory lane is about to end. Then I catch a glimpse of Lena rushing by, fighting against the few people who are still trying to run away.

She drops to her knees next to Calisto's body, then throws herself at her, wailing. That's the last thing I see before I'm thrust into my own body.

With a gasp, I sit up, my hand immediately going to my shoulder where Calisto was hit by the arrow. There's still a faint throb there. *No. It must be my imagination.*

A loud grunt on my left catches my attention. Tristan is on his knees, body folded forward while his arms hug his middle. Dark veins are spreading throughout his body, just like I witnessed happen to Valerius.

"Tristan!"

When he swings his head toward me, his eyes flash with a tinge of red. His canines have descended, too. "Red, he's back, and he's trying to take control of my body again. You need to run."

Chapter 48
Dante

"I'm not leaving you. There must be something we can do to help you," Red says, inching closer to Tristan.

I hold her arm, preventing her from advancing. Sam stands on her other side, ready to defend Red if Tristan succumbs to the power of Harkon. He falls forward, letting out a guttural scream. Red struggles against my hold.

"No. Don't get any closer to him."

"We have to do something," she pleads, her eyes already brimming with unshed tears.

Tristan rolls onto his back, holding his head as his face twists in what I can only guess is pure agony. There's no way I can just simply watch and do nothing. I have to help him.

Letting go of Red, I hurry to him, then drop onto my knees by his side. When Tristan focuses on me, his pupils are not completely red yet, but the dark veins around them are spreading down his cheeks. It means he's losing the fight against the demon.

"Run, Dante. Run," he begs as he tries to push me away.

"No. I won't lose you to Harkon again."

Acting on pure instinct, I hold Tristan's head between my hands, then do something I've never done before, at least not on purpose. I barge into his mind, breaking his natural barriers, which, at the moment, are as strong as a sheet of paper. Once inside, I sense Harkon's presence immediately. It's a dark seed he somehow left behind, dormant and undetectable until now.

"*What are you doing here, vermin?*" Harkon hisses as he tries to forcefully evict me.

Grinding my teeth, I use all the mental power I have to stay. "*You won't turn my brother into a puppet again.*"

"*You're a fool. Can't you see it's too late? He's corrupted beyond help. I made sure of it.*" The demon laughs, which only fuels my hate for him.

A great power unfurls in the pit of my stomach. I don't know where it's coming from. Maybe Artemis decided to help, for I'm sure this extra strength doesn't belong to me. But I don't care about its origin. Without wasting another second, I hurl the ball of energy at the darkness in Tristan's mind, rejoicing when Harkon shrieks. A violent, dark vortex forms, bouncing against Tristan's walls. Harkon is trying to stay in, but I won't let him. Bringing forth the mysterious power again, I hit the dark mass with bright light bolts, not stopping until the vortex loses momentum, finally vanishing from sight completely. A sense of relief washes over me, but it's fleeting. Harkon isn't completely gone. The damn chip is still embedded in Tristan's brain, and for as long as it's there, he'll be in danger.

"*Dante? What are you doing in my head?*" Tristan asks, sounding confused.

"*I managed to detain Harkon for now, but I couldn't extricate him completely from your head.*"

"*It's all my fault. When I entered his mind, I inadvertently created a link between us. I brought that dark seed with me.*"

I sense Tristan's loathsome feelings toward himself. It couldn't have been easy to remember all his past lives' mistakes. But I can't let him succumb to the guilt that's eating away his soul.

"*Don't fucking blame yourself for it. And don't you dare think for one second that you're weak or worthless. I don't care what Artemis said. You're my hero, Tristan.*"

"*I'm nobody's hero.*"

"*Yes, you are. You've never fooled us, brother. You've always put Sam and me first.*"

"*You don't know what you're saying.*"

"*Really? Shall I make a list? Our entire lives, you've always wanted to try everything first, not because you were a cocky bastard, but because you wanted to protect us from harm. You took the helm of Wolfe Corp—even though that job bored you to death—because you knew Sam and I would hate ourselves if we had to do it.*"

"*Why are you telling me all this?*"

"*Because I don't want you to give up on yourself. We'll find a way to remove Harkon and that blasted chip from your head.*"

"*You need to take me where they're keeping the wolves*

from Shadow Creek. I have to be put in quarantine."

I hate the idea of locking Tristan away, but we really don't have much choice. *"Okay."*

Finally, I pull myself out of his head, then sit on the balls on my feet, feeling drained.

"Is he gone?" Red asks.

"For now," I say. "Let's go. We need to get Tristan to Brian's place."

"How you were able to send Harkon away?" Sam asks.

"I don't know. Some new power awakened inside of me. Maybe Artemis decided Tristan deserved to be saved."

"No. She didn't help you, Dante," Red says. "It was all you."

I shake my head. "That's impossible, Red. That kind of power... it couldn't have come from me."

Red and Sam share a meaningful glance before they turn to me again.

"You were glowing for a moment," Red adds.

"That's true. I also saw it."

Running a hand through my hair, I search for my clothes, not wanting to dwell on who is right about what happened to me.

"We can talk about this later, but right now, we need to get out of here."

Tristan staggers to his feet, glowering at the broken arrow discarded to the side. "I shouldn't come near that thing again."

Red walks around me, then bends to retrieve the arrow. She stares at the two pieces for a second, before facing us. Her gaze drops to my crotch, and then she clears her throat. "I have no issue with you riding back to Brian's in your birthday suit, but Tico's B&B guests might not be as appreciative."

"Right." I grab my clothes, which ended up scattered all over the place. It's a miracle they aren't in rags. By the time I'm done collecting everything, Tristan and Sam are all dressed.

We leave the barn in a single file. Red takes the lead, followed by Sam, Tristan, then me. This is a precaution in case Harkon returns. We don't want Red anywhere near him.

Red once again slips behind the steering wheel. When we're all sandwiched in the backseat, she takes off. The ride is silent, but from time to time, Red glances at the rearview mirror to check on us—or to make sure Tristan is still himself. The dark veins have faded from his face, but not completely.

I catch Sam touching his eye patch, which is stained red and peeling off already.

"How is that?" I ask.

"It's beginning to itch. Now I know why Harkon aimed for my eye. It was payback for what Calisto did to him."

Red shakes her head. "I can't believe Lena betrayed Calisto like that. I want to know why."

"Well, I'm sure your grandmother remembers every single one of her past lives. You can ask her," Sam replies, not hiding his bitterness.

"Oh, I will."

There's a lull in the conversation. I believe everyone

is trying to process what we saw in Red's memories. After a moment, I ask, "Do you think you will ever be able to forgive her?"

"Red lets out a loaded sigh. "I honestly don't know. I don't even hold a grudge for what she did as Lena, but the lies and deception she carried on as my grandmother? That's a hard pill to swallow."

"It will be more than okay if you tell her to fuck out of your life, sugar. I say good riddance." Sam scowls out the window, his jaw tense.

"I second that," Tristan says.

Red peeks in the rearview mirror once more, and our eyes connect. "What do you think, Dante?"

"I wish I knew how to answer that. Have an honest conversation with her and then decide. I'll support you no matter what." I sense Sam and Tristan staring hard at me. "What?"

"Way to make us sound like total unfeeling asshats," Sam replies.

"I don't think you're that at all," Red replies. "You all have reasons to feel that way about my grandmother. She's manipulated me since the start. First, lying about her illness, making me worry about her needlessly. Then by setting me up to be attacked by that Shadow Creek wolf. She never once stopped to consider what those events would do to my psyche. That attack was one of the most terrifying moments of my life."

Guilt sneaks into my heart because I also never stopped to think about what those events did to her. Everything happened so fast, and Red, being the badass woman she is, took everything in stride, even when her new life as a wolf became harder and harder.

"I'm sorry," I say.

"What for?" she asks.

"For not helping you more," Sam adds.

"For not being more sympathetic," Tristan chimes in.

"What is this now? Why are you all apologizing? I don't like this."

"Why not?" I ask.

"Because it sounds like you're asking for absolution before you… before you die." She chokes up on the last part, but manages to contain the sob trying to escape.

I have no comment to that because I'm not sure if we're all going to survive this. Plus, Sam and I also have the pledge we made to Artemis hanging over our heads. We promised to return to her when our time in this plane is over. Desperate that we were to breach the barrier and enter the cave, we agreed. But deep down, I'm aware it was a foolish decision. How can I live with Artemis when I'm bound to Red, not only with my mortal body, but also with my soul?

The familiar signs on the road indicate we're getting near Brian's place. I stop worrying about my promise to the deity. Instead, I focus on the situation at hand. Red turns onto the dirt road that will lead to Brian's house. When we pass where Brian's wards start, I barely sense them. Damn it. They still haven't been able to find a way to keep the wards up for extended periods of time.

"Do you know where the building they're keeping the

wolves is at?" Red asks.

"No. But I don't believe we can get there by car. Let's just park in front of the main house and see if anyone is around," I reply.

There are a few cars already parked in front of the building, including Sheriff Arantes's cruiser and Mom's car. But also Mayor Montgomery's black sedan.

"Great. The witch is here," Tristan snarls.

Chapter 49
Red

We all know the mayor's presence here doesn't bode well. With apprehension, I exit the vehicle, then look over at Tristan and Dante on the other side. Sam stops next to me, placing a hand on my lower back. It's a relief that his touch no longer makes me crazy with lust, just the normal butterflies in my stomach—a feeling I hope to never cease having around my guys.

"Are we ready for this?" Sam asks, the question directed to all of us.

"Let's get this over with. If the mayor is here, then it means she wants to move the wolves to her domain."

"If that's the case, then shouldn't we rethink you volunteering to be taken away? I don't trust her," I say.

"Yeah, I'm with Red. My vote is to keep the truth about your condition to ourselves until we know what's going on." Sam crosses his arms, frowning at the house as if he's seeing the mayor in front of him.

Tristan opens his mouth, but Dante cuts him off. "No, Tristan. This is not your decision. If the Shadow Creek wolves are being moved, we'll not disclose that Harkon still has a hold on you."

At that precise moment, Alex, Daria, and Max emerge from the house. Daria twists her face into an expression of disgust, making me wish she were the enemy so I could punch her in the throat without feeling bad about it. Maximus smirks, and Alex simply stares at me without giving any hint to his thoughts—no surprise there.

"Are you done with your nasty business?" Daria asks, curling her lips.

"Don't be a hater because you can't get laid. I bet if you worked on your awful personality, you could find a willing poor bastard," I reply.

"Burn." Max laughs, and Daria switches her ire to him.

"Is everything okay now?" Alex asks, studying Tristan. I tense. Will Alex be able to sense that Tristan is still vulnerable to Harkon?

"Yes, everything is dandy," Dante replies, sarcasm at one hundred percent.

Things are getting more intense by the second. We can't let this animosity get in the way of destroying Harkon. Determined to bring everyone's focus to what's important, I edge around the car toward Alex.

"Where's everyone?" I ask.

"With the quarantined wolves. The mayor showed up and demanded to see them," Alex replies.

"Nice lady, that one," Max adds.

Tristan takes the lead, circling around the house. There's a stone path that leads deeper into the woods surrounding

Brian's. I follow closely behind, sandwiched between Sam and Dante.

"They could have at least showered before coming here," Daria whispers behind us, and it takes a great amount of self-control to not put her into her place once and for all. But I must swallow the angry retort. The reason why we had to rush here must not be revealed yet.

Once we leave the path, I'm shocked to discover there isn't a building housing the wolves from Shadow Creek. They've created a makeshift housing of sorts by erecting a massive tent. The deceit, even if not done purposely, makes me angry. I let out a growl, increasing my pace. My gums ache. If it wasn't for Dante's light touch on my mind, the canines would have fully descended.

"What's the matter, Red?"

"I've always assumed there was a proper building. I didn't realize the quarantine space was a flimsy tent."

"It's not too bad, not if you think about it. It's still summer after all. Mom wouldn't let them be in any discomfort."

"I hope you're right." I push the flap of the entrance to the side, bracing for a depressing scene. My imagination doesn't disappoint. There are cot beds everywhere, placed side by side with only a little space between them, barely enough to allow a person to walk in between.

The shifters have their wrists and ankles bound to the beds' railings. Some are sleeping, but others are moving restlessly, trying to get free. The most troubled ones are caught in mid-shift, but they either can't completely shift into wolves, or something was done to halt the process. I don't know what situation is worse. I remember too vividly how impotent and violated I felt when I couldn't tap into my wolf.

With a quick glance, I find Dr. Mervina, Brian, his wife Carol, Sheriff Arantes, and Mayor Montgomery arguing pretty loudly. I catch the tail end of the subject before they stop talking abruptly and glance in our direction. The mayor wants to move the wolves, but Dr. Mervina, Brian, and Carol are completely against it. I'm not sure what stance the sheriff will take on this one, but my bet is she will side with her boss.

"You're back already?" Dr. Mervina asks, and my face immediately becomes hot. Shit, I wonder if everyone is privy to why we vanished for a day and a half.

"Yes. What's going on here?" I ask, playing stupid.

"We want to move the wolves to a safer location, but Dr. Mervina doesn't agree," the sheriff replies. "Maybe you can convince her, Red."

"What makes you think you can take them to a safer location? Whatever is causing the wards to weaken will have the same effect on your protective spells," Dante replies.

Mayor Montgomery raises an eyebrow in an arrogant gesture. "Dear Dante, you obviously don't know how powerful the Midnight Lily Coven is. Druid magic doesn't compare to ours."

"Indeed it doesn't. We didn't steal anyone's powers or keep an entire race enslaved," Carol replies, fire flashing in her eyes.

Whoa. What the hell is she talking about now?

The mayor narrows her gaze on Carol. "Careful with what you say, Carol. Don't forget the only reason you have your precious family is thanks to my mother's soft heart. But she's old and probably won't live much longer. I'm not as benevolent as she is."

"Is that a threat?" Carol takes a step forward, but Brian wraps his arm around her waist and pulls her back.

"Calm down, love. She's not worth it."

I'm definitely curious about this new revelation since I made a vow to Demetria Montgomery, but it will have to wait. I search for Victor, regretting I couldn't bring Nadine with me. He's all the way at the back of the tent, isolated from the other shifters. He still has not returned to human form.

Dr. Mervina must have followed the direction of my stare for she says, "I don't know what to do to help him."

"That wolf ought to be put down," the mayor says, tone dismissive, as if he's just a rabid stray dog.

I whip my face to her so fast I might have pulled a muscle. "You touch one strand of his fur, and I'll rip your throat out. I swear."

"How dare you threaten me like that? I've had people arrested for less."

"I'm sure you have," Tristan says, and the sheriff fidgets on the spot, appearing uncomfortable as hell. I've always gotten along with her, but right now, I have to remember she's not Kenya's mother. She's first and foremost the mayor's minion.

Turning my back to them, I stride toward Victor. I'm not surprised when my mates follow me. Their presence infuses me with strength and courage, two things I'll need more than ever in the days to come.

I stop by Victor's cot. He's lying on his side with his eyes closed. It pains me to see how emaciated he is now. He's so thin, his rib cage bones are visible under the fur. When I touch his shoulder, he opens his eyes. I let out a breath of relief when there isn't any sign of red in his pupils.

"Oh, Victor. You need to change back to human."

He whines, closing his eyes again.

"Maybe Dante can try to speak to him mind to mind," Sam suggests.

I gaze hopefully at Dante. "Would you try?"

"Yes, of course. I can attempt to open a conference channel like we've done among ourselves."

"Let's do it," I say, but some disturbance in the air surrounding us makes the hair on the back of my neck stand on end. "What was that?"

"The wards, they just vanished completely." Dante faces outward, his eyes narrowed as if he's searching for danger.

At the precise moment, howling can be heard not too far away. All at once, the shifters who had been sleeping a moment ago wake up and try to break free. A dangerous growl comes from Victor. He tries to bite my hand, and he would have succeeded if Sam hadn't pulled me away.

"No, no, no." Tristan drops to his knees, visibly shaking, and then begins to shift.

"Tristan. You can fight it," I urge him.

Mayhem issues all around us. The rowdiest shifters manage to flip their beds as they begin to shift as well. Whatever magic was keeping their wolves bound was also destroyed. Somewhere in the melee, the mayor accuses Dr. Mervina and Brian of being irresponsible. Shit, I have to help Tristan or get him out of here before everyone realizes he's under Harkon's control. I approach him, knowing the demon hasn't taken full control of him yet.

"Tristan, my love. You can fight him off. Please don't let him win. I can't lose you."

"Red, look out," Dante yells, making me turn.

Free from his bindings, Victor jumps in my direction, but he's intercepted by Sam, who tackles him to the ground, still in human form. He can't fight with Victor in that vulnerable state. During my moment of distraction, I don't realize Tristan is no longer in control. His savage growl is the only warning I get before he pounces. I fall with him on top of me, bracing my hands against his chest to keep his sharp teeth away from my face.

"Stop it, Tristan. Please."

I have to shift, but I can't do it with him on top of me. Plus, I still have Artemis's arrow in my possession. I can't lose it. Dante body slams Tristan from the side, pushing him off me. They snarl and bite one another in a vicious dance. Dante won't stop until Tristan is subdued, but under the manic frenzy Tristan is in, only death will stop him.

Somehow, I need to get him unconscious. Maybe if I can conjure up a ball of energy and hit him with it, it will do the trick. Focusing on my powers, I bring my hands up, facing each other. Crackling energy forms on the tips of my fingers, and I begin to knit my ammunition. I'm ready to throw what I created in Tristan's direction, but they're moving so fast I might accidentally hit Dante. No, I have to do something else.

Dante manages to get the upper hand, throwing Tristan off him. He loses traction on the floor, then slides toward Alex. Everything happens in slow motion. Alex turns with his special dagger in hand. His gaze drops to Tristan's form on the ground, and I watch in horror, knowing exactly what he'll do. He raises his weapon over his head, ready to strike Tristan while he's down. Not giving it a second thought, I send the ball of energy in Alex's direction, hitting him square in his chest. He flies backward, falling on top of an overturned bed. His friend Daria sees the whole thing, running to assist him.

She will be the one who tries to kill Tristan next. I need to get him out of here. I scramble to him, jumping over tumbled mattresses and beds. He's already back on his paws, ready to charge Daria. I pick up a metal container, then throw it at him to get his attention.

"It's me you want. Catch me if you can."

Tristan peels his lips back and flexes his leg muscles, preparing to give chase. Not knowing if I can get out of this tent before he catches up with me, I sprint toward the canvas wall. I believe the obstacles between me and my destination are what helps me in the end.

Not knowing how securely the canvas is attached to the metal poles, I jump, tearing through the fabric. I hit the stony ground in a semi-crouch, but stagger to my feet fast and bolt to the forest. Truthfully, I have no idea what I'm doing, but whatever it is, I have to think fast before Tristan reaches me. I make the mistake of looking over my shoulder, then, as fate would have it, I trip over something and fall like a demented sack of potatoes. Because my life wasn't already a fucking mess, I had to go and become a horror-movie cliché, the dumb blonde who gets killed by the monster. The scream that leaves my throat is instinctual, only serving to punctuate my damsel-in-distress moment more.

But one thing the fall makes me remember is the arrow tucked inside my jacket pocket. I won't have time to shift before Tristan is upon me, so I have to use it as a weapon. His savage snarl announces I might be too late in my realization. I roll onto my back, and Tristan lands right where I was. In the few seconds it takes for him to readjust, I pull the arrow from my pocket. When he comes at me again, I slam the pointed end into his shoulder, piercing his skin.

He lets out a pain-filled howl that reaches deep into my soul. Tristan is being controlled by Harkon, but he felt the agony of that blow. Other wolves answer his call. Soon, I find myself surrounded. I get back on my feet to come face to face with Seth, who appears from behind a tree, carrying a rifle.

"Well, well, well. Look at what we have here." There's so much hatred in his eyes that it gives me chills. His eyes are not tinged red, but there are dark veins on his skin. He's also under Harkon's influence. What a damn fool.

"So you really have given up fighting as a wolf, huh?"

"I don't need to fight when I have slaves to do the dirty work for me."

"So what did Harkon promise you that would make you betray your friends and your own kind?"

"I know you can't possibly grasp wanting something that, by all rights, should be yours, but is given to someone weaker by default."

I snort. "You think you have the qualifications and strength to be an alpha? Oh my God. You're not only a snake, but you're also fucking delusional."

Tristan begins to convulse and make a sound that's a mix of howling and human groans. The arrow stuck in him is glowing, turning brighter with each second. Then, black smoke pours from his mouth, eyes, and ears. It rises into the air, taking the exact shape of the archdemon that came for Calisto. Harkon.

"Filthy whore. You think you can beat me?" he yells.

The wolves whine at his presence, beginning to retreat. Seth is trembling, staring wide eyed at Harkon. The demon pins the traitor with malicious eyes, then, faster than lightning, he zaps into him. Seth drops his gun as his body begins to shake. Dark veins spread all over his face and arms, the screams tearing from his throat terrifying in their clearly agonized decibels.

"Seth! No!" Billy's voice sounds in the distance. I didn't even know he was here. He's coming fast, running toward his brother, not caring that Harkon has taken possession of Seth's body. If Billy gets too close, Harkon will take him, too. I can't allow that to happen. Moving as fast as I can, I manage to wrap my arms around Billy before he can pass me.

"You can't go to him. Harkon will kill you, too."

"Let me go." He struggles in my hold.

"It's too late. You can't help your brother, Billy. I'm sorry."

Seth's screams become louder when his body starts to disintegrate as if he's being burned from the inside out. Billy shouts and cries desperately in my arms. Then Nina, Dante, and Sam catch up to us, stopping to witness the former enforcer's demise. Seth finally turns completely to dust, his ashes quickly blown away by the wind. Harkon's dark presence, on the other hand, becomes more tangible. My guess is that he increased his strength by consuming Seth.

He laughs, then says, "This isn't over. You *will* be mine."

His nearly formed shape becomes black smoke again before he zaps away through the forest, leaving behind his putrid stench and those ominous words.

Chapter 50

Samuel

When I see Red baiting Tristan, then taking off, I almost lose my shit. Unfortunately, the scarred son of a bitch won't stop attacking us, his wolf unnaturally savage. I know how important it is to Red that he survives. He's Nadine's brother, and Red doesn't want to see the teen suffer more. But it's getting harder and harder not to kill the motherfucker.

"*Dante, can't you get into his head and try to reason with him?*" I ask.

"*I've been trying to all this time. But the damn chip in his head has formed a wall around his consciousness. I've never seen anything like it.*"

"*Well, we've got to immobilize him soon, because if we don't kill him, one of those trigger-happy druids or Sheriff Arantes will.*"

Victor lumbers up after I push him against a turned-over bed. Despite banging his head pretty hard, he doesn't seem one bit fazed. His eyes are glowing red, and the venom from his snarl is pretty telling. He won't be stopped. Shit, we need someone with a tranquilizer gun.

Out of nowhere, a dark shadow leaps in front of Victor. It's that damn black jaguar that stopped Alex from attacking Xander. But instead of helping us out, she positions herself in between us and Victor. I want to yell 'get out of the way,' but unfortunately, I can't communicate with other shifters telepathically. I yap at her instead. In response, she growls, bringing her body lower to the ground. I look over her shoulder to make sure Victor is not about to maul the big cat to death, but he seems frozen. I don't know why this shifter is hell-bent on protecting Victor. She's not one of Harkon's minions as far as I can tell. Her pupils are not crimson. Wait a second.

"Holy shit. I think Nadine is the black jaguar," I tell Dante.

"How is that possible? She's a wolf."

"I don't know how, but I'm almost one-hundred-percent sure. Take a whiff and tell me you don't recognize her scent."

A second later, Dante huffs. "Holy shit. You're right. It's her, but it doesn't make any sense."

"She could have been adopted."

"I thought the entire pride was extinct."

"Apparently not. Shit, and she's defending her big brother. Can't she see he's deranged?"

The sound of a gunshot explodes, and then Victor falls with a whine. Nadine swings around, loping to him. I search for the shooter, surprised when I see Nina on the other side of the tent with a tranquilizer gun in her hand. Billy is by her side, and he hasn't shifted either. He's also carrying a gun.

I'm sure there's a good explanation for that, but now that Victor is taken care of, I need to go after Red and Tristan. Dante shares the same thought. Together, we leave the battle scene behind, our instincts to protect Red overriding everything else.

But as soon as we veer into the forest, we encounter the wolves we heard in the distance. I don't recognize their scent, but it's clear they're under Harkon's influence. Savage and lost to their bloodlust, they attack us. We're outnumbered, four against two. Not the worst odds, but considering those chips also increase their natural strength, this is not going to be a walk in the park.

The wolves split, and two come at me at the same time. I face them head-on, because getting on the defensive until I find an opening will take too long and we don't have the time. The first wolf to reach me bites my shoulder, but I also got a big chunk of his flesh. My grip is better than his, so I sink my teeth in deeply while shaking my body from side to side. It serves two purposes. One, to get free from his hold on me, and two, to shred his muscles. I drop him when I sense his strength is beginning to wane, and because the second wolf is pressing down on me. Swiveling just in time to avoid getting bitten on my hind end, I flex my legs, jumping on the small wolf and using my larger body mass and momentum to hold him down. He's pinned under me, but still putting up a hell of a fight.

I hear Red's scream, and that pushes my priorities to the front of my mind. *Sorry, buddy.* I sink my teeth into the soft skin under the wolf's jaw, slashing his throat open and leaving him to bleed to death. My hatred for Harkon increases by tenfold if that's even possible. Damn him for turning me into a murderer.

The sound of someone running in our direction makes me tense, but it's only Nina who's coming after us.

"Have you seen Billy?"

I howl. How am I supposed to answer that?

"Ugh, never mind." She takes off in the direction we heard Red's scream.

"Why do you think Billy left the tent? It looked like they needed all the help they could get," I ask Dante.

"Take a good whiff, Sam. Can't you smell him?"

I do as Dante says while biting back the angry retort. Gee, like I had the chance to stop and separate the different scents all around us. But then, when I do, I catch Seth's stench. *Fuck.* No wonder Billy took off and now Nina is going after him. If those two aren't an item yet, it's only a matter of time.

In another minute, we find Billy. Red is holding him still while his brother is being... what in the hell... I don't even have the words to describe it. It seems like he's turning to dust while he's still alive. His screams of agony make my fur stand on end. When Seth's body disintegrates completely, Harkon reappears, no longer a shapeless shadow, but almost the full corporeal demon he once was.

"Did he just consume Seth?" I ask uneasily.

"I believe so."

The demon laughs, then he announces that Red will be his before he disappears. Billy collapses on the ground, taking Red with him. Kneeling, she hugs him tightly while the kid cries his eyes out. My eyes begin to burn. Sure, Seth was a piece of shit and he deserved the death he got, but Billy didn't need to witness that. From the corner of my eye, I catch Nina wiping her cheek. When I cock my head at her, she twists her face into an annoyed grimace.

"What are you looking at?"

I don't hear any more wolves nearby. Sensing the danger has passed, I shift back. Now that I can see things from a higher vantage point, I spot Tristan's crumpled form near a rock. He's also in his human form. Wait a second…

"Is that Artemis's arrow sticking out of Tristan's shoulder?"

Red eases off the embrace with Billy and glances at me, her eyes shining with guilt. "It was the only thing I could think of to purge Harkon from Tristan's head."

Nina approaches them, then helps Billy up. For a moment, they only stare at each other before she grabs his face between her hands and brings him down for a kiss. Okay then. I guess they *are* coming out as a couple. Free of Billy, Red returns to Tristan.

Dante is checking his pulse, and the tick of his jaw doesn't bode well to me.

"Is he…okay?"

"He's got a pulse, but it's weak. He's lost a lot of blood."

Red makes a sound in the back of her throat. She covers her mouth, suppressing a sob. I throw my arms over her shoulder, bringing her flush against my body.

"It's all my fault," she says.

"How can this be your fault? You saved Tristan from Harkon."

Loud shouts reach us, and I recognize Sheriff Arantes's voice.

"We're down here," I reply.

Mom emerges from the path first, her keen wolf eyes scanning the scene fast. Sheriff Arantes, Brian, and Simon, the London pack's alpha, follow close behind. Unlike Mom, the British shifter is not in wolf form. He's also dressed, which means he never shifted.

"What happened? Where's Seth? Santiago said he spotted him running in this direction with a few of his wolves," Sheriff Arantes says.

"He's dead," Red answers, and Billy grimaces. "Harkon killed him. As for the other wolves, you can see for yourself." Red points at the carnage of what's left of them. Dante also killed his opponents with precise efficiency.

Mom's body begins to wobble and shimmer before she returns to her two-legged version. She approaches us, then drops to her knees to check on Tristan.

"We managed to contain a few of the wolves that attacked us. One told us who was supplying the chips to Valerius," Brian says.

"I take it that it wasn't Blake," Dante replies.

"Blake was involved, but he wasn't the leader of the operation up North. After Blake was caught by your friend," Simon looks pointedly in Nina's direction, "I interrogated Martin extensively. It just didn't seem logical that the little pup would have the brains to pull some covert operation like that."

"So that piece of shit druid finally gave the information?" I ask. I know he was an undercover agent, but he let terrible things be done to Red, Nadine, and Rochelle, and I can't accept that.

"It was difficult, but with his sister's help, we were able to breach through the block Harkon put in his mind. That bloody demon is powerful."

"Martin didn't know who was providing the chips, but he did know they were coming from Canada," Sheriff Arantes adds. "We've put a tag on Francois per Simon's suggestion."

"So let me guess, Francois was the bad guy this whole time. It makes sense. He must have set Blake up to stop us from looking too closely in his direction," Nina says. "When did you have proof that Francois was the guilty party?"

"Not until this morning. I came here to warn Dr. Mervina and Brian, but to my surprise, the mayor was here. The discussion diverted to the relocation of the wolves, and then the wards collapsed," the sheriff replies.

"Where's Francois now?" Red asks with a frown.

"Unfortunately, we don't know." The sheriff gestures at Tristan. "What happened to him?"

"I had to stop Harkon from using Tristan to exact his revenge." Red places a hand on his cheek.

"And you used a broken arrow to do so?" Simon raises an eyebrow.

"That's not an ordinary arrow," I reply, leaving it at that.

"I need to take care of his wounds ASAP," Dr. Mervina

announces.

With a nod, Dante lifts Tristan's body. Together, we return to Brian's house. We pass what is left of the makeshift hospital—a mess of broken metal poles and torn canvas.

"Where are all the wolves?" I ask.

"The mayor and her witches took them," Simon replies, and I catch a hint of annoyance in his tone.

"You're not a fan of her either, huh?" I ask.

"She's a stuck-up bitch. So, no, I'm not a fan."

"You'd better not let her know how you feel," the sheriff chimes in.

"I'm not afraid of her."

The sheriff clamps her mouth shut, but I bet she wanted to say more.

The mood is absolutely the worst inside Brian's house. Carol is busy helping to patch up those who need it. Mom announces she'll get supplies and will be right back to treat Tristan. Dante heads to the rear of the house, no doubt in search of a room. He passes in front of Alex, who scrutinizes Tristan with an indecipherable expression on his face.

Suddenly, Red's wolf aggression flares up. She strides across the room in Alex's direction, stopping in front of him. Without a word, she rears back and slaps him hard across the face.

Chapter 51
Red

I'm still riding the wave of wrath even after I smack Alex across the face. Covering his cheek, he raises his head slowly, disbelief and anger in his eyes. No one speaks, probably waiting to see how this is going to play out.

"Are you done taking out all of your frustrations on me?" he asks sarcastically.

"That's what you think this is about? You tried to kill my mate!" I curl my hands into fists, fighting the urge to strike Alex again.

"I was trying to save you!" He takes a step forward, his eyes sparkling with fury now. "He was not Tristan; he was one of Harkon's puppets."

A hand curls around my forearm, then drags me away from Alex. I'm surprised to see Kenya there. "Red, you need to calm down."

I'm so confused to find her here, and talking to me to boot, that my anger deflates. "What are you doing here?"

"While you were gone, I had the chance to think things through. Gain some perspective. I've also learned a few things about myself, but we can talk about them when this mess is over."

"Are you saying you're not mad at me anymore?"

"How can I stay mad at you when you're fighting for your life? What kind of horrible friend would that make me?"

I get teary-eyed, but now is not the time for sentimentality. All I can do is hug my best friend, glad we'll be able to go back to what we used to be before everything changed.

Easing off, she whispers in my ear, "Now, I want to know why you never told me your ex is a hottie."

I laugh, even though Kenya is bringing up Alex. I'm still fucking mad at him. "I'll tell you another time. I have to—"

"See Tristan. I know. I'm not going anywhere, and I'm going to help."

Opening my mouth to tell Kenya what we'll be facing is too dangerous, I close it instead. By the determination etched into her face, I can tell I won't be able to convince her to run and hide.

"Okay. I'll talk to you soon."

When I turn around, Alex is nowhere to be seen. Now that the anger has receded, there's room in my heart for the guilt to sneak in. I do believe he was trying to protect me.

My gaze connects with Max. In his eyes, I see something I don't think he's ever directed at me before—disappointment. He shakes his head, then mutters under his breath.

"You know the reason he did it, Red. Way to dig a

dagger into the poor guy's heart." Max pushes off the wall he was leaning against, leaving the room without a second glance.

Sam touches my shoulder. "Don't worry about the Blade. The guy is a douche, and he totally deserved that slap. He was lucky it was you who got to him first."

I give Sam a pitiful smile, doing a terrible job at hiding my turmoil. He can sense it, I bet, but he doesn't call me on it. Together, we head to where Dante took Tristan. I follow the bond, which is mercifully as strong as ever. When we enter the room, Dr. Mervina has already pulled the arrow out of Tristan's shoulder and set it aside on the nightstand. The tip is still coated in Tristan's blood, and that makes me a little nauseated.

"How is he?" I ask.

"He will live. Thank you for saving him from that monster."

"Are we sure Harkon is gone from his head for good?" Sam asks.

"Yes," Dante, Dr. Mervina, and Brian say in unison.

"I entered his mind, Red. There's no trace of Harkon or the chip," Dante adds. "I believe when he was struck by Artemis's arrow, you severed the link Harkon had to Tristan's mind."

I let out a relieved sigh, but it's too soon to celebrate. However, the knowledge that Artemis's arrow, even broken, purged Harkon completely and destroyed the chip, too, gives me an idea.

To Brian, I ask, "Have you made the sacred stone into a

weapon yet?"

The druid gives me an apologetic glance. "No, I'm sorry. There hasn't been time. I spent every ounce of my energy trying to keep those wards up."

"Good. Do you think you can fix Artemis's arrow and embed the stone to it?"

Brian's eyes widen a fraction, and then he smiles. "Yes, I can do it."

"What are you thinking, Red?" Sam asks.

"We know that one stone alone won't defeat Harkon, but if we combine its power with the arrow, I think we have a chance."

"You'll only have one shot at striking his heart," Dante points out.

"I know they're completely different sports, but I have rather good shooting aim. While Brian finishes the weapon, I'll practice my archery skills."

Dr. Mervina finishes patching Tristan up, then addresses Sam. "Now it's your turn. Thank God for shifters' resistance to germs. You would have gotten an infection by now if you were human."

Sam rolls his one eye, then smirks at me.

"Now that the Shadow Creek wolves are gone and the wards are back in place, you should all rest," Carol announces.

"I wouldn't mind a shower," I say, suddenly realizing I don't remember the last time I had one.

"Of course my dear, come with me. You too, Dante."

Dr. Mervina pushes Sam into a chair, firmly holding him

there when he tries to get up. "Hey, don't you start anything without me."

Mortification makes my face hot. I can't believe that after thirty-six hours of non-stop sex, Sam is still thinking about doing it, and here, of all places, where we're surrounded by people.

Carol leads Dante and me to a room down the corridor, passing several doors along the way. I didn't realize how big their house was until now. The druid couple have several children, but I don't know how many.

"How many people live here?" I ask.

"Oh, you've counted the number of doors, huh? Well, Brian and I have five sons and a daughter. You've met Jared and Kirian already. Kirian is the only one who still lives at home. He's the youngest. Jared has his own place in town."

"What about the others?"

"Saoirse is the oldest. She lives in Dublin and works for the Council of Druids. Patrick, Connor, and Sean are wanderers. Honestly, I have no clue where they are at the moment. From time to time, they send me a postcard or call."

"You don't worry about them?"

"I do, but I can't force them to live in Crimson Hollow."

Just because they don't want to live in the same town as their parents doesn't mean they can just fall off the face of the earth. But I swallow the comment. If I say those words out loud, I'll be a hypocrite. It's been months since I last spoke with my parents.

"Here we are." Carol opens the door, revealing a cozy

room with a king-sized bed covered by a plush comforter and pillows. I don't know what I yearn for more, getting clean or sleeping until the end of times.

While I stare at the bed, Carol goes to the wardrobe. She removes a few items, and then places them on the bed. There are a couple of towels and clean clothes.

"You don't need to lend us clothes," I say, then shrug when I notice Dante is still wearing his birthday suit. "Well, maybe Dante needs them."

He smiles at me, the gesture creating little creases around his eyes, which sparkle with mischief. And just like that, the familiar seed of desire unfurls in the pit of my stomach.

"The bathroom is through that door, and it's stocked with whatever you need." She suppresses a smile. Maybe I'm imagining things, but she seems to know exactly what's going on in my body. Damn it. My face is probably giving me away. "If you feel up to it, you can come out and grab something to eat once you're done."

As soon as she closes the door with a resounding click, I head for the shower. I can't possibly entertain the idea of having sex, at least until I wash off the grime I've accumulated in the past few days. The bathroom is small, but the shower is good-sized, no chance I'll bang my elbow against the door if I moved too much. I soak under the hot stream of water for a good minute before I reach for the shampoo, then drench my hair with the stuff. When the first rinse reveals muddy water, I wince in disgust. Shit, I was indeed filthy.

My eyes are closed, but I sense the moment Dante enters the bathroom.

"I'm not done yet," I say as I rinse my hair again.

"You were taking too long, sweetheart, and I'm a dirty, dirty wolf."

His voice is husky and sexy, like whiskey over crushed ice.

When I rub my thighs together, the familiar throbbing between my legs commences. I'm still sore from our marathon, but I want him like I haven't had sex in months.

Dante slides the glass door open, crowding into the small space.

"There's no room," I say, my words a mixture of a whine and laughter.

"There's always room for one more." He pushes me gently against the tiled wall, pressing his body against my back. His erection is evident against my butt. "Ah, this feels good."

"What—the hot shower or me?"

He chuckles. "Both."

"You're hogging all the water. I'm getting cold."

"Hold on." Dante reaches for the liquid soap, then he runs his hands along my arms, over my belly, heading lower toward my navel until his fingers are between my thighs, teasing my clit. I lean against him, arching my back. Dante places an openmouthed kiss on my neck, continuing the sweet torture up until he captures my earlobe between his teeth at the same moment he fills me with his finger.

"Oh my God." I moan loudly, the sound echoing ever

the sound of the shower. "How can I want you so badly after what we did in that barn?"

"This is how it feels every time I see you, my love. This is not my wolf nature, or the fact you are going into heat. It's only you who awakens this insatiable hunger in me."

"We're so bad. Sam did tell us not to start anything without him."

"Sam will just have to suck it." Dante inserts another finger into me, curling both in a way that now has him rubbing that magical spot. My legs turn to jelly. Even though I'm bracing my arms against the wall, I'm covered in soap and super slippery.

"As much as I think sex in the shower is hot, I would like to be fucked properly in a bed this time."

"Say no more, my love." Dante turns the water off, then lifts me off the floor. I don't know how he manages to walk out of the bathroom with me in his arms and not drop me, considering I might as well have been covered in butter. He places me on the edge of the bed, and I shimmy back to make room for him as well. When he gets onto his hands and knees, he resembles more of a wild cat than a wolf with the way he stalks me. His eyes are glowing amber, and it makes my mouth go even drier than it already is. I lick my lips, drawing Dante's attention to them.

"I don't remember half that stuff we did in the barn." I don't know why I said it, but by the way Dante's lips twist, I can guess he took my words as a challenge.

"I'm sure we can recreate every single thing we did in there given time. We can start now." He wraps his fingers around my ankle, then spreads my legs apart. Moving closer, he runs his hot tongue up my calf, then places a kiss in the sensitive spot behind my knee. When he reaches the top of my thigh, I'm panting so hard it feels like I've been running for hours.

"Dante, you're killing me. Please don't be such a terrible tease."

"What would you have me do?"

"Anything, just make this pain stop."

"But I thought you were sore, my dear."

"Then shouldn't you kiss it better?"

With a darkly seductive laugh, Dante brings his face closer to my sex, his hot breath fanning over my overheated skin. I twitch, but he places a hand on my pubic bone, keeping me in place.

"Dante...."

"You smell so divine, Red. I must have a taste."

His tongue darts out, the tip barely touching me. He lets out a groan, then gives me a good lick that sends a zap of pleasure down my legs to my toes. I buckle—or try to—but Dante is keeping me in place while he feasts on me. The room begins to spin as I become lightheaded. With each swipe of his tongue, Dante urges me closer and closer to the edge. But I'm also hungry for him.

"Switch," I whisper.

Dante lifts his face, peering at me with wolfish eyes. "What, my love?"

"I want to taste you, too."

His lips curl into a wicked grin. "As you wish."

We change our position. I'm on my knees, holding the base of Dante's cock while I suck his length. As much as I love doing it, it's hard to concentrate when Dante's tongue and fingers are so damn distracting. But the groans from deep in his throat are sexy as hell. As much as I would like to prolong this moment, I can't keep the orgasm at bay. When it hits, it blasts me hard. I would have screamed if I could. Dante finds his release next, fucking my mouth to the end as he rides his climax.

Boneless, I collapse on top of him with my eyes closed. I can't move. Can barely breathe. I just need a moment to recover. And that's the last thought I have before slumber claims me.

CHAPTER 52
RED

I didn't mean to fall asleep after Dante and I had our fun in and out of the shower. When I wake up, I'm hot, my back is sweaty, and there are definitely more than one pairs of arms wrapped around my body. My legs are also trapped under the weight of someone. But the feeling of utter bliss and completion clues me in on who it is. Sam and Tristan found their way into bed with Dante and me sometime during our nap. Unfortunately, my bladder is killing me. I have to get up.

Tristan has his face hidden in the crook of my neck with his arm across my belly. Dante spoons my other side, his arms across my hips. So it means Sam is the one lying across my legs. Shit, that can't be comfortable. The first order of business once we defeat Harkon is to buy a bed big enough to fit the four of us comfortably. We might have to custom order it.

Not wanting to wake them, I gently push Tristan's arm off, then do the same with Dante. It's a task that takes me at least a minute. Those boys are packing solid muscle and are heavy. Dislodging Sam from his position without waking him is trickier. As a matter of fact, when I try to pull my knees up, he hugs my legs tighter.

Ah shit, there's no helping it now. I have to get out of bed or there will be an accident. Sitting up, I shake his shoulder. "Sam, I need to use the restroom."

Mumbling something I can't comprehend, he shifts his face away from me. Damn it. I tried to be gentle, but it seems only brutal strength will free me from his sleepy grasp. It takes a couple of hard shoves to dislodge him, but it's only when my legs are free at last that he opens his eye to a slit.

"Where are you going?"

"I have to pee." I jump out of bed before he can trap me again.

When I return to the room, all my boys are up. I catch the tail end of Tristan's arms stretch, which emphasizes his washboard abs and wide chest. Desire unfurls deep in my belly, so I switch my attention to Dante, but that doesn't help either. He's staring out the window, completely naked of course, and giving me a nice profile view of his backside. Sam is… wait, where is he?

He grabs me from behind, placing a kiss on my neck, tongue sliding over my skin. I shriek like a silly girl. "Sam, shit, you scared me."

His warm laugh tickles my neck, and the fact his hard-on is pressing against my ass doesn't help my case one bit.

"You must still be tired, or you would have sensed me behind you."

Dante and Tristan are now regarding me with the unmistakable glint of need in their eyes. The mating bond is getting stronger, too, and I'm afraid we might have a repeat of what happened in the barn.

The loud knock on the door saves me—or not—from having another four-way with the brothers. My pussy isn't happy, but the human in me is glad for the interruption. It's bad enough Dante and I had our fun under Brian and Carol's roof.

"Who is it?" I ask, motioning for them to get dressed. Tristan raises an eyebrow, pointing at my naked body. Oh, shit, right. I forgot I'm not wearing anything either.

"It's Carol. I'm sorry to interrupt, but your grandmother would like to have a word with you."

A mix of guilt and anger kills my great mood. It sucks because I haven't had many moments where I could enjoy my guys stress-free since I was turned.

"Hey, it's best you talk now before shit goes down with Harkon," Dante says, probably sensing the change in my mood.

"Right." I grab the clothes Carol had gotten for me before. They were on the floor by the foot of the bed, rumpled into a pile. "I'll be there in a minute, Carol."

"All right, honey. Take your time."

I get dressed as fast as I can, ignoring the guys who can't seem to take their eyes off me. Finally, when I can't take their attention any longer, I snap, "What?"

"No matter what you decide, we'll support you one hundred percent," Tristan says.

"You worry too much. It will be okay. *I* will be okay."

I half believe my own words, but it's clear they don't buy my bullshit. Before they can say or do anything that will break the steel wall I've erected around my heart, I slip out of the room.

My stomach is tied into knots while my chest feels too tight. Finally, I'm going to hear the whole truth about why Grandma hid so much from me. The living room is empty for a change. The sun has set, which means I've slept for most of the day. Carol walks into the room, drying her hands on the apron she's wearing.

"She's waiting for you in Brian's study. I thought it would be best if you could talk without interruptions."

Carol guides me to the aforementioned room, taking a different hallway than the one that leads to the bedrooms. Without knocking on the door, she pushes it open. "Red is here."

She lets me through, then closes the door. Grandma is sitting on the small leather couch with her hands folded on her lap. She appears fine, which means her encounter with the poltergeists didn't leave any visible wound.

"You look well," I say, unable to hide the bitterness from my tone.

"You too."

The silence stretches, then I finally ask. "I know you betrayed Calisto."

Grandma grimaces before dropping her gaze to her lap. "I truly wish you'd never learned that."

"Because you were afraid of what I would think?"

"That and because I was so ashamed."

Yeah, typical half-baked excuses. "Whatever. There are few things I want to know. Did you work with Valerius? Did you set me up on purpose?"

Grandma raises her head, her eyebrows arched. "That's absurd. I had nothing to do with that vermin."

"But you did set me up."

"Yes, I did. Under Artemis's orders. Do you remember the pledge Calisto took?"

"Yes, that she would serve Artemis through the end of times."

Grandma nods. "Artemis was tired of getting involved with humans, but she didn't want to leave her wolves unprotected. So she granted Natalia some of her powers. It's the reason she was able to lead the wolves without causing a fight among the pack. She had a special connection to them. She could feel what they felt."

That explains a lot. There have been several occasions where I felt when other wolves were in pain. The first time was the mysterious wolf who was running from Valerius's hunters. Then I felt when Victor and Rochelle were in pain, too.

"I see. Who were you in that lifetime?"

"I was not around then. Despite being bound to serve Artemis, she doesn't control the cycle of life and death. I wasn't reincarnated when Natalia was. Maybe that's why Artemis gave her extra powers. When you were born, Artemis came to me and made me remember everything. She told me I would have to one day help you change into a wolf shifter. I loathed what I had done to Calisto, and I tried to convince Artemis to let you live your life as a human. But she wouldn't hear my pleas. I only learned the reason when you were bound to Sam and Dante, and I recognized them. They were Artemis's favorite wolves."

"She wanted to make sure I would become their mates."

Grandma nods. "She loved them dearly, and even though it must have killed her to let them come to the human world, she wanted to make sure they were happy."

Hearing that almost makes me believe Artemis is a benevolent goddess, but I don't forget how she decided to make me feel Calisto's terror firsthand. She's capricious and mean, which leads me to believe she can't be trusted.

"Why did you betray Calisto on that day?"

"Because I was jealous."

"Of her affair with Alesandro?"

Grandma scoffs. "No. I was jealous because I spent my entire life serving the goddess, yet all it took was one request from you for her to give you one of her arrows. Do you realize how significant that gesture was?"

I nibble on my lower lip. "I suppose it was a big deal. But how was that Calisto's fault? Shouldn't you be mad at Artemis?

"Yes, that would have been the logical thing, but I was only human and so flawed."

"You're the reason Calisto died. The reason Harkon is still terrorizing everyone till this day."

"Don't you think I know that? I've been doing everything in my power to rectify my mistakes. I hid the arrow when Calisto fell. When Artemis restored my memories, I flew to Greece to retrieve it."

"Good for you." My reply is filled with sarcasm. "You hid Artemis's arrow from me, knowing it was the only way I could kill Harkon."

"You don't know that. The sacred stones would work, too."

"No! They won't. Natalia died trying to defeat Harkon using the sacred stone. Brian believes more than one could work, but no one knows that for sure. The only thing we know will work is the arrow, and you had it all along."

Grandma's eyes fill with tears, but she's still watching me with her chin raised stubbornly.

"Fine. I'm not perfect. I haven't been able to move past old sentiments. When Artemis made me remember my past lives, I also retained all the ugly feelings Lena harbored in her heart. I've been trying to get rid of it, and there were many moments I wanted to tell you about the arrow and about our connection, but I just couldn't bring myself to do it."

My nose burns, and my own eyes fill with tears. "You don't regret any of the painful things you made me go through, do you?"

Grandma looks away, but doesn't answer. I guess that says it all. "I did what had to be done."

Any illusion I had that I could patch things up with Grandma evaporates. When Artemis made her remember her past life as Lena, she ceased to be my dear grandmother.

"You'll help in any way that you can, but once Harkon is

defeated, I want you out of my life for good."

Grandma's face blanches, and she starts to blink fast. For a moment, I think I see a flash of true regret in her gaze, but it disappears as quickly as it came.

"As you wish, Amelia."

Not wanting to spend another minute in her presence, I turn on my heels and leave. Once I hit the hallway, I break into a run, slowing only when I'm outside and deep into Brian's forest. Finally alone, I let the waterworks run freely, crying so loudly I sound more like a hyena than a person.

It takes a good minute for the sobbing to stop and my breathing to return to normal. My nose is stuffed, and my face is a wet mess. Wiping it with the sleeve of my shirt, I prepare to return to the house when I hear a twig break nearby. My heart jumps up my throat as I swing around, ready to fight.

"It's only me, Red," Alex says.

My heart returns to its designated spot, only to begin hammering fast. Great. Fucking great.

Chapter 53
Red

"What are you doing here?"

"I went for a walk to clear my head. Are you okay?"

"Does it look like I'm okay?" I point at my face, then turn to the side, folding my arms.

"Do you want to talk about it?" He moves closer.

"With you? I don't think so."

"I get you're still mad at me, but we used to be friends, Red. You were my best friend."

I peer at Alex, not knowing where he's going with this. He's not looking at me, but toward the woods. His arms are hugged around his middle, and there's a slight tremor in his jaw. He's grinding his teeth, something he used to do when he had stuff to get off his chest.

"You were my best friend, too, which is why it hurt so much to learn you had lied to me all these years."

His eyes are wide and anguished when he lifts them to mine. "I didn't want to lie to you. As a matter of fact, I was ready to tell you the whole truth once we came back from our trip to Scotland. But…" He runs a hand through his hair.

"But what?"

"You don't remember because they made sure of it."

"What?" My heart is hammering now. I have a bad feeling about what Alex is going to say next.

"On that trip, we were attacked by marsh fairies. I was outnumbered, and you were only a human then. You got hurt badly, Red. If it wasn't for Max finding us, you would have died. It took you a week to recover enough to fly home."

"No, that's impossible. We were only in Scotland for ten days, and I have memories of every single day of that tr—"

My blood grows cold as the truth finally dawns on me. "You scrubbed my memories."

Alex closes his eyes briefly, shaking his head. "I didn't. The elders in the Council of Druids did. I was completely against it, Red. You have to believe me."

My eyes burn as the urge to cry returns. Once again, I'm finding out people treated me like I was nothing but a puppet. But this time, the violation went too far.

"You should have told me after the fact!" I'm frustrated and angry, and I don't care who hears me. Nor do I give a damn about the fact tears are rolling freely down my cheeks.

"I couldn't do it. They put a silencing spell on me." Alex is crying now, too. Whether I want to or not, damn it, I do believe he was also a victim in all this.

"And you still choose to work for them?"

"Being a druid is not a choice. If you don't fall in line and follow the Order, you're stripped of your powers and shunned by your kind. It's the worst kind of punishment there is. So I decided to become the best of them so no one would dare to hurt the people I love again."

With trembling fingers, I wipe the tears that won't stop falling. "You destroyed me when you ended things. I honestly didn't think I could ever fall in love again."

Alex's lips twist sardonically. "Yet, here you are, in love with three hunky wolves." His smile wilts as his eyes narrow. "I broke up with you because I couldn't take the chance of something awful happening to you again. I did it because I loved you."

I understand that now. Alex was not like Grandma, not in the least. She lied to protect her own ass.

"You said the elders put a silencing spell on you, so why can you now tell me what happened?"

"You're no longer human. The spell doesn't work anymore."

My back muscles tense when I sense the approach of my mates. They find us the next moment, and I can already guess how they're going to react.

"Is everything okay?" Dante flicks his gaze from me to Alex, eyes narrowed.

"Yup. I was distraught after my conversation with Grandma, so I came here for a bit of fresh air. Alex found me."

Tristan stops in front of me, then wipes my cheeks with his thumb. "You've been crying."

"Some truths are pretty hard to hear."

"What did you tell her?" Sam rounds on Alex, glaring.

"Relax, Sam. Alex and I are good. I was referring to Grandma."

"Oh?"

"Did she explain why she didn't help Calisto and why she kept the arrow from you?" Dante asks.

"Yes, but her reasons aren't noble."

"I knew it. Shady fucking Grandma," Sam mutters.

I shake my head. "I don't want to talk about it any longer. The important thing is that we have the arrow. Soon, we'll have a weapon strong enough to defeat Harkon."

"We just have to wait for him to show his ugly face." Sam cracks his knuckles.

Jared comes running from the house toward us. "Hey, there you are. My father was looking for you. He's finished with the arrow."

A great weight is lifted off my shoulders. I hadn't realized how worried I was about transforming the stone into a weapon until now.

"That's really great news. I've got to practice hitting the target."

"I can help you," Alex says, receiving snarls from three angry wolves.

"Guys, cut it out," I say in exasperation.

"I can teach you, too," Jared offers. "I'm not as good as Alex, but if it will help keep the peace…"

"Thanks, Jared. Maybe both of you can help me."

I take the path to the house, and the guys follow me closely. Dante brushes my mind with his touch. Begrudgingly, I drop my barriers.

"Sorry," he says.

"I understand that kind of behavior coming from Sam,

but from you?"

"Hey, why did you single me out?" Sam complains.

"Because you're the baby," Tristan replies.

"Seriously, guys. Alex and I are cool. There's no need for jealousy."

"Well, I know we don't have to worry about your feelings, but that guy is still seriously in love with you," Sam continues.

"It doesn't matter if he is. He's not trying to win me back."

"And if he were?" Tristan asks.

"Then he would just have to cry his eyes out, because the three of you aren't getting rid of me."

"Red, wait up. Dad is not in the house. He's in his workshop. Follow me," Jared takes another path that leads to a chalet-style building with an attached covered work area.

Piles of firewood are stacked next to it. There's also a woodcutter that seems to have been recently used. Brian emerges from the workshop with the arrow in his hand. It's in one piece again, but besides the obvious difference, I can also sense the power emanating from it. It's much stronger than the stone alone. It has to be enough to kill Harkon. Brian also has a bow with him, along with a quiver with regular arrows. Jared hurries to the covered workspace, then retrieves a practice target from behind a few logs.

He sets the target down. Tapping on it, he asks, "Have you ever used a bow before?"

"A few times in high school. I wasn't terrible."

"Good. You'll only have one shot at Harkon. Most

likely, he won't be standing still."

"I know. So basically Jared and Alex must turn me into Robin Hood in the next couple of hours."

"Precisely." Brian's grin is rueful.

"Let's hope my wolf's dexterity helps."

Jared picks the target up again, then places it around twenty-five yards away from me. Shit, it's far. My confidence wanes a little. After I get the bow and quiver from Brian, I prepare to try my first shot. It takes me a while to get used to the feel of the bow. I haven't held one in years. Closing one eye, I take aim, pulling the string back. My muscles flexing, I let the arrow fly. It hits the target, but nowhere near the bull's-eye.

"That sucked." I lower the bow, glowering at the arrow stuck on the outer ring of the board.

"No, don't say that. You're just rusty," Alex replies, and one of the guys makes a disgruntled sound in the back of their throats. I cut a glare in their direction, focusing on Sam because he's the most jealous one.

"If you're not going to behave, then you'll have to leave."

He lifts his palms. "This time, it wasn't me. I swear."

Dante points silently in Tristan's direction, and I fight the laughter. I don't have time to be amused by their antics right now.

I pull another arrow from the quiver, then try again. I still miss the bull's-eye by a mile—not really, just inches—but it feels like a mile. Artemis said I have to hit Harkon straight in his heart. I spend hours practicing, refusing to take a break. My mates stay with me the whole time, giving me support when tiredness and hopelessness begins to affect my aim so badly that I miss the target altogether on the last few tries.

"Red, you really need a break." Jared pulls the arrows from the board, then returns to me.

"I'll take a break when I hit the bull's-eye."

"Forget it, man. I've never met anyone more stubborn than Red," Alex adds, shaking his head.

"Well, Harkon seems to be winning in that department. After centuries of failed attempts, you'd think he would have given up by now." Frustrated, Sam kicks at a random pebble on the ground, then shrugs.

"He's an archdemon. His only goal is to cause pain and destruction." Alex frowns, even though Sam isn't paying attention to him.

"He's kidding," I say, knowing Sam's joke flew right over Alex's head.

The roar of thunder makes me jump. When I glance up, I see that the sky has turned dark grey. My nose picks up the scent of approaching rain. Damn it. I really don't want to keep practicing, not under a summer storm.

Okay, Red. You can do this. I take a deep breath, ignoring the ache in my back, shoulders, and fingers. Instead, I bring to the forefront of my mind the terrifying memory of Calisto trapped to that offering pole as she watched Harkon approach without the means to defend herself. This has to end now.

Before I let the arrow fly, I close my eyes and take a

deep, steadying breath. When I peel them open again, I feel more energized than I was a second ago. My body is warm, and my feet are tethered to the earth, to nature. It's then I realize what I did without intention. The great wolf apparition steps out of the shrubbery. It stands tall and magnificent in all its blue light glory.

"*You can do this, Mother of Wolves. We believe in you.*"

It vanishes in the next second. Since I didn't hear gasps of surprise from my companions, I guess the great wolf only appeared to me. It doesn't matter. I can still feel our connection, and it reminded me that I've been approaching this practice all wrong. I never once attempted to use my powers—the ones Artemis gave me—to hit the damn target. I was trying to do it by using my motor skills alone.

Focusing on the swirling energy, I let it spread throughout my body. Suddenly, I become one with the bow and arrow. When I let it fly, I immediately know it will pierce that target right in the middle. I didn't expect the arrow to break the wooden board in half, though.

"Holy shit! You did it, Red." Sam runs to me, picking me up in his arms and twirling me around like a deranged person.

Through giggles, I say, "All right, all right. Put me down, silly."

He does so with a resounding smack to my lips. As soon as my feet are on the ground, I take a step back, not wanting to turn this into a make-out session.

Jared and Brian have smirks on their lips. Alex, on the other hand, is just staring at me with his enigmatic, intense eyes. Whatever. I swing to Dante and Tristan, grinning.

"Let's get everyone ready. We have a demon to hunt."

Chapter 54
Red

Brian's living room is extremely crowded with all of our allies present. Sam's bandmates—Armand, Jared, and Leo—are standing next to him, while Nina and Billy are closer to Dante and Tristan. It breaks my heart to read the deep sadness in Billy's eyes, but other than that, his face is a steely mask of determination. Zeke is also here. For the first time, he's wearing clothes sensible enough for a battle—if the sequined, camouflage pants are ignored, anyway. His succubus friend isn't here, for which I'm grateful. Nina would probably kick her ass for sucking face with her brother—and also for taking a part of his soul.

Xander and his brother-in-law Derek are in corner as far away as possible from Tristan. That doesn't stop either from sending nasty glances in his direction. I hope one day they can forgive Tristan for what Harkon made him do.

Nadine is sitting next to me, and Kenya is on my other side. I haven't told anyone that Nadine is a black jaguar. Sam figured it out on his own, so right now, only my mates, Zeke, and I know about her secret. I let her attend this meeting, but I was able to dissuade her from joining me on the frontlines. I can't face Harkon and worry about her.

We're waiting for Santiago and Sheriff Arantes to return from their patrol. So far, no one has seen or heard anything. Brian has just finished giving us an update from the mayor. The Shadow Creek wolves are safe for now, and the mayor has witches working around the clock to make sure the wards hold.

The front door opens, and everyone's attention shifts to the entrance foyer. Sheriff Arantes enters the room with Santiago by her side.

"Any news?" I ask.

"Nothing. I have my entire force out. The town has never been more peaceful."

"I don't like this," Tristan says.

"So what are we supposed to do? Just sit around and wait for Harkon to surprise us again?" Daria clenches a fist, glowering.

"No. We can't wait for that. We need to draw him out," I reply.

"Yes, we definitely can't wait. The mayor is on my case. She wants the situation resolved as quickly as possible. She was already forced to cancel the Summer Carnival."

"Of course, all of her concerns involve money," Sam says in disgust.

"Oh, shit. The Cartwright Circus was scheduled to come to Crimson Hollow in two days. They're mega popular and draw a lot of tourists into town," Kenya says.

"Exactly, and the mayor does not want to cancel that."

"Tough shit, she'll have to." Dr. Mervina's expression darkens.

Suddenly, an idea occurs to me. "What if she doesn't?" I ask.

"That would be extremely irresponsible. We can't have tourists flooding the town when Harkon could reappear at any moment," the sheriff says.

"Harkon feeds off the suffering of innocents. That's why he set Tristan to attack Xander's nephews. A circus would be the perfect place for him to feast."

"You want us to use children as bait?" Daria asks, accusation in her tone.

"It's the perfect trap," Dante replies. "Harkon will show up, but we'll be ready."

"It's genius." Sam smiles at me, giving me warm fuzziness in my belly.

"That's devilish. I like it," Zeke says with an approving grin. I'm not sure if I should take that as a positive, considering he's an imp.

"You're all insane. We can't risk innocent lives like that." Daria throws her hands up, then shoots daggers at me with her eyes.

"We're risking lives every second that we don't kill that monster. What's your suggestion? Wait for Harkon to attack a mall or the hospital where people will perish for sure?" I spit back.

"Red has a point," Alex says, earning a disbelieving glance from the druid girl. "I don't like putting innocent lives at risk, but if we're prepared, no one will get hurt."

"I still don't like it." Sheriff Arantes rests her hands on her hips, her gaze going a little out of focus.

"Mom, this is the best plan we've got. I trust Red," Kenya chimes in, making me feel better about my idea. It's risky, and maybe I *am* being a little heartless to suggest it, but I don't see any other option to draw Harkon out.

"Me too," Xander announces, to my surprise. I didn't expect support from him. Dante must have noticed my astonished expression, because he speaks to my mind.

"He didn't forget my vision, love."

The vision where Dante saw me charging Harkon. Now Xander's support makes more sense.

"Right, but that vision could have already come to pass. It could have been the battle in Shadow Creek."

"True, but he doesn't know that. And if the only reason he's here is because of that vision, I won't say a word about it. We need his help."

"We should put it to a vote," Brian interjects. "All in favor of Red's plan, raise your hands."

The majority does so. Sheriff Arantes takes in those in favor, finally raising her hand as well. Only Daria and Derek don't. I'm not surprised.

"It's settled then," Brian says. "Sheriff, we're going to need a detailed map of the circus space. We need to cover every single exit."

"I can send that over as soon as I return to the precinct."

"We'll need more bodies on the ground, too. I can get my best enforcers here within a day," Simon adds, speaking for the first time since the meeting started.

"That would be extremely helpful, Simon." The sheriff nods approvingly.

After the meeting adjourns, Sheriff Arantes returns to the precinct so she can send us the map. The rest of us spend the next few hours planning. We don't return to the alpha's manor until the wee hours of the morning. I again share a room with my mates, but this time, all we do is sleep. For real.

Chapter 55
Red

The circus is coming to town today, and all I can do is toss and turn. At the crack of dawn, I give up, managing to slip out of the bedroom without waking up any of the guys. On tiptoe, I return to my former room where I still keep my clothes. We've been sleeping in Tristan's bedroom because it's bigger than mine.

We spent the past two days strategizing. Provided that Harkon does take the bait and attacks during the circus show, we're prepared. Still, the heaviness in my chest won't ease off. I'm afraid something will go wrong, or he won't show up at all.

I walk outside, needing the fresh air. The sky is tinged pink. The sun hasn't broken through the horizon yet. With bow and arrows in hand, I head toward the quad next to the training facility. It's where I've been practicing every hour that I wasn't in a meeting. This will be our only shot to end Harkon, and the pressure is sitting heavily on my shoulders. I can't fail this time. This is my last chance. I feel it in my bones.

I practice without magic in case I can't tap into my powers for some reason, managing to hit the bull's-eye a few times without it. It's an improvement for sure, but I won't be robbing from the rich any time soon. When I use my powers, I don't miss once. I'm about to let another arrow loose when the hairs on the back of my neck stand on end. I turn around, still keeping the arrow ready. The compound is protected by wards, but one can't be too careful these days. I lower the bow when I see it's only Nadine.

"What are you doing out here?"

She signals that she couldn't sleep. She's not using sign language because I wouldn't understand. For now, we have to rely on gestures that attempt to show what she's trying to say.

"Yeah, me neither."

She approaches, then points at the bow in my hands.

"What is it?"

She mimics the motion of someone using the bow.

"Would you like to try?" I ask, and she nods.

I give her the bow and an arrow. She stares at them for a moment before she snaps both in two.

"Nadine. What the he—"

She turns on me so fast I don't have time to defend myself. Clutching my throat, she lifts me off the ground. Her pupils are no longer green. They are a malevolent red. My wolf awakens, and I start to shift while trying to get free from her hold. She squeezes my neck harder until dark spots appear in my vision.

How could I have been so stupid? is my last thought

before I pass out.

Dante

Waking with a start, I search for Red in the bed. I find Sam instead. Still deep in his sleep, he throws his arm around me, thinking I'm her. I push him off.

"What?" He opens his eyes lazily, then seems confused. "Oh shit. Sorry, Dante. I thought you were Red." Turning to the other side, he asks, "Where is she?"

"I don't know. I just woke up with a terrible feeling in my chest."

Sam yawns, then rubs his eyes. "It must be the anticipation."

"God, will you two shut up? It's still early," Tristan complains from his spot on the floor. He lost in rock, paper, scissors, and had to sleep in the sleeping bag last night. We can't all fit on the bed—*his* bed, which is ironic.

"Red is gone." Throwing my legs to the side, I sit up.

Tristan's face appears by the foot of the bed so fast he must have jolted to a sitting position. "What do you mean she's gone?"

"Dante means she's not in the room. She can't be that far; the bond is steady and strong." Sam gets out of bed, then heads for the bathroom. I hear the shower being turned on, which means he will be in there for a while. He loves his long showers.

"I don't feel anything wrong," Tristan says, but then frowns as he stares at nothing. "But it wouldn't hurt to go check on her."

"Agreed."

I stand as well, when I get hit by a blinding pain in my forehead. Hissing, I close my eyes and pinch my nose.

"Dante, what is it?"

"I think I'm getting a vi—"

My words are cut short by the image that pops in my head. Red and Nadine are outside by the target. Then Nadine morphs into Harkon.

"No, no, no." My eyes fly open.

"What?"

"It's Nadine. Harkon is using her now as his new puppet. Come on, we might still catch them." I run out of the room, then fly down the stairs.

Tristan shouts Sam's name, then he's right behind me. The pain in my chest hits as soon as I burst out of the manor. The vision I saw must have just happened. Without slowing, I shift, blazing through the deserted courtyard. In a few seconds, I arrive at the spot Red and Nadine were. Red's quiver is on the ground, next to a destroyed bow.

Sniffing the air, I catch her scent and Nadine's, but I also smell sulfur, which means Harkon is here. I'm ready to take off when Sam's voice shouts in my head.

"Wait. We need Artemis's arrow."

"Without a bow, it's useless," I reply.

"We have another in the training facility. I'll get it. You two go after her. We can't let Nadine take her out of the

compound," Tristan replies.

Sam and I take off after Red's scent. Bitterness pools in my mouth. All that preparation for nothing. Harkon was a step ahead of us the entire time.

"It wasn't your fault, Dante. None of us saw that coming," Sam says, probably picking up on my mood.

"I should have seen it, though."

Sam doesn't reply for a second, then he says, *"Their scent is getting stronger. We'll get to them in time. Have faith, Dante."*

I wish I could.

RED

When I come to again, Nadine is carrying me over her shoulder. Even with the added weight, she's running faster than I ever could. However, we're still inside the compound, which means we're safe from Harkon for now.

I can't believe I was so stupid that I never asked anyone to check if Nadine was okay. Harkon must have managed to corrupt Nadine while she was in Shadow Creek. He bided his time, not using her until now.

"Nadine, please. If you can hear me, you have to fight Harkon's influence."

She doesn't slow, and if she continues at this pace, we'll reach the compound's border in less than a minute. I have no choice but to shift and fight her. The change happens fast.

Only when Nadine senses it does she stop moving and drop me to the ground.

Now in my wolf form, I attempt to reach her mind, but there's nothing but a void. What did Harkon do to her? Her human features morph into the black jaguar, and then she drops to her knees.

She leaps on me as soon as she's finished with the shift, moving so fast she's nothing but a blur. I don't have time to evade her attack. She pushes me down, trapping me under her. Without mercy, she bites my shoulder, then begins to drag me toward the ward's perimeter. She wants me out of the protective barrier. Harkon must be waiting outside. I let out a howl, hoping there are sentries nearby.

My heart leaps to my chest when two distinct replies sound in the distance. Sam and Dante.

"Red, where are you?" Dante's voice is loud in my head.

"I'm near the edge of the compound. Nadine is being controlled by Harkon. She's dragging me to him."

My blood turns cold when I sense the ward's energy as we cross it. *No. They're too late.* Immediately, I feel Harkon's presence and smell his scent. Nadine lets me go then, moving away. I leap to my feet, wincing in pain from the wound she inflicted. My heart begins to beat at staccato. Harkon is standing not even a couple of feet away from us, almost as tall as he used to be in his glory days. Worst of all, he's fully corporeal.

"You can't escape me now, Calisto. But that animal form of yours won't do."

He attacks me with his demonic energy, hitting me on the side as I try to leap away. A painful shockwave goes through my body, then my bones crack and my muscles rearrange themselves. Harkon just forced me to shift back into human.

Breathing hard, I brace on my elbows, glaring up. "How did you manage to gain your body back?" I ask, trying to buy time.

"Once I consumed that vermin's soul, I realized I didn't need to use lowly shifters as vessels any longer. So I devoured the rest of my allies." Harkon laughs, the sound chilling.

"You killed the alpha from Montreal?"

"He was the first, then the others. My only regret is I didn't acquire the ability to do so when I had your mate in my hands. It would have given me great pleasure to consume his soul."

"You can try now," Tristan announces as he breaks through the trees.

"Tristan, no! Get away." I raise my arm, as if I'll shoo him away by doing so.

"Red, Tristan is just buying you time. He brought Artemis's arrow and new bow," Dante explains in my head.

Then he and Sam join us in wolf form.

"I don't have time to deal with your pests. You're coming with me now."

Harkon runs toward me, clawed hands outstretched. I leap to the side at the same time that Tristan charges him. In his hand, he's carrying a long sword. What the hell does he think he's going to do with that?

Tristan jumps, bringing his sword down in an arc. He slashes at Harkon's shoulder, but the archdemon doesn't even flinch. Instead, he backhands Tristan, sending him flying.

The sound of angry roars and snarls draws my attention. Nadine is poised to fight Dante and Sam. This is going to get ugly in a second.

I concentrate my senses on the arrow, letting its energy guide me to where Tristan hid it. When I make a beeline for it, Harkon is faster and blocks my way. I call my special gift, creating a ball of crackling magic between my hands. As I hurl the power ball toward him, he moves too fast and avoids it altogether. At least he's out of my way. I sprint for the arrow, making the mistake of not checking to see where Harkon is. He sends one of his own demonic shots at me. It hits me square on my back, sending me head-first to the ground. Before I can leap back on my feet, he grabs my ankle and lifts me off the ground, dangling me upside down.

Grunting, I attempt to create another ball of white magic, but the demonic spell must have depleted me somehow. A dark portal begins to form behind Harkon. He's going to drag me to hell. If that happens, I'm doomed forever.

"Red!" Tristan yells as he runs in my direction. He hasn't shifted yet, but I don't think it matters. None of my mates can fight Harkon in either form.

"Get back, Tristan. Don't come any closer. He'll kill you."

Tristan doesn't slow—of course he wouldn't. Closing

my eyes, I focus on my power again. It stirs in my chest, but I know it won't burst out in time. I need help. I need the guardians. Focusing on the great wolf apparition, I call out to it, praying I'm strong enough to summon the magical being. The air changes around me. A dark energy is reaching out, trying to kill any fight I have in me. My nose picks up the stench of brimstone, which means the portal must be getting wider.

Hot tears fill my eyes as a great sense of defeat washes over me. Almost begging now, I send my call for help as far as I can. This is my last attempt. My time is running out. Suddenly, my body becomes warmer, and it's has nothing to do with my body temperature. Opening my eyes, I see tendrils of blue energy sprout from the ground, growing bigger until they wrap around my hands. The moment I'm connected to it, it's like my powers kickstart. With the bands of energy still wrapped around my wrists, I create another power sphere. Harkon won't be able to evade my attack this time. Letting out a battle cry, I hurl the concentrated energy at him, hitting the demon squarely on the chest. With an enraged roar, he drops me to the ground. The portal he summoned vanishes.

Scrambling to my feet, I run to where the Artemis's arrow is. Tristan left it behind a tree, next to a bow. Harkon lets out another a roar, turning my attention to him. The great wolf apparition is fighting with the archdemon, buying me time. With trembling hands, I grab the arrow and bow, then run back to where Harkon is.

Now that the guardians are keeping Harkon occupied,

Tristan has fallen back. He focuses on Dante and Sam, who are trying their best not to harm Nadine. She's acting just like her brother Victor did, attacking in blind fury. Surprising me, Tristan runs in the opposite direction. I don't know what he's planning, but I trust him.

A sharp pain in my chest brings me to my knees. Clutching at my breastbone, I lift my gaze to where the archdemon is. Harkon just hit the great wolf apparition with one of his red bolts, breaking the guardians into pieces. Tethered to them, I felt the blow as well. Their spirits scatter. Harkon's jaw opens impossibly wide, and he begins to suck the guardian's souls toward his gaping mouth.

No! I can't allow Harkon to consume them.

I use what's left of my power to yank them away, planting my feet into the ground when I begin to slide toward the archdemon. To end this once and for all, I need to shoot him, but he's not facing me.

"Let them go," I shout.

Finally, Harkon turns on me, forgetting the guardians for now. He laughs, the sound so foul it sends shivers down my spine.

"Haven't you learned anything, Calisto? You can't kill me with a pitiful sacred stone. I'm more powerful than ever. You won't even scratch me with it this time."

I let a smile unfurl on my lips as I take aim. "Good thing I've leveled up. Artemis says hello."

The arrow flies, striking Harkon's chest. It all happens in a split second. Startled, the archdemon drops his eyes to the arrow sticking out of his chest, then throws his head back and roars with laughter when nothing happens. *What the hell!* It was supposed to work. My heart drops. *This is it. We're all doomed.* I search for my mates so I can urge them to flee. Then, from the corner of my eye, I catch an out-of-place brightness. I swing around just in time, catching when the guardians' spirits converge, becoming one. Their combined energy zaps into the arrow, making it glow with a bright blue light. Harkon's skin begins to crack, and his laughter ceases abruptly.

"No!" he rages as the cracks spread at a rapid pace.

A great light seems to be growing from inside him. He takes a lumbering step in my direction, but then his legs crumple from underneath him. The explosion that follows sends me flying backward. I hit something hard, maybe a tree, and everything goes dark for a few seconds. When my sense of awareness returns, my ears are ringing. The stench of sulfur is almost unbearable. With a cough, I open my eyes, instantly regretting it. The entire area has been covered by a dark miasma that stings my eyes. I cover my nose as I stagger to my feet.

"Tristan, Dante, Sam!" I shout their names as I stumble to the spot where I had last seen them.

Not not too far from me, I hear a cough, which makes me swing around. Tristan emerges from the dark fog. With a cry, I jump into his arms, thankful he's in one piece.

"You're okay. Thank God," I exclaim.

"I'm fine." He runs his hands down my arms, then he cups my face. "Are you all right? Did he hurt you?"

"I'm fine. Where are Dante and Sam?"

"The last visual I got of them, they had managed to pin Nadine down. I think they were over there." Tristan points to his left, and we head that way.

The fog finally begins to dissipate, and I manage to discern Nadine's shape first. She's back in her human form, sitting with her knees up and her arms wrapped around them. I don't realize she's crying until her eyes meet mine. When her gaze switches to a point to her right, my stomach bottoms out. Sam and Dante are on the ground in their wolf forms, both deathly still.

"No!" The anguished scream tears through my soul.

I run in their direction, dropping to my knees between them. There's a gaping hole in my chest as I shake Sam first, then Dante. Tristan crouches next to Dante, then presses his fingers to his brother's neck. His face spasms before his eyes meet mine. A slight shake of his head tells me what I already knew. With trembling fingers, I try to locate Sam's pulse as well, finding nothing.

Sam and Dante are dead.

Chapter 56

Red

"No!" I scream while hot tears roll down my cheeks. "You can't be dead. You can't leave me."

Tristan wraps his arms around my shoulders as he pulls me tight against his chest. His body is shaking like mine.

"They can't be gone," I brokenly sob.

Tristan kisses the top of my head, then begins to rock back and forth. Stopping abruptly, he says, "Red, look."

I turn to see bursts of light leave Sam's and Dante's bodies. Their souls. Then, in the distance, she appears with her flaming red hair and flawless skin. When she raises her hand, their spirits float in her direction, making me jump to my feet.

"No. Stop it. You can't take them from me," I shout.

"Oh, but I can, child. You see, Dante and Samuel made a bargain with me. In exchange for me breaking the wards that prevented their entrance into the witches' cave, they agreed to return to me when their time in the mortal lands was over."

I know Nadine didn't kill them. There's no sign of a

mortal wound on their bodies.

"You killed them, didn't you?" I take a step forward, curling my hands into fists.

Artemis smiles, chilling me to the bone. "I may have cut their mortal lives short. You don't need them. You have your soulmate." She switches her attention to Tristan.

"They're all my soulmates, and I won't let you take them away from me."

Artemis laughs before fading away, taking Sam and Dante with her.

"No!" Tristan leaps forward, but I stop him.

"I'm the only who can go after them."

"How?"

"Artemis bestowed upon me some of her powers. She made me the Mother of Wolves. I'm bringing them home."

Closing my eyes, I focus on my mates' essences. They're not far yet; the bond has not been broken. I become as light as air when my soul detaches from my body. My senses become much sharper, and I can see through a great distance. The landscape is different in this plane. I can still gaze at the mortal lands below, but it's hazy, as if they're covered by white fog.

The sky is blue save for scattered clouds here and there, but it's the golden trail of light that has my undivided attention. I fly after it as fast as lightning. Everything around me becomes a blur until I cross an invisible barrier into a different place. A beautiful garden greets me. Colorful flowers and aromatic trees are everywhere. I land softly on my feet, recovering the feel of my body, though I'm aware the sensation is not real.

The tug of the bond is beginning to weaken, so I hasten my steps toward it. When I turn the bend in the path, I glimpse Artemis seated on a chaise lounge, eating grape while Sam and Dante rest at her feet as wolves. They both perk their ears when they sense my presence.

Artemis's eyes sparkle with fury as she sits straighter.

"*You!* How did you find this place?"

"Did you forget that you gave me some of your powers? I told you I wasn't going to give up my mates."

The goddess stands, summoning her deity powers. Immense energy crackles around her body as she stalks menacingly forward. By all means, her stance should terrify me, but I won't back down, not when Sam's and Dante's fates are on the line. They leap to their feet and howl.

"Stay away, my precious wolves. I'll deal with this intruder in no time."

Flexing my leg muscles, I prepare to fight with a goddess. I must be crazy, but Sam and Dante are worth it.

"So you think because you have a bit of my powers, you can defeat me? Humans are so arrogant."

"I am a wolf."

"Because I made you so."

Out of nowhere, a bow and an arrow appear in Artemis's hands. Fuck. I'm as good as dead. Sam and Dante leap to their feet, nipping at Artemis's heels in an attempt to stop her. With a flick of her hand, she shoves them away. Vines erupt from the ground, trapping them.

"It's for your own good. I do not want to shoot you by

accident, my darlings."

A familiar presence blooms behind me. The guardians—they've followed me. But how? I thought they disappeared after they helped defeat Harkon.

"We had thought our duty was fulfilled. We were ready to follow the golden angel. But when we heard your desperate cry, we returned to your aid. Let's us help you."

"How? I can't survive being pierced by one of Artemis's arrows."

"Accept our spirit force."

"What? You want me to absorb you like Harkon wanted to? I can't do that."

"It's our choice, but it's no sacrifice. Becoming one with you will be an honor."

Overwhelmed with emotion by their offering, I don't see when Artemis pulls the string of the bow back. The arrow flies in the next second, but it stops less than an inch from my heart. A blue energy shield protected me. Sparks fly from the tip of the arrow as it attempts to pierce the barrier. I grab the shaft, receiving an electric shock in the process, but I don't let go. Using all my strength, I slowly begin to pull the arrow away. Once I manage to, I curl my fingers tightly around it, breaking the shaft in two.

"No! That's impossible." Artemis lowers her bow, her shocked eyes wide as she stares at me.

The shield disappears, and the guardians' life forces enter my body, making me tingle all over. A great rush flows through me, making me dizzy. But I can't get lost in the feeling. Taking advantage of Artemis's distraction, I create the biggest energy ball I can draw from my enhanced powers, and I aim it straight at her chest. The impact sends her flying, ending up yards away from where she started. She falls into a heap. At the same time, the vines trapping Sam and Dante loosen. They jump onto their paws, rushing to me.

Overwhelmed with relief, I drop to my knees to receive them into my arms. They lick my face, nuzzling my neck with their noses. I open my mind, but I can't communicate with them.

"Why can't I talk to you?"

"Because they aren't your wolves anymore." Artemis is back on her feet, eyeing me with so much hatred that it makes me tremble on the spot.

I unfurl from my crouch, standing proudly in front of my mates. "They will always be my wolves, no matter who or what stands in our way."

Artemis glances at them, and the emotion on her face changes. It's almost like she's sad.

"You gave me your word you would return to me. Yet, at the first chance you got, you chose to protect her from me."

Dante howls, followed by Sam.

To my surprise, Artemis sheds a lonely tear. She wipes it off hastily, then turns her gaze skyward.

"I thought your desire to live with the mortal girl was mere curiosity. Now I understand you genuinely love her." She studies them again, seeming to drink in the sight of them. "I cannot keep you here if your heart has chosen her."

They howl again as they move in front of me, rubbing

their bodies against my legs.

"Are you letting them go, then?" I ask hesitatingly, still not believing this isn't a trick.

"Yes, but be warned. If you do not treat them as they deserve, I will hunt you down." It's not a threat. It's a promise, but it's an unnecessary one.

Lifting my chin, I reply, "Then I'll never be seeing you again."

Artemis turns on her heels, slowly walking away. A great force begins to drag me back. I hesitate for one second before I gaze at Sam and Dante.

"It's okay, Red. You can let go now," Dante says in my mind.

I almost weep with the joy of hearing his voice before I do as he says.

With a gasp, I open my eyes. I'm on my back. Above me, the familiar trees of Crimson Hollow are there to greet me.

"Red, my love, you're alive." Tristan lifts me in his arms, cradling me like a baby.

"Of course I'm alive, silly."

Groans in our vicinity draw my attention. Sam and Dante are coming around as well, fully human already.

Sam's gaze is the first to connect with mine, awe apparent there. Love, too. "Did you really challenge a goddess for us, Red?"

"You betcha. And I'll do it all over again if I need to."

"No," the three of them exclaim at the same time.

Tristan adds, "The only fighting allowed for the next few

decades is to decide who gets to spoon with you first."

I chuckle, because the notion is too ludicrous. "How about you take turns?'

He smiles, then kisses my cheek. "Deal."

"Yo, stopping hogging the girl. We want our share, too," Sam jokes.

Tristan helps to me to my feet, then I open my arms to Sam and Dante. "There's enough of me for the three of you. Maybe we can even add a fourt—"

"Hell to the no." Dante is the first to reach me, pulling me into his arms. "I'm only cool with sharing you with my two annoying brothers. No one else."

"You got that right," Sam crosses his arms, watching me with suspicion now.

I roll my eyes. "Oh, stop acting like a baby. It was a joke."

"A terrible joke. Please don't make them anymore," Tristan says somberly, but then he winks.

My gaze travels past Sam. Nadine is standing near a tree, hugging herself as she attempts to appear smaller. Stepping away from Dante, I go to her.

"Hey, everything is all right now. Harkon is gone. He can't harm you anymore."

Nadine throws herself in my arms. She shakes as sobs rack through her body. My hatred for that fucking demon doubles. In the end, his death happened too fast. I wish I'd made him suffer more. It would still not be enough for all the suffering he caused.

The sound of footsteps approaching makes my spine go

rigid, but once I take a good whiff, I realize exactly who's coming.

Dr. Mervina and Billy find us, bug-eyed and on high alert.

"What happened?" Dr. Mervina asks.

"Harkon decided to make a surprise appearance. He's gone."

"You killed him?" Billy asks, stunned.

"Sure did."

"Why is Nadine crying?" he asks.

"It's a long story, kid." Sam throws his arm around Billy's shoulders. "Come on, let's head back to the compound. It's best if we don't have to repeat the same story a thousand times."

Tristan snorts. "Who does he think he's fooling? He's probably going to write a song about it."

Dante chuckles, and the whole interaction gives me warm, fuzzy feelings in my belly. We'll be dealing with Harkon's evildoings for many months to come, but with my mates safe, the task is not so daunting.

Chapter 57
Red

No one speaks for a good minute after we finish telling them how we defeated Harkon in the end. I left the whole ordeal with Artemis out of the story. It's no one's business what went down with me and the goddess.

Finally, Zeke taps his knuckles on the table once before standing up. "Well, I don't know about you, but I feel like a round of shots is in order. Where do you keep the good stuff, Dr. Mervina?"

Sam jumps to his feet, "I'll show you."

Xander rubs his face, then peers at me. "How is the little wolf?"

He's asking about Nadine, but for once, there's no contempt or animosity in his tone.

"She's asleep now. I gave her a sedative. Poor child." Dr. Mervina shakes her head.

Her words are loaded with meaning. Nadine was distraught when we returned to the alpha's manor, and Dr. Mervina thought it was best to sedate her before she and Brian did a read of her aura. I suspect Dr. Mervina saw something in Nadine's psyche that profoundly disturbed her. Maybe she discovered Nadine is a hybrid shifter, but Dr. Mervina didn't comment on it.

Xander's countenance becomes troubled, but when he notices my stare, he clears his throat and asks, "So, you're absolutely sure the archdemon has been dealt with?"

"Yes, I destroyed him. As for his allies, I don't think we need to worry."

"Why is that?" Alex asks.

"Because Harkon killed them in order to regain full power."

The doorbell rings, halting the conversation for a second. Dr. Mervina moves to get the door, but Dante lifts his hand. "I'll get it, Mom."

Tristan makes a disgruntled sound in the back of his throat, drawing my attention to him. He finds my hand under the table, then gives it a gentle squeeze, but he doesn't tell me why he reacted like that. The answer is given in the next moment when Dante returns with Mayor Montgomery.

As usual, she's dressed to the nines, not a single strand of hair out of place. "Good afternoon. It seems we have everyone here." Her hawk eyes take a sweep of the room, missing nothing. The woman gives me the chills.

"What news do you have about the Shadow Creek wolves?" Brian asks.

"After an extensive reading performed by my witches, they found no demonic trace left in the implanted chips. I believe they can be removed safely."

"That's good news." Dr. Mervina turns to Zaya, the head

nurse at Crimson Hollow's Hospital. "We'll need to book an operating room to conduct the procedures."

"I'll arrange it."

"Once the chips are removed, we'll destroy them using Eternal Fire."

"Speaking of fire, did we discover who used clingfire to set the warehouse on fire?" Alex watches the mayor closely.

"We're still investigating. Clingfire is forbidden, and only a few supernaturals know how to conjure one," she replies.

"Maybe Harkon killed whoever did that," Kenya offers with a shrug.

"I don't operate on maybes." The mayor's reply is sharp, which prompts Sheriff Arantes to narrow her gaze in her boss's direction. "Now, I would like a word with Amelia. Alone."

"Why?" Tristan asks before I can.

"Because I sense the magic binding her to my mother."

By Dante's expressions, I'm aware they're going to object again. However, I'm curious what the illustrious mayor has to say to me in private.

"That's fine. We can use Tristan's office." I stand.

"Red, are you sure?" Dante asks telepathically.

"Yes. I'm sure. Don't worry. I faced a goddess and an archdemon, the mayor is small league in comparison."

"Don't underestimate her. She's dangerous."

"One more reason to hear what she wants to say. Keep your enemies close, right?" I wink at him, an action I don't try to hide.

During the walk, the mayor doesn't say a word. When we're finally alone in the office with the door closed, I sense the malice Dante was warning me about.

"So. You're the one who killed an archdemon, all by yourself."

"Not all by myself. I had help."

The mayor waves her hand in a dismissive way. "Shifter are the lowest of supernaturals. In a game of chess, they're pawns."

"Does that make you queen, then?" I straighten my shoulders, watching her through slits.

The chilling smile she rewards me with is answer enough. Of course she thinks she's the queen.

"About the bond you made with my mother. I want to know what that's all about."

Raising an eyebrow, I smirk. "Shouldn't you be asking her that question?"

"My mother is…peculiar. And also very old. Her mind doesn't work as it used to."

"I'm sorry, but the details of my bond with Demetria is none of your concern. That's between your mother and me."

My answer is not what the woman expected if the flash of ire in her eyes is any indication. "Be careful, Amelia. You don't want me as your enemy."

"With all due respect, Mayor, I'm not trying to make enemies. You're the one who's drawing the line."

"You have power, more than is normal for a wolf shifter."

"I'm part witch, too," I say, not wanting the mayor to

ever find out my powers come from Artemis.

She laughs. "Well, that's what Wendy wants everyone to believe, but you can't fool me, girl."

It's hard to keep my face impartial, especially when the woman keeps staring at me with her cold eyes.

"I'm not sure what you're talking about."

"Unlike your grandmother, you're a terrible liar."

Well, the mayor has me there. Grandma turned out to be a master of deceit.

"Who was feeding you information about the pack?" I ask, since I don't know when I'll be alone with the woman again.

"I'm not sure I follow you."

I raise an eyebrow, unable to resist. "Who is being the bad liar now?"

It seems my reply amuses the woman. She's smirking now. What the hell?

"You won't tell me what the deal was with my mother, but you want me to give you information? You clearly don't know how things work, do you?"

Shit. I could just blow her off and keep my mouth shut, but in the end, knowing who betrayed the pack is more important.

"Fine. I'll tell you what my bond with your mother is if you tell me who your informant was."

The mayor grins from ear to ear. Somehow, I think I just made a deal with the devil. Damn it.

"It was Lyria. I heard you killed her."

Now I understand the mayor's smile. Lyria is already

dead, so her information is pointless now.

"I sure did. Traitors deserve no mercy."

"On that regard, we're in agreement. Now, about your deal with my mother. What did she ask from you?"

"She wants me to keep an eye on your daughter Erin when she comes to town."

The mayor's eyebrows arch in surprise. The reaction is fleeting. In the next beat, she's sporting her resting bitch face.

"Oh, I see. And did she tell you why Erin would need protection from a wolf shifter?"

"No. Honestly, I thought her request was strange, too. Things are not about to get better, are they?"

"I don't know what you mean. But like I said earlier, my mother is old. You can't take her words at face value."

Bullshit. The mayor is lying through her teeth. Something major is about to happen in Crimson Hollow. I can feel it in my bones.

"You'd better return to your mates. They must be frantic already. Imagine when they find out…" She grins once more, satisfaction blooming before she begins to turn toward the door.

"Find out what?"

She stops suddenly to scrutinize me again. "Erin is almost the same age as you. You two could become fast friends, but I'm afraid with the litter you're carrying, you won't have much time to socialize."

The woman sweeps from the room, leaving me alone to deal with her words. Confused, I scramble to figure out what she's talking about. Looking down, I place my hands on my belly. Oh my God. How could I have been so careless, so stupid? I never asked Dr. Mervina if there was a way to avoid getting knocked up during the heat.

My head feels light, and there's a sudden buzz in my ears. I'm one hundred percent having a freak-out moment. Was the mayor telling the truth? Am I pregnant? And how could she know?

Oh my God. Oh my God. I'm starting to hyperventilate.

"Red!" Sam calls my name, standing in the doorway with wide eyes.

He strides in, followed by Tristan and Dante.

"What happened? I felt a disturbance in the bond, and when that snake came back to the meeting without you, I thought—"

"She didn't hurt me," I say numbly.

"Then why are you looking like you've seen a ghost?" Tristan asks.

"Holy shit. I can't believe I didn't see it before." Dante is watching me with awe now.

He stops in front of me, dropping to his knees, then presses his hand on my belly. Gazing up, eyes brimming with tears, he whispers, "Red, did you know?"

I shake my head. "Not until a minute ago. How can you and the mayor tell?"

"Wait a minute." Sam's eyebrows fly up. "Red, are you preggers?"

I answer that I don't know at the same time Dante nods. Sam lets out a howl, then engulfs me in a bear hug. Dante stands, turning me into a human sandwich. My eyes connect with Tristan's, who is watching me with a curled hand covering his lips, his eyes shining with emotion.

He drops his hand, then whispers, "I love you," before hurrying over to join our group hug.

"Is this really happening?" I ask, dazed.

"Yes, my love. I can sense their life forces." Dante kisses my neck.

"Their?" I gasp. "H-how many?"

Suddenly, they're all staring at me. "What's wrong?" Sam asks.

"I... this is going to sound terrible, but I don't know if I'm ready for this." I close my eyes, hating that I feel so insecure. I'm not ready to be a mom. Heck, I've barely gotten used to being a shifter.

"Hey, look at us, sweetheart." Tristan rubs my cheek. "You killed an archdemon, you saved Sam and Dante from Artemis's clutches and you defied a high fae, yet motherhood is the thing that terrifies you?"

"Those bad guys will feel like a walk in the park compared to this."

Sam chuckles. "Aw, love. It's going to be a piece of cake."

"That's easy for you to say. You don't have to carry I-don't-know-how-many babies in your belly for nine months, or worse, give birth to them." I pinch the bridge of my nose. "I'm already getting panic attacks thinking about it."

"You don't have to feel this way, my love. We'll be right

next to you through it all."

I start to cry, and I don't know why. Gee, could it be the hormones already? Humans don't feel symptoms until at least a few weeks into pregnancy. Why must everything with shifters be faster and more intense?

"What about college? I was planning to go back once things calmed down."

"And you still can. Red, you're not alone." Tristan grabs my face between his hands. "You have me, Dante, and Sam. We're a family, my love."

Family. That's right. We *are* a family. Not in my wildest dreams had I pictured falling in love with three amazing, kind, and strong brothers. But now, surrounded by them, feeling their immeasurable love, I realize I wouldn't trade this for any other scenario or any other life. I'm right where I'm supposed to be.

THE END

About the Author

USA Today Bestselling author M. H. Soars always knew creative arts were her calling but not in a million years did she think she would become an author. With a background in fashion design she thought she would follow that path. But one day, out of the blue, she had an idea for a book. One page turned into ten pages, ten pages turned into a hundred, and before she knew, her first novel, The Prophecy of Arcadia, was born.

M. H. Soars resides in The Netherlands with her husband and daughter. She is currently working on the *Love Me, I'm Famous* series, and the *Crimson Hollow World* novels. She also writes SciFi and Fantasy under the pen name Michelle Hercules.

Join M. H. Soars VIP group on Facebook:
https://www.facebook.com/groups/mhsoars/

Connect with M. H. Soars:
Website: www.mhsoars.com
Email: books@mhsoars.com
Facebook: https://www.facebook.com/mhsoars
Twitter: @mhsoars

Sign-up for M. H Soars newsletter:
http://mhsoars.com/sign-up/

ALSO BY M. H. SOARS:

LOVE ME, I'M FAMOUS SERIES:

WONDERWALL

SUGAR, WE'RE GOING DOWN

WRECK OF THE DAY

DEVILS DON'T FLY

LOVE ME LIKE YOU DO

CATCH YOU

ALL THE RIGHT MOVES

ALSO BY MICHELLE HERCULES:

ARCADIAN WARS SERIES:

SAVAGE DAWN

OZ IN SPACE SERIES:

LOST HORIZON (COMING JUNE 2019)

Made in the USA
Monee, IL
09 May 2021